ESCAPEMENT

KRISTEN WOLF is an author, filmmaker and wondernaut who lives in the Rocky Mountains. Her debut novel, *The Way*, was hailed by *O, The Oprah Magazine* as "A Title to Pick Up Now!" As a graduate of Georgetown University she was nominated to the Phi Beta Kappa honor society and holds an M.A. in creative writing from Hollins University. She is currently working on an innovative venture in storytelling. Follow her creative passions here: www.kristenwolf.com.

PRAISE FOR KRISTEN WOLF'S NOVEL, *THE WAY*

"This imaginative novel may make you a believer."
—*O, The Oprah Magazine*

. . . .

"The Way is a daring and passionate debut from an author to watch in the future."
—Historical Novel Society

. . . .

"Wow, is all I can say. This novel blew me away!"
—Book Pleasures

. . . .

"I don't think I could rave anymore about this book ... truly one of a kind."
—Chick Lit Plus

. . . .

"THE WAY is a magical, evocative first novel that I plan to buy a carton of to give to my family and friends. This message of compassion, healing, and respect for women could indeed transform our world."
—Joan Borysenko, Ph.D., author of *A Woman's Journey to God*

. . . .

"Are you looking for a book that will stay with you long after you've closed its pages, a book that will transport you into an exotic world filled with intrigue, faith, and courage? You're looking for Kristen Wolf's THE WAY, a remarkable story, beautifully told."
—Mary Johnson, *New York Times* bestselling author of *An Unquenchable Thirst: A Memoir*

. . . .

"THE WAY is an intriguing coming of age... Fascinating..."
(★★★★★)
—AMAZON #1 Reviewer

. . . .

"...sure to be a book-club darling."
—Booklist

"A young girl in ancient Palestine struggles with her calling as a spiritual leader in Wolf's audacious, deftly woven debut."
—Publishers Weekly

. . . .

"This book took me on a journey... I was surprised in more ways than I ever could have imagined. THE WAY is one of those rare novels that makes you think."
—Javier Sierra, *New York Times* bestselling author of *The Secret Supper*

. . . .

"THE WAY will invoke some deep thinking and soul searching...pick it up."
—*Rhodes Review*

. . . .

"The Way is a unique and ambitious debut novel, certain to provoke passionate discussions."
—John Shors, bestselling author of *Beneath a Marble Sky*

. . . .

"...page turning and utterly creative."
—Maria's Space

. . . .

"Wolf's voice, vision, and verve combine to make THE WAY an emotional and action-packed debut."
—Alice Peck, author of *Bread, Body, Spirit: Finding the Sacred in Food*

. . . .

PRAISE FOR KRISTEN WOLF'S NOVEL, *ESCAPEMENT*

"Wolf is a masterful storyteller who has created an enchanting novel. ESCAPEMENT is a symphony of words, marked by lyrical phrases and exquisite rhythm. It will resonate with anyone who has ever felt passion."
—*IndieReader*

Publisher's Cataloging-in-Publication

Wolf, Kristen, author.

Escapement / Kristen Wolf.

LCCN 2017961244

ISBN 978-0-9996103-0-5

1. Fiction. 2. Music. 3. Piano. 4. Women's Fiction.
5. Queer Fiction. 6. Romanticism.

Published by Pixeltry

Printed and bound in the United States of America

Cover design by Andrej Semnic aka semnitz | semnitz@gmail.com
Book layout by Kerry Ellis | www.coveredbykerry.com

PIXELTRY

ESCAPEMENT

a novel

Kristen Wolf

The soul that sees beauty
may sometimes walk alone.

—*Johann Wolfgang von Goethe*

PROLOGUE

I have but only once seen a grand piano stripped of its keys. Its soul gouged and gaping.

The utter paralysis of spirit—the inflicted and eternal silence suggested by that image—is terrible. Were it not for my undying fidelity to that instrument whose tones still pierce my heart, I would flee in terror.

Comparable in its horror is the image now before me.

And yet I stand. Without retreat. Surrounded by a thousand comrades. Leapt to our feet. Applauding. Tears streaming down reddened faces. Our cheers having reached a deafening roar. As if the great clamor could scare off death. Could frighten the profound and oncoming tragedy. The immeasurable silence that had come to reclaim our prophet.

Standing beside us in unity is the orchestra, the players, who have only moments ago finished performing the final movement of Cristofer Vaughn's last symphony. The entire ensemble leans awkwardly, gripping at instruments. The act of ushering through their bodies the ache and artistry of our peerless composer has left them more undone than we.

Yet dismantled as all are, players and audience alike, we hold our ground—in reverence—acknowledging the Creator's presence among us.

Rumors had circulated that our cherished composer was sick. That he was, in fact, dying. No one, however, took the news seriously. In our minds no calamity existed of vigor enough to bring down his magnitude. No darkness enough to quell his obstinate and searing light. He had reigned for nearly one hundred years. Outlived nearly everyone he loved, including his beloved Clara.

His music—hailed as genius by luminaries as great as Richard Thorne—had risen to overtake and captivate an entire era. Yet what stood to pass from us in that hour was not just one individual. Not just an acknowledged wizard of the tonal arts.

No.

The reason we in that concert hall rose, cheering though our sobs, was because we felt within our very marrow that when Cristofer passed, a doorway that opened upon the Source of All would close.

Forever.

As we gazed up to the director's box, where the spindly husk of our virtuoso stood, clung to the railing, tears streaming down sunken cheeks, there remained no doubt. The force of life was leaving him. All that remained was strength enough to be among us. To hear his music performed one last time. And, mercifully, to witness our granting upon him the most extravagant, grief-stricken display of gratitude this city has ever known. A display that, in my mind, had been far too long in coming—but arrived, nevertheless, before the end.

I will leave it to historians and biographers to qualify the massive body of work Cristofer left to the world, its scope veering from the thundering majesty of existential angst to the intimate whispers of a child. I will also leave to better minds the task of detailing the enduring effects his talents brought to bear not just upon this age, but on those to come.

That I lived to observe his journey toward this triumph I will forever count as my greatest privilege.

For my part, I can only speak to my liege's spirit. To the indomitable character that enabled him to overcome a lifetime of terrifying expectations, trials, and rejection. Though I could not know all the mysteries that unfolded within the interior of his great mind, of what I am certain is that at some point in his life my Cristofer made a choice: to sacrifice his entire being in pursuit of the art to which all other arts aspire. To channel sounds and energies from beyond. To open his chest and grant that his body, mind, and soul serve as conduits for the Creator. And from that moment forward he suffered, with his usual candor and gruffness, the deep joys and dark isolation such a contract entails. To that end, he has at last bestowed upon us all the treasures and beauties he could gather. His every physical and emotional foible forgiven in light of this daring odyssey.

And now, after decades spent funneling divinity and the profoundest human longing into a music that both soothes and unsettles, he is depleted.

It is the passing of such rare individuals that lies among the greatest of human tragedies. For their absence delivers a collective loss unlike any other. And while I do not believe in angels, perhaps this is from where the myth of them arises.

Even as I am thinking these things, the cheers and applause surge upward to a rousing din as Cristofer lifts a hand in farewell.

At this, I am overcome.

Unable to bear the sight of his dwindling, I drop my eyes. Rub my face with my coat sleeve. Soaking it.

It is then that I feel her.

I turn. Find her gaze.

Being able to speak without need of words, I know what she is thinking, what she is wishing to suggest.

But I will not have it.

Not now, not ever.

What Cristofer is, he has become through the enormity of his own grace and effort.

And what I am, I have become because of Cristofer.

CHAPTER 1

" God, you are Beauty itself," I said before I could stop myself.

And I wasn't speaking to the Creator.

I was speaking to Her.

Though she stood across the drawing room, distant enough not to hear me. Not to notice my bewildered stare. And watering mouth.

We had just arrived at the estate, Cristofer and I. Footmen were busy whisking the capes from our shoulders when I saw her. *Felt* her, rather. For the encounter sent flames roaring through the hollows of my body. All this before I became fully aware of what I had beheld. Of what the aspects caught in the net of my periphery might embody.

It was the mere suggestion of her that impaled me.

Dark hair glazed with sunset. Green eyes aflame. Cheekbones

aroused. Stem of delicate throat. Collarbones spread like wings. A velvet gown, the color of blood, low at the neck. A ruby seeping from her heart.

The footman dropped my cape. Bowed and apologized profusely, no doubt expecting an outburst. But I had no words.

No sooner had the saliva poured into my mouth than it dried. A swift and distressing drought.

"Our pianist has arrived!" someone called from across the room.

Heads turned.

Cristofer blushed.

A small crowd gathered and cinched around us. Unable to look in her direction, I concentrated on those before me. It was the usual beau monde. Overstuffed, middle-aged men about court, all frill at the collar and daintily shod, ladies in waiting lashed with jewels, fluttering coquettes, nervous dilettantes, swarthy gentlemen from abroad, a gaggle of spectacled intellectuals.

Each wanting to touch the rising star of Cristofer Vaughn. The dashing young musician. My companion for the evening.

A jumble of questions billowed from the crowd: Have you brought the Haydn sonata? Is it true you despise Liszt? I understand you are highly selective, I have a daughter who might suit you ...

Cristofer stared blankly as into a distant cloud. His lion's mane of hair gallantly swept back.

I laid a hand upon his forearm. He was not a social animal by nature. Which was why he insisted that I, his housekeeper, accompany him on such outings. My presence, he claimed, steadied him.

When I touched him, the onlookers dropped their eyes to my person. Aghast. No one addressed me or went so far as to acknowledge my presence. Those simple acts would have suggested an approval they were not prepared to bestow.

In the imagination of an adoring public, no great artist can be truly possessed. The balloon of their talent, the very buoyancy of their spirit, holds so many aloft that to believe a mere mortal could command their affections would be to puncture the airship and send every soul crashing.

The crowd pressed further. Cristofer swallowed.

Anticipating the advance of a well-endowed vixen, I angled my body in front of hers. Thus rebuffed, she threw a scowl in my direction, her red lips plumping like angered slugs.

"Monsieur Vaughn! Welcome to our home!" a handsome voice called. At his words, the crowd parted.

It was Jacque Bertrand. Statesman. Diplomat to the French. Lover of fine art and food—and exquisite women.

He was Her husband.

The pair had recently arrived from Paris.

Jacque stepped up to my companion. Towered over him. My

Cristofer had been endowed with many blessings, but height was not among them.

"I hope you will make yourself comfortable, monsieur. Ava and I are indeed honored."

Ava.

Her name singed my lips.

Our host took Cristofer's hand and shook it firmly. In his excitement he had forgotten that keyboardists do not partake in this sometimes dangerous social custom. Think of our dear friend Richard Thorne who sustained significant injury after the Duchess of Wales crushed his knuckles in her ham-boned mitts.

When released, Cristofer laced his precious digits behind his back to prevent others from attempting the same.

Jacque turned and bowed in my direction. Halting. Perfunctory.

It was then that I noticed a small deformity scarring our stately host. Missing was the top nugget of his left ring finger. A shiny stub poking just above his wedding band.

"Ah ... yes," Cristofer stumbled, noting his oversight. "Monsieur Bertrand, please, meet my good friend ... Nesvelda."

I threw Cristofer a sideways glance.

Nesvelda?

But this was my fault. I usually provided an identity before we attended such occasions. Given that I kept to myself, and no one in Vienna's upper echelons knew of my existence, I could easily masquerade as Cristofer's escort. However, being in a rush that evening, I had failed to provide a fictitious moniker. Nesvelda it was.

"Charmed to make your acquaintance," Jacque said, lifting my hand, his gestures cool as silk.

I watched his eyes sweep the narrow shelves of my merchandise. Unimpressed, he threw me a half-lipped grin. I am well accustomed to the indifference. Broad-shouldered, lean as an oar, and thinly hipped, I am not to most men's liking. Compared to Ava, who embodies the lushness of a violin (and a Stradivarius at that), I am the female equivalent of an oboe.

Turning back to my companion, Jacque's face lit up. "You must come see her," he declared, his eyebrows reaching for the chandeliers. He gave Cristofer a slap on the shoulder. "Her beauty is unparalleled!"

My eyes cut to Ava. Naturally I thought he was speaking of her. Cued by the sound of her husband's voice, she politely broke free of conversation and made her way toward us.

Upon seeing her approach, the bottom dropped out of my belly.

I spun, looking for escape. I found an opening beside the vixen. I grasped Cristofer at the elbow and pulled his ear to my lips. "Someone to meet. I'll find you later," I whispered. He looked utterly bereft at my departure. I fled before he could protest.

Having absconded to a corner, I wielded a flute of champagne and pretended to admire the furniture. It wasn't an unreasonable charade. Monsieur Bertrand had imported pieces from all over Europe. Carved in cherry, ash, myrtlewood, and mahogany, their artistry was undeniable, though not particularly to my taste. I am less touched by the heavy-footedness of appointments fit for kings and more compelled by the airy curvatures wrought by modernists. I like my art to encourage ascension, not anchor me to the ground. I guess one could say that is my credo.

Shielding myself behind an inlaid armoire, I spied on events unnoticed. The drawing room's first-rate acoustics allowed me to eavesdrop on the entire span of the crowd, even those milling at the farthest edge.

That phenomenon was why I could hear Jacque say, clear as though he stood beside me, "Monsieur Vaughn, I would like you to meet the love of my life. She has just arrived from Paris." He waved his arm in a dramatic swath. The crowd faded back as from a magician. When the floor had cleared, the object of Jacque's affection was revealed. For composed in the heart of the clearing stood Ava.

My breath shuddered.

Concealed from view, my eyes were free to roam. And roam they did. It becoming immediately clear why the merest glimpse of her had untethered me.

In my experience, women are composed of two elements—Beauty and Light. Of the two, the former is the most celebrated. The most readily observed. It is the physical tidings, the graceful arcs, the beneficent swellings that make men swoon and artists weep. It is the physical majesty of a woman's body that lures. The conduit that transfers sudden heat into the lover's core.

Then there is the Light. This is a somewhat more ephemeral element but no less vital. I suppose I could describe it as a certain cast of character. A measure of aliveness. A discernment. A complicity. A manner of beholding one's world—and of being beheld. Outwardly, it arises as a brilliance radiating from the eyes. A carving shine.

Finding such luster in the eyes of a woman is an intoxicant, and one a thousand-fold more potent than physical beauty. It is a treasure bestowed on whoever learns to cherish it. An eternal power that never surrenders, never dims—even as time fades the raw beauty.

I almost feel I am wasting my time in trying to portray the nature of this Light. That by so attempting I am diminishing its vigor. But God help me, I know it when it comes before me.

Suffice it to say, then, that when Ava lifted her green eyes in my direction, I was struck blind for the Light of her. For the cunning feline luminescence.

Stumbling back, the flute slipped from my hand and shattered.

I am here reminded of the story of the apostle, Paul, traveling the road from Jerusalem whereupon he is blinded by a sudden blaze of light. This is not unlike what occurred to me in the drawing room. And is, perhaps, the best evidence yet that our Creator may indeed be female.

"My God," I heard Cristofer exclaim. (And he *was* speaking to the Creator.)

My sight restored, I was surprised to find that my companion was not gazing upon Ava at all. As it happened, she was not "the love" Jacque had referred to.

For standing alongside her, and captivating my poor Cristofer, was a magnificent instrument. A piano. Exceptional in every detail. Her flawless wooden flanks shone like charred nectar. Her slow curves shivered with whorls. Her strings trembled, taut and measured. Her keyboard invited approach, a ready ladder of ivory and onyx.

Cristofer circled her as if in a trance.

Jacque threw his wife a knowing glance, pleased with their guest's reaction.

I wanted to look upon Ava, to gauge her response, but could not bear to see her lighted gaze fall upon her husband.

In the short time it had taken for the butler to sweep the glittering shards from my feet, Ava had become the great artist and I her adoring public. For already the idea of a mere mortal possessing her had me shaking.

Cristofer stood back. "From where have you acquired this?" he managed, extending a cautious hand.

Jacque peeled open a conspiratorial smile. "It was built for Beethoven," he said.

Cristofer's hand retracted from the keyboard as from an open flame.

There were those who had predicted that Cristofer would inherit the mantel of that foremost composer. That he was Ludwig's rightful successor and would bring a glorious and powerful new music to the world. Richard Thorne, in particular, regularly fanned this notion in public. But this massive expectation, I knew in confidence, weighed terribly on my liege. He was terrified of the comparison. Just as he was driven by it.

Jacque went on. "She was in Liszt's possession when I found her. But I convinced him to seek out a more robust instrument. A model more suited to his *athleticism*," he said, referring to the pianist's famously explosive style of play. "But I think you, Monsieur Vaughn, will find her well suited in tone and balance to your distinctive touch."

I looked up. It was a sensitive and astute comment. It almost made me admire the man who had made it.

I resisted.

"I could not possibly—" Cristofer began.

"Nonsense," Jacque replied. "You are in my employ this evening. And I insist. Besides," he added, lifting his disfigured hand, "ever since the fall from my stallion robbed me of that pleasure, I relish in the sharing of it."

I could see the tremble in Cristofer's palms. A swift pain clutched my heart. I felt sick for having abandoned him when he so badly needed me by his side.

"Go on," I whispered, encouraging him. Hoping the room's miraculous acoustics might carry my words. Might assure him of my presence.

Jacque and he exchanged glances. After a moment, our host lifted his intact hand and snapped the air. At the signal, two footmen dashed to the piano's bench and slid it backward.

Cristofer breathed deeply and approached. He slipped between the bench and keyboard. As the footmen nestled the seat behind his knees, he flipped up his coattails. Thus situated, he unfurled his chest, his shoulders, his spine, as if readying to ascend heavenward.

The crowd pressed forward.

"Will it be Haydn, you think?" someone whispered.

"Mendelssohn, perhaps?"

I wondered the same myself.

Cristofer tossed out his wrists. Yanked back his cuffs.

The crowd hushed. A collective anticipation lifted the ceiling.

His fingers arched and settled, forming bridges to the keys.

I drew a breath.

The first notes burst into the air. Wild. Turbulent. Uncontained. A vintner cracking the cask and the wine bubbling free.

The audience drew back.

I fell against the furniture. Only I knew how necessary his success that night. How frayed his nerves. How tenuous his esteem.

But to my relief, Cristofer did not crumble. Did not surrender. Instead, he wrestled.

Mid-stroke, he attuned himself to the keys' skittishness and, with effort, held the glass before them, training their flow into an even arc. A steady, seamless pour.

After the first few refrains, the notes lined up as they should and began to sing.

The onlookers noticeably relaxed. I pulled myself upright with a sigh.

The piano sang with a lush tone, rich and expressive. A voice laced with time. With wisdom. Listening, one almost fancied the instrument might begin to speak. Its sound blossomed within the space. The notes rushed upward, beating their wings against the windows, seeking sky.

It was only after the first refrain that I noticed the music itself. It was not Haydn. Nor Mendelssohn.

It was Vaughn.

The sketch of a rhapsody he had been grappling with as of late. Or, rather, that *we* had been grappling with. A melody heard on earth solely by the composer, myself, and our cat.

To play an untested and unfamiliar piece before such an esteemed audience was a mark of courage. A sign of daring and overt confidence.

It was also extremely risky.

My eyes shot to Jacque. He stood, finger to chin, eyebrows knit, his face unreadable.

Was he baffled? Furious? Did he fear that the unfamiliar and challenging composition would alienate his guests? The very ones he had promised to impress?

I swallowed what felt like stones.

Cristofer, unaware of the audience, rode the wave. The musical theme unfolded along bursting petals of tension and restlessness. The piece would not relax. It sped onward. Percussive. Daunting.

No one moved.

After several more refrains, the tension slackened. The theme shifted. And I knew he had sailed into uncharted territory.

His hairline began to shimmer. Beads glistened at his sideburns.

Where would he go next?

I closed my eyes. If the worst were to befall my friend, I did not want to stand witness.

Then he found a chord. A minor chord. Sweet. Aching. Familiar.

Another followed. He held it. Gave the sound its due before advancing. Each compelled the next, tugging upward. A smooth elevation. A rising twist of smoke.

I recognized it immediately.

My mouth fell open.

It was *my* theme. My creation. I had conceived it alongside him. And now, he had possessed it.

I smiled.

I did not begrudge him ownership. Indeed, such were the terms of our agreement: that I provide whatever creative material and inspiration I could, along with the full litany of domestic duties, in exchange for residing at his spare cottage. It seemed a fair trade. And had proven agreeable for years.

So while I was not unaccustomed to him claiming authorship of material I had wrought, I *was* surprised to hear him attempt it within that particular forum.

Naturally I blushed with pride at his selection. But felt, too, a measure of sadness, as it meant he had abandoned his own voice. Having launched himself into the fray with bold confidence, he had wavered, mid-performance. Had lost heart in himself, and his talents, to fall back on mine. And, given the day's disappointing news, this was not a positive development.

His arms sailed open. His chest broadened. The music swelled into the upper and lower registers simultaneously. A division of aching dichotomy.

I closed my eyes, carried adrift.

The theme's anguish had arisen from a broken heart. From the recent dissolution of a coupling that had enflamed me. And nearly consumed me.

We had met in the butcher shop. She, hovering behind a thick oak block diced with knives. Me, incognito, dressed as a dandy. (It is often my pleasure, being androgynous, to dress as a man.)

I ordered six links of sausage. She wiped a bloody palm across her apron. Tugged a meaty chain from a floating hook. Moved languidly. As though simply being in her body brought pleasure.

My attention lingered on her magenta fingers. Long and finely jointed, they dressed a sheaf of brown paper around my purchase. She said nothing as she worked, but her lidded eyes pursued mine. After a moment, her father knocked an elbow into her ribs. He gestured and spouted something gruff in a foreign accent. She had wrapped the paper inside out. She cursed and pushed him away. He shook his head and moved to the next customer.

We shared a smile.

I never did learn her language. Nor she mine. Our tongues failed us in this regard—yet spoke fluently beneath the sheets.

So feral was our passion that she had divided me against myself. So deep my craving for her, my insatiable hunger, that I often lost track of the days. Emerging from the cottage dewy and spent.

When my creative collaboration diminished, Cristofer took me by the scruff. Locked me in his room. Served me forceful coffee. Begged me to wake up.

Naturally I did not listen.

For months I had ears only for her song. For months we carried on. Body on body. Laughter and prosciutto. Champagne and bare toes. Let the rest of the world go to hell.

And then it did.

Cristofer lost a commission and I took the blame. He had asked for assistance and I was out of my head.

Soon afterward, the artist's ache began to scrape again at my craw. And I returned to Cristofer's cottage. To work beside him at the piano.

My sudden departure ignited banging fits of rage in my lover. I'm not sure how one becomes jealous of an inanimate object. But she was. She loathed the instrument. If she could have pecked out its eyes, she would have. Had Cristofer not guarded the door, she most likely would have taken her butcher's axe to the ivory.

Then she made me choose.

Pent up and exhausted, I made the only choice I could.

She threatened to leave. I begged her to stay. (Exhausted though I was, the hunger for her still clenched my belly.) She ignored my pleading and tore my suits to shreds.

I now frequent a different butcher. But there are days when I will stroll by the shop, if only to catch a glimpse of her vermillion fingers in the glass.

All this explains the tension of the piece unfolding in Jacque's drawing room. The one lifting from Cristofer's hands. For it contained within it not only the seeds of loss but the heady froth of regained freedom. The buzzing, clear-headedness that follows nervous collapse.

The crowd swooned.

I surged with joy.

Then sunk into panic.

It was not the result of having music of my making performed publicly. Many had heard my melodies and enjoyed them, however unsuspecting of their author.

What had me unhinged was that tonight *she* was hearing it. The woman of Light.

I could not bear to look in her direction.

What if her face bore disgust? Disapproval? Or, worse yet, disregard?

I steeled myself. Snatched yet another flute of champagne.

Then turned.

There are faces that transport us. That belong above altars. Hers was one.

I stared in utter disbelief. Her spirit had loosened. Her shoulders softened. Her face melted with emotion.

I gasped. Knowing it was my sound entering her. My music nesting inside.

It was then I saw a tear. It swelled in the far corner of her eye. And when it fell, it rode the slope of her cheek. I saw her raise a gloved hand to clear it, disguising the gesture as sweeping wisps of hair from her forehead.

Seeing her response, I struggled to restrain myself. I wanted to speed to her side. To console her. To commiserate. "There, there," I would say. "You mustn't cry. Just tell me what you heard. What it was that moved you ..."

Does not every artist long to be appreciated? Understood?

Is it not this yearning that grinds the spices inside us?

As I contemplated this, the music swerved. Cristofer had introduced the final refrain. And, I noted happily, returned to his original theme.

Panting, he planted the final chord. It hovered, shimmering above the instrument, then receded slowly, down its legs, soaking into the ground.

He released the pedal and silence prevailed.

The moment of transition.

The agonizing comma.

Then, as I'd hoped, the room erupted. The walls clamoring with applause. Shouts of praise.

"Bravo! BRAVO!!" the crowd cheered.

Cristofer started as if from a dream.

Jacque scanned the ecstatic faces on his guests. And smiled.

"Well done, Cristof," I said aloud. "*Well* done." I set down my flute and cheered. Glancing toward Ava, I found her damp-eyed and shining.

Then I noticed how she looked upon him.

Not Jacque.

But Cristofer.

And the green knife entered me.

I have seen a thousand women gaze upon him this way. Adoring him. Beguiled by his keen, eagle eyes. His soft lips. His physical earnestness. And never had I begrudged my friend this attention. In fact, I facilitated it whenever I could. And brought many ladies to his door.

But tonight was different.

Tonight I had beheld Light.

The candles had softened and dribbled down the iron. Well-booted butlers hurried between the flames with snuffers. The scent of smoke lingered along with late-staying guests.

"You look enchanting in that dress," a voice said from behind.

I turned. The man who had spoken was hidden within deep folds of drapery. I lifted my flute and found it empty. I was irritated. I had been most of the night.

"I imagine you would look more so without it," he added.

I scowled. The man laughed and emerged. He was heavyset, baggy-eyed, and greasy as a garden toad. His finely tailored suit dripped with riches.

I had been down this road before.

I looked about seeking a fresh flute of champagne, but all the butlers were busy overseeing the extinguishment of candles.

My pursuer leaned in. His breath smelled of liver. "As you can probably tell, I am an avid admirer of women. And, I must say, you strike me as a very unique specimen."

If only you knew.

I dragged tongue across teeth, sharpening the edges.

He pressed a hand to my elbow. His palm felt spongy. "Come this way," he urged. "I have something wondrous to show you."

Bubbling from champagne, I prepared to stab a verbal blade into my greasy admirer when a second hand tugged forcefully at my other elbow.

"Nesvelda! I've been looking for you," Cristofer announced. He faced my company. Gave a bow. "I beg your every pardon, sir," he said. "But I must speak with this lady at once."

The toad frowned. His look swung from me to Cristofer and back again. His eyes narrowed and he departed with a huff.

Cristof's intrusion made me even more surly. "You could have let me have my way with him first," I snapped.

Cristofer shook his head. "Don't bother with that," he said. He appeared pale. "You enjoyed the performance?"

"Very much," I said. "You played masterfully, as always."

"Yes, good, *good*," he said. He looked across the room. Seemed distracted. That further irritated me.

"I'm tired," I said, and made for the door.

"Wait! Not yet!" he said, chasing behind. "She has requested to meet you."

I turned around and gave him a thorough looking over.

Ahh, I thought. During his mingling, he had found for me a willing hussy. An empty head lashed to open legs. Salve for my broken heart.

"I appreciate the sentiment. But—"

"No, no, not that. It's our hostess. Madame Bertrand."

Ava?

"She wants lessons. Jacque insists that she take a female instructor. I mentioned you and they both seemed pleased."

"You *mentioned* me?"

The implications rippled through my brain.

"Are you *mad*?" I hissed, infuriated.

I tore from his grip and bolted for the door.

Cristofer stared after me. Dumbstruck.

Of course my reaction would baffle him.

How could he know the root of my fury?

Behind my back, I heard her call out, "Monsieur Vaughn? Have you found your companion? May we meet her?"

I halted. My ankles set in stone.

Should I turn back for one more look?

Then.

But what if she were to see me? And know me as I am? Would I never be able to meet her as I wished?

Then.

Have you lost your mind?! You could never pursue her. She is wife to the wealthiest man in Vienna. A virtual empress. An enchantment! What value could she possibly perceive in you—a penniless housekeeper loitering in your employer's cottage?

Then.

But could I truly live without beholding her once more?

Startled by my haste, the footman dropped my cape. He and

the butler scrambled at my feet.

Numb with terror, I fled into the cold. Uncloaked. Exposed.

Never looking back.

CHAPTER 2

I lay in bed, awake. Waiting for twilight to drain from the sky. Listening to the bubbling song of a scarlet-throated honeyeater. He was alone but optimistic. Certain the sun would hear him and rise.

It was not that I had woken early. It was that I had not slept.

In the ceiling above, I listened to mice treading through the thatch. Busy expanding their kingdom.

There was little point remaining in bed, sleep having avoided me. But I could not rise. Did not want to.

All I craved was to lie still, close my eyes, and let her face appear. Each recall of her quickening my pulse. Heating my belly.

After awhile, I was drenched in sweat.

When the power of repetition faded, I felt drained and despairing.

The truth was, I would never see her again.

But what life was worth living if not in the presence of such beauty?

What purpose more truthful than to worship at its feet?

To the uninitiated, this sounds like madness. But those who have savored understand.

I am a fool for Beauty. A ferocious connoisseur. A glutton with a hole in my gut.

A former lover once told me I was Beauty's whipping boy.

I prefer to think I am her honored servant.

Though it's true I have felt her lashes, I have borne every one with pleasure. I am not a religious person, but if I had to claim a spiritual creed, it would be: *To seek, honor, and emulate Beauty.*

There is no limit upon what is beautiful, of course, and my spirit is enlivened by a reverence, a vast sensitivity, for every detail. Such that even the slightest aspect of a person or object can occupy me for hours.

My most ardent enthrallment, however, is for the beauty of the female. It has been so since I can remember.

When I was three, my mother noted how deeply I gazed upon her sister, a tall red-haired enchantress. Troubled by my intensity, she hired a fortune-teller. The mystic, a freckle-faced woman with a cloak smelling of peat and wood smoke, told my mother that her eldest child would have trouble in love and would spend much of her life alone.

When my mother began to weep, the fortune-teller cupped her palms over her crystal dome and said, "Do not weep, madame. Though your daughter may grow alone, she will not be unhappy. For she possesses a gift that will enable her to conjure untold treasures."

I squeezed my eyelids and returned to my perch in the drawing room. There I again beheld her hair, those waving rays of auburn. Her cheekbones, their full blossoms gilded with candlelight. Beneath, her delicate throat trembled.

Hypnotized, I watched her glittering lashes as they swept upward.

Infused with heat, I could not remain a spectator.

I took hold of the memory.

And altered it.

Through sheer force of imagination, I willed her neck to turn. Watched her gaze drift to meet mine.

The fantasy unnerved me. Left me starved for breath. Trapped at the peak of a bridge between ecstasy and despair. While the conjuring of such beauty sent my spirit soaring, the knowledge that I could never encounter it directly flooded me with melancholy.

I know it is not rational, but it is the truth. And because unattainable female beauty abounds, I often find myself drowning in sorrow—in a sadness unlike any other—one that gnaws the bones and drains the will.

A cry issued from the ceiling. I opened my eyes just as a length of straw dropped to the floor.

I shook my head. I had become too distracted. Too immersed in delusions. And avoidance.

Tired of myself and my usual tactics I pushed back the covers and stood. I had learned from experience that the antidote for melancholy, however hateful, is movement.

My limbs dragged as though lined with lead, but I forced myself to move. In the corner, I bent before the bowl and splashed water on my burning cheeks. The mirror above confirmed the damage.

I tossed on a shirt and breeches and left the mice to their business.

Outside, the sun had begun to suggest herself, draping the trees in gauzy, purpled tints. The air smelled spicy sweet.

The honeyeater chirped from his perch, joined at last by a scattered chorus. Above the fray he pealed out a three-noted call. I froze, struck by the temperate warmth of his phrase. He called again and each note spilled a color before my eyes. The first, a D, shone the innocent green of poplar leaves. The next, a C-sharp, bloomed with a scarlet that matched the bird's own throat. The last, a B, trembled with ripened indigo, the same dressing the sky at its edges.

God knows, I had heard his simple song a thousand times, but never had it affected me so.

What had come over me?

I hummed his phrase aloud. My imagination orchestrated a harmony beneath. To my surprise, the music had merit.

Such is the reward of melancholy. Her twin sister, lesser known though no less delicious, is ecstasy. Strangely, both often come to call at the same time.

I smiled and filled my lungs with lilac.

Perhaps I would live after all.

The front door creaked as I let myself in. I heard the thump of paws as our cat dropped from the table. He blew across the floor and wove through my knees like long-haired smoke.

Seven years old and possessed of perfect pitch, he found us one rainy night. A ravaged kitten with steely eyes. We let him in and when he lapped a full bowl of milk and curled to sleep between the trusses while Cristofer ripened a ballade, I dubbed him Signore Minore in honor of my employer's two profound loves—the land of Italy and minor keys.

I knelt to scratch between the cat's ears. "What shall it be this morning, Signore? Catfish or quail?" Like his owners, he had a most discerning palate.

I glanced toward the bedroom. Cristofer had not yet risen.

I tied on my apron. Before long the stove was crackling and the kitchen filling with the aromas of coffee and bacon.

Into this fracas stepped our composer.

Signore and I looked up.

Cristofer appeared dim-eyed and drained. His hair flat. His buttons mismatched.

"It's warm today," I said.

"Yes." He took a seat. Spread his napkin.

I leaned over to pour his coffee. Strong, as he liked it.

The eggs frying in the skillet snapped between us. Signore hopped to the windowsill. Purred ferociously.

We fell into silence. Not the usual kind. Not the easy silence of old companions. But an unsettling lull. A scab over infection.

Cristofer fingered a chip denting the rim of his cup. I jellied a crust of bread.

The silence lingered.

"She initially asked for Clara's instruction," he said finally. Gave a shrug. "The madame knew of my friendship with the Thornes and wondered if I would recommend her as a student."

"So why didn't you grant our fair hostess her request?" I challenged. Knowing, of course, that the renowned pianist Clara Thorne had neither time nor inclination to take on an amateur student. Her hours already bursting at the seams with rehearsals, tours, wrangling children, and managing the affairs of her famous husband.

Cristofer looked up. Searched me with his eyes.

"Ah," he whispered. "I thought so."

"What?" I snapped. Defensive, I sprung to my feet. Hurried to the stove. I could tell by the look on his face that he'd found me out.

Before my Cristofer, I am naked. I am only what I am. Nothing more. Nothing less. Our intimacy and confidences having come to extend beyond our outward roles.

"I apologize for my oversight," he said. "I did not realize you fancied her."

I flipped the eggs. There was no point denying the truth. After a moment, the tension left my body.

My head dropped. "I'm sorry I abandoned you."

Cristofer shrugged. "I would never have suggested the introduction had I known. Had I seen—"

"No, no, no," I protested, returning to the table. "You needed to focus on your performance. There was no time for me, or my needs."

Have I mentioned my mercurial tendencies?

Ignore me and I play the brat. Hear me and I am yours. And can cycle between these two extremes at least three times per minute.

"There are no excuses," I continued. "I should have been at your side. It was bad form. Especially after ... the news. At any rate, I am truly sorry."

I slid the eggs onto his plate. They were cooked as he liked. Three perfect suns.

He smiled.

Signore Minore stretched along the sill. He knew the routine. Knew that in our strange little way we had cleared the air between us.

Cristofer picked up his fork. "Yes," he sighed, "the *news* ..."

"Put it behind you," I suggested with some force. "The loss is theirs."

We were speaking, of course, of his rejection.

For years, Cristofer had supported himself directing women's choirs. Now, having gained modest recognition as a pianist and composer, he sought a conducting position—an orchestra of his own. A greater challenge and one that, to his mind, carried increased respectability.

But his inquiry had once again been passed over. As was often the case, the orchestra's benefactors were admirers of the Liszt/Wagner school of dis-tonality. And not of the more conservative classical form—to which Cristofer and the Thornes adhered.

Cristofer's cheeks reddened. "They would rather scald the air with dissonance than endeavor true artistry!"

I laid a hand on his arm. On this we stood as comrades. And, therefore, had agreed to avoid unleashing polemical tirades on the other.

He calmed.

I poured more coffee into his cup. Twirled the chipped edge away from him.

"You realize," I began quietly, "that if you conduct, you will have precious little time to compose." It was an intentional pinprick. I watched it take effect.

"Compose? Why compose when no one has a taste for my music?"

He was goading me. We both knew he could not resist the desire to create. To divine and reflect the cosmos. Just as he knew I could not resist being near a woman such as Ava. But still, the game had to be played. The gushing compliments offered. The fears quelled. We were artists after all. A direct march toward self-assuredness bordered on the impossible.

"You *must* compose, Cristofer, because you were born to it. Because the world would be impoverished without your music," I assured. "Your gift is beyond question. The height to which you can lift the human spirit unparalleled. Do you think Richard and Clara and all your various supporters incapable of recognizing true talent? Do you think that they of such high taste and refinement would bother to falsely inflate your ego? And what of your performance last night? Did you see people's faces? Their ebullience? *Did* you?"

I noticed the strain in his forehead relax. "It was the elegant intensity of your theme to which they responded," he tried.

"Nonsense! It was the power and emotion of your performance. Not the few supplementary notes of mine."

We were both lying, of course, and both telling the truth. And, in this way, both receiving the nourishment we needed to survive.

"Compose. Perform. Expand your base of support and then inquire after the conductor position again, if you feel so inclined. But do not be surprised if in a year's time it is they who come begging at your door and *you* who turn them away."

Cristofer looked up at me, his eagle eyes pearling with gratitude. He reached for my hand.

"Thank you, sweet Henri," he said.

I pressed his palm. "I'm not doling out charity. Just relating the truth. Perhaps one day you, too, will believe."

Signore Minore jumped into his master's lap. Cristofer bent and nuzzled in soft fur.

Signore and I locked eyes. The feline and I have an agreement: We will, at whatever expense to our pride, work to keep the man of our house happy—and in so doing, protect the comfort and stability we have come to enjoy. Having both arrived at his home on the tail of desperate episodes, we knew his contentment vital to our security.

Cristofer sat up in his chair. "Have we any more bacon?" he inquired.

I nodded and wiped a bit of egg from his lip.

On my way back to the stove, I combed my fingers down Signore's back. All had been righted in our world.

The afternoon drifted along as it normally did.

Cristofer settled in at the piano. Needing to spend a few hours over the keys, to lose himself in fugues and shifting tones. That, more than anything, would repair his injured spirit.

As for myself, I didn't have the heart to listen, or assist. I felt frazzled and scooped out. The effort expended to lift my liege's mood had drained the last from me. Today I wanted only to be alone.

And to rinse her memory from my body.

The soil gave way beneath my boots as I pressed onward, following my usual path through the forest. Its winding avenue lined with slender beech trees. Their leafy canopy filtering the sun, stirring the path with breezy shadows.

In my mind, I replayed the honeyeater's song. And with each recall, expanded upon it. Feeling heavyhearted, I thickened the harmony with minor chords. Jumping over a small stream, I found my pace slowed by the water-logged ground. Striding forward, I extended the melody between steps, each drawn out with effort. When I had committed the several lines to memory, I listened to them repeat over and over. I then waited for the instruments to present themselves. To sing out and lay claim to the phrases fated for their tone. I drew in deep breaths as strings rang from under pebbles. Horns bellowed from tree trunks. Flutes scurried between the leaves. Soon, the very sky opened and music began to pour around me. I lifted my face, letting sunshine and notes splash on my cheeks.

It was through this strange collaboration of solitude, nature, and longing that all my ideas were born. Upon completion, such melodic morsels remained tucked inside my memory or, as with the themes for the butcher's daughter, found their way into a work of Cristofer's.

For I myself do not compose. Do not manifest with paper and ink the melodies of my making. That endeavor is for far greater spirits than those of a self-appointed housekeeper.

Again, I listened.

The forest shuddered with orchestras of light and song.

Phrase tumbled after phrase.

Lost to myself, my eyes glazed with inwardness. Which was why I failed to see the man kneeling in the bush.

When his hunkering shape caught my notice, I gasped and drew back.

Generally speaking, men kneeling in bushes are scheming something wicked. And I anticipated the worst.

"Sorry, mademoiselle—" he said. "Er, *sir*. So sorry to have frightened you!"

It was my breeches that had confused him.

I glanced down at the ground and noticed a strange contraption set between his knees. At its center sat a barrel suspended on its side like a miniature wine cask. One of its ends gaped open onto the world, while a smaller one on the opposing side was aimed at a floating black cylinder. Both the barrel and the cylinder were affixed to a board with hooks and clamps of hammered brass.

I frowned, on guard.

"Please," he started, his eyes enlarged behind thick spectacles. "Do not be alarmed. I know ... I realize ... it is an oddity, but I assure you its purpose is of the highest scientific virtue."

I scoffed, assuming the device to be an illicit machine. Most likely used to amuse the male organ. Though I could not discern in what manner.

"Then what, pray tell, does it *do*?" I challenged.

He had begun to answer when a bird landed on the branch above us. It called out and I immediately recognized the song. Another scarlet-throated honeyeater!

I dizzied as the ground shifted beneath me, swelling once again with music. Fortunately, the man did not notice my disorientation. His attention becoming fixed entirely on the bird. Having all but forgotten me, he pulled a pin from the machine and tilted the barrel's open mouth toward the creature.

The honeyeater cocked an eye and shuffled along its limb. Then, apparently determining that we posed no threat, opened his throat to the sky.

When the bird sang out, the man turned a crank, setting the machine in motion. As the song lilted above the trees, a pointed bristle at the barrel's smaller mouth shivered along the cylinder's blackened surface.

I stood bewildered.

Watching him, I would have sworn the man had ceased breathing, but still his hand spun the crank gently, evenly.

The bird then closed its throat and flew off. In the silence, the bristle fell still.

The man exhaled and dropped along the ground. "That was the lengthiest specimen yet!" he cheered, slapping a knee, his face ruddy with excitement.

A scientist? A madman? (Does a difference exist?)

Before I could inquire after what he meant, he urged me forward with enthusiastic pumps of his arm.

"Come look!" he said.

He knelt again alongside the device. With swift movements, he released a row of hooks and drew away the cylinder. He cradled the piece by its edges, taking care not to touch its surface.

"Look here," he said. "Can you see the sound?"

See the sound?

He urged me forward.

I bent closer. Then wondered if I were falling for the clever ploy of a robber. And half expected to feel his accomplice club the back of my head.

"There! Can you see the tracing left by the bristle?"

I squinted and could indeed see a delicate white line etched into the black. It curved around the cylinder, running straight in some sections, pulsing with jags in others.

My mind returned to what I had witnessed: the bird opening its throat, the cylinder turning, the contraption's bristle vibrating along with the creature's sound.

I stared into the man's eyes. Dumbstruck.

He smiled. "You understand."

I said nothing. Uncertain if what I thought were indeed true.

The man extended a finger and pushed up his spectacles. "The idea came to me after reading about photographs," he said, referring to the infamous invention that had taken Paris by storm. "I thought to myself, if we can fashion a permanent and palpable record of light, can we not do the same with sound?"

He gave a strange laugh. "It seemed a simple idea at the time, but that was nearly seven years ago!" He dropped the cylinder into a velvet sleeve.

"Wait. Are you saying that the bird's song is now—*contained*—on that cylinder?"

"In a manner of speaking," he said. He lifted his contraption and placed it inside a small trunk.

I thought for a moment. Tried to imagine that particular honeyeater's voice as a silent engraving. As a physical thing that could be carried. A piece of past kept ever-present.

It wasn't possible. Was it?

The man hefted the trunk onto his shoulder and turned up the trail.

"But what will you do with it?" I asked.

He shrugged. "I don't know yet. The ideal, of course, would be to make the line sing again. Maybe by reversing the process? Altering the bristle's shape? Connecting the etching to the barrel? Maybe employing some mechanism of reverberation?" he mumbled, sifting through various ideas. "Ah well, what's the use," he said finally. "The solution will come to me eventually. It always does."

I stared. Struck by his confidence.

"Enjoy your walk," he called over his shoulder, disappearing with his trunk of abducted song.

By the time I returned home the air had thickened with evening perfumes. As the cottage slipped into view I heard Cristofer at the piano. His music flowered above the roof, its tendrils trailing from the windows. I could tell by the weave of chord progressions that he was inspired.

Inside, a candle burned on the mantle. Cristofer leaned over the piano, his body curving to meet the keys, his shirt undone. He played a few bars then stopped and brought pen to paper. Scribbling furiously along the staff.

Beneath the instrument, Signore Minore lay stretched and purring.

I closed the door, dropped my coat, and sat quietly on the bench alongside my employer.

"It's coming," he said, his voice fevered.

I scanned the paper, noting that the score featured multiple staffs.

"A concerto?" I asked in disbelief.

"Yes," he said.

My eyes widened.

In the entire volume of his output, Cristofer had yet to attempt a piano concerto. His avoidance due entirely to the fact that any work approaching such a length and complexity would immediately draw comparison to that of Beethoven. A terrifying prospect.

For whom, then, was he attempting the piece?

I could think of only one person.

He fanned the fingers of one hand across a chord and with the other expanded his score.

"Richard came by," he said, his eyes on the page. "He and Clara will be coming for dinner tomorrow."

"They have returned from Munich, then?" I asked.

The famous couple had gone to attend the premiere of Wagner's opera *Tristan und Isolde*.

"Yes, and the trip seems to have ignited them."

I nodded. "I'll roast a chicken."

Signore Minore opened his eyes at the mention of food.

"And Henri?"

"Yes?"

"Richard has made a most wondrous request."

I waited.

Cristofer swallowed. "He has asked me to compose a work for Clara."

Ahh, I thought, my suspicions confirmed. That explained the flush in my companion's cheeks. The sudden and daring rush at a concerto.

"How exciting!" I cried.

"Yes," he said with a sober nod. "She intends to perform the piece on her grand tour through Germany. It seems they found the *Tristan und Isolde* work wholly devastating. And have become convinced that a concert of music composed solely by Richard and myself will fire a necessary fusillade for our philosophy."

"While advancing *your* name in the public," I added.

Cristofer's blush deepened. "He thinks I am ready."

I crossed my hands in my lap. "This is a momentous day."

Aside from being one of the age's most respected composers, Richard Thorne also served as an ardent advocate of rising musical talents. To have him not only laud Cristofer in public but request that he compose a piece for his famous wife was an honor of the highest degree.

Cristofer set his quill on the sideboard. His fingertips stained with ink.

"What do you think of this?" he asked. He played the introduction in which he rolled out a five-note motif. "Then the horns answer, or perhaps the bassoon, with this ..." He echoed the motif in a lower octave, adding a crescendo. "Then the strings carry us here, to the first point of departure."

"Heroic," I said.

His growing movement, the first, the allegro, was indeed bold. It raised an impressive wall of tonality, a clear attempt at grandeur.

Leaning in, I placed my fingers on the keys and replayed his introduction. Exactly. Then I carried it in a different direction. "What if you leapt up to an F-sharp here?" I suggested. "Just before the bridge." His theme broadened beneath us.

Cristofer scooted forward on the bench. "Yes," he whispered. "Excellent."

I withdrew my hands, letting him assimilate and expand upon my suggestion. A drop of sweat slipped beneath his sideburn. He had entered the magical place. The holy temple. And was thoroughly absorbed in creation. I suggested a few more divergences, but my heart was not fully engaged. His song was his song.

Somewhere in the trees outside, I could hear my newly discovered melody lingering. I longed to stretch my hands along the keys and render a body worthy of the honeyeater's music, something more than a scraggly line etched in lampblack. But today Cristofer needed the instrument to bend to *his* imagination.

My hour of communion would have to wait.

The scents of rosemary and roasting potatoes drifted along the walls. Cristofer moved between desk and piano, wrangling the feral concerto he hoped to tame. I listened critically, spooning preserved apples from a jar and sipping wine.

Hours later, two plates sat on the table. Our dinner growing cold.

I nestled in my chair, reading poetry. Though hungry, I was happy to wait. This was not the first night our dinner had sat untouched. Nor would it be the last. We shared such mutual thirst for inspiration, such longing for her approach, that a chilly meal seemed a pittance.

When Cristofer finally arrived at the table, his eyes were ringed with red, his hair wild, his shoulders hunched. He looked as if he'd wrestled a lion.

I lifted the silver dome from his plate.

His eyes widened at the sight of food. I lit the candle between us and maintained a respectful silence.

Cristofer tore off a leg of chicken and gorged. I poured him a glass of wine.

When he was done, he pushed back slightly and groaned.

I waited patiently then finally asked, "It was good?"

He closed his eyes. "Yes," he whispered, knowing I meant the music.

I smiled. Feeling joy at his success.

I watched the waves in his hair come alive in the candlelight. His gray eyes lambent, staring inwardly.

It was in such moments that I wondered how my brother might have appeared, had he been granted the years to manhood.

Would his heart beat with equal parts tenderness and brilliance as my Cristof?

Staring at the floor, I replayed a memory. Not of a grand event. But a simple moment. I was standing in my mother's larder. On the floor, beneath jars of preserved peaches, sat my two-year-old brother. In his small, square hands he held a tin of elderberries. Devouring them one at a time. I watched his ample lips cup the round fruits. Pump them eagerly into his mouth. I saw his eyes light at the burst of flavor when flesh gave way. Saw his crooked smile and stained palm.

I squeezed my eyes until the vision vanished behind stars.

Years had passed, yet still I could not look back. Could not endure the pain it tendered, the cleaving of heart from chest.

What was the point in looking back?

The etched line, according to its inventor, could not sing again.

I looked out the window. Above, the stars knit into the sky, jewels interrupting velvet.

Nothing remained forever.

Beauty waned. Breath faded. Light dimmed.

"I will make a fire," Cristofer said from behind an empty plate.

I started. "Yes. Of course."

Hearing the catch in my voice, and seeing me in some distress, he remained seated. He passed me his napkin. I dabbed it at my dampened cheeks. We were silent for several minutes. I had never told him of my past, and he had never pried, but being gentle in some part of him, he had intuited its sadness.

I cleared my throat. "You will work tonight?" I asked. It was a pointless question. We both knew he would tangle with his new piece well into the small hours.

He nodded.

I stared into the candle. "And what have you decided about our hostess?" I asked.

"Our hostess?"

"Madame Bertrand. You offered me as her instructor."

"Ah. Yes," he said. Thought for a moment. "I suppose I will inform her that you had to leave the country. Unexpectedly. Perhaps a death in the family?"

I winced. "A worthy excuse."

He looked over his shoulder. Eager to return to work. "Perhaps Richard will know someone who would suit her. I shall ask him tomorrow."

Ava's eyes flashed before mine, and for a moment I felt as though I might fall apart. Instead, I carried away our dishes.

Not wanting to further interrupt his evening, I tidied the kitchen, set out a warm slice of strudel, and headed for the door. "Good night, then," I said softly.

"Good night, Henri," Cristofer said from the fireplace, already ushering the flames.

Inside my cottage, darkness concealed the outlines of things. I did not bother lighting a candle. There was nothing I wanted to see.

I lay down along the feathered mattress. The mice above were still. Only the crickets were awake, their churring at every window.

I stretched a hand underneath the bed sheet, longing to feel the warmth of flesh returned.

But I was alone. My heat dissipating into air instead of into the limbs of another.

Normally I relished my life of solitude.

But that night, I felt only ache. And unsettledness. As if a small force were trying to escape from my heart or, perhaps, break its way in.

CHAPTER 3

*T*he cottage was silent when I stepped inside. Hungry and ready
for breakfast, Signore brushed at my shins.

The piano room showed signs of a late night. Sheets of manuscript
damp with ink lay drying atop tables, chairs, and the instrument's
lid. An even larger number rested in crumpled balls on the floor. A
plate of crumbs sat on the sideboard. A row of once-thick candles
spread in a shallow riverbed.

I tossed a chicken's neck into Signore's bowl and lifted my market
sack. There was no point in cooking breakfast. Cristofer would not
rise until the afternoon. And I needed to gather provisions in order
to prepare dinner for the Thornes.

On my way out, I felt the piano tugging at my back. The promise
of her tones luring me. I turned. I could not play the instrument, of

course, as the sound would wake Cristofer. But I could touch her. Run my fingers along her slotted spine.

I sunk to the bench and breathed in. Heard the honeyeater's song coursing through my body and silently depressed the matching keys. The ivory felt cool on my fingertips. Somewhere in the cavern of my inner ear, the song came to life. I bent to the music, my hands instinctively carving the harmony's chords.

I played in silence for nearly an hour, gathering the finger patterns and chord shifts into my memory. With those in hand, I could mold and shape the song in my imagination whenever I wished.

Yet as the honeyeater's melody coursed through me, I felt a sudden and unsettling compulsion. The prodding of a root. Inside my gut.

My eyes swept furtively to Cristofer's tray of quills.

I kept to my seat. Surprised to find I was trembling.

Then, without warning, the floor tipped.

Thrown off balance, I reached for the piano.

After a moment, the world stabilized.

Relieved, I rose hurriedly from the bench, lifted my sack, and departed, silent as I had arrived.

The path through the forest appeared much as it had the day

before, though a golden dust laced the earth. Fallen clouds of pollen from the wild lilies.

I arrived at the area where I had spied the scientist and his strange device. He was not there. I doubted if I would ever see him again. Nor would the bird whose voice he had taken.

I arrived at the bridge. A boy stood fishing on its peak. His oversized pants were lashed round his waist with a cord. His shoes stepping two sizes beyond his feet.

"Step lightly or you'll scare the fish," he pronounced as I passed.

I tipped my hat and floated across on tiptoe. On my way I noticed his pail, empty but for river water.

As usual, I could smell the market long before it came into sight—the scents of yeasty breads, sugared cakes, dusky coffees, salted pork, candied fruit, dried tobacco, all blended into a sultry mix that hovered above the cobblestones.

"Hello again, sir. Might you like some carrots?" the farmer asked, lifting a bouquet of orange fingers, the dirt still clinging to their roots.

I nodded and dropped the vegetables into my sack. "What do you have for greens?" I asked.

He looked over his goods. "Swiss chard, this morning, sir. Strong crunch. Bitter. Sauté with French butter and you'll weep."

I smiled. "Three bunches, then," I said.

It felt good to be in motion. To be in open air.

I stopped by the coffee trader. Burlap sacks stood swollen and open-mouthed. Mounds of chocolaty beans filled the air with the spice of Turkish and Arabic hillsides.

A young woman with black eyes and caramel skin stood nearby wielding a silver scoop. "What would please you today, sir?" she asked. Her glances suggested she was not referring to the coffee.

Before I could answer, her sister jumped down from their wagon to lend assistance. She arrived flushed and panting. Waiting for my reply, she pressed her body along her sister's.

They were young, but their ways were not.

Wound together they appeared as a two-sided creature of the sea. A maritime vixen. Seahorse eyes and mermaid skin.

What was it about women selling wares?

I felt my heart skip a beat. Under normal circumstances, I would have relished these miracles of the deep. Would have shucked the oysters from their shells and sipped the brine. But just at the moment when I might have let an invitation slip from my lips, I found myself unable to speak.

The young women leaned forward, churning with anticipation.

I looked again into their fishy eyes and felt lost at sea.

They were ravishing indeed. But they were not Her. And their beauty failed by comparison—a most unjust but certain defeat.

I turned from the stall shaking my head.

Was I ruined for life?

Chained forever to an impossibility?

To a treasure beyond my reach?

Such were the worries preoccupying me when I ran headlong into a wall of breasts.

"Why not tangle with someone your own age?" they grumbled.

I looked up into a black hole. A mouth vacant of teeth.

Their mother.

She lifted a metal scoop over her head as if to flatten me.

I covered myself and fled, the sisters laughing in my wake.

I came to rest at my new butcher and had him fill the rest of my sack with chicken. Thus provisioned, I turned again for the forest, eager for its cover.

Drifting under the canopy of beech trees, my steps found a regular rhythm. As I drew further from town, I felt my breath ease. Above the spine of my measured pace, the music finally broke free and began to sing. While the minor chords and various melodies held sway of their own accord, my own aching began to seep inside. Drawing out deep strings and plaintive woodwinds.

Inevitably, the piano arose.

Its opening melody a descending chain of fragile, silver-sided thirds. With nearly unbearable ache, each chord sunk into place. Above them, rose a phrase that strained upward to reach passing clouds, then tumbled down to mingle in the dens of wild crocus.

Slipping back over the bridge, I tipped my hat again to the fisherboy. He eyed with suspicion the bright carrot tips poking from my bag. As I clamored across the boards, I peered down once again into his pail. Inside writhed two speckled curves. Their fins sweeping the metal walls.

From the height of the bridge, I looked upriver. There, flowered hills rolled upward to a clear-faced crest. Perched at its top stood a white castle, flags shouting from the towers. Its only visible attendants the hawks drifting in slow cyclones.

Somewhere inside, her voice echoed along stone walls.

My feet yearned to turn me in that direction. To the slow climbing spiral that would deliver me to her door.

I felt a tug as sure as the young fisherboy's hook.

But what would I do if I were to arrive at her home? Haunt the perimeter? Stare in open windows?

Perhaps I could arrive as myself, give her lessons, let nature take its course?

Take hold of yourself, Henri, my inner voice cautioned.

Behind me, the young boy yelled and a breathless fish slapped on top of the bridge. The creature whacked its tail against the boards, fighting the airless void.

Feeling my own breath shallow, I clutched my sack and hurried on.

The silhouette of her castle burning beneath my hat.

The cottage was silent upon my arrival. I called out. Signore Minore glanced up through sleepy slits. No response from Cristofer. I thought that odd.

I dropped my provisions on the table and searched the rooms. In the kitchen basin, I found coffee grinds. In the bedroom, an unmade bed. Atop the piano, Cristofer's manuscript.

He must have stepped out to clear his head.

Intrigued by the manuscript, my eyes dropped to the lines of notes on its first page. As I drew across them, each instrument came to life until an entire orchestra swelled inside my ears. I stepped back as the theme ballooned like the ego of a self-proclaimed prophet. The percussion bantered with brassy boasts, the strings stretched toward the showiest of octaves.

I shook my head and sifted through the pages of what would become the concerto's first movement, its allegro. But the phrases were relentless. Each unfolding with an oppressive glare. With self-conscious showmanship.

As I'd feared, it sounded like an amateur striving to mimic the magnificence of Beethoven. But without the gravitas of mastery and self-knowledge.

It was not impressive. It was not tasteful.

And it was most certainly not Cristofer Vaughn.

I glanced over at the chickens, their necks cinched in the mouth of my sack. I knew I should begin to prepare the evening meal. But could not resist the compulsion to assist.

There were no two people on earth Cristofer wished to impress more than Richard and Clara Thorne. Most especially Clara. It was clear, however, that emotion had overcome his sense. Intimidation strangled his genius.

I sunk to the bench. The world forgotten.

Several hours later, Cristofer burst through the door, a pained expression on his face.

He set his hat on a bench and removed his boots. Their soles caked with mud and flowers.

He charged toward the piano but, his vision not yet being adjusted to the dim interior, collided with me instead.

"Henri! I'm so sorry—" He fell back blinking.

"Sit down, Cristofer," I urged.

He dropped slowly, his eyes following mine to the manuscript.

"What is this?" he asked.

I drew in a breath. "Your masterpiece," I said.

His eyes remained on the manuscript. On the introduction that I had reworked. And the piano's first theme.

Having crossed out and rewritten so many notes, I hoped that he could see the brilliance behind the damage.

I heard a sound issue from his throat. He was humming.

I remained silent, allowing him to hear the various instruments.

He dabbed finger to tongue and leafed through the sheets.

Seeing the look in his eyes, I wondered if I should have waited to confront him with the truth of his misguided efforts. And to share my suggestions at a later time.

"My God ..." he croaked.

I cringed.

"What have you done?"

My head fell. I should have waited.

"I thought I was doomed," he said. "But now, with this, I am *saved*."

I swallowed. "You approve?"

He pressed a palm against his forehead. "I left here believing I had unleashed a disaster."

"Oh no, no," I countered quickly. "Quite the contrary. I found many jewels within your pages. But they were buried beneath an

uncharacteristic pomp and circumstance. It were as if you were trying to woo a woman with a circus drum. Most unbecoming. And
certainly unworthy of your talent."

Cristofer fell back with a sigh. "Henri, you have once again
spared me from myself."

I, too, fell back in relief. "Do not over-credit me. I didn't really
contribute anything. I simply mined the vein that was already present." I hesitated. Then made one further observation. "I did notice,
of course, that the piano does not enter for quite some time."

He chuckled through nerves. "For a while, I wasn't certain she
would lift her voice *at all*."

I rested on an elbow. "I cannot begin to imagine the strain this
commission has leveled upon you," I said. "It would present a challenge to anyone's equanimity."

"Yes. And now even *more* pressure has been heaped upon me."

"How so?"

"This afternoon, Monsieur Bertrand requested that, as soon as
possible, I perform a preview of the piece for him and his wife." He
buried his face in his hands. "On the way home I had to restrain
myself from jumping off the bridge."

My limbs chilled.

"You visited the Bertrands' today?" I managed. Looked over at
his dirty boots.

He nodded. "It was at Richard's suggestion. Knowing of the madame's appreciation for Clara, and the monsieur's for me, he thought they might be convinced to provide patronage for the concerto's premiere."

"I see," I said. But I didn't. My mind was whirling. Perhaps at the very moment I had been eyeing her castle, mulling its impossibility, my employer had simply walked inside.

I blinked. Unseeing. "And what of the madame?"

Cristofer shrugged. "She was not at home. But I did leave word that, regrettably, you would be unable to serve as her instructor."

We both fell silent. His eyes drifted again to the manuscript. Mine to the floorboards.

"Your boots need cleaning," I said finally, and headed for the door. On the way, I felt the house turn upside down.

Clara and Richard arrived with a bouquet of ferns they had collected on their walk.

"What a delicious aroma!" Clara said, removing her bonnet. "Henri must be working her usual magic."

I liked Clara immensely. She was young and brilliant. And though not overtly attractive, the intensity of Light that shone through her eyes could melt glass.

Richard carried an armload of gifts into the kitchen.

"Two bottles of Chianti, a loaf of Clara's molasses bread, and some spicy chocolate I found in the market," he announced.

"Marvelous!" I cheered.

He smiled. Lifted my hand. Planted an affectionate kiss.

The Thornes are one of those couples a person feels compelled to admire. The beginning of their life together had been wrought with adversity—Clara's father having refused to give Richard his daughter's hand, even going so far as to take the matter to court. But since then, the two had blossomed into perfect unity around their careers and the raising of their several children.

And when Richard looked upon his wife, one could see that the years had not dulled his ardor.

I busied myself setting the ferns in a vase. In so doing, one of my cufflinks popped loose and dropped into the water. Irritated, but needing to baste the chicken, I decided to fetch the accessory at evening's end.

Engrossed in conversation, Cristofer and Richard stepped outside with a bottle of Chianti. I offered Clara a glass but she declined.

As was her way when entering a room, she gravitated immediately toward the piano. Having learned to sit at the instrument before she could walk, the keyboard compelled her instinctively. Light to a moth.

"So tell me, Henri. What are your latest escapades?" she asked, walking past the keyboard, skimming her fingers along ivory.

I grinned.

Being an aberrant and independent spirit herself, Clara thought nothing of my wandering yet reclusive ways. Nor my love of women.

"There is painfully little to tell, I'm afraid."

"Oh surely there must be something!" she insisted.

Given Clara's relentless schedule and the constant demands of her family, I knew she derived a vicarious thrill hearing of my adventures.

"Well," I began, "I did recently encounter a pair of mermaids at the market."

"The ones who run the coffee stall?"

"The very same."

"Do tell!" she said. "We have just now seen them. Quite an extraordinary pair, I must say. And those *eyes!*"

Not wanting to disappoint, I offered up a story, exaggerating the interlude, as well as the height and weight of their mother and her metal scoop.

Clara roared with laughter. When she settled, she shook her head with maternal admonishment. "You really should be more careful, Henri," she said. Then added, "Though a coffee scoop is certainly an improvement over a meat cleaver!"

I winced with self-deprecation. "How true."

Unable to further resist the piano's magnetism on her person, Clara dropped to the bench. Without warning, she shot out a series of rapid-fire scales, adjusting her touch to the instrument's particular action. When satisfied, she launched into a bagatelle of Richard's that lifted the roof on bubbles of joy. Her playing elevated my mood. I set about preparing a cheese board.

Later, when the piano fell silent, I looked over and saw Clara leafing through various stacks of manuscripts. After a bit of shuffling, her attention fell to a single piece. This she drew down and commenced to study with some interest. After what seemed an unusually long time, she set the sheets upon the rack. Bent close to the keys. Began.

I froze at the peal of the first chord.

It was not her selection that had startled me—her having chosen Cristofer's most recent rhapsody—the one he had performed at the soiree. But rather, it was the section of the piece where she had begun—having skipped Cristofer's theme entirely to sweep directly into mine.

The one inspired by the butcher's daughter.

Her arms spread quickly across the aching, roundabout battle between octaves.

Had she chosen that passage on purpose?

No, of course not!

Her choice could only have resulted from coincidence.

As far as anyone knew, I was employed solely as a housekeeper. That I happened to possess an average musical aptitude meant I could also assist with the copyediting and transcribing of Cristofer's scores.

The rest of our arrangement we carefully safeguarded.

For example, to prevent accidental discovery of my creative assistance, Cristofer and I immediately destroyed any and all evidence. Therefore, if I were to enhance one of his manuscripts with my scribbles, as I had that day on his concerto's allegro, I would transcribe a fresh copy, in a single hand, and burn the other. In this way, no trace remained of our mutual efforts.

Clara stormed on. Unrelenting. Pounding through percussive sequences with gusto. Her face flushing with effort.

I stared out the window, trying to keep the memories the piece evoked at bay.

When she came to the moment of transition, where Cristofer's theme overlaid mine, she abruptly stopped. Turned toward the kitchen.

"Well!" she huffed. "That was certainly a provocative passage."

Saying this, she set an elbow on the piano to focus again on the music.

"Yes," I agreed absently, bending to scrape a bit of mold from a cheese rind.

After another long silence, she said, "Have you ever noticed our Cristofer's propensity for arrhythmic and somewhat jarring thematic shifts?"

"What?" I said, feigning a lack of comprehension. For I did not wish to give the impression that I could grasp the complexities of musical theory. Nor did I feel at ease with her insights.

Ignoring me, she held up the sheets of Cristofer's score. "In here, as in a great deal of his work, one can almost detect two distinctive personalities. One, conservative and calculated, the other rhapsodic."

I shrugged. "Cristofer is a complex man."

Clara laughed aloud. "I'm certain we can both attest to that!"

I grimaced. Turned my attention to the roasting chicken.

The pianist sighed. "Composing is such a mystery to me," she confessed. "Yet when I hear a piece like this, rife with gravitas, with such reverence and ache, I feel as though I can almost grasp the nature of the endeavor, and it makes me yearn to try."

"I think your public would welcome that effort from you," I said, hoping that I had not overstepped my bounds. For who was I, the mere keeper of the house, to make suggestions to the great Clara Thorne?

I felt relief when she laughed.

"Henri, in the entire history of music there has yet to be a great female composer. I really cannot see any reason why I should be the first," she said. Then added, "Especially when I suspect strongly that this mantle belongs on the shoulders of another."

I met her leading statement with a blank stare.

Seeing it, Clara let out a sigh. Slapped down the fallboard. Strode into the kitchen.

"I will take that glass of wine now," she huffed, her flinty eyes sparking.

Despite the distraction, the chicken arrived moist and tender, the vegetables crisp and deftly herbed. Richard paid high compliments in particular to the chard.

As always, the esteemed musicians insisted I join in their feast. An invitation that never failed to humble me.

Talk at the table progressed easily. Not wanting heavy topics to weigh our pleasure, the conversation danced around the weather, recently discovered walking paths, and children.

In that vein, Richard related a story about their second son, Ferdinand.

"He has phenomenal powers of observation that, I must admit, I failed to notice earlier on," he said.

He went on to tell how one afternoon he and Ferdinand had

dropped by the neighboring farmers who were in the field running a threshing machine.

"It's a complicated device," Richard noted. "Full of levers and knobs. Very difficult to operate."

During the visit, the elder Thorne reported that his son seemed entirely disinterested in the machine, focusing instead on the crickets clicking through the grass. "I never once saw him look directly at the contraption," he said.

"Two days later," Clara continued, "our neighbor stormed up to our house leading Ferdinand by the ear. Turns out he'd strayed back into the field and gotten the machine up and running all by *himself*. And apparently had gotten up such a head of steam that he'd knocked down an old lady's clothing line!"

"Did demonstrable damage to her undergarments," Richard added with a wink.

When our laughter died down, Richard wagged his head in disbelief. "I would have sworn he hadn't taken any notice at all."

While I, too, was delighted by the story, I could not help but be distracted by another drama unfolding simultaneously.

It was Cristofer's gaze.

The more animated Clara became in her storytelling, the more my companion's eyes smoldered.

Only I knew of the secret love shadowing in his heart. His

overwhelming desire and noble restraint.

Being a woman, I had to believe that Clara could sense his longing. Could feel it pressing against her flesh. But seeming certain of her life and marriage, she never once reciprocated. For which I was truly grateful. Though I knew this lack ate at my liege from the inside.

Richard, fortunately, remained unaware of his friend's ardor. And I further doubt he would have believed anyone who suggested it, being such a loyal friend and admirer of Cristofer.

But the tension crackling between the two always unsettled me.

After dinner we retired to the drawing room. I poured sifters of brandy for myself and the men. Clara returned to the piano and began to play a series of nocturnes. The rest of us ringed the fire.

Richard turned to me. "Cristofer has told you about the commission?"

"Yes. I was most pleased to hear of it," I said.

"Clara thought of it while in Munich."

"Were you much displeased with the opera?" I asked.

"*Displeased?*" Richard spouted, his face reddening. "We left after the opening movement. A hideous, discordant thing. An abomination. The effect was entirely tortuous. I insisted they return the cost of our admission!"

Clara stopped playing. She looked suddenly serious. "It was the most repugnant thing I have ever heard," she said.

On and on it went, the Thornes detailing Wagner's musical trespasses.

Such conversations, either in support or opposition to the Wagnerian school, were occurring in drawing rooms throughout Europe. The speakers' arguments and tempers were enflamed enough to burn books in their shelves.

The acrimony that existed between the opposing schools cannot be exaggerated. The first, advocated by Cristofer and the Thornes, among others, honored the upholding of the classical music tradition: pure harmonic scales, unmodified chord progressions, uplifting melodies, and harmonic resolution. Above all, its proponents served as guardians for music of substance, that which attained the highest human aesthetics of grace and beauty and intelligence.

The second school, advocated by Wagner, Liszt, and others, was eager to sweep away the cobwebs of "the old guard," including the likes of Beethoven, Bach, and Handel. Its ardent supporters hoped to inspire and invent an entirely different music, a new aural experience that pushed the limits of human ingenuity. They were chemists of sound, slaving away in their labs to mix never-before-heard compounds. They staunchly rejected boundaries and balance and favored discomfort over pleasantries. Decoration over virtuosity.

The two schools could not be more diametrically opposed. Mutual hatred and venom rose from each camp as from troops engaged in civil war. And, like that most treacherous brand of conflict, the fighting made enemies of brothers—pitting musician against musician, patron against composer, artist against audience.

Though no shots had been fired, stories of sabotage abounded. Violins disappearing. Piano strings cut. Scores left in the rain. And the rumor of a possible poisoning—a young, outspoken cellist found face down in a tureen of soup.

As for me, I refrained from the debate. I longed, of course, to believe in the enduring truths of Vaughn and Thorne. To believe that great music would stand through the ages. But sadly, life had taught me that nothing remained forever.

Agitated, Cristofer got to his feet and began to pace. "Every note Wagner pens is a strike against the pillars of past genius and human decency. And yet he persists!"

Clara nodded. "I agree entirely," she said. "Which is why I insisted on the commission."

Cristofer halted. He stepped back and eyed her intently. It appeared that just the simple act of her agreement had aroused him. My attention dropped to his empty glass. He had consumed more than his normal share. I suddenly wished he would retake his seat. He himself would be mortified at the obvious exposure of his passions.

Fortunately, Richard had also imbibed a fair bit more than usual. He hoisted his glass into the air. "To preserving the pillars!"

he cheered, his alacrity breaking the tension.

I sagged with relief and raised my glass.

Staring into the fire, her face flushed with wine and flame, Clara said, "Henri, you've been reticent this evening. Perhaps to make up for it you will play something for us?"

I started.

"Wonderful idea, Clara!" Richard cheered. "I don't believe we've ever had the pleasure, have we?"

Cristofer flinched. Firstly, he would not wish the Thornes to learn of my abilities. And secondly, he most certainly would have wished Clara to have made the request of *him*.

For my part, I balked at her strange and unprecedented request.

Why on earth bring a dilettante to the bench in the presence of luminaries?

I looked over at my disappointed employer and thinking quickly said, "What a waste of your ears when you could have Cristofer play a bit of the concerto instead!"

Cristofer's head snapped up in fear.

"I have already transcribed it for you," I said, assuring him quickly. "The manuscript is on your desk."

My liege visibly relaxed.

I had, in fact, produced a clean copy of his draft that afternoon, having burned the one marked with my revisions.

"Yes! Yes! An even more wondrous idea!" Richard insisted as Cristofer went to retrieve his score.

Clara frowned, but said nothing more.

The first chord struck at the roof and shuddered down the walls. Heads turned. A hush fell over our group.

Emboldened, Cristofer leaned into the opening passage. Scrubbed of flagrancy, the bold heroism he'd originally intended shone through.

As the piece progressed, Richard's head bobbed with pleasure.

Strangely, Clara sat facing away from the piano. While the music unfolded, she stared openly into the flames, her hands folded in her lap.

At one point, just before a slight melodic digression, I saw Cristofer turn toward his audience. Saw him take note of Clara's distant stare. Saw him fill his lungs and sweep along the keys, building a crescendo that cried out with the agony of romance—one he no doubt hoped would provoke a response.

And it did.

As I looked over, I noticed the surface of her dark eyes begin to glisten.

Was it the drying effect of the flames? Or was she, too, harboring a hidden passion, a secret love?

I looked away, not wanting to bring attention to the silent drama.

I'm not sure if it were real or imagined, but the music bloomed with a new intensity, with almost unbearable emotion. I assumed it the result of Cristofer having seen Clara's reaction.

When he came to the end, he sagged along the bench. His breath uneven. "That's all I have," he said.

Richard leapt to his feet. "Bravo, my friend!" he cheered. "It is fine and lush and heartrending!" He turned to his young wife. "Do you not think so, my dear?"

Clara started as if from a dream.

"Yes," she said. "It certainly is." She stood and headed to the kitchen. "Might I have a glass of water?" she asked. "Sitting so close to the fire has left me singed."

It was not the fire that heated you, I thought, but kept this to myself.

I noted the blaze about Cristofer and knew he'd reached the same conclusion.

"Just wait until they hear Clara play your concerto in Munich! That will set the tides right again!" Richard said, chasing his comment with a full swig of brandy. "You must hurry and finish, Cristofer. Pour everything you have into it," he urged.

"Yes," Cristofer said. "I will."

The four of us stood at the door, flushed, saying our goodbyes.

Cristofer turned first to his friend. "Thank you, Richard," he said.

Clara approached as the men spoke. She peered over at the piano then turned to face me. Her cheekbones shimmered in the firelight. She held my look for what seemed a long time, then smiled weakly.

Closing her eyes, she leaned forward and grazed my cheek with a kiss.

When she drew back, Cristofer stepped in. He gently took her hand. But being unable to look her in the face, glanced down at her feet. When he gathered the courage to lift her hand to his lips, I turned away. I could not bear to observe the desire leaking from his body.

"My dear Henri," Richard said. The composer wrapped me into his arms. "You have fed us another beautiful meal. And warmed our souls with your hospitality."

"It was my pleasure. I only wish it could be more frequent."

"I assure you, you are not alone in that wish," he said. His attention drifted to the other two then back to me. "Oh!" he started. "I almost forgot." He reached into his breast pocket and removed a small item. "Give me your hand."

I spread my palm. Into it, he dropped my cufflink. The one that had tumbled into the vase.

But how had he found it? I was certain no one had seen it fall.

He smiled at my bafflement. "Like father, like son," he said with a small laugh. He then pressed Clara's hand along his forearm and together they stepped into the night.

CHAPTER 4

*F*ollowing our evening with the Thornes, life took shape around the rigor of Cristofer's work schedule. With the allegro well established, he feverishly began plotting the second movement for the concerto, the adagio, laboring at the piano until the evening's candles had reduced to misshapen pools.

I, on the other hand, threw myself into the arms of monotony, hoping she would lure me from my obsession. Each morning I rose before the sun and strolled to the market. I returned carrying sacks laden with meat, vegetables, and sweets. Unloading my hoard, I would sequester myself in the kitchen and set about preparing lavish meals for Cristofer and Signore.

Since I had little access to our piano, I continued to compose through food. Blending flavors as though they were sounds. Building chords of fig, orange zest, and mint. Crescendos of beef and asparagus. Beneath my hands, meals swelled like edible symphonies.

As I worked, I listened inwardly, letting the piece stirred by the scarlet-throated honeyeater play out. And, to my pleasure, the piece continued to grow.

When I wasn't at the stove, I distracted myself with long walks through the woods. Each day I watched groves of birch and alder richen with the maturing of spring. I heard bundles of newborns crying from their nests. Watched afternoon rains wet the grass. Every day I glanced behind bushes and copses, hoping I might again encounter the man and his sound machine. But he had yet to return.

Suspended in my patterns and culinary pursuits, I barely felt the wolf at the door, the occasional knocking of heart on rib cage.

Then the long-awaited day arrived. The afternoon that Cristofer would travel to the Bertrands' to present selections from his concerto.

Unable to sleep, I woke just as the stars began to fade. Dizzy for lack of rest, I splashed cold water on my cheeks and dressed.

I convinced myself that I had risen early so that I might be first to market and therefore certain of acquiring fresh cilantro—a critical ingredient for that evening's dish. But the truth was, the thought of Cristofer paying a visit to Ava's home had me disheveled.

It was not yet light when I arrived at the bridge. It rose over the river alone, the hour too early for even the fisherboy. Skirts of fine mist shrouded its arch and stanchions, making it seem as though one could cross over into thin air.

As I approached the high point of its spine, I had to force my thoughts away from the castle looming on the hillside. For weeks I had passed by without incident, but today its shrouded turrets tugged again on my person. When my mind's eye stowed away in the pocket of Cristofer's overcoat and he stepped across the cobbled threshold of her domain, I knew I had to take hold. Even imagining such an encounter carried too great a hazard.

Unsure if I could control myself, and suddenly disoriented by the mist, I decided to turn back and forgo the market. After all, I had amassed enough foodstuffs in my previous forays to prepare many meals. There was no need to put my sanity at risk for a few fresh greens.

By the time I arrived home, my head was spinning with imagined menus and exquisite combinations. I could not wait to get my hands on the spices.

But when I opened the cottage door, Signore bounded out as if fleeing a horror. Alarmed, I ran inside. Found Cristofer in his bedroom, bent over a copper bowl. Retching.

I ran to his side and held tight to his shoulders as he hacked and sputtered.

After a moment, he moaned and rolled to his side. "I'm ... sorry."

"Shh," I told him. "Be still." When it seemed he had reached a respite, we shuffled him to a chair.

"Is it nerves?" I asked.

He nodded.

I'd been worried about that possibility. After overexerting himself for weeks, he now faced the thing he most feared—promoting his work. Every time he had to step before a selection committee or patron, he fretted. It wasn't that Cristofer lacked confidence in his abilities. Or his music. It was more that he was possessed of a chronic desire to render perfection. What he dreaded was error, or a sub-adequate result of any kind. And this fear hobbled him whenever he faced assessment.

I poured him a glass of water. He sipped through pale lips.

"Better?"

"Yes."

I sat in the chair across from him.

"When are they expecting you?"

"In an hour."

"Have you selected the sections you will play?"

"No."

He listed onto the arm of the chair. "There is so much, so much that is incomplete, that is not ready."

"The parts I have heard are excellent," I countered.

"Because you wrote them!" he shot back.

"I'm not composing, Cristofer. I'm refining. Fleshing out. No more."

It was what I had to say. As a supporter. A co-conspirator. Though we both knew the truth of the matter.

"I need to rework the dénouement in the second theme."

"What you need is to get dressed."

He shook his head.

"Cristof, they have the means to provide patronage for the entire concert. You must go up there and secure this reward for yourself."

He drew shaky fingers through his mane.

"Have you forgotten that it is Clara Thorne who will perform your piece, not some half-pissed brothel buzzard? If you can't seek funding for your sake, seek it for *hers*." I hoped this entreaty would fan the fire in his belly.

After a few moments, he dropped quickly from the chair and knelt at my feet.

"Come with me," he begged.

"What?"

"I'll tell them you're my accompanist. A visiting cousin. *Something*."

I shrunk back. "You're mad."

"Please, Henri!"

My head spun to recall the tantalizing imagery from the soiree: her hair, her throat, her *Light*.

"But they have seen me before," I protested.

He shook his head. "Only once. As a *woman*."

I stared as his meaning crystallized. I got to my feet and pushed past.

"I can't."

He pursued me into the piano room.

"But you *must*, Henri," he said, his tone taut. Desperate. "If I fail at this, I will be ruined. Not only will word of Jacque's rejection spread throughout Europe but, without funding, Richard will be forced to retract his offer. And then Clara will not—" His voice thinned to nothing.

I stared out the window, numb with terror.

But for the heat prickling the back of my neck.

"I don't have any clean suits," I said.

He smiled.

"I'll give you one of mine."

The gravel cracked under our boots as we approached the portico. Beneath the castle's shadow, two stable hands busied themselves unhooking a team of steaming horses. Seeing foam at the animals' mouths, I swallowed. Glanced down at my costume and carefully observed every seam. Being somewhat smaller than Cristofer, I had pinned parts of the suit in place. Fortunately the alterations seemed to be holding.

Cristofer took a deep breath and dropped the solid metal knocker upon the door. He stepped back and laid a hand upon my shoulder. "I'm glad you're here …"

The sound of hurried footsteps echoed from inside. The door gaped like a dragon's mouth.

"Good afternoon, Monsieur Vaughn," the footman said. He cast a suspicious eye in my direction.

"This is my attendant," Cristofer said. He tipped his head toward the bulging portfolio beneath my arm. "The size of the manuscript necessitated assistance," he explained.

"And how may I introduce you?" he asked, a paunchy gut stretching his vest tight.

"Pleased to make your acquaintance. Henri Worth, I am," I said cheerfully, dropping a confident bow.

The footman lifted his eyebrows then gathered himself. "Very well. Follow me."

We made our way through the foyer toward the cavernous drawing room where Beethoven's infamous piano lay in wait.

Cristofer drew his hands behind his back, his fingers fidgeting.

"Steady now," I whispered.

As we drew closer, I saw the armoire behind which I had hidden the night of the soiree. A jolt of fear knocked against my breastbone.

Would they recognize me?

Would my false disguise result in arrest?

Or worse?

Such thoughts fled the moment the instrument came into view. Cristofer and I froze in our paces, the footman advancing alone.

The piano blazed with silent élan, her flanks glistening.

"You may re-acquaint yourself if you wish," the footman said. He slid back the bench. "I shall fetch Monsieur Bertrand."

I looked up at this announcement. Forgetting myself, I prepared to ask after the madame. Cristofer grabbed my forearm and squeezed. A silent warning. "If you would arrange the music here," he said, indicating the piano's gilded music stand.

Snapped to my senses, I unwrapped the portfolio and set to fanning out the pages.

"Monsieur Vaughn! So happy you've arrived!" Jacque shouted. He sped across the room furiously buttoning his jacket which for some reason had come open. He appeared red-faced and preoccupied. I worried that his jubilant welcome would unnerve Cristofer, but my liege met our host with equanimity, accepting the friendly slap on his back with a smile.

Jacque turned to face me. "And who is this handsome young man?"

I flashed what I hoped was a charming yet deferential grin.

"Henri is here to manage the manuscript for me," Cristofer said.

"Ah, very good." Jacque offered his hand but I stepped back with a polite bow. "A fellow pianist, I see," our host spouted, amused.

I watched his eyes travel along my frame and felt a great sense of relief when he appeared satisfied with the legitimacy of my person.

Further pleasantries followed while two servants positioned a richly upholstered chair for the honored spectator.

After a moment, Jacque dropped into his seat. "Please," he said, motioning to the piano. "My ears are yours."

"Are we not to wait for the madame?" Cristofer inquired.

Jacque rasped the knobby stub of his finger with the two that flanked it. "I'm afraid she's been delayed," he said.

I cast my face aside so as not to have anyone notice my distress.

Cristofer acquiesced and sunk gently to the bench. I knew I must attend to his performance immediately but was unsure if I could command my limbs.

When I felt the weight of Jacque's unwavering gaze, I sprung to action. Pressed close to Cristofer. "I have prepared both the first and second themes from the allegro," I whispered. Held my breath. Waited for him to choose.

My work, or his?

He tossed his wrists into the air and swept back his cuffs. Digging in his boots, he sat up tall and gave a sharp nod. "The first," he said.

Mine.

"Of course," I replied, and quickly removed the unwanted sheets. I obediently returned to his side. By the time I settled into position, I could feel his absence. He had already dissolved into the future. Into unborn sound.

He launched immediately, without warning. Throwing himself off the precipice before he could reconsider.

The sudden start shook off the last of my disappointment and I, too, fused with the oncoming tone.

He began with a sweep of intently oscillating minor chords. The sound of footsteps at night. Of uncertainty. And ache. The phrase repeated several times, creating a hypnotic effect, holding the listener's heart tight in its fist. Until it finally released upward in a grand crescendo capped by a hovering trill.

From there, the music began to wander, but with control, as if unfurling an intricate tale.

I swiftly pulled the pages as Cristofer progressed. Watched the keys give under his fingertips, the piano's curves shudder, the sweat gather on his brow. He was playing brilliantly.

At a slower point, I looked over to gauge our host's reaction. Jacque leaned forward, bent over his thighs as if shielding himself from some discomfort. As if fighting back deep emotions.

I was glad for his response, but thought it a bit extreme given that the music had yet to reach its peak.

Cristofer was unrelenting. The theme sped forward on a gathering pace. Floating on impossible runs of complex chords.

At last, the moment of finality arrived. His hands swept up and down the keyboard in explosive lengths, one melding into the next, unleashing an extraordinary ascent. The effort left both Cristofer and the audience breathless.

When he released the pedal, Jacque leapt from his seat, applauding as though in a concert hall, tears streaming down his cheeks.

"Bravo! *Brav-o!*" he called at the top of his lungs. Both Cristofer and I leaned back from our labors. Satisfied with the result. He tossed me a slight nod, acknowledging our collaborative success.

Then Cristofer stepped from the piano, leaving me behind.

Jacque rushed up and fell into his arms. "Magnificent, utterly *magnificent*, my friend," he sputtered, overcome. He lifted a silk handkerchief from his breast pocket and wiped his face. When he had regained control, he draped an arm across Cristofer's shoulder. "Come. We must speak immediately. In my study."

The partners disappeared behind a thick velvet curtain. Two footmen trailed them, one carrying cigars, the other decanting spirits.

Alone in the silence, my eyes dropped again to the piano. The scent of warm ivory rose to my nostrils, the keys having softened from recent attention.

I did not know whether I would be trespassing were I to touch the instrument.

No one had strictly forbidden it.

And it had been so long since I had felt keys beneath my fingers.

I checked around the great room, confirming that I was, indeed, alone. I tried to stave off temptation, but when my knees folded to the bench, I felt the familiar posture shape my body and could not resist.

At last I would hear the song that had, for weeks, been germinating inside my head.

My fingers curled into position. I set them down slowly. The keys surrendered with a suppleness I had not expected. Soft and silky, they yielded like flesh. Like the swells beneath a woman.

I moaned.

The silver-sided thirds descended haltingly. Heavy dew slipping from a leaf. The forest waking from slumber. Somewhere above, the honeyeater waited on a branch, hidden from the listener.

I elongated my playing, letting each chord enjoy an extended audience, a deep shimmer. The instrument's sound emanated from its maple curves, the vibrations returning from the walls and ceiling with enriched timbres. Tucked inside this aural halo, I felt quickly subsumed.

And then the melody of the honeyeater flittered from the branches. My right hand floating singly as if lifted on wings.

The piece, though greatly enhanced by the splendid piano, sounded much as it had in my head.

As the introduction began to dissolve into the central theme, a strange wave of feelings flooded over me. I had no idea what had caused the overwhelming rush—the piano's glorious tone? Joy for Cristofer's success?—but from that point forward, the music steamed with a passionate vitality the likes of which I had not felt in years.

The song drew in air and took shape around its breath. As it did, my eyes closed and my spirit cleaved in two—half creating the piece, the other grasping at the music, committing it to memory so that none would be lost.

I could have remained missing to myself for hours. And probably would have had I not heard from behind me the slightest gasp. My hands froze atop separate arcs.

Whoever stood watching did not speak.

Was it Jacque and Cristofer?

A searing heat fanned up my neck. Rippled across my cheeks.

I sat still, cursing myself.

What had I done?

It was my sworn habit never to play music of my own making, at full capacity, in a place where strangers might overhear. To do so risked unwanted attention. And raising questions that might threaten the arrangement with my employer.

I turned slowly. But did not see the men.

Instead, my eyes fell upon Ava.

The shock of her presence left me momentarily deaf.

"I beg your pardon. I did not mean to frighten you," she said, noting my distress. "Are you alright?"

I calmed somewhat at her concern, realizing that she was more likely a dilettante than connoisseur and, therefore, unable to judge gradations of talent.

But I had touched her piano without permission.

"Perhaps you should retake your seat," she suggested.

I stared blankly. Unaware that I had leapt to my feet.

"There is no need to stand on my count."

Oh but indeed there <u>was</u>.

She looked me over. Gave a curious smile.

I cleared my throat. "I beg your pardon. It was presumptuous of me to touch your instrument."

She laughed. "On the contrary. Anyone who plays music of such beauty would be *invited* to touch her."

I glanced up quickly.

What had she meant by that?

"Was it yours?" she asked.

"I beg your pardon?" I stuttered, my thoughts elsewhere.

"The music."

"No, of course not!" I said, recovering. "It was composed by Cristofer Vaughn."

Her lids lowered. "Ah."

I looked toward the velvet curtain wishing, suddenly, for Cristof's return.

"Would you play more of it?"

I shook my head. "No, madame. Those keys were made for finer hands than mine."

"Nonsense! My very own fingers have touched them."

"My point exactly."

She grinned.

I looked down, unable to bear the sheen of her.

A painful silence unfolded.

Finally, "Do you offer lessons?"

The clatter of boots echoed in the hall. Cristofer and Jacque burst through the curtains, rowdy with enthusiasm and spirits.

They halted when they saw both of us at the piano.

Ava broke the spell by casting a glowering look at her husband. "Darling," she said flatly, "I'm told you enjoyed your preview of the concerto."

I had said nothing of the kind.

Jacque slapped Cristofer on the back. "This man's a genius! Richard Thorne was entirely correct about the brilliance of his future!" He pushed his artist forward.

I busied myself collecting the sheet music.

When the men neared, Ava offered Cristofer her hand. Out of the corner of my eye, I watched his lips press her flesh. Inwardly, I cringed. That pleasure had been denied me.

"All of Europe will be talking about this!" Jacque said, his cheeks shining. "And the Bertrands will be known as patrons of Beethoven's heir!"

Cristofer smiled and adjusted his collar with a tug.

"I am certainly glad to hear this," Ava said. She turned to Cristofer. "Do you share my husband's enthusiasm, Monsieur Vaughn?"

"Of course, madame. And am honored to have your most generous patronage."

"Nonsense, it is *we* who are privileged," Jacque insisted. He turned to his wife. "My dear, please take your seat. You must hear this man's creation."

As if suddenly remembering his presence, Ava cast a sharp look upon her husband.

At that moment, someone coughed in a nearby doorway.

I looked over to see the toady man who had accosted me on the night of the soiree. I then watched in horror as he entered the room and strode toward Jacque, his cheeks as swollen as they had been that evening.

I turned as if to peer out a distant window, hoping he had not noticed me.

He bent toward our host, said something in his ear.

"Ah yes," Jacque said with a nod, maintaining his composure. "Thank you, Sarkov."

When he had finished delivering his message, Sarkov snapped his fingers at the footman waiting stoically in the corner. The youth dashed from the room on his errand.

Jacque addressed his wife. "My sweet, we must be off. We've been called to the chancellor's."

At that moment the footman returned, a coat draped along each forearm. He helped the madame into hers first, with all efficiency.

Sarkov stepped back to watch from a distance. When I felt his attention shift to me, I averted my face, feigning lint on a cuff.

"Monsieur Vaughn, my apologies for this intrusion. A most unavoidable matter," Jacque lamented. "But when we meet again, may we expect to hear the concerto in its entirety?"

"Of course," Cristofer said with an officious bow.

"Good. Then back to work with you!" Jacque cried with mock exasperation.

Cristofer grinned weakly.

Uncertain what to do, but sensing we needed to depart, I stepped to the piano, slid the bench underneath, and lifted the portfolio into my arms.

Ava turned to Cristofer, approached him. "I greatly regret missing your performance but will most certainly look forward to the next."

Cristofer dropped a graceful bow. When he rose, she offered her hand. Again. This time I was close enough to catch the scent that rose from between the folds of her dress. It was unusual. Fragrant.

Jasmine?

"A true pleasure, Monsieur Vaughn," she said.

"Equally, I assure you."

Ava turned to face me. My eyes fell into hers and the walls rushed outward, swallowing us in space.

I waited, yearning for the reach of her hand, the heat of her flesh at my lips.

But to me she offered only a cursory nod.

"Let us be off," Jacque called.

In a whirl of auburn and scented skirts, she was gone.

That afternoon Cristofer did not play the piano.

Nor did I.

While my companion paced up and down the drawing room, I set about cooking a meal of extravagant proportions. Heaps of turnips, vats of yams, a flock of quartered chickens, a pan of sliced beets, three shepherd's pies, and a thick bean stew. Despite the amount, I kept cooking, hoping the food would ground me. Since returning from the castle, I felt as though I could not trust the earth. As though dimensions had broken loose of their frames.

"Do you offer lessons?"

Her words played in my ears.

Had she really said them?

Cristofer sat for dinner. His forehead furrowed. Signore Minore draped himself across the windowsill, happy to avoid us.

I lifted my wine glass. "To your victory."

Cristofer tightened his lips. "She does not support the patronage."

"What? Who doesn't?"

"Madame Bertrand. She was irritated."

I scoffed. "From what I observed, she was irritated with the monsieur. Wives are often annoyed with their husbands. The reason most likely had nothing to do with your music."

He wagged his head in frustration. "No. She was late and showed only tangential interest. It was a bad sign. A very bad sign indeed."

You think she does not favor your music. Yet she gave her hand to your lips.

Twice!

"I think you have misread her. I would remain on your course. Continue working on the second movement, then start the third. After all, it is Jacque, not the madame, who controls the purse."

"True, true," Cristofer agreed. He stared into the scarlet orb of his wineglass.

Then, in a bout of selfishness, I said, "She asked if I gave lessons."

"Who did?"

"Madame Bertrand."

"Ah," he said, setting down his fork. "But Jacque will never allow a male instructor. He has said so many times."

I froze, felt my throat tighten. "Are you certain of this?"

"Oh yes. He is quite adamant about it."

I fell silent. My thoughts crashing.

Had I ruined my chance to meet her? Should I have accepted her first offer the night of the soiree?

No!

I could not make her acquaintance as a woman. Just imagining the encounter made me feel off-key.

Yet ... what if that were the only way?

Despite the amount and variety of food, Cristofer picked sparingly at his meal. For my sake, he tried not to appear anxious to go to the piano, but I could see him losing the battle.

Within minutes, his chair scraped the floor and he went to work.

Alone and restless, I returned to my dwelling.

When I opened the door, the air pressed in. Pillowing my senses. Even the mice in the roof felt unbearably close.

My fingers twitched, seeking the focus of the keyboard. But Cristofer would undoubtedly work through the night.

I looked at the empty bed and knew I had to leave.

But where to go?

I went and stood before the mirror. Still dressed in my employer's suit, I cut a handsome figure. I lifted a comb and smoothed my short waves with drops of scented oil. Satisfied, I lifted a hat and sped into the night.

CHAPTER 5

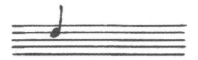

*T*he tavern was already crowded when I arrived. The air dark. Wooden crates leaned in stacks along a far wall. A tense, unwelcoming odor drifting about.

Peering around, I noticed that the clientele had the usual look in their eye, a vagueness—something between thirst and desperation.

As I sidled up to the well, I heard little Bonnet's murderous screech. Dressed in a purple skirt with red knickers, the devil-faced monkey clattered on a shelf high above, weaving her way between surplus liquor bottles. Seeing the restless creature put me at ease.

As did the barmaid's gaze.

"What'll be, lad?" she crooned, nestling on an elbow.

"Whisky," I muttered.

She lifted a chipped glass to the light. Eyed me over its rim.

"Looks like you might be needing a double."

She wasn't a beauty. But her quick eyes shed a feisty glint.

She set down my glass. "You live nearby?" Her smock fit snugly, stretched tight by a strong back and firm bosom.

I shook my head. "Just passing through," I told her.

She grinned. "That's what a man says when he's out looking for trouble."

I couldn't disagree. The glass of whisky went down swiftly. Another followed. Soon, lines and shapes softened. Colors drifted between objects. And, for the first time, I forgot about Ava.

"So are you?"

"Am I what?"

She leaned in. Lowered her voice. "Looking for trouble."

I marveled at her cascade of soft blonde curls. Her pouty lips.

"Eh, Tess!" a patron shouted. "Where's my bourbon?"

The barmaid stood up quickly. Speared a hand to her hip.

"Can't you see I'm busy with a customer?" she called out.

"Not as busy as I'm guessing you'd like to be!" the patron retorted.

The men at the well broke into laughter.

Tess tossed a hand. "Pay him no mind," she said. "He's only got half of one."

"Yes! And she's duller than he is!" another man chimed.

I felt numb from the senseless chatter. I needed air. So dropped a few coins alongside my glass.

"Aw, come on now, love. It's not time to go yet, is it?" she cooed.

I slipped uneasily to my feet.

"How about one more? This one's on me." She was already pouring.

Not feeling entirely stable, I relented, sought again the top of my stool.

She pushed the drink forward. Kept an eye on me while I sipped.

"What is it that's on your mind, lad?" she asked, a tone of unexpected tenderness coming into her voice.

I looked off. Thought for a moment. "Mortality, I suppose."

She cocked an eyebrow. "Ahh, mortality," she said, as if she'd expected that answer. As if it were a common complaint.

"So tell me," she continued. "What do you do for a living? An undertaker, are you?"

I shook my head. "A musician."

"A musician!" she cried. "You've hit upon my very passion. I *love* music!" She quickly dropped her voice. "I used to go with someone who was quite a talent on the Jew's harp. Sometimes I'd drum an accompaniment on the washboard."

Hearing this, my eyes flew to her fingers. They were strong, like little arms, each with a bulge where the bicep would be. Normally this would not appeal to me. But tonight I was not myself.

Tess sighed at her recollection. "Good times those were," she said. "Ah, but I don't go with that one no more," she added with a wink.

I stared into my whisky. "Nothing lasts," I said.

My statement made the buxom barmaid frown. She lifted a tray and idled around to where I sat. Pressed up close. I felt the rough weave of her shift scrape the back of my hand.

"I'm off in twenty. Why not come home with me?" she whispered. Clasped her powerful fingers around my knee. "I'll make you forget whatever it is that's troubling you."

She gave a squeeze then sauntered off. The men at the end of the bar cheered and whistled.

I didn't want to go home with Tess.

But neither did I want to face my empty bed.

The old farmhouse was dark when we arrived. Inside, it smelled of wet dog and root vegetables.

A cyclone of panting hounds greeted us at the door. Tess ushered them out with a fresh ham bone. She returned and lit candles. Put a pot of water on the stove.

"Sit where you'd like," she said.

I dropped into an overstuffed chair.

She worked furiously at the stove. Opening jars, pouring contents into the pot, stirring. As the water came to a boil, she threw me a lascivious grin.

Afterward, she handed me a cup of steamy, foul-smelling liquid. "Here you are, love. You'll be of no use to me without some fortification."

She waited for me to drink it down then took back the cup.

"You play the piano, don't you?"

I winced at the bitter taste along my tongue.

She nodded toward my lap. "It's your fingers. They're unusually fine for a gentleman."

I gazed up at her buttery curls and felt the sudden urge to have them spill across my cheeks.

Had she dowsed me with a love potion?

Seeming aware of my thoughts, Tess dropped to her knees. Kneaded my thighs within her muscular hands.

"I've never had me a pianist before," she said, leaning forward. "But if you're good, you'll hear me sing."

She drew apart the buttons on my pants. I closed my eyes as a sharp heat ran the cleft of me.

"That's it, love. Let ol' Tess take your troubles away," she crooned. Then sat back with a start. "What's this?" Her finger-arms rummaged through my pants. Her palm pressed against my sex.

She looked up. "Where is it, then?" she asked. Her eyelids lowered into a squint. "Well I'll be a three-legged ass. You're not a lad at all!"

I opened my eyes. "I-I thought ... I thought—"

Tess rocked back onto her heels. "You certainly *look* like a chap. And a handsome one at that," she said. "But seems God forgot to arm you with the proper tools."

I didn't know what to say. But knew where things were headed. I got to my feet.

"Thank you for the tea," I said. Stumbled toward the door.

Tess waited until I had turned the handle.

"Aw now, hon. Don't look so heartbroken. I didn't mean to hurt your feelings. Honest." She led me back inside and laid me out on her sofa. From a nearby closet she drew down a stack of heavy blankets. "I wouldn't feel right tossing you out. Especially since you're in no condition to find your way home." She set me back into the chair, propped a pillow behind my head. "I've nothing against you, understand? It's just that, when you're in the mood for a chunk of beef, a sliver of cod won't do. You see that, don't you?"

Her hounds scratched at the door. She strode over and threw the latch. They spilled across the floor, a river of floppy ears and paws. Two of the beasts leapt onto the sofa and laid down atop my legs. With wide tongues they swept strings of drool from their chops. I could smell ham on their breath.

Tess put more water on the stove. She then returned to the room with her own cup of potion. Curled on the floor in a puddle of warm hound.

"So why do you do it, then?"

"Do what?"

"Go about as a man."

I stared into the directness of her question.

"Is it because you think women will fancy you more?"

I shrugged. I didn't feel like talking. I had come for another reason. Tess, on the other hand, being denied a lover, seemed content to have acquired a friend.

"Seems I know women who don't mind either way. Might save you some trouble is all I'm saying. And I'm sure you cut just as dashing a figure in your own skin."

I looked up.

"Don't act surprised! I didn't say I don't fancy you at all. I said I don't fancy you *tonight.*"

She crumpled a furry ear in her hand. The dog groaned and kicked the air in pleasure.

We sat in silence.

My eyes drifted across her shelves, past bins of barley, biscuits, and balls of string to the corner where there sat a clear glass orb.

"Bit of a clairvoyant, I am," she said.

I thought back to my mother's fortune-teller. Her scent of peat and wood smoke. She'd been right about me having trouble in love, and living alone.

But she'd been wrong about my brother. In that case, she had assured my mother that he would grow up to marry a princess. And occupy a spectacular castle in a far-off land.

It might have been the setting of my mother's expectations at such a high pitch that made her son's sudden death all the more unbearable. And which gave her the strength to drown herself in a bucket when no one was looking.

"Do you want to ask about her?"

I flinched. "Who?"

"The woman who's crushing your heart."

I gave her a funny look.

"I told you. Bit of a clairvoyant." She grinned.

When I didn't get up to leave, she brought down her crystal ball. Stared into its watery prism. After a moment, her eyes grew wide.

"What do you see?" I asked.

"Hmm. I see that you are in some danger," she said, her voice shadowy, hovering above us.

"What kind of danger?"

She turned her head, as if someone else were speaking to her. "You are a lover and seeker of beauty," she said. "Yours is a practice of deep attention. There is no other manner in which you can live. And this is your gift," she said. Closed her eyes. "But it seems as though … how can I say this? … Your candle has been snuffed."

I shrugged. Feeling the familiar twinge of melancholy. "What does it matter? Nothing in this world lasts."

Tess snorted with disapproval. "Don't talk to me of impermanence," she snapped. "You're far too young to have been tainted with the undertaker's gloom, no matter what you've lost. Or who. No, that's not the trouble. Nor is your longed-for lover the cause of your pain. Those are just masks you're hiding behind." She stared off again. Cocked an ear as if listening to a distant sound. "It's something else. Something that has drained your will. And got you hiding."

"And what's wrong with hiding?" I asked, made surly by her prying, by her scraping forbidden corners.

"What's wrong? Ha!" She glanced over at her dogs. "Just imagine if a flower hadn't will enough. Why, then, would it bother risking the bloom? And, for that matter, why would birds sore their throats? Or trees seek sky? Or people fall in love? In fact, why would anything happen at *all*?"

Her words came quickly. I dizzied. Felt like a tortoise tipped on its back.

"Tell me, then, how long have you been living like this?"

"Like what?"

"Without your *shine*?" she asked.

I said nothing.

Tess remained silent.

After what seemed like a while, she took my eyes again into hers. Whispered. "Do you want to tell me what the trouble *truly* is?"

Before I could stem it, moisture leaked from behind my eyes. I shook my head. I wasn't sure what she was asking for, but it felt scary. Water deep and dark enough to drown.

She smiled. Tipped her head gently. "Maybe, then, you want to ask a question?"

I peered out through burning eyes. Nodded.

"Please." She opened her palms.

I gave her request some thought. Cleared my throat, hoping my voice would not fail. Then asked, "Will I give her lessons?"

Tess sat back and thought for a moment.

"Yes," she said.

A blinding light flashed inside my skull. Sightless, I stared into the distance.

Tess watched me carefully. Leaned forward, her brow tightening. "Yes. *There* it is," she said softly. "Not entirely extinguished, I see."

Saying this, she settled back. "Have you another question?" she asked.

I hadn't really intended to ask her more. But there was something about Tess's way that was loosening me. Offering a hand.

I closed my eyes. Braced. Then asked, "Why was the fortune-teller wrong about my brother? Why didn't she warn us?"

Tess nodded without expression, without any surprise about my asking after someone of whom she knew nothing. Without a word, she dropped her gaze to the smooth crystal. For several minutes she kept it there. Slowly, her eyes lit up as if she were watching some magical, faraway scene. When she looked back up at me, she smiled.

"Who says she was wrong?"

The next morning, I didn't go home.

I stayed.

It wasn't that I preferred sleeping with damp hounds. It was that I liked how Tess listened.

She insisted I tell her everything. All of my past. All of my present. And she didn't just want to hear the good. She wanted the ugly, too. Especially that.

"Seems to me you're not really this or that. You're a bit of both, or everything, really. Maybe that's what has you so confused," she said. We were sitting on a blanket alongside the river, tossing crumbs to the fish and livers to the hounds.

Her attention compelled me. Made me feel tussled. And refreshed. Like a recently turned garden.

I knew I couldn't go home in that condition. Especially with Cristofer constantly at work, needing my ministrations and leaving me no access to the piano.

I much preferred to accompany Tess while she gathered ingredients for our breakfast: fresh eggs from the hens, milk from her cow, and dried sausage from the smokehouse. These she brought to her kitchen and transformed into a feast that spread across the table. She was a model of industrious self-sufficiency and I quickly succumbed to the unfamiliar joy of being looked after.

In the evenings, when Tess slipped into her shift and ambled to work, I would take the hounds out walking in the fields. While they yelped and cavorted and thrust their snouts down holes, I thought over the things she had told me. The insights she'd revealed. The layers peeled back.

And I wondered at myself.

At night, Tess took to letting me sleep alongside her. Though we were not lovers, I took comfort in the regularity of her breathing, in the quiet strength of her slumber. She perhaps felt the same as I sometimes woke to find her arms draped around me, her warm breath at my neck.

When it came time to leave the farmhouse, I felt lighter in my bones than when I'd arrived. And sensed I might be in the thrall of a new emotion. One that had not touched me in years.

Tess said it was hope.

I stepped into the cottage, hoping I would not find Cristofer too upset by my absence.

Instead of finding him hunched over the piano, I saw a note atop the keys.

Dearest H—

Have gone to the Bertrands'. A new and brilliant development to share! Hope you had a restful stay wherever you landed.

Fondly, C

Brilliant development?

Might Ava have found a way around her husband's restrictions and made a formal request for lessons?

Could Tess's prediction actually be coming true?

I dared not think it. Not until I had proof.

I looked down at the multiple sheets of music on the sideboard. Cristofer had been productive while I'd been away.

With a strange sense of euphoria, I set on my apron and bent to my labors.

Having set Cristofer's cottage right, I lifted my market sack and headed out. Intent on refilling our cupboards.

The afternoon air was drenched with the perfumes of young flowers and fresh grass. Feeling a lean toward liberty, I set off down a side path. One I did not usually follow.

While strolling, my thoughts drifted back to Tess and her predictions.

Will I give her lessons? I'd asked.

Yes, came the answer.

I plucked a tall blade of grass and set it between my teeth. Its sweet flavor brought water to my mouth.

Then came a sobering thought.

What if I were asked to provide lessons? What then?

I had nothing prepared. No curriculum. No materials.

On top of that I was not, by any stretch, of a pedagogical bent. And could not boast a single student.

Yes, I knew how to play the piano.

But to teach someone?

Where would I begin?

And what, beyond the basic tenets, could be taught?

I, myself, had always held the belief that good musicians arose from practice, whereas genius arose from a certain cast of the soul.

Perhaps, then, I could only hope to make her good.

I sighed.

How I would gladly settle for that chance.

I shifted the grass between my teeth and tilted my face toward the sun. My eyes were closed when I heard what sounded like a grunt.

An animal? The sound collector?

I looked about, my vision hazy and reddened.

"Henri!" she called out. Even in her distress I recognized her voice.

Clara lurched forward, her hair unpinned, her dress damp with sweat, her shoes muddied and torn.

Winded, she fell into my arms.

"We must get Cristofer," she gasped. "It's Richard!"

I shook my head. "Cristofer is not at home. He's with the Bertrands."

Her eyes widened. She clasped my wrists. Despite the heat, her palms were cold. "You must come, then," she said, tightening her grip. "Please help me. He's alone. With the children—"

"But your shoes, your feet," I protested, pointing down at torn leather and bloody flesh.

"There's no time for that," she said, pulling me with remarkable strength.

A cluster of children met us at the door. Wide-eyed and silent, the littlest ones clutched faceless dolls in tight fists.

Marie, the eldest, had been left in charge but she seemed just as rattled as the others, her composure askew, her quiet eyes darting about.

Clara set her hands on her daughter's shoulders. "Take the children to play outside. We're going to go see to your father."

Marie looked me over. Suspicion darkened her eyes.

Clara urged her on. "It's alright, Marie. Henri's here to help. Just take the children."

When we were alone, Clara led me to Richard's study. She tried the door but found it locked.

She knocked gently. "Richard? My love? Will you let me in?"

Silence.

"Please open the door, my sweet. Someone's here to see you."

No response.

I braced myself, preparing to break down the door. Clara shook her head. "I have a key."

The hinges creaked as the door swung open.

Inside, it looked as though a squall had battered the study. Books had been thrown from shelves. Chairs and tables upended. Glass broken. Manuscripts torn.

Three yellow songbirds dove in and out of the wreckage, chirping frantically, their cage toppled.

In the middle of the turmoil lay Richard, fallen across the desk, his face buried in the crook of an elbow.

Clara rushed to his side. "Oh, my love, my love, what have you done?"

She lifted his face to the light. His eyes were closed, though he was still breathing. Small streaks of blood issued from in and around his ears. Closer inspection revealed a spray of minute punctures. For a moment I thought he might have contracted measles until Clara picked up his writing quill, its tip crusted with blood.

He had stabbed his own face.

"Help me bring him to bed," Clara insisted, rolling up her sleeves. She spoke calmly, with stark efficiency.

Richard mumbled and thrashed as we carried him down the hall. We laid him on top of the bed and worked to remove his shoes, his overcoat. Once he was tucked under the sheets, Clara applied a cool cloth to his forehead. His breathing fell into a rhythm. She bent to kiss his cheek.

Clara led me back to the kitchen. Set water on the stove. "Will you stay for tea?" she asked.

I nodded, in a daze.

"Let me look to the children first." She lifted a handful of apples from a basket and headed outside.

Uncertain what to do, I searched their home, looking for answers. Despite its diminutive size and large number of occupants, the dwelling spoke of order and efficiency. Everything nestled in its proper place, nothing rolling about on the floor or atop the furniture. Of note were the number of small plants lining the windowsills—flowers, sprouts, cuttings suspended in bright watery jars.

Just off the living room, the Thornes had built an addition to house their piano. A great, masculine beast, an Érard grand, dominated the room. One could barely slip between the piano and the rows of books and sheet music lining the surrounding shelves.

Beyond the instrument, two windows opened onto the garden. I wanted to sit and play the piano, to experience her particular tone. But when I heard the spit of boiling water, I rushed over to the stove.

I had just finished steeping two cups of tea when Clara returned. She looked worn but otherwise in control.

"Are they well?" I asked.

"They're sturdy little souls," she said, leading me to wonder whether the incident with Richard was not the first.

We huddled at the table. She bent to remove her boots. The skin around her ankles shredded.

"Clara, those wounds are ghastly! You must rub them with olive oil. If you tell me where it is, I'll apply it."

She looked up quickly, her eyes alight. I was halfway to my feet when she said, "No, no, please. That won't be necessary. Thank you for the offer, but I'll tend to it. Just have your tea."

We sat in silence for several minutes. The sound of the children's singing floated through the windows.

Clara sighed.

I did not want to upset her but sensed she needed help.

"Will you tell me what's going on?"

She stared out the window. Took a long breath. Her face bore the strain of hesitation. Yet after a moment, she relented. "Richard has a history of battling the darker moods," she said. "As of late, he told me he's been hearing things. Voices. That when he's alone in his study they speak to him. He's tried everything to ignore them. To silence them. But they won't stop. Sometimes they deliver music. And sweet it is. But, most recently, they've been telling him to do things."

"What kind of things?"

She shook her head. "They're too heinous to speak of."

I frowned.

"He's never been violent. But lately, he's had a few bad episodes. When they come, I can't control him. Can't communicate. He goes somewhere else." Her fingers ringed her cup. "When it's over, he has no recollection. And when I tell him what's happened, he becomes profoundly upset." She paused. Looked me dead in the eye. "He thinks he's going mad."

I winced. Waited a proper moment before asking, "Do *you*?"

She looked off. Shrugged. "I don't know. Nor do the doctors. One suggested, in private, that someone might be poisoning him."

"A supporter of Wagner, perhaps?"

She shook her head. "Possible. But unlikely."

I looked out the window. Watched the children gather about a swing.

"He worries that it weighs on me. That it burdens the children." She tapped a finger on the table. "I can't bear the thought that one day he might ... harm himself."

I struggled to hide my distress.

"Henri," she said, leaning toward me. "I have your word you will tell no one of this?"

"You have my word," I assured.

I knew well of Clara's desire to protect her husband's name.

Her head fell in relief and, no doubt, exhaustion.

"Would you like me to stay the night?" I asked, thinking she might be afraid to be alone under the circumstances.

At my suggestion, Clara looked up. A strange expression clouding her face. Without warning, she burst into laughter. Unable to contain herself, she bent over, caught in throes of hilarity.

I stared with something like horror. Unable to imagine what she could find so amusing.

Perhaps the stress had unbalanced her?

Wiping tears from her eyes, she said, "Oh … no. I'm so sorry, Henri. I just— never mind. It's too absurd. I am not myself today."

"That's understandable."

She sat back. "I've already taken too much of your time. But I cannot thank you enough for coming."

"I am happy to help more. If you need assistance with the children—"

"No. Please. Go home. You do enough caregiving."

She saw me to the door. Took my hands in hers. Lifted each one to her lips and kissed it gently. "My sweet Henri. I shall never forget this kindness."

I shook my head. "It doesn't feel right, leaving you alone."

She ignored my protests. "There's a chill. Take this." She threw one of Richard's capes around my shoulders. Smiled as I buttoned the collar.

"Tell Cristofer what has happened," she said.

I nodded and began the journey homeward.

Having walked the last mile in the dark, I was greatly relieved to see the flicker of candlelight in the cottage windows.

And to hear Cristofer at the piano.

When I entered, he sprang to his feet. "Henri!"

"We have to talk," I said, shucking off Richard's cape.

"Yes, yes, I have grand news. Grand news indeed!"

"Cristofer, I—"

He held up a hand. "Please! I've been waiting all afternoon for you."

Knowing that my report would cast a pall over his good spirits, I decided to wait. What harm would another few minutes bring?

"Is it to do with the Bertrands?" I asked.

"Yes! Entirely." He tugged down his cuffs and began to pace. "Unbeknownst to me, Monsieur Bertrand has been working to obtain a significant contribution from the Duchess of Salzburg, as she is a well-known admirer of Clara's. Today he told me the duchess has granted his request. And you'll never guess what he has asked of her."

I stared, unable to imagine.

"He's requested that she arrange for transport of the Bertrands' phenomenal piano to the concerto's premiere! Both he and the duchess absolutely *insist* that Clara have it. Isn't that just brilliant?"

"That is wonderful," I said, numbly.

His smile lit the room. "I cannot wait to share the news with Richard and Clara. They will be as overcome as I!"

"Yes."

He paused. "What is it, Henri? You've gone suddenly pale."

I looked down. "It's Richard," I said.

He rushed forward, his joy cut short. "What is it? What's happened?"

"I don't know. Clara came looking for you. We found him locked in his study. He'd made a mess of the place. Stabbed himself about the ears."

Cristofer's face fell open. He took my shoulders. "What of Clara? And the children?"

"Everyone is well. But notably upset." I had barely spoken the words when he hurried to the door. Threw on his hat and cape.

"Are you going to her?"

"Yes," he said.

I knew I could not stop him.

But imagining him at Clara's side stirred something within me.

"Cristofer!" I called as he strode down the walkway.

He turned back.

"Was there any word from Madame Bertrand? Any further inquiries into lessons?"

I felt shallow for asking but could not restrain my hope.

His head shook beneath his hat. "Jacque informed me that she has already obtained an instructor," he said. "A woman. Recommended by Clara."

CHAPTER 6

*T*he piano is a magnificent but ambiguous creature. When invented, musicians debated whether it belonged among the percussion or the strings. The controversy arose as a result of the action used to create its sound. On the one hand, the instrument's tones issued from the vibration of strings, arguing that it would be most comfortable among the violins and cellos. Yet the piano's strings vibrated due to their being struck by hammers, much as mallets hit the resonate head of a drum. A fact arguing that it belonged in the percussion section.

No matter its proper classification (I have no mind for calculating such things), the piano is a beast whose cry tumbles the heart. Whose voice embodies the passion of poems. Who breathes harmonies between sonorous ribs. Who speaks a myriad of languages.

Plaintive. Joyful. Heartbroken. No matter one's mood, a listener cannot resist such range. In fact, I know of no other instrument that can so readily seduce.

And, that night, seduction was on my mind.

Dressed in my trusty breeches, I fled to the market. To the coffee stall with its twin mermaids. When their lumbering mother slipped away to carry on with a customer, I endeavored to lure one of the girls into the night. Looking over my shoulder, I soon discovered that both had followed. One, it seemed, could not be cleaved from the other.

When we stumbled through the door, the men topping the barstools sat up. Their eyes widened at the beauties dangling from my elbows.

Tess looked up from behind the bar. She tried to catch my eye. I turned away without acknowledging her.

I led the girls to a table. From there they could look up and see Bonnet's latest trick—pouring water on a man's head.

Tess stormed toward our table. She grunted and dropped a bowl of nuts between us.

"How kind of you to bring schoolchildren on an outing," she

said. Her lips curled back. "Where are you off to, then? The zoo, perhaps?"

The twins looked at each other, then at me.

I laughed with a snort. I was angry. With her. With Clara. With everyone. But Tess seemed the easiest target.

"No need to be hissy," I told her. "When you're in the mood for lean meat, a fatty brisket simply won't do."

Tess's eyes widened. For a moment I thought she might slap me.

I picked a nut from the bowl, lifted it to one of the girls' lips. She scooped it from my fingertips with her tongue.

"Three whiskies," I ordered.

Tess scowled. Vanished in a whirl of buttery curls.

"Who was *that*?" one of the twins inquired.

"A bit churlish!" the other noted.

"I would be, too, if my thighs were big as ham bones!" her sister replied.

They giggled.

My eyelids dipped.

A different barmaid brought the drinks. Set them down gruffly.

I took my whisky in a single shot. The girls sipped theirs and commented on the bar's unsavory patronage.

Suddenly remorseful, the liquor having dulled my anger, I looked beyond my companions' matching profiles to seek out Tess.

It wasn't her fault Ava had found another instructor, was it?

She hadn't made any promises about her predictions, had she?

I thought of the night she had taken me in. And the week we had spent together, embracing amidst her hounds.

I prepared to stand, to approach my friend and apologize, when a spark burned my calf.

I glanced across the table to find one of the twins looking in my direction. Her gaze nailed me to my seat. Lust darkening the rims of her eyes. Underneath the table, she slipped a toe inside the leg of my breeches.

When her sister noticed our silence, she grinned and swept her hair upward. As if slipping underneath a waterfall, she tipped back her head, closed her eyes, and let her lips part.

With thoughts of Tess forgotten, I surrendered my attentions fully to the creatures before me.

They were twins, of course, but careful observation revealed subtle differences between them. Most noticeable were their scents—one of honeydew and coffee, the other of iron and cinnamon. One possessing the most delectable nibs for earlobes, the other, finely jointed fingers stretching in languid repose along the table, like long, naked women.

Why is it that the beauty in one woman speaks to that found in all? So that upon discovering the grace in the one before you, others you have admired come instantly to mind? It is as if Beauty speaks to itself. As if all women are spun from a single flesh and therefore serve as conduits, through geography, through time, to the Source that inspires them.

"Would you like another drink?" I asked the girls, my mouth suddenly dry.

The twins shook their heads. "We're not thirsty," one said. "We're *hungry.*" Her searing stare made clear her meaning.

I signaled for whisky.

When the barmaid set the glass before me, I took the liquor in one heady gulp.

"Let's go," one of them said when my empty glass chinked down on the table.

I could not tell if I was leading them or if they were leading me. In any case, I took care to avoid Tess, which wasn't hard, as anything beyond the end of my nose suddenly seemed difficult to discern. Whether from the heated attraction, the turmoil with Tess, or the potency of the liquor, I found my steps swayed, my vision blurred.

"Where shall we go?" they asked, snuggling into me. The question hit like water in the face.

Where *would* we go?

"This way!" one of them coaxed, tugging at my arm.

I was relieved to have someone take charge, as I could think of no place suitable for our mingling.

The light in the alley slanted sharply toward darkness. Beneath this sinister hood, I sensed hands lifting my jacket. Palms spreading along my belly, fingers sifting my waistband, digging at my hips. Their advances stoked the coal in my belly. My knees weakened as hot breath entered my ear.

Moans echoed off the cobblestones.

Mine? Theirs?

I reached forward, seeking flesh.

Then I was falling. Tumbling through space.

Where had the ground gone?

There was a sudden *crack!* of chin on stone. Warm liquid dribbled from my lips.

Laughter. Hurried whispers.

Uneven cobble denting my cheek.

Then.

Blackness.

I woke with a tongue at my lips. Not mine.

I flinched. Found myself gaping into the face of a hound.

"Eh, there, leave her alone," someone said.

I looked up into a familiar swirl of blonde curls.

I touched the corner of my mouth. It flamed as if on fire. I cried out.

"Leave it be," she said. Pushed away my hand. "Now open up."

I tried but the pain made my eyes water.

Undaunted, she slipped something between my lips. "Suck on that. It will bring you to your senses." She paused. "If anything can."

I felt the lozenge crack and begin to dissolve. A metal flavor leaked between my teeth, stealing my consciousness with it.

When I woke again, I heard bubbling. A pot on open flame.

I bent forward. A blade of light cut through the window, tore behind my eyes. A door opened, flooding the room with an even sharper blaze.

"Well, look who's awake!" she said, the dogs milling at her knees. She nudged them back.

Hulking in the doorway, she removed her hat, her cheeks flushed with sun and effort. A basket of freshly picked vegetables swung from one elbow.

The dogs yelped outside.

"They've been eager to see you," Tess said. "I've had a hell of a time keeping them out."

Tears of gratitude gathered in my eyes.

"Oh, for heaven's sake, don't do that," she said. Lifted her apron and dabbed it at my cheeks. "The salt will sting like the devil if it gets in those wounds."

I had yet to see the damage but could imagine its extent. My whole face pulsed with ache. Out the corner of my eye I saw taut, swelling bulges of cheek and lip.

Then I had a ghastly thought. Holding my breath, I drew up my hands. One of my fingers, the smallest on my left, was wrapped in bloody gauze.

"No!" I cried.

Tess grasped my hand gently and guided it back under the blanket. "One of 'em sliced you to get at your coins," she said. "Leave it alone and it will heal good as new. Trust me."

Light-headed, I fell back against the pillows.

Tess stepped into the kitchen and returned with a bowl of soup. She sat and blew across the steam.

"We'll have to let that cool," she said, setting the bowl on the crate she used as a table.

I said nothing. I was afraid to speak. Not only because of the pain, but because I recalled how I'd treated Tess. And felt ashamed.

She peered over at me. Passed a knowing look. "Aw, don't worry about what you done," she said. "I'm stronger than I look."

I smiled. It hurt.

Several minutes passed. The hounds wailed in the fields.

Tess's eyebrows wrinkled. "I'm guessing she didn't ask for lessons?"

I said nothing, but the tears welled again.

Tess lifted her apron. Wagged her head. "You've as much sense as the dogs."

I still said nothing.

She ran a spoon through the soup. Blew lightly across its noodled surface.

"Tell me, love. What can we do to see you gleaming again?"

I looked up, confused.

"Don't see it, do you?"

I shook my head. I wanted her to be quiet.

She lifted a spoonful. Tilted the liquid until it spilled down my throat.

I swallowed.

She lifted another spoonful. "Tell me about your brother."

My brother? Why my brother?

In all our conversations, somehow I had managed to avoid talking about my deceased sibling. Tess knew of him, of course, but I had never really given her any details, nor had she pushed. Until now.

I drank the soup and tried to swallow my words with it. But, as always, Tess's attentiveness disarmed me and drew out a reluctant confession.

In mottled phrases I told her of our childhood. Of my brother's bravura. And my solitary ways. Of how he charmed the ladies while I traded bread for piano lessons and sonatas.

I told her of our unbreakable bond. And how he served as a bulwark between myself and my mother. How he'd weathered her screaming tirades and her shaming of me for my pursuit of music.

"You'll not be chasing any such foolishness!" she would yell, cornering me with my secondhand sheet music. "In all my days, I've never heard of anything more frivolous! More *pointless!*"

Prone to kicking me out of the house at all hours, her face purpled, her breath fuming spirits, she'd chide, "So you think you deserve to dabble in pretty notes while the rest of us grovel, eh? Treacherous slap to my face, that is! After all I've done to stuff your mouth and hang a roof over your scabby head? Not on your life!"

When her fury reached a deafening pitch, and my knuckles became the target of her crushing rod, my brother rented a small flat for us. He found work as a cobbler's apprentice and I tended our home.

When he went to work, I would set off to scour the city for an unattended piano upon which I could work.

At night, while he ate dinner, I would sing to him the music I had conjured. Without fail, my efforts would bring a wistful, far-off look to his face.

He was the only one who understood.

In those days, I'd dreamed of earning my place in the pantheon of great composers.

It had been, I told Tess, the happiest time of my life. And never had I let a day go by without acknowledging his sacrifice.

But when a horse broke loose from its carriage and trampled a group of passersby, the pulse of my dream, and the core of my heart, met an abrupt end. Causing the greatest loss I'd ever known.

My mother's assault came in the dead of night. Half-naked and drawn with despair, I fled her fury.

"Murderer!" she raged, cleaving the door to our flat with an axe while I leapt out its window. "How can you bear to draw breath?!" she screamed. "Come out here, you pathetic coward! Pay for the blood on your hands!"

Homeless, penniless, and sickened with grief, I retreated to the city's underbelly.

Disguised as a young man, I haunted the most notorious brothels. Night after night I rattled tuneless keys on sour pianos, scrounged for meals, and slept in alleys with razor-toothed rats.

Until one fateful night.

Having just learned of my mother's suicide, I arrived at the brothel's piano, writhing and sickened with rage. Not only had she taken her life, but she'd done so in the very bucket she'd used to douse the bonfire upon which she'd burned every last sheet of my music.

Paralyzed with loss, I spent my last coins on a flask of third-rate whisky.

Tensing above the keys, I fired a bass note then unleashed a sweeping crescendo, a lengthy escalation that ran the length of the keyboard. It was the opening of a nocturne I had been in the process of composing for my brother. Knowing now that all my music had been destroyed, I had only memory to rely on.

Heated by liquor and the effort of detailed remembering, sweat soon streaked down my cheeks. Pushing forward, the nocturne began to open, bursting with new petals. I stared into its beauty.

So enthralled and overcome with my endeavor was I that I nearly jumped from my skin when the brothel's owner slapped a hand on the back of my head.

"Look what you done!" he growled.

Stunned, I looked out to where he was pointing. There I saw the brothel's clientele (and not a few of its well-painted employees) leaning between oversized velvet pillows, sobbing.

"I hired you to liven things up, not sicken the customers with despair!"

I blinked. Felt my body rise. Slowly. As though emerging through thick liquid.

He hit me a second time. "I won't warn you again, Henri!"

"Right, right," I mumbled, and set my hands to unrolling a bawdy Bavarian folk tune. The room's mood swung instantly so that when I looked up again, I beheld the more usual scene—men lolling among the pillows, their hungry palms cupping womanly parts, tears and despair long forgotten.

But their gain was my loss. And for the rest of the night, an internal urgency gnawed at my guts.

I drank. And drank again.

Clenching my teeth, I managed to produce a stream of glaring, twinkly tunes. Songs to keep the women entertained and the men awake. But as the evening aged and clients slipped behind thin wooden doors, my restraint began to unhinge.

When only a few men remained thrashing between the pillows, I stopped playing. And stared into the dark gaps between the keys. As my eyes lost their focus, images began to bubble up from between the cracks: my brother's body smashed atop cobblestones; sheets of music aflame; inky notes evaporating into smoke; my mother, stricken, her lifeless head submerged.

I sunk onto the keys. Felt death at my door. Took yet another shot of whisky. Its effect fanned my limbs.

To hell with it!

I sat up straight, limbered my wrists, and swept again through the nocturne's opening crescendo. When no one came to stop me, I traveled onward, into a theme of unusual grace and weightlessness.

Unable to keep up with the blur of my fingers, I closed my eyes. And listened.

The song climbed and dove, a kerchief in soft wind.

A long farewell.

Inwardly, I let the current carry me.

Until I felt a presence.

I opened my eyes and found a set of boots standing not more than two feet away. Above them hung a pair of breeches, unusually short.

I looked up and took in the young man before me. He was more handsome than the usual clientele. His gray, eagle-sharp eyes peering from beneath a mane of golden hair. His suit clean but not expensive. He said nothing, merely stared, a queer look on his face.

I expected him to complain or call for the owner. He did neither. He just watched me. Or, rather, watched my fingers.

Perhaps he was the kind who preferred men?

I approached the dénouement of the first theme. As I did, I became aware of my abilities deteriorating—the harmonies I could hear playing in my head were no longer corresponding with those entering my ears.

I then felt a solid ball swelling inside my belly. Shoving my innards to one side.

The next thing I knew, I had dropped to my knees and begun retching on the stranger's boots.

The man kept still. When I had finished, he allowed me a moment to wipe my mouth. Then he offered his hand and helped me to my feet. At that point I felt certain he was the kind who preferred men. (And a particularly desperate member of that breed.)

For who else would assist the man who'd just vomited on his boots?

"Bloody hell, that's *it*!" someone yelled.

The owner.

"I want you out of here, Henri! Now! And don't come knocking for your pay. I'm withholding for damages!" he added, thrusting a finger at my mess on the floor.

When I cocked back a fist, the strange man grabbed my arm and laid it across his shoulder, restraining me on the one hand while simultaneously keeping me upright.

Dragging me toward the door, he called out, "What's his address?"

The owner spat. "Lives with the rats, far as I know. Which is where his kind belong!"

Tess leaned forward with another spoonful. "Did you know that he was Cristofer Vaughn?"

I shook my head.

She sat back. "Have you an angel, you do," she said.

When she said nothing more, I went on.

"The next thing I remember I was lying on a bed with the man yanking off my boots. He turned to loosening my cravat and fiddling open the buttons at my collar. It was then I felt cold air rush across my exposed chest. I heard him gasp. Then burst out laughing. 'I knew it! I just *knew* it!'" he cried.

Tess leaned in. "It was your music that saved you," she noted.

I shook my head. "It was Cristofer," I corrected. "Were it not for him, I would not be here."

Tess sniffed. "Seems he might not be where *he* is, either."

I looked down. Knew what she meant. But could not accept it. She did not understand. Not my need of Cristofer. Nor the nature of our attachment. Nor did she understand the height of my despair when we'd met. "Had he not taken me home that night, I most certainly would have ended it."

Tess wagged her head. Stood and took the uneaten soup to the stove. Poured it back into the pot.

As she worked, her eyes narrowed along a thought. "And what, then, of your composing?"

I lowered my face.

Tess grunted in her knowing way. "Too busy hiding yourself up ladies' skirts, I suppose," she said, but her tone sounded more hurt than disdainful.

It was then I realized that she loved me.

Tess lifted her basket and gloves and shears and readied to go into the garden. After opening the door, she turned in the threshold. Waited a moment. Then said, "Mark my words, Henri. No matter the guilt you shoulder, the mortality you blame, the subservient you play, the dalliances you pursue, the holy gift you deny—or whatever else you conjure to endure—the sacrifice will never, ever be enough."

I stared at Tess. Hard. Grit my teeth.

I knew she wanted me to ask the obvious question.

It hung there, in the air, an unspoken miasma between us.

I was terrified. Both of the answer. And of not knowing.

As usual, she broke me down.

"Enough for what?" I dared.

She smiled.

"Your desire did not cause anyone's death, Henri," she said softly. Then pinned me with a stare. "Though denied much longer, it may bring about yours."

Even without a crystal ball her voice carried the ominous tone of prophesy.

Such a loud ringing overtook my ears that I did not hear the door close behind her.

When she left, I shook as though stricken with fever, the covers shaking violently above me.

Finally, feeling faint, and unable to withstand the strain of consciousness, I drifted beneath the world.

Under Tess's ministrations, it did not take long for my wounds to heal.

At night, as we laid beside one another, I could feel the heat of need rising from her skin. Yet she never reached for me. She refrained, I assumed, in order to speed my recovery. For this I admired her.

Had our stations been reversed, I doubt I could have commanded the same self-control.

On the day of my departure, Tess left the farmhouse before I had risen. She'd told me that saying goodbye was unnecessary. And that I was always welcome.

Walking toward home, the road seemed wider, more open than I'd remembered. Above, the afternoon clouds ambled the sky in puffy herds.

I lifted both hands in front of me and wiggled my fingers. Thankfully, due to the effects of Tess's homemade balm, the blade did not seem to have rendered permanent damage.

On my way through the fields, I hummed through a new transition for the honeyeater piece. The chords had come to me quite unexpectedly during one of the many sleepless nights in my recovery. The transition began with the piano falling silent. Into the void stepped a stringed bass. The instrument moaned in its lowest register while a flute cried plaintively several octaves above. The resulting harmony rose thick with haunting. Yet it ended upward, on a curve of optimism.

Increasing my pace, I rushed homeward, my boots whisking through the grass. All I could think about was sitting to work, alone, at the piano.

My palms flexed in anticipation.

Growing ever more anxious as the cottage neared, I prayed Cristofer would be off somewhere, granting me a bit of time.

"Henri, my God! Where have you been?"

Cristofer was pacing before the piano. He looked tired and disheveled, his hair wild and unkempt.

I peered past him into the kitchen. It stood in utter disarray. Dirtied pots lined the tables, vegetables wilted in the open, coffee accouterments lay scattered about.

Signore Mignore bounded from under the bed as soon as he heard me. He brushed against my legs, purring and frantic.

Cristofer stepped closer, looking as though he might chastise me, then suddenly stopped.

"Henri ..." he croaked. Lifted a hand toward my cheek. Gaped at the still obvious bruises and swelling. "What happened? Your *face*!"

I shrugged. "A run-in with duplicitous mermaids."

He frowned. Spotted the bandage on my hand. Cried out and cradled my fingers. "Oh, Henri ... *no*! Please, no!"

I drew back my hand. "Not to worry. It's healing. All will be well," I assured him.

Not wanting to dwell on my misfortune, I waved an arm about the cottage.

"You've been working?"

Cristofer dropped to the bench. "Floundering is more the word," he said. I noticed a distinct lack of vigor in his eyes, a more sullen gray. I observed the pages on the rack. Cristofer normally placed his notes in a precise and mechanical manner. But his most recent chords and phrases appeared to waver with uncertainty.

"You're still at work on the second movement? The adagio?"

He shrugged. "I have nothing to show for it. The idea seems reluctant to appear. I don't understand why. I'm well pleased now with the first movement. It presents with a bold and clear direction.

But *this*—" he moaned, spreading a hand across the manuscript— "is abysmal."

Reading the melody sketched along the staff, I had to agree. I laid a hand on his shoulder.

"Why not approach the third movement?" I suggested.

Cristofer swiveled on the bench. "What? But that would be ..." He trailed off. I could tell from his bewildered expression that he thought the idea mad. That was where we differed. Cristofer operated in a linear fashion. He sought—no—he *demanded* logical succession, and would often not advance within a piece until all that came before had been buffed to high polish.

Not so me. Without the restraints of tradition or formality, I was free to meander.

"Look at it this way," I began. "You've been granted the commission of a lifetime. Your nerves are aroused. You're in a heroic frame of mind. Capitalize on that. Rather than reining yourself in, embrace your high spirits and tackle the grand finale, the presto. Then, when your nerves have steadied, you'll be better positioned to go back and address the adagio."

Cristofer raised his eyebrows. He sat for another moment in silence, thinking. Sifted a hand through his hair. "Henri, you are a genius."

"No. Not a genius. But I *do* understand my Cristof."

I could see that the idea of a new approach, a permission to step beyond his usual bounds, had ignited a creative spark within him. I could see, too, the ensuing hunger to return to work.

But then I saw him take hold of himself. And struggle with his human side, with his sense of decency and the duty of friendship. All he wanted was to work, but his faithful servant stood beside him, injured and in need of attention.

To which should he attend?

I was not unfamiliar with the battle.

"Return to your work," I said, absolving him. I looked about the cottage and added, "I have plenty to occupy me."

His expression drew inward. He was trying his hardest to accommodate me. To acknowledge my significance in his world. But I could already feel the wall rising between us. And knew all too well how tight its perimeter. How well-constructed the creative shell—allowing within its narrow skin only one.

I turned and strode toward the kitchen. Signore followed, bellowing at my ankles.

Having fed the cat, scrubbed pots, stored vegetables, and set the kitchen generally in order, I turned my attention to the piano room.

I tried to ignore Cristofer and his work. While dusting, I attempted to concentrate on the honeyeater piece but could not focus with Cristofer banging out notes and chords. The effect was torturous as I very badly wanted to be the one seated at the keyboard.

When I knelt to sweep ash from the fireplace, he glanced up from his labors.

"What do you think of this progression?"

He played a band of six notes that stepped outward from a bass of G.

"A solid phrase indeed."

"But what of this as the cello accompaniment? It seems too, well, too derivative."

He played the harmony intended for the strings. It was indeed unremarkable.

Covering the dustpan to prevent the ash from blowing away, I glided to the piano. Scanned the passage of music. Listened as the piece unfolded inside my head.

"There," I said, indicating a phrase. "Try two quarter notes and make the chord a half. That should lift its effect."

He scribbled down my idea then reproduced it on the keys. Repeated the phrase several times, each with a slight variation.

"Yes!" he cried triumphantly. "Then to here," he said, moving to a second phrase.

I smiled. "You've got it."

"Good. Now listen to this," he urged, setting down yet more chords.

Standing there, listening, I felt a sudden and strange pang in my belly. A sourness. I did not recognize it at first. But its nature soon became apparent.

It was resentment.

I stepped back at its foul tang.

Never before had I begrudged Cristofer his time at the keyboard.

It was his instrument. His *house*, after all.

What in heaven's name had come over me?

I knew exactly.

It was Tess. Her words. They'd burrowed beneath my skin.

I looked down at the tray filled with ash. The bandage about my palm. And felt the sourness swelling upward, taking root behind my teeth.

Cristofer continued to labor. "What do you think of this? And *this?*" he asked, pounding his ideas into the keys.

I became immobilized by restraint. Clamped my jaw against the urge to scream.

"Henri," I heard Cristofer whisper.

I turned to find him staring up at me.

"You're sweating. Please sit," he urged, taking my elbow and guiding me to the bench. "Perhaps you should be resting."

I was unable to speak, unable to accept the feelings holding sway within me.

With a gentle hand, he lifted the hair from my ripening bruises. "My God, Henri. They've made a mess of you."

I closed my eyes. He meant to be kind, but his words grated at the last of my self-possession.

Cristofer's lips tightened into a troubled line. "Whatever will we tell the *madame*?" he asked.

The ash slipped in my hands.

"What?" I stuttered.

He wagged his head. "Madame Bertrand. What will you tell her has happened?" He rubbed a hand across his forehead. "You most definitely cannot reveal the truth, as Jacque will vehemently disapprove."

"The madame?"

Seeing me in distress, he snatched away the dustpan.

"Did I not tell you? I thought I mentioned it just before you left. My God, where is my head?" he rambled as he carried the pan out the front door.

"She has asked for ... *lessons*?"

"Yes, yes," he said, tossing the ash. "Apparently the instructor Clara recommended did not suit her. Aggravated, she implored

Jacque to allow her an instructor of her own choosing. It would appear her entreaty was successful, as she requested that I inquire as to your availability."

Owing to an increase in the number of strings, their thickness, and tension, the amount of pressure a piano's body must endure has increased exponentially. Reaching upward of fifteen tons. To accommodate this growing stress, piano makers have devised a number of grand technical innovations. The most notable being the replacement of the wood frame with one of solid iron. Sitting atop the soundboard, this formidable metallic collar resists the strings' colossal force. Without it, the piano would violently implode, cracking itself to pieces.

How I wished, in that moment, to have an iron collar sustaining my frame.

Cristofer set down the pan and sat on the bench alongside me.

I was frozen.

How had he replied to her request?

Had he refused her?

Had he thought the charade too dangerous?

Cristofer slapped a hand on my knee. Gave it a playful squeeze. "I hope you don't mind," he said. "But I accepted on your behalf."

The ground beneath us gave way.

He grinned. "You give your first instruction in three days."

There are moments that arise unexpectedly in one's life to alter its course forever. Such events catch us unaware—a chance encounter, a comment overheard, a glance met across a room.

Then there are the events that approach in full view, laden with fanfare and expectation. And it is these, perhaps, that are the most difficult to face.

Such was to be my first encounter with Ava, as her instructor.

I tried not to let panic get the best of me. Tried to prepare with all efficiency.

It was, after all, everything I had wanted, everything I had yearned for. Yet secretly I was terrified that the day of our meeting might actually arrive.

At the outset, I determined that the detail most critical to success would be my physical appearance.

Facing her with bruises and swelling could not be helped. I would have to concoct a suitable excuse. But the rest of my charade needed acute attention.

Having lost all my money to the seafaring twins, I had to approach Cristofer and, with great reluctance, borrow funds. I made promises to pay him back with what I earned from the lessons. But

I must say, he did not seem in the least bit concerned.

That same day I bought the finest three suits I could afford and had them fitted by the city's most prominent tailor. Fortunately, I had frequented the well-known clothier in the past and he, a crooked button of a man, thought nothing of my request to be fit in men's clothing.

Two days later, I assessed the suits' appearance before my mirror. The shoulders fit snugly, the coattails spilled elegantly. As I sometimes did, I rolled up a ball of socks which I stuffed down my britches. Having had my hair cut in a short style by Cristofer's barber, I had to admit that the overall effect struck me as quite dapper.

Still.

This was not a simple social gala, nor a dim night of brothel trolling.

Given all that lay at stake, I decided it would be prudent to take my disguise one step further.

When I entered the costume store, the bells secured to the doorframe rang out. I spotted the elder clerk at the back taking his tea. He made no motion to assist me.

"Do you have a mustache?" I called out.

He looked confused. "Eggs and hash?"

"No, no. A false mustache. And perhaps a beard."

The clerk cupped a hand behind his ear. "Beads? You want beads?"

I took a few steps forward. "I'm looking for a false mustache," I said, rubbing a finger along my upper lip.

"Ah! A mustache! Why didn't you say so?" He shook his head. "We don't carry those. Most like to grow their own."

"Well, then, do you know where I could obtain one?"

The clerk shrugged.

Frustrated at having wasted time, I made for the door. Just as the bells rang out, I heard him say, "You might try Therese. The costume designer."

I approached the theater. Given that it was daytime, its doors and windows were shut. Its lights unlit.

Does anything appear more dejected than a theater between per-formances?

I stepped up and knocked on the door. There was no response. After a few more attempts, I located the alley and headed back. The rear door had a buzzer alongside it and a small gold placard: "Mme. Therese Zakow, Costumier."

I knocked and this time someone answered. Therese. An ample-breasted, red-haired vixen. The glint in her eye enough to blind a dead man.

"Hello," she said with a grin. She refrained from using sir or madame.

God help me, another woman selling wares.

"Please come inside," she said, the lightest accent tracing her words. She glanced about the alley before closing the door behind us.

"How might I be of assistance?" she asked, a weightless gown of silvered chiffon hovering in her arms like a late-evening cloud.

Fretting over how much remained to be done, I decided not to mince words. "I need a false mustache. Of the highest quality. It must be foolproof."

She drew her gaze up my person.

I stood my ground. I could not afford to lose more time.

Her lips parted as if she might say something. Then, apparently thinking better of it, she turned and stepped behind a cabinet. On its glass top rested glittering wands and masks wrought in rubies, greens, and golds. Alongside these rose mannequins, one strapped in a corset, another jangling in the bells and silks of a court jester. Farther back, powdered wigs rose on stilts, hats and bonnets perched on pegs, capes swung from hooks, and shoes of every description lined the floorboards.

Therese opened the glass case. She removed several items and cradled them as if they were the most extravagant confections. Standing before me, she opened her palm to reveal a mustache and matching sideburns.

"I wove these for Claude Lemond, our troupe's newest lead. Still too young to grow enough of his own," she said. She lifted a tin of liquid adhesive. "Would you like me to apply them?"

I hesitated, then relented. Presumably she possessed the necessary expertise.

She directed me to sit on a stool. Leaned in, her eyes within inches of my own.

She drew a brush along my upper lip. Then pressed the mustache onto my skin.

Afterward she sat back to assess her handiwork. "Good. But a bit out of balance. Would you mind if I applied these?" she asked, lifting the sideburns in the cup of a hand.

I shrugged. Why not?

Again she ran the brush along my skin. Again she leaned in. Closer. Enabling me to peer down the deep gully between her breasts.

She then sat back slowly. Took in my new appearance. A smile of delight rolled across her lips. "Perfect."

She lifted a mirror. We gazed into its orb.

I flinched. Startled by the handsome stranger looking back. His jaw cut sharp by the dark frame of chops.

Therese nodded. "Will you be hoping to draw a kiss?"

"What?"

She laughed. "Don't feign innocence with me. I work in the theater, remember?"

She pouted her lips, full and red. She clamped my cheeks between her fingers. "Would you like to practice?" she purred.

I drew back. "No, no. I must be going. Someone is … expecting me."

Therese sighed, swept back her hair. "I'm sure she is."

I shook my head. "It's not like that."

Therese laughed out loud. Gruff, throaty laughter. "Of course it isn't," she said. Wagged her head. "It never is. At *first*."

Cristofer and I sat to eat. I had roasted lamb chops and blanched a mix of sweet greens.

He moaned at his first bite. "Oh, Henri. It's delectable."

I filled his glass with wine.

Earlier I had dressed in my disguise for him, donning the mustache and sideburns (for which, upon Therese's advice, I had purchased extra adhesive), as well as my carefully placed ball of socks.

His face had beamed with astonishment. "Henri? Is that you?" he'd asked. Then cheered, "Brilliant! Just brilliant."

I allowed a small smile then grew serious. "Were you able to speak with Jacque? To inquire after the madame's preferences and level of play?"

Knowing nothing of her abilities, I wanted to mentally prepare for what we might cover in our first lesson, as it would occur the very next day.

"Yes, yes," he said. "Jacque told me that his wife is devoid of proper musical instinct. That she has attempted lessons on a few occasions but the instructors have consistently given up and departed in exasperation. Apparently, she possesses an almost quixotic view of her abilities."

I ran a finger along my lip. Leaned back. "I see. Thank you for that."

He shrugged as if it were nothing.

It impressed me how supportive he remained of my endeavor.

Curious about this, I asked, "How is it that you can retain such enthusiasm for my charade when it clearly entails considerable risk for you?"

Cristofer's face clouded over. After a long moment, he said, "I must confess, I would not have allowed it had I not thought of a way to protect myself should things go ... awry."

"And that would be?"

"I will pretend that I'd known nothing. That I'd been equally deceived."

I tipped my head. "And you will make a great show of turning against me?"

He hesitated. Gave a slight nod.

So that's to be the way, I thought.

I will not pretend that his honesty came without a sting. But before I could dwell further upon it, a new thought entered my mind.

What would be my line of defense—to protect my own life and interests—should things go awry?

And, for just a moment, I considered withdrawing from the entire affair.

Cristofer lifted a chop to his lips, bit along the bone. "Thank you again for your marvelous suggestion, Henri. The third movement is coming right along. In fact, maybe you would have time to look it over before you retire?"

I started. "What? Oh, of course. I would be happy to have a look."

Would I?

My thoughts and interests had drifted so far from his creations. His needs. In fact, his constant requests for attention were beginning to irritate.

Still, I had to remember, it had been Cristofer who had brought me into contact with Ava and whose efforts would make our future meeting possible.

Those realizations helped soothe my mood.

"What material will you prepare for your first lesson?" he asked, dropping a bit of meat onto the floor for Signore.

I pondered the question, having little notion of what would be required. "What do you recommend?"

"Some charts, simple finger exercises," he suggested. "Perhaps a short melodic piece or two to facilitate early recognition of note and finger patterns. I have a great deal of material left over from my teaching days," he said. "Everything is stored in a box to the left of the fireplace. Use whatever you wish."

"Thank you."

Staring off, as if listening to something in the distance, he wiped his fingers vigorously on a napkin and pushed back from the table. Without another word, he returned to the bench, and his work.

I spent the rest of my evening sifting through sheets of elementary music.

In the morning I was surprised to find Cristofer already awake and at the piano.

When I walked inside, he was taken aback.

"Good God, Henri," he blurted. "I thought you a stranger!"

I laughed, ran a finger along my mustache.

He quickly returned to the keyboard. "I took your suggestion on the descending quarter notes for the transition. That section now sounds like this." He played a stirring passage.

"Stunning," I said. "Far improved."

Though, truly, I hadn't heard a thing. My mind and heart being elsewhere.

Shaky with nerves, I set about feeding Signore and preparing breakfast. As I whisked eggs and diced chives, I found myself unable to tolerate the blare of Cristof at the keyboard, the pounding chords, the swelling crescendos.

I set out his meal and coffee.

"Come eat," I urged, noting the pallor of his skin.

But I knew he would not rise. Despite my intrusion, he had already re-entered the rapture of struggle, of discovery. And would likely not emerge for hours. Noting this, I covered his eggs and poured the coffee into a carafe.

Though ample time remained until the madame would expect me, I gathered my pile of music and went to the door to fetch my cape.

"Wait!" Cristofer called from the piano.

He looked me up and down, a scowl setting his jaw.

What did he see?

Had my mustache come loose? My sock shifted?

"Where is your satchel?" he asked.

"My what?"

He shook his head at the loose sheets of music under my arm. "No proper instructor would travel to a lesson without one."

He strode to the fireplace. From a nearby cabinet, he lifted a case he had purchased while on holiday in Italy. Its soft chocolate leather was fractured with age. "Take mine," he said. Then slid my sheets of music into the case and snapped its silver buckles.

I thanked him and lifted the strap to my shoulder.

"Good luck," he said, but his attention had already drifted elsewhere and he burst into a rapid arpeggio.

I smiled at his having taken the time to perform a simple act of friendship. It was because these came so infrequently, that some people attributed a rather cold temperament to my Cristof.

But I knew the truth to be otherwise.

CHAPTER 7

When I arrived at the castle, the sun was still nestled along the horizon, causing the grand portico to cast a frigid shadow.

I glanced up at the door. I did not want to be caught lingering in the entranceway but hadn't yet summoned the vigor to announce my presence. My hands dashed over my hair, my mustache, my cravat. Assessing, smoothing.

I lifted the watch from my vest pocket. Despite having set out with a surplus of time, I now risked being overdue.

How had that happened?

I shivered and found myself wishing the sun would rise faster.

The clatter of horse hooves sounded behind me. I whirled and saw a stable boy galloping through the main gate. He tipped his head in my direction as he glided past astride a finely saddled stallion. The beast skidded to a stop before the hitching post. The rider leapt off and lashed the reins through an iron ring. The animal blew froth from its nostrils. Its flanks shimmering with sweat and gloss.

The stallion had no doubt been primed for Jacque's morning ride. Soon, I thought, the statesmen would appear in the plaza adorned in his equestrian costume.

Not wanting to risk such an encounter, I wheeled.

No sooner had the leaden knocker dropped from my hand than the great door opened and the butler appeared.

"Greetings, Monsieur Worth. The madame is expecting for you. If you would follow me."

I fully expected him to deliver me to the drawing room, and to Beethoven's glorious instrument, but to my surprise his path took us into an unlit antechamber stacked with folded tapestries. Passing quickly out of that room we wound through yet another. This one housed the castle's massive candelabras, all standing at attention in soldier-like rows.

I thought to protest our direction when the butler suddenly halted at the top of a staircase. He nodded down the narrow passage and said, "Please take care as you step."

He then descended.

I hesitated. My confidence wavering.

Had my charade been discovered?

Was I being led into an ambush?

Below, I heard the screech of door hinges.

"Monsieur?"

"Coming presently," I croaked. Headed downward.

No sooner had the darkness enveloped me than I beheld a distant shaft of light.

The butler spun in a doorway.

"You may wait in here," he said.

Stepping inside I was taken aback. The room was cozy and suffused with gauzy light. A bank of tall, mullioned windows opened upon the castle's rear gardens. These were lush and less manicured than those at its entrance, displaying a jungle of unfettered roses, flowering vines, fruit-laden trees, rivers of ivy.

Opposite the windows rose a wall of shelves shingled with books. Near these sat a small fireplace ringed by an armchair and ottoman. Comfortable furniture, unassuming, of a different breed altogether from the opulent pieces adorning the upstairs rooms.

I took another few steps into the room. My eyes feasted.

Beneath the windows sat a desk. Its top littered with random delights: trays of butterfly wings, pressed flowers, colored stones, spice jars, a magnifying glass, scalpels, a hummingbird's nest, an inkwell and paper, a decanter of sherry.

I could not help but wonder at the hungry and marvelous mind that would gather such pearls.

To my right, opposite a wall of silken drapes, I spied yet another treasure.

A cottage piano.

Its wood a dark nutty chocolate. Its adornment minimal yet assured.

Delighted, I approached. Pressed a finger to the key of middle C. The note sounded with a rich, burnished tone. To my surprise, the action felt sensitive and sure. Far superior to what I had expected. The piano maker's name appeared gilded beneath the music rack. I did not recognize it.

Perhaps they had acquired the unusual instrument while abroad?

Strangely, I could not locate a single sheet of music anywhere.

I was tempted to sit and run through some of the honeyeater piece but did not want to risk the madame catching me at the keyboard.

I would not make that mistake again.

Instead, I strolled to the bookshelf. The titles printed in the spines washed over me with warm familiarity. I noted that we shared a similar taste in literature. Aside from the works of the masters (Shakespeare, Dostoyevsky, Dickens, Bronte, Goethe, Blake, Eliot), she had also collected a mélange of less-familiar works. Some written in English, some in French and German. Even Russian.

Clearly her intellect possessed a keen agility.

I tried not to allow this fact to unsettle me.

After much perusing, I began to wonder at the time. I lifted my pocket watch and found it twenty-five minutes beyond the hour.

I looked over to the door. Felt prickles along my hairline.

Had she forgotten? Changed her mind?

What if she did not appear?

Determined to extend my wait, I drew down a slim volume and slipped between its pages.

After what felt like an unbearably long time, a figure rushed into the room.

"Monsieur Worth," she said, her breath coming fast.

The book slipped from my hands. I bent down to retrieve the volume.

"Madame," I managed.

"I am at a loss how to apologize, how to compensate you for this delay," she said.

As on the first occasion, I found it difficult to look fully upon her.

I rose slightly into a bow. "Your presence is reward enough," I assured.

When I stood upright, she drew a quick breath at the sight of my bruises. "Monsieur! What on earth happened?"

I cast my eyes downward. "I apologize for the insult my appearance must be inflicting upon you."

She cringed. "I imagine the effect is somewhat worse for *you*," she said. "I will, however, accept an explanation of your injuries as compensation."

"Yes, of course," I blurted. "You see, it was circumstance that forced me into the position of defending a woman's honor. Unfortunately, I was badly outnumbered," I said, adhering to the script Cristofer and I had devised.

"A woman?" she asked.

I gave a slight nod.

"Yours or another's?"

"Oh, very much another's."

"I see," she said. Arched an eyebrow. "Are you in very much pain?"

"Not presently," I said.

If only you could know the pleasure of standing before you!

"And what of your adversaries?"

Having no further embellishments, I looked to the floor, a picture (I hoped) of humility. "Please do not ask me to elaborate further, madame," I said. "It was a difficult and complicated encounter. And I would not wish to mar your impression of me."

"Very well," she said, seeming content with my answers.

Silence followed.

Feeling awkward, I prepared to make some effort at pedagogy when, suddenly, I sensed her moving closer. Circling me.

I held still, sensing that I was under her inspection.

"You've grown a mustache," she said. Sounding amused.

My hand rose unconsciously.

She came to a stop in front of me. Dusted fingertips along her throat.

"It suits you," she said.

After what seemed a very long moment, she turned and indicated the space about us. "I hope you find the conditions suitable?"

"It is a lovely room indeed."

Hell itself would be a fine place to meet you.

She gazed out with affection. "This is where I satisfy my many curiosities. It is my private oasis. My refuge."

I considered her words.

Curiosities? Refuge?

From what did she seek escape?

I kept silent. Made a study of my boots.

It was only with the greatest effort that I did not stare. But even looking upon her with stolen and measured glances, I felt overcome.

What had made me believe I could carry out such a mad scheme?

"Please know, Monsieur Worth, that today's delay was unavoidable and not at all the manner in which I wished to begin with you."

Begin with me?

She swept wisps of hair from her forehead. Sought to lift my eyes with her own. "I am almost afraid to ask, but have you still time?"

I swallowed.

Madame, I have Eternity if you but so asked. And would sacrifice my limbs to elongate Forever if such a trade were possible.

"I have time."

She smiled. Swept to the piano bench. Her silk dress whispering as she settled.

To the piano? Already?

"Wait!" I cautioned, realizing I had lost control of my pupil, an occurrence Cristofer had counseled me to avoid. I was, after all, the man between us. The master musician.

I stepped close as I dared and lowered the fallboard.

Her lips pouted as the keys disappeared.

Unable to bear our proximity (*can one's skin actually crackle?*), I slipped to a safer distance.

"There is time enough for music-making," I said, "but by way of initiating the journey, I prefer to know something of my students first—their hearts, goals, expectations."

My students?

She sniffed. Twisted to face me.

I tried not to notice how the bands of sinew swelled gracefully in her neck when she did this.

"What is it you wish to know?" Her green eyes flared, spewing sparks of gold.

Certain they were trembling, I stuffed my hands into my pockets.

"Your ... goals," I repeated.

She turned back to the fallboard. Ran her fingers thoughtfully along the dark polished wood. "Since I have hired an instructor, would it not be reasonable to assume I wish to have you evaluate my playing and chart a course of practice designed to enhance my musicality?"

A barbed reply.

I strained against the confines of my suit.

"Of course," I mumbled.

Had I offended?

The mustache on my lip heated to an almost unbearable scald.

"So will you?"

"Will I what?"

"Evaluate me?"

"Right now?"

"Yes. Right now."

I flushed.

Were we speaking of the same thing?

I struggled to remember the other inquiries I had planned, the other directives.

I wanted to suggest a different avenue entirely but she seemed eager, if not anxious, to approach the instrument.

"Of course, madame."

Seeking a measure of control, I stepped forward, curled my fingertips under the fallboard. Set it flush against the rack.

Her eyes lighted atop the keys as if on a banquet long denied her.

I would have wondered longer at this reaction but at that precise moment the mist of her perfume had risen to encompass me. Fearing for my composure, I breathed in as little as possible.

Yet even a trace aroused.

It was the same scent she had worn in the drawing room. A bewitching fragrance of nectar and spice. Jasmine harvested in a foreign land.

"What would you wish me to play?" she asked, her eyes bearing on the keys.

I thought back to Jacque's inference that his wife harbored a grossly unrealistic opinion of her abilities.

Not wishing to overwhelm her with a request she could not possibly fulfill, I sought a more basic direction.

"I will have you play in a moment," I said. "But let us first conduct a course of exercise. To prepare wrists and fingers. As is good practice."

At my suggestion, she rolled back the sleeves of her dress.

How can I admit the effect her exposed wrists had upon me?

There is no point in trying to describe them—other than to say they curved with an alluring elegance. Yet it was not their physicality that affected me, but the confident manner with which she moved them, the graceful arcs by which they swept the air.

I didn't *dare* look upon her fingers.

Lifting my hands before me, I modeled several exercises. As I did so, I explained the significance of each and its effect on performance.

"Do you notice a difference in pliability?" I asked when we had finished.

She wriggled her fingers, gave a mild shrug. "I suppose I shall know when I have something to run them along."

She looked up. Her lips parting.

"You are eager to play, then?" I said, wishing I had not.

Why did everything sound like innuendo?

"I am eager, yes."

I gave a little laugh. Mainly to relieve the unbearable pressure.

"Let me then retrieve something for you."

I stepped to my satchel. Wary, I drew out a Clementi exercise. It was the easiest selection I had found in Cristofer's collection and, I hoped, the least daunting.

I lowered the rack and set the sheet of music upon it. "There you are," I said. "Let us begin with this. A study of scales in the key of C."

I stepped back. Waited for her to begin.

When she did not, I looked down.

To my shock, she was staring wide-eyed. Her cheeks drained white.

Aghast, I leapt to the most obvious and horrifying conclusion.

She could not read music!

I faltered.

Had I insulted her beyond repair? Had I trampled on the most tender shoots of her enthusiasm?

"Madame, my deepest apologies," I stuttered, not knowing what to say.

"Is this what you think of me?" she asked, her voice small, breathy.

"Perhaps we can begin with something else entirely ..." I offered.

I watched in horror as a blush swept up the sides of her neck.

Without so much as a glance in my direction, she reached for the service bell. Rang it over her head.

The butler appeared swiftly, as if he'd been waiting outside the door.

"Madame, please," I begged, my heart pounding. "If this music is not to your liking, I can adjust in whatever manner—"

"Audric, Monsieur Worth has finished his lesson. Please see him out."

Audric swept his arm toward the exit.

I yearned to protest. To offer reparations.

But that would be unseemly.

Instead, I gathered my satchel and cape and departed.

With all efficiency, Audric led me back through the maze of dim rooms. The candelabras looming with solemnity, as if overseeing a gallows.

"Good day," he said, holding open the great door. No sooner had I exited than he shut it with a bang.

The fiery morning licked my face. Burning, I sped across the plaza.

I spat all manner of curses as I strode down the flowered hill. My heart clogging the back of my throat.

Inside, my soul curdled.

I would never see her again.

When I returned home, I rushed into Cristofer's cottage. Even if he were lost in the concerto, I would shake him from his efforts. I needed to speak with him. To yell. Sob. Regurgitate the poison of anger and confusion and despair.

Then I worried he might be angry with me. Might view my failure as a risk to his arrangement with Jacque.

But my employer was not home.

I stared through reddened eyes at the vacated piano. The saddle of its bench polished to a sheen by the friction of our endeavors.

It had been so long—and yet—I could not bring myself to engage.

At that moment, her solemn tone would surely break me.

Late afternoon sunlight slanted through the bedroom window. Kissed the edge of the bed. I rolled over and opened my eyes. I must have slept for hours.

In the distance, I heard a man yelling. Calling my name.

Cristofer!

I listened more carefully. He sounded distressed.

Had he caught wind of the madame's upset?

I'd just leapt from beneath the covers when he appeared at the door, his suit wet, his eyes wide and rolling.

"Henri! Thank God you're here. Come with me. Now."

"But—?"

"*Now!*"

He ran from the door and I rushed after him.

At the end of the walkway I spotted a covered dray. Two horses frothing at the reins.

Without a word of explanation, Cristofer hopped onto the rear of the carriage and extended his hand. I pressed my palm into his and mounted the vehicle.

The driver threw me a sideways glance—I was still in my instructor's costume—then fired his team with a yell and crack of whip.

The jolting departure nearly threw me overboard. Fortunately, Cristofer caught my elbow and, with a strong pull, conveyed me beneath the canopy.

It was dark underneath the canvas, the only light spilling through torn holes.

Then the smell hit me.

A dank odor. Of stagnant water and river sludge.

I heard a moan.

I stared into the dark and could just make out the perimeter of a figure. He was lying down. Shivering. His suit heavy with water, the wool plastered to his limbs.

"Is it *Richard*?" I whispered.

"Yes."

"What in God's name—?"

"He jumped. From the bridge."

The dray hit a rock and lurched. The famed composer laughed aloud. Wild, discordant laughter. The shriek of furies.

I stared in horror.

Cristofer said nothing as the dray sped along.

Shortly thereafter, the horses ground to a halt outside the Thornes'.

"Clara has taken the children to a neighbor's," Cristofer said. "Help me bring him inside."

In what felt like an insidious déjà vu, we bore the drenched and nearly unconscious Richard into the house. Once we had him settled in bed, Cristofer took the driver aside. He dropped several coins into the man's hand. "Remember. Not a word of this to anyone."

"Is he famous?" the driver asked.

"That's of no concern," Cristofer barked.

The driver threw a last look toward the bedroom door then departed.

Cristofer turned to me while Richard mumbled. "Boil water. I'll dress him in dry clothes."

In the kitchen, I steeped three cups of tea, ardently hoping Richard would recover enough to drink with us. I set out biscuits, sugar, fresh cream.

Waiting for Cristofer to re-emerge, I went to the window. The sky had thickened with dark clouds. Soon the raindrops began. Their rhythmic patter clicking against the roof.

I looked to the far end of the hall. Richard's door remained closed.

I put a hand to my heart.

What cruel disorder had reduced our man of genius? Our gentle soul, father, and friend?

Seeking distraction, I stepped into the music room. There I found an unusual silence. Not the usual hush that lingers between sessions, but the weighted stillness that accompanies tragedy.

Or death.

I shivered at the feeling and fought to brush it aside.

Richard would recover. It could not be otherwise. He was too powerful a beast, too bold a force, to be extinguished.

I went and stood above the piano. There I noticed a stack of music set on the rack. The sheets appeared to have been recently created, the notes still damp, the phrasings incomplete.

A work in progress. Written in Richard's looping, meticulous hand.

The title, inscribed at the top of the parchment, read "Clara's Variations."

I sat and fanned out the sheets. Scanning the staffs, I played the music inside my head. The piece set off with a clear and forthright theme. A musical lilt in a major scale. A nod toward purity of spirit.

I continued to study the music for some time. Still Cristofer did not appear.

Intrigued by the music and eager to hear it aloud, I stood and closed the piano's lid, thus decreasing its volume. I then sat in position and played with the lightest possible touch.

The tune unfolded readily. The melody enriched by a fast and challenging undercurrent. I continued, swimming atop the opening theme until, quite unpredictably, a second theme imposed itself. The second one had a different weight entirely from the first, suggesting an almost tragic yet somewhat grand bearing. Its sudden intrusion was ungainly and unlike any device Richard had utilized in previous works. Stylistically, it stuck out like a sore thumb.

As these observations raced through my mind, the first theme regained supremacy. But no sooner had it begun to spread roots and develop than the second theme reared again. Galloping alongside the first. My hands swept back and forth. Taxed by dueling moods, I leaned into the keyboard. The piece was proving not only technically challenging but increasingly stressful, the embattled melodies threatening at every turn to dissolve into dissonance.

It was almost as if the composer wished to force the pianist to choose one theme over the other. The making of that choice being the only way to prevent harmonic disaster.

I began to perspire as the tension reached a fevered pitch.

Then.

A woman's voice.

"Please stop."

I whirled to find Clara at my shoulder.

For a moment I panicked at her having heard my playing, but soon realized she had taken no notice of it whatsoever.

"Henri..." she whispered, absorbing the full effect of my disguise.

She observed my bruises and a hand flew to her lips. "My *God*—"

"It's nothing," I said. Drew her hands into mine. "The children are safe?" I asked.

She nodded slowly. Appeared half out of her head. Yet something in her eyes shimmered.

"Cristofer is tending to him," I assured. Then helped remove her coat. "You're soaked," I said. "Come and have tea." I put my arm around her shoulders and led her to the kitchen. She moved like a phantom beside me.

We sat for several minutes in silence. Double twists of steam braided between us.

"He was writing that piece for me," she whispered. "To try... to tell me—" Her eyes reddened. She wagged her head. "But he couldn't ... *doesn't* ... accept the truth of things."

I remained silent.

She pinned me with a stare. In that moment, I understood how a sheet of music might feel when placed before her.

"No one understands," she whispered. "*No one.*"

I wanted to blurt out that *I* understood. That I had seen the passion flowing between her and Cristofer.

But I could not.

Given the circumstances, what good would come of such an accusation?

Cristofer stepped into the kitchen. His expression spoke of what he could not. He lifted a shaky hand to his lips.

When Clara saw him, she rose and rushed into his arms. He pressed her to his chest. When their embrace approached an inappropriate length, I saw Clara draw back. Straighten the front of her dress.

Cristof stumbled into the silence. "He's safe now. He's resting," he said.

We sat with our tea. Cristofer lifted what I'd intended as Richard's cup.

For a while, no one spoke.

Then Clara, "Did anyone witness it?"

Cristofer shook his head. "Just the two who helped pull him out. Passersby. Not from here, fortunately."

Clara tapped a rhythm on the table with her fingers. "Richard would be mortified to know you have seen this."

"I don't think he will remember," Cristofer offered quietly.

Clara's head fell into her hands. Her shoulders shuddered. "He was just working ... at the piano ... Ferdinand was in the corner reading ... Marie dressing dolls ... It was a day like any other," she groaned.

"Did he not say anything unusual?" Cristofer asked. "Or act strangely?"

Clara shook her head. "He'd been feeling better as of late. Taking long walks. Working well into the evenings. When I saw him this morning, he took me in his arms, said that he loved me, that he would always love me, and wished only that I—" Her throat closed with emotion.

Cristofer rose to his feet. Frazzled. His eyes bore into mine, giving me the distinct impression I was no longer welcome.

I cleared my throat. "I should be going."

"Yes, of course," Cristofer muttered, as if he hadn't influenced my decision.

At the scrape of my chair, Clara looked up. "But the *rain*, Henri—"

"It will cause no harm," I said. "And you need to rest." I bent down. Kissed her cheek. Felt my false bristles yield to her softness. "Take care of Richard, and yourself, too," I counseled.

She pressed her hand into mine.

I nodded to Cristofer and made my way quickly to the door before any more could be said.

Under the clouds, I turned up my collar and drew in a shuddering breath. It was only then, feeling a measure of relief under the open sky, that I realized the conflicting tensions wiring one end of the Thornes' cottage to the other. Hope and despair. Passion and restraint. The known and the untasted.

Seeking the shelter of the forest's canopy, I could not help but wonder at the fate of the three souls left behind me.

}

I filled the tub to its brim, poured a cup of perfumed salts, descended into the pearly milk.

The water pooled around my neck. Its warmth drew the ache from inside me, though I could not tell if the pain arose from body or heart.

Lying there, I felt an audience of eyes upon me:

Ava, fuming with shock and betrayal.

Richard, stormy with despair.

Clara, frantic, split in two.

And Cristofer. My poor Cristofer.

I could not begin to imagine the torment inhabiting his soul.

On the one hand, his loyalty and love for Richard would bring him nothing but grief over his mentor's suffering. And yet, what of the window that such madness might open?

I dared not think of it. But knew the grim possibility had gripped my liege by the throat. Filled him with a dark and delirious temptation. That afternoon, as he leaned over his fallen comrade, I'd seen the realization seep slowly into his eyes, until they glinted with a madness all their own.

And had I not seen the same take root in Clara?

Yet nothing between them could be possible—nor realized—as long as their hero drew breath.

While I mulled these difficult considerations, the water cooled and receded, exposing my thighs and hipbones to the air. Part of me wanted to refresh the bath, to infuse it again with warmth. But another part wanted to endure the chill, wanted its sharp teeth to pierce my skin.

The day's events had left me tangled.

How I wanted to mourn the loss of Ava, to weep over my carelessness and idiocy.

But what did such loss matter in the face of Richard's tragic surrender?

I began to shiver uncontrollably. The chatter of my teeth echoing off the porcelain.

I thought again of Richard's "Variations." Of the maddening thematic battle. My mind then recalled the night he had come for dinner, and his quiet gesture of returning my cufflink.

Connecting these errant threads led me to an inescapable conclusion.

He knew.

How could it be otherwise?

And, by way of farewell, he had enfolded his knowledge into a piece for Clara.

And she had heard it.

Only Cristofer had managed to avoid the "Variations'" damning agony. Its raging counterpoint.

I ached to think of Richard's anguish. Of his divided loyalties. To himself, to Clara, to Cristofer, to his music. He loved them all fiercely. With devotion and adornment.

Yet perhaps he had come to suspect that life might soon force a choice upon him. Or force one upon Clara—or Cristofer.

Whatever the case, a choice made by one would alter them all.

Perhaps this inevitable and impending damage was what he wished to convey in the "Variations."

Such things were impossible to know, living only in the great heart and mind of Richard Thorne, which that day he had nearly extinguished.

The sound of a slam nextdoor broke into my thoughts.

Cristofer had come home.

Not more than a minute later, I heard the sharp slap of the fallboard.

Followed by the crash of heavy chords.

Thirds. Fourths. Sevenths. They shattered the upper register like glass.

From there he began to drill downward. Anguished minor chords, thick with ache, driven down the piano's throat. The technique, one of his favorites, usually thrilled the listener. But tonight he ran the chords down with such force, such violence, as if he might choke the piano, that it created a terrifying effect.

I continued to listen as the chords, having initially sounded with clarity and force, began to warp and misshapen.

Alarmed by this uncharacteristic blurring, I leapt from the bath. Drying quickly, I slipped into my breeches and bolted for his cottage.

When I opened the door, the piano's roar hit me like a wall.

Cristofer battered the keyboard. His blonde hair tumbling about his purpled cheeks. His tears pelting the keys.

I rushed to his side.

When he felt my shoulder, he turned and collapsed into my arms.

His sobs wracked the both of us.

I held him until, shuddering, he drew out an agonizing moan. Thus emptied, he pressed his face along my chest.

"What will we do? What will we do?" he moaned.

I pressed a palm to his cheek, uncertain of which "we" he was referring to.

Perhaps he meant all of us.

He began again to weep.

"I cannot—she will not ... release her hold ..."

"I know, Cristof," I whispered. "I know."

He gripped my sleeves. "For the love of Richard I cannot look. And for the love of her, I cannot look away."

I held him tighter.

"I know she is not a grand beauty. I have even tried to use her plainness as a balm against the flames. But I cannot. Because what she possesses inside is what lures me. The force of her, the shine of her that pronounces itself in her music. By all that is holy, I swear, it cracks the bones in my chest and tears the heart from my body."

My own heart ached at his words. Knowing something of what he felt.

It is her Light, I thought.

He drew the back of a hand across his shining face. "It is a cruel, *cruel* trap fate has used to snare me."

I could not disagree.

Hearing us, Signore appeared and wound a path between our legs.

"Cristofer," I said quietly, "you are trembling. Let me draw you a bath. Cook you dinner. Then we can—"

"No," he said, pulling away. "You don't understand. You couldn't."

I glared.

Was he suggesting that my heart could not love as deeply? That my attachments amounted to mere infatuations?

I felt my mood swing toward resentment, the day's stresses having worn me thin.

"As you wish," I said. "I only thought to help. I will be in my cottage. You may call if you need me."

If he wanted to hit his head against stones, what could I do?

He whirled around at my curt words. "Henri. No. Please stay."

"Whatever for? My offers of assistance only seem to incite—"

"Henri, *please!*" he begged. He drew a hand to his mouth. "It is worse than you can know. Worse than you can imagine."

Worse? I wanted to scream.

How can it be worse than donning a counterfeit costume in order to approach the object of your desire only to be thrown out like a dog?

Enraged, I lunged for the door. Threw it open with such force that its wooden slats cracked against the stone.

"Henri!" he shouted after me.

I said nothing. Stomped into the rain, the rage and anguish I had kept buried billowing through me.

"Henri, wait! Please listen!" Cristofer wailed. Then groaned, "Clara is … *with child*."

CHAPTER 8

A man's legs hung out of our piano, cut in half by its giant jaws. The rest of his burly torso remained buried deep in the belly of our beast.

Ever since Cristofer had unleashed his storm of anguish onto the keyboard, the instrument had sounded decidedly off.

Hideous knocks and twangs issued from the piano's interior. Shortly thereafter, the piano tuner re-emerged. Though white-haired, he stood to an impressive height, his leather apron straining to contain him.

He twirled a curious tool in each hand and delivered his diagnosis. "I'm sorry to say, but there's a good bit of damage to a number of the escapement mechanisms."

"Is that a complicated repair?"

He squinted. "Do you know how escapement works?"

I shrugged. "I have a general notion."

The truth was, having never owned my own piano, I had only a vague idea of how the internal machinery operated.

He laughed. "You players are all alike," he said. "You create the most beautiful melodies but have no idea what it takes to make them possible!"

He leaned back inside the instrument. "I've gone ahead and removed several strings to relieve the pressure on the frame, so you'll have to refrain from playing until I can return."

"And when will that be?"

He drew a sweaty palm across the bib of his apron. "Oh, I'd estimate a few weeks or so."

"*Weeks?*" I blurted.

"Well, parts will have to be brought in from Hamburg. This can take some time." He looked over at the stacks of manuscripts blanketing the furniture. "Of course I understand the significance of Master Vaughn's work. So I'll do my best to hurry things along." He chuckled lightly. "My daughters seem to think he walks on water," he added with a wink.

I scoffed. "As do many others more illuminated than your daughters. Hence the need to expedite this matter."

He sobered at my slight and bent to collect his tools.

The task of overseeing the instrument's repair had fallen to me since Cristofer had disappeared. I knew where he had gone, of course, and could easily have found him rummaging amid the city's rougher women, but left him to his devices. Knowing they served as an acrid but necessary medicine.

In the meantime, denied the use of our piano, and seeking a curative of my own, I collected the dried sheets of Cristofer's manuscript and sat to study his progress.

From the sounds his work conjured inside my head, the concerto's third movement had begun to gain momentum. His presto stormed forward along a jutted spine of demanding rhythms and walls of brass.

I sighed with admiration. At last, my liege had found his feet.

Feeling roused by the music's elevated spirit, I began pacing.

For a moment, Ava's eyes rose before me.

I winced.

Suddenly desperate for greater distraction, I gathered my hat and cape and set off for the woods. There, hopefully, I might find inspiration or, at the very least, exhaustion enough to dim my anguish.

Hours of circuitous turns eventually brought me to a glen of linden trees. Their roughly grated bark and pea-shaped fruits lent a sudden festivity to the forest. Beyond them leaned tall rows of sunflowers, their thick stalks supporting wide, bright flowers circled by clouds of bees and goldfinches.

Mesmerized by the glen's busy orbits and vivid scents, I lowered myself into the grass. Doing so, I felt simultaneously settled and lifted.

Seemingly unaware of my presence, the bees continued to curve paths in the air. Watching them, I began to sense a pattern in their racing spirals. As often happens, the visual pattern transformed into sound. I closed my eyes as the music ascended of its own accord, rising on a major chromatic scale of buzzing beauty, drifting between my ears then flooding outward to inhabit my limbs.

I let the music hold me, float me. And in that moment felt as though I was cared for.

Perhaps even loved.

Soon my tears found themselves released and falling.

A single human can only contain so much sentiment without springing a leak.

I shook my head at my display, thinking how ridiculous I would appear to anyone who walked by—a woman looking handsomely like a man—spread in the grass crying at nothing.

And what would be my defense?

Some days I wish not to feel life so deeply. It is the blessing and the curse of the artist. An artist being, in my mind, no one greater than someone who practices reverent attention. Someone who allows their powers of observation to stray beyond the normal bounds into a domain usually reserved for worship.

As a breed, rightly or wrongly, we artists do not survive on bread alone. We feast instead on the banquet of elements that surrounds us. On common details of extraordinary beauty. With these we become fascinated, fixated, obsessed, enamored—lured by the electricity, the animated pulse emitted by a specific curve, scent, light, hum, touch, and so forth. These drive us to distraction with their particular twists of grace.

Thus, a stand of sunflowers, haloed with honeybees, can reduce me to tears.

It is unknown if we artists could survive without imbibing such details, but I suspect strongly not. And so we clutch them, root them out with hungry eyes and mouths, as if without them our very breath would cease. Believing that it is the devouring of such elements that enables us to distill novel melodies, brushstrokes, shapes and verses that never before existed. And which we could not invent by any other means.

Does any of this convey what I wish it to?

As usual, I am not certain if my rambling has done my subject more harm than good.

But I suppose what I'm trying to describe is a rare vein of love.

For eventually, an artist's appreciation for a particular thing will ignite their passion. After all, who can dissolve one's self in profound admiration and not fall in love? And this love can either rest quietly in the heart or, in more unfortunate cases, spawn disaster.

In the case where the particular object is an inanimate one—say, a river or a landscape—no difficulty will arise, as the artist simply returns there to abide and relish.

But should an artist's appreciation be for a trait or forte of another human being, trouble may ensue. For in loving a single trait or aspect, the artist cannot help but fall equally in love with the being who possesses it. We have no faculty, it seems, for cleaving a single beloved quality from the entire person. One measures a face for the other. And the artist's passion arises, quick and heady, as though they were one.

While such hunger alone is no cause for concern, and can lead to wondrous romance, when the object of desire is beholden to another, torment is assured.

This was the desperate predicament Cristofer had found himself in.

As had I.

Cristofer had fallen for Clara's gift. For her profound musical genius.

I had fallen for Ava's luminosity. For the shine of her spirit.

Yet neither of us could sip the nectar that drew us. To attempt even a taste would risk not only our standing in the world, but would tarnish the very thing we cherished.

So each of us, in our own way, had vowed to restrain. To rein our desire.

A sweet and devastating torture.

Though for Cristofer, now, a possibility, an awful crack in circumstance. One that lured with the promise of a stolen word. Or touch.

And for me?

For me all hope had departed. Never would I know the lovely incandescence that had seduced my eye and heart. Never would her essence nest in my bones.

Thinking this, I rolled onto my back and from that vantage heard a sound that raised goose flesh along my arms.

It was a honeyeater's song.

But not just any honeyeater.

The honeyeater. The specific bird whose voice I had seen the scientist carry off in his strange case.

I listened again, certain my ears had failed me. Or fooled me. And not a little concerned that I might also be going mad.

After the turn of recent events, who could blame me?

But no. There it was again. Ghostly in its repeat. The sound a vapor of what I remembered—but authentic in detail, nonetheless. There could be no mistaking the specific character of that one bird's song—its unusual tremolo between phrases, a hiccup to punctuate its end.

I bolted upright.

How was this possible?

Could that same bird have traveled to this remote location so far from its hunting ground?

On my feet before I realized it, I advanced toward the clearing. Fearing that my efforts might scare the creature, I moved with all possible stealth.

Soon I was upon him.

When he saw me, he let out a loud, whooping cry.

Not the bird, but the scientist.

"Ahhhh!"

We tumbled mutually to the ground.

In the fall, the machine he'd been holding sprang from his hands.

"Heavens!" he blurted.

Scrambling back to his feet, he rushed to retrieve the device, its parts now scattered in the bush.

"Please, let me help you," I offered.

"No!" he cried. "It would be best if I did it. Things are delicate … cannot be touched … must be handled a certain way…"

Fanning open a cluster of tall grass, he placed a hand inside and lifted a dark round object.

I recognized it immediately. It was the cylinder. The very one on which I had seen him etch the bird's song!

"Isn't that where ...?" I tried, unsure how to phrase my question.

But the scientist ignored me. Engrossed in collecting his machine, he seemed to have forgotten my presence. When he had piled the various parts at his feet, he began to reassemble them.

After what seemed an eternity, he righted his little device. In many ways it appeared of similar design to the one I had seen him operating during our first encounter. Yet the various mechanisms seemed more refined. More precise. From what I could see, the cylinder still rested in a central position, a fine filament angling as before toward the lines etched in its surface. But rather than balancing between two barrels as before, the filament now hovered beneath a single horn whose broad mouth opened entirely on the forest.

I studied the contraption, trying to imagine the path a vibration might make through its entrails.

Relieved at the successful reassembly, the scientist turned to face me.

"You heard him sing?" he asked.

"What? I—I don't know," I stuttered, unwilling to make a fool of myself.

He laughed out loud, his tone unexpectedly joyful. "My friend, meet the Phonautograph!"

"The what?"

He bent an ear to the horn's vessel. Smiled as though possessing a grand secret. Then turned a crank.

Nothing happened.

Or rather, the machine released only the dull echo of metal scraping wax.

He glared. "No, no," he said with obvious frustration. He fiddled with the device. "She's not perfected, of course. A number of improvements need to be made, along with tolerance and fitting adjustments," he added. "Ah, *there* …"

He retook his position before the horn's mouth. Closed his eyes. Turned the crank.

Again. Nothing.

His shoulders sagged with disappointment. "I cannot fix her here. I need my tools back at the lab," he said and began to dissemble the machine. Doing so, he turned to face me. "But you heard him sing again, did you not?"

I shook my head in disbelief. I had no idea what I'd heard. Perhaps nothing. Perhaps a parlor trick.

It could not be possible for the past to speak again.

For the dead to occupy princely castles.

It simply could not.

Could it?

I sat at the kitchen table shelling peas. Staring into space.

For the life of me, I could not remember how I'd found my way home.

Had the encounter with the scientist even occurred?

Had I been dreaming?

On the other side of the cottage, the piano glowed with the peach of arriving sunset.

As a small mountain of peas rose in the bowl, so rose thoughts of my brother.

Before me I saw again the stain of elderberry on his palm.

The fortune-teller had said he would grow up. Would marry and inhabit a castle.

I recalled the words spoken by Tess: *"Who says she was wrong?"*

I peeled another pod.

Imagined again the honeyeater's song, echoing within the horn's mouth. Returned somehow from the grave.

Could some essence of our life actually linger?

And could this essence bend time? Wrap the past back into the present?

*Were our souls, then, like rounded cylinders, etched by the Creator,
ever revolving?*

I shook at the improbability. At the sense of gravity releasing
its hold.

When something rustled outside the window, Signore leapt
onto the table.

Thinking Cristofer had finally come home, I slipped the peas
into a pot of boiling water.

Then came a knock.

Realizing it was not Cristof, I answered with caution from
behind the closed door.

"Who is it?"

"A messenger, ma'am."

I opened the door. Found a wiry young man on the step. Stared
at his brooding features, trying to place him.

I could see him doing the same with me.

Behind us, a horse let out a piercing whinny. At the end of our
walkway I spotted the steed, black and flashing, tied to the lamppost.

Jacque's stallion!

I glanced back at the young man and made the connection. He
was the stable boy who had ridden past while I delayed outside the
castle door.

"I have a message for Monsieur Worth," he said.

"For who?"

"Henri Worth," he repeated.

I was not in costume.

"Ah yes," I began. Wiped a hand across the face of my apron. "Unfortunately, Henri is not here at present. But if you give me the message, I'll see it delivered."

The rider glanced over my shoulder as if seeking someone more respectable with whom to deposit his missive.

"Give it here," I said. I didn't want to play games. Nor risk him catching a glimpse of my trembling hands.

"'Tis a verbal message, ma'am."

"That says?"

I waited for him to speak, hoping the roar in my ears would cease long enough for me to hear.

He cleared his throat. Stood tall. Boomed, "Monsieur Worth, Madame Bertrand requests that tomorrow's lesson occur an hour later than scheduled, owing to a previous engagement."

"Tomorrow's *lesson?*"

Was this a joke?

The boy appeared bewildered by my confusion. His request, it seemed, was genuine.

I thought quickly.

"The message is received and understood," I said. "And you

may inform the madame that Monsieur Worth will gladly honor her request."

The boy dipped a polite bow. Then dashed down the walkway, unhooked the rearing stallion, and leapt to its back. Tossing me a wave, he galloped off, divots of turf flying in his wake.

When he was gone, I spun in the threshold and fell against the doorframe.

As the meaning of the message unfolded, my heart thumped against my chest.

But how was it possible she would continue with her lessons?

After my abject insult and her violent reaction, what had transpired to change her mind?

Try as I might, I could not conjure a satisfactory answer.

But if she truly did wish to resume her instruction, there were preparations to be made!

I strode to the fireplace to locate my satchel and review the contents inside. As I did so, my attention coiled around a single thought:

Soon I would see her again. Soon I would gaze into the eyes of Light!

My cheeks swelled atop an insistent smile.

Then other thoughts intruded upon the first, causing my sudden joy to fade. I thought back to the scene in the doorway. To the stable hand's wandering eyes.

Had he recognized me? Seen through my pretense?

And, if he had, would he feel it his duty to inform the madame?

Or worse yet—Jacques Bertrand himself?

CHAPTER 9

*T*he next morning as I slipped beneath the castle's shadow I looked furtively about, searching for the stable boy, desperate to avoid him. Thankfully, he did not appear and I hurried to the portico.

Audric opened the door. I looked into his eyes, trying to gauge whether my secret had been revealed. But he only returned my stare with the usual surplus of ennui. His features an impressive void.

As he had previously, he guided me through the labyrinth of rooms and down into Ava's hidden study.

"The madame promises to be along shortly," he said, and disappeared.

Glancing about, I found the room much as it had been. The ottoman still stacked with books, the desk littered with curiosities.

Struggling against the lure of the piano, I paced the room's perimeter. To my alarm, I found the air alight with the madame's scent.

I tugged at my collar, resumed my pacing.

In a far corner just beyond the garden windows, I spotted the screen of thick silk. I had given this element little notice on my previous visit. Facing the door, I made certain no one was coming. Then, with all haste, slipped the back of a hand inside the silken seam. Peering between the curtains, I saw a long, low-slung chaise. Luxurious pillows stitched with gold and ebony threads lay strewn along its plush mattress.

The sight of this accouterment—roomy enough to accommodate two persons—sent a shiver down my spine.

I had barely recovered when I sensed someone behind me. I immediately retracted my hand.

"Hello," she said.

I turned. Swooned as her presence washed over me.

"Close your eyes," she said.

What?

"Madame," I began, armed with my apology, "I—"

"Close your eyes," she commanded again.

"Madame, I feel I must—"

"Please. Not another word."

I fell silent. Closed my eyes.

What was this game?

Unable to see, I found the faculty of my hearing much enhanced. My ears widening like open-mouthed horns.

I heard the rustle of skirts. Silk brushing skin. The squeal of hinges. The fallboard lifting. A tap as it set against the rack. The rhythmic creaking as a body—her body—nestled along the bench's back.

Oh to be that bench!

Tangled in this thought, I was hardly prepared for what I heard next.

A single, solemn tone. Vibrating deep in the piano's chest. Followed swiftly by a chain of notes rising from this lower octave along a breathy arpeggio. Bubbles ascending through water.

The chain repeated, a haunting bracelet that returned again and again to itself. Above this chain rose a delicate melody, stitched hesitantly in the piano's upper register.

I recognized the tune immediately.

Chopin.

His Nocturne in E Minor.

I swallowed with difficulty. My throat suddenly swollen.

But it was not the identity of the piece that affected me.

It was the unrestrained and unblushing mastery with which the madame was playing.

Despite her request, I opened my eyes. My gaze fell along the open wings of her.

She carried the music forward with steady seriousness. With restrained rhythm. Until she unleashed herself entirely in a frothy, well-timed crescendo.

I watched in disbelief as she tackled the rapid runs, one hurtling into the air after the other.

The music swelled. Encapsulating us.

There is no embrace, no world, or womb as subsuming as that defined by music's membrane.

Together, we floated.

Then, with the gentlest touch, she lulled the melody back to earth. Coaxing it down, a little at a time, to the silence from which it had risen.

We held still as the final note diminished.

She waited.

Then turned.

Her eyes were glowing. Pulsing between green and gold.

I stared. Speechless. To attempt an apology seemed pathetic—I had offered her elementary scales and she had given me Chopin.

But I must explain myself. I must!

"Madame," I croaked. "I had no idea ... Your husband led me to believe—"

"Never speak of him in this room," she hissed, her eyes cutting to the door. She swept her hands nervously along her skirts. After a few moments, her features relaxed.

"Whatever you thought, you were obviously misinformed," she said.

I wondered at this. Said nothing.

Waited. Unsure what to do.

She looked at me again. Her eyes wandering across my face. "Your bruises have healed."

"Yes."

She cocked an eyebrow. "And how is she?"

"She?"

"The woman whose honor you were defending."

I looked off. "I am told she is quite well."

"Ah. Good."

Did not a coy smile play at her lips?

She tipped her head toward the piano. "Upon review of our first lesson, I remembered you saying you like to begin by knowing something of your students. I then realized that I had declined to provide this insight. Putting you at a disadvantage."

I kept still.

"I therefore decided to begin our efforts anew, this time offering you a small performance. To reveal something of myself."

She dropped a silence between us. Inviting me to speak.

"It was exquisite," I said. I was not lying.

I drew a finger along my mustache. Hoping the sweat breaking along my lip would not loosen its hold.

She reclined slightly, folding her hands in her lap.

"The emotional tenor that shapes your playing seems to arise from instinct. A difficult thing to bestow."

Her eyebrows creased. "And you approve of such emotion?"

"Very much so!" I blurted. "For what other reason do we come to the piano than to communicate? To express ourselves in ways words can never afford?"

In my earlier years I, myself, had been accused of possessing an over-emotional style of play. But never by those who truly understood the power and purpose of music. In this, she and I seemed comrades.

"That is an unusual opinion," she said. "For a man."

I bit down on my tongue. Said nothing.

She peered outside as if held in a dream. "Ever since I was a child, I have felt drawn to music," she said. Then added quietly, "But for various reasons never had the opportunity to undertake proper study."

I listened intently, straining to hear what lay behind her words.

Her tone made me feel as though we were discussing something other than music. Something illicit. And dangerous.

She whisked her fingers along the keyboard's slotted ivory. "For this reason, I am limited in my technical abilities," she said, her eyes dropping as though ashamed.

For the first time I noted a chink in her armor. A catch in her confident breath.

What had caused this sudden humbling?

She went on. "From you I hope to gain the mastery that will enable me to express what I feel inside the music. Entirely." She glanced up. "Do you understand?"

I nodded. "Of course, madame."

Did I?

I took hold of the instructor's persona and said, "From what you have shared, it seems we do already agree on one thing—that music is possessed of a duality. A double nature. That it begins first and foremost as the notes, structure, and composer commands. But that it also thrives as a living thing, one that arises spontaneously from within us, from the very soil of our hearts and souls. I myself have always thought of music as a chimera—the mythical creature—born of two distinct species, technique and spirit. Living neither as one nor the other. But embracing half of each. Certain to perish without both."

"Yes," she whispered. Her eyes glistening.

Or had I imagined this?

It was then that I had the strangest sensation of being watched. I looked quickly to the door but found it closed.

If something were awry, the madame did not seem to notice.

After a moment, her eyebrows furrowed. "Tell me, monsieur, can you provide me with what I desire?"

I flinched.

If only ...

"I believe so. Yes."

"And you have no hesitation at my request?"

I shook my head. "None, madame. Only the regret that it has taken me this long to discover the true scope of your ability."

She expanded into a smile, setting the diamonds beneath her ears in motion. Dazzling metronomes.

Encouraged by the positive turn of events, and not wanting to risk further complications, I extended my arm toward the keyboard.

"Let us begin."

She whirled at my command. Took a position before the keys.

I observed her posture. Let my eyes drift along her curvature (God help me how I wanted to linger). I noted that she held her carriage too near the instrument. To create a spaciousness of tone, she would need to allow greater distance.

That was easily corrected, of course.

But I dared not touch her.

Instead, I began barking out drills.

"Scale of F sharp. Left hand."

She ran the octave. It was crisp. Consistent.

"Now the right!"

I ratcheted up the difficulty of my requests a bit at a time—from various hand positions to double notes in major and minor chords to mirrored arpeggios, single notes first, then advancing to double and triple chords.

As she assailed the keyboard, I shouted above the din, instructing her where to correct her motion, where to alter finger position, articulation, wrist movement.

Each time she sought to rest, I urged her on.

"Push through your errors!" I commanded. "Concentrate!"

She drilled ahead, the notes pummeling the walls like cannon fire.

"Again!" I shouted.

Her hands blurred.

"Do not roll the knuckles! Keep them afloat!"

She flubbed two chords in the D major scale.

"To A minor! Staccato!" I called out, pushing her onward.

She hammered out the new scale, her head bowed with effort.

Standing above, I felt the warmth rising from her. Distilling her scent. Intensifying it.

Unable to see her eyes, I looked down along the back of her neck. For a moment I became lost in the delicate border where creamy skin met auburn hair. I traced its path from the nub of her spine to where it slipped behind her ear.

There I had to stop.

I could scarcely breathe for the heat rising through my britches.

Then I noticed the silence.

I looked down and saw Ava heaving beneath me.

She had finished the last round and I neglected to supply another.

She drew the back of a hand across her brow. Spun to look up at me. A flush dressing her cheeks with fire.

"I'd like to try the F minor triads again. Legato," she breathed.

Overwhelmed, I glanced at my watch. "Our time is up," I told her.

She frowned. "But we have barely begun!"

In that moment, I sensed how vast her hunger.

"Mastery cannot be conferred in a day," I advised, clinging to my instructor façade.

The truth was, our encounter had exhausted me. Having thrown myself into the enterprise, I felt disoriented. Dizzied. As if having climbed too close to the sun.

I stepped to my satchel. Lifted out pencil and paper.

"I shall keep a record of our progress," I said. "And herein list your assignments."

She watched me write. Swept fingers through her hair.

"You are left-handed," she said.

I kept my eyes on the page.

Her tone sounded innocent.

But my heated imagination made it not so.

The walls pressed close.

I set the sheets on the music rack. "It might be best if you kept a diary in which to house these notes."

She tilted her head in agreement.

"Practice what I have assigned with care. Next time we will review what you have done and expand upon it."

That seemed a sensible thing to say.

Ava remained seated on the bench. Ran her eyes over the sheets. A dreaminess softening her features.

I packed my satchel. Snapped its buckles. Then stood awkwardly before her, hoping she would see me ready for departure and ring the butler.

She did not.

Instead I caught her looking intently about my waist.

"You have unusually beautiful hands," she said, almost to herself.

Heat flared under my collar.

Why would she say that?

I looked toward the door.

And where was that infernal butler?

Ava's brow furrowed, as if she would say more.

"Madame, I'm afraid I will need assistance in finding my way out."

Her hand floated to her breast. She laughed lightly. "I suppose you will."

So saying, she drifted across the room and rang the bell. As before, Audric entered in an instant.

"Our lesson is finished. Please see Monsieur Worth safely to the door."

Safely?

I dropped a respectful bow. "Well played today, madame," I said. When I stood back up, she was gone.

The market bustled with its usual activity. The scene a chaos of vegetables, livestock, street urchins, magic makers, farmers, and moneylenders.

Wielding my sack, I stepped into a stall.

"What is it today?" I asked the vendor.

"Golden beets, sir!" he chimed. "Spheres of bullion, I swear to you."

I smiled at his hyperbole. "I'll take two bunches."

"And for dessert? Why not a bag of plump cherries?"

"Why not indeed? Make it three." I could not contain myself.

On my way out I passed the coffee vendor. The mother leered at me, brandishing her scoop. Her daughters nowhere to be seen.

Walking home, I felt light-headed, disoriented.

I had slept little. Eaten even less. Like an exotic plant, I'd been living on air and longing.

With my employer yet to return, I hovered above our broken piano, staring down at the waiting keys. Marveling at their equal slashes of black and white. Realizing this might be my only time alone with them.

My eyes drifted up to where Cristofer's manuscript awaited fresh assessment. I began to read the notes, humming them aloud as I scanned the staffs. After only a few bars, I stopped.

Held in a strange tension, I realized I could either review his work in the way I had become accustomed.

Or.

I could devote these rare hours to my own invention.

Uncertain as to when Cristofer might return, I curled to the bench.

Waited.

Attuned myself to the silence.

Then gifted to it a tone.

As my fingers wended along silent keys, my mind conjured the music. The physicality of my connection with the piano serving as catalyst.

Dropping slowly, the silver-sided thirds melted along the facets of things. Wetting edges like dew.

Soon the theme of the honeyeater entered. Lifted to the top of the song. But with contemplative steps. Searching for a better view. Needing to believe, perhaps, that one could be found.

As the piece progressed, the thirds heavied. Shuddered with heft. Setting down mightier steps.

Still. Their final destination alluded them.

The chords rose and fell, a tide seeking arrival. The shoreline aching in anticipation of some landing. Some end to the cyclic anguish.

From above, I watched my hands perform of their own accord. Taking their cue from some unknown part of me—for who knows the true origin of song? Is it mind, heart, soul? None of these? All of them?

As I moved forward, I strained to memorize.

During a particularly stirring passage, the sight of Cristofer's quill hooked itself into my periphery.

The music rushed onward, seemingly unaware of my straying attention.

Yet the quill's allure would not abate.

I would describe its hold as a discomforting prickle. An irritating itch beneath the skin that no amount of scratching could alleviate.

I re-focused. Hoping to rid myself of the sensation.

But the itch spread.

I grew angry.

Why? Why write it down?

The piece rang out with tremolos and mighty chordal shifts.

Into the fray stepped Tess.

"How long have you been living like this?" she demanded.

I braced. Bit down.

The urge had been dead to me for so long.

Why was it resurrecting? Why making itself bold with insistence?

Again, Tess.

"Listen to me, Henri! What reason is needed to pursue one's desire?"

My fists came down. Crashing against silent keys.

I could not answer the question.

Nor ignore the call.

Almost as if someone other than myself, I reached up and drew down the quill. Opened a jar of ink. Fanned parchment along the rack.

Within seconds I had meticulously lined out the staves. Scripted key and time signatures.

What force overtook me to perform these actions, I cannot say. But it had a reflexive quality more akin to instinct than intention.

Having set my marks, I reviewed the first page.

Something felt incomplete.

My eyes drifted to the upper-right-hand corner. Lingered with discomfort.

In my previous life, I would have thought nothing of inscribing my name in this space. Such an act, at the very outset of a composition, seemed nothing more than an administrative duty. A formality.

And yet.

Did the act not also signal an assertion?

A conscious undertaking?

A certain ... resolve?

I paused before the weightiness. Assessing its significance. Its hazard.

Stepping again into the silence, I closed my eyes.

Drew a breath.

Gripped the quill.

And, with trembling hand, wrote: *H. Worth.*

The hours shed like minutes.

When I looked up, the sun's light leaned along a dramatic slant.

I had worked well into the late afternoon.

My belly grumbled.

Spent and desperate for movement, I gathered the sheaf of papers into a stack. All of the music that had been floating in my head had been transferred, at long last, to manuscript.

Afraid to leave any trace of my labors vulnerable to discovery, I strode to the wall of drawers alongside the bookshelves. After a short perusal, I located an unused drawer toward the bottom, far from prying eyes.

Into it I placed my fledgling effort.

CHAPTER 10

I stood outside the Thornes' front door wiping mud from my boots. Cristofer had sent word for me to come.

I knocked but felt certain no one would hear me. Someone had just sat to the piano. A spirited romance of Richard's dappling the rafters.

I let myself in and removed my cape. Stepped quietly into the room and found Clara at the keyboard.

I held still, flushed with awe.

Her fingers leapt along wild progressions, swift as gazelles. Her focus flashed from one hand to the other, like a shepherd steering her flock.

The piano rumbled with gusts of harmonic finesse.

I stopped breathing. Wanting only her sound to enter my body.

For Clara's was the music of the elusive chimera—fully aroused.

During a pause, I spotted two of her younger children beneath the instrument. Hunkered alongside the pedals. One cradled a picture book. The other pinched a dead beetle. Neither seemed bothered by the roar overhead. Or their mother's foot pumping ardently beside them.

As the romance rose in pitch and tempo, I became distracted by an underlying sentiment I had not noticed at first. In Clara's phrasing, I now sensed a strain. A syntax of worry.

Something, I felt certain, had happened to Richard.

Just then, I spotted Cristofer standing in the opposite doorway. His cheeks ruddy. I glanced toward the fireplace, thinking he had been standing near it. But the hearth sat cold.

Clara was the open flame.

Given the ebullience of her sound, the graceful force of her body, I could not condemn his response.

Having arrived at the end of the piece, she wound up her shoulders and prepared to attack again from the beginning.

Cristofer stopped her with a single word.

"Henri," he said, having caught sight of me. Clara spun atop the bench. The children also looked up. "Thank you for coming."

"Of course," I said efficiently, not wanting to incite the children's concern.

Cristofer looked to Clara. "Shall we go into the study?"

"Yes," she said. But in the vacancy of her stare I saw that she remained embedded in the music. Watching her rise, I could almost hear the membrane tear.

Possibly sensing this, Cristofer lifted a hand. "Let me speak with her, Clara. You can continue to rehearse."

Clara gave a ghostly nod and sunk back to the keyboard. Before we had left the room, she launched again into the romance. As if my arrival had never occurred.

Cristof closed the study door behind us.

I sat in a chair by the window. He leaned on the edge of Richard's desk. Folded his arms beneath a furrowed brow. It was then I noticed the bags weighting his eyes.

"Richard has requested that he be taken to Endenich," he said.

I drew back in shock. "The *asylum?*"

Cristofer nodded. "He told Clara he's no longer in control of his person. That he doesn't wish to harm anyone." He watched the songbirds flitting in their cage. "I wish only that I could disagree."

"But what are you saying? " I blurted. "This is Richard Thorne we're talking about!"

He sagged. "Perhaps he has inherited a vile disease. Or is the victim of an attempted poisoning." He became quiet. "Or perhaps his flesh can no longer withstand the fire of his genius."

Cristofer did not look up. I knew the latter was a hard possibility for him to consider. As it was a condition that could afflict any number of those he loved. Himself included.

I listened to Richard's romance bubbling from the piano. Its rising insistence.

I found it impossible to believe that such a noble creative spirit could be silenced. That fate would mute the magnificence yet inside him.

"Perhaps, after some time, he will recover and resume his life entirely," I suggested.

Cristofer shrugged.

"At Richard's insistence, I've made the necessary arrangements," he said. "The facility has requested that he be accompanied there by someone less intimate than Clara or myself. To prevent upset upon admission."

"And you wish for me to do this?"

"Yes."

"When?"

"Today."

Clara reached the end of the piece, began again.

"For what is she rehearsing?" I asked.

"She has arranged a series of concerts. Of Richard's music. She departs for Bonn in a week's time."

"Concerts? *Now?*"

"She's concerned about the family's finances. Especially since they must now live without Richard's income." He ran a hand through his hair. "I, of course, am of no use to her in this regard."

Having learned to scrape by on his lean earnings, I knew this to be true.

But was Clara leaving because of monetary concerns? Or because she feared what might happen were she left alone with Cristofer?

"And the children?"

"They will stay with cousins."

I thought of the young lives huddled underneath the piano's rib cage. And the nascent one tucked inside Clara.

I noted the stack of manuscripts on Richard's desk. The spectacles lying atop his books.

"Where is he?" I asked.

"In the garden."

"Shall he come once more to Clara?"

His hand drifted across the windowsill. "The doctors have recommended against it."

I pushed slowly to my feet. "I will see him safely delivered."

Cristofer choked back tears.

I departed before he could stop me.

We sat across from one another in the swaying carriage. Richard, upright and vacant. Me, slouched and despondent.

Neither of us spoke.

An hour into our journey, Richard turned toward the window. The landscape flickered at the pace and rhythm of the horses' hooves. He smiled. As if delighted.

But when I looked over moments later, I found his eyes welling with tears.

Feeling the weight of the moment, I laid a hand upon his knee.

"Richard ..." I tried.

What could I say?

I waited.

"Are you certain this is what you want?"

He sniffled and drew out his handkerchief. Then fell into the bowl of his palms and sobbed.

I kept my hand pressed to him.

After what seemed a long time, he sat back and wiped his eyes. I noticed that his focus seemed to have sharpened. A lucidity having sliced through the fog.

He cleared his throat. Breathed softly. "She always feared this day would come," he said, dabbing at his cheeks.

He did not say her name. But I knew of whom he spoke.

After a moment, he went on.

"Genius, by its very nature, belongs to the public," he said. "No one individual can possess it, nor claim ownership. Such titles are not permitted. Every lien denied."

His eyes reddened. "She knew this truth. I tried to deny it." He leaned forward abruptly. "How on earth did I think I could ...?"

He left the question unfinished.

I reached for the strap dangling from the roof, seeking balance.

After some time, I sensed another altering of his mood. In an instant, his brow clamped as rage descended upon him. He turned to stare me dead in the eyes.

"Do not be fooled, Henri!" he boomed. "The artistic urge is a monster. A demon! An ungodly alien that takes up residence within the unlucky few. Its only want is to torment and exhaust us as it propagates beauty through our efforts. It is nothing but a gilded parasite. An infernal worm. A quick-rooting hell!"

I drew back, frightened by his bellowing. By the rolling madness in his eye.

Fortunately, the outburst wrung from him what little strength he had left and he soon slumped back against the seat.

I held still, not wishing to aggravate him.

The driver slid open the small window above our heads. "One

minute to Endenich!" he shouted.

The carriage swayed steeply to the right. Richard's head knocked against the door. He righted himself. Cleared his throat. But I could see a tremble rising to his lips.

The gallop of the horses pounded like an erratic heartbeat, charging us toward our destination. Richard looked once more outside. The lush landscape had diminished to sparse desolation.

He pursed his lips, lost in thought. "The urge to create," he said in a much quieted voice, "is both a privilege and a curse. After all these years, I can find no other way to view it. Try to tame the urge, and you suffer. Deny it, you shall suffer worse. Attempt to own it and you risk your sanity. Perhaps even your life. And yet even still, the price of her occupation seems a bargain to those held in her sway. To those who hear the glory of angels, who leave this world to engage the other."

The carriage jerked to a stop.

Richard's head drooped. He rubbed his hands as if unsure to whom they belonged. "The demand of genius is that she be allowed to flourish in one's life without bonds. The surrender to her needs must be utter and complete. There can be no other before her." He glanced up, held my eyes with his. "I was never able to do this, Henri. My heart was too big for the task. It made me love too deeply. I could never forsake those I cared for. And this will be the ruin of me."

"Richard," I said, taking hold of his hands. "It is the greatness of your heart that will see you through. That will restore you fully. You must believe this."

He offered a weak smile. But the fight, I could see, had gone out of him.

He reached over and took my sleeve, drew me close. Whispered with insistence, "See to yourself, Henri. See to *yourself*."

With that, the carriage door opened. Two white-suited attendants approached. Richard's eyes lit up as though meeting long lost friends.

"Sweet angels! Come for me at last, have you?" he said.

I watched as the attendants led him down a walkway lined with linden trees.

Arm in arm, the three shuffled through the front door and disappeared.

CHAPTER 11

With Richard and Clara gone, Cristofer spent more and more time at the Thornes' home, composing at their piano. Working there, he told me, allowed him to upkeep their residence and grant the children occasional visits.

I suspected, however, that the moments spent in their domicile helped ease the ache caused by the dual absence of his hero, and his love.

Whatever the case, he continued to compose the concerto's third movement, its presto, at a furious pace. Soon he got into the habit of rushing home at all hours, imploring me to evaluate his work.

Hunched beneath candles and lamps, focused by the night's hush, we sifted through sheets and sheets of notes. Our piano still silenced, we took turns vocalizing particular sections, mimicking the horns, strings and woodwinds. Testing and adapting the counterpoint, the tonal depth, the color.

I found the work inspired. Unlike anything he had yet produced. His chords had thickened, ripened to a majesty that, to my ear, diluted even Beethoven's symphonic grandeur. Yet it wasn't just the innovative musicality—the chord progressions and key shifts and rhythmic sorcery—that seized at me, that tore my heart. But something else. Some other elusive quality I could not yet identify.

We had just sounded out a major portion of the first theme's development when I jumped to my feet. "Cristof, I am overcome!" I said. "The orchestration is sublime. The coloration heroic. The shift in keys provocative. And the piano, my God, the courage and bravado are irrepressible."

The composer grinned, gave a modest toss of his head. He did not suffer compliments well. But knowing I had no inclination whatsoever toward flattery, accepted mine.

The moment did not last.

A scowl soon muddied his smile. He set his quill alongside the inkwell. "This success in the third movement, I fear, will only cast an unflattering light on the first. Until now I thought the allegro was going rather well," he said with a laugh. "Perhaps, though, with the first movement being acceptable, and the third extraordinary, no one will notice the absence of a second!"

I joined in the laughter. It was late. We were tired.

But I knew Cristofer too well to think the joke a weightless one. Behind his offhand humor hid real fear. A terror that he could not rise to the challenge laid before him. That he could not tackle the massive intellectual undertaking that was a full-blown orchestral piece. And that through this failure the world would discover he was not—as Richard had so publicly predicted and Jacque publicized—Beethoven's heir.

At this thought, the lamp beside us faltered.

I took this as a sign it was time to retire.

But Cristofer only grumbled and relit the flame. He would not surrender.

Despite his somewhat fair appearance, Cristofer was no dandy. His willingness to provoke and engage difficulty was one of the things about him I most admired.

Humming, he took up the quill.

Eager for sleep, I stood and bent over him. Laying a kiss on each of his cheeks, I whispered, "Goodnight, fair Ludwig."

He grunted in response. Lost already to the world.

I rose somewhat later than intended and found myself rushing to prepare for the madame's lesson. Despite the lateness of the hour, I took time to select a new suit and sprinkle scented oil along my throat.

I strode to the cottage and fed Signore his breakfast, knowing that Cristofer would sleep well into the afternoon. That done, I gathered the sheets of drills I'd stacked near the fireplace and packed them inside my satchel.

My boots clattered as I crossed the bridge. Turning, I hurried up the hill.

For some reason, I felt curiously optimistic. Perhaps it was the handsome cut of my new suit or the fresh haircut that was lifting my mood. Perhaps it was Cristofer's rousing crescendos billowing in my ears. Whatever the case, when the butler opened the door, I did not shrink. But inclined toward the frontier.

As if, in plunging ahead, all things might be made possible.

Alone in the madame's private refuge, I approached the piano and lined the rack with sheets of complex drills. The material, I knew, would present her with considerable challenge.

Pleased with my preparations, I wandered to the window. On the way I kept my eyes averted from the curtains of silk. Contemplating what lay behind would only unsettle me. I focused instead on the garden, hoping to draw serenity from the lush plantings.

Shortly, I heard footsteps. Recognized the rhythm of her gait.

Drawing a breath, I spun to greet her, wanting the sight of my new costume to make a favorable impression.

It did not.

Ava stormed into the room. Her cheeks reddened with agitation.

I bowed. "Madame."

Her eyes swept up. Lingered at my appearance. Flit away.

"Good morning," she huffed.

She moved to the piano. Eyed the staffs dripping with trills and arpeggios. "What is this?"

"Material for your lesson," I said.

She shook her head. "No."

Wringing her hands, she backed away from the instrument.

"No drills. Not today. Remove them."

Startled, I rushed to the rack and fulfilled her request.

She turned to the window. Her eyes open but unseeing.

I held still. Baffled.

"Today we must have music," she said. "Only music."

"Why not begin with Chopin?"

"No. Not another's music," she said firmly. "*Yours.*"

"But madame, I do not compose," I protested.

Her eyes cut to mine. "Then play something by Cristofer Vaughn. You seem intimate with his repertoire."

A wreath of prickles wrung about my neck.

I could not play for her!

She grew frustrated at my delay.

"What is it? Why do you not begin? Is there something you hide?"

"I beg your pardon, madame. I'm merely considering which piece might most please."

She laughed. "If your selection does not gratify, I will request another."

I dizzied at her venom.

Steadying myself against the back of a chair, I sensed the fulcrum of the moment. Depending on how I performed in that instant, the balance would either remain or be forever upset.

I may never know from where I drew the strength, but somehow I marshaled my best. And determined to grasp at the possibility before me.

Damn the consequences.

I sunk to the keyboard searching desperately for the ideal piece. One that would speak of my heart. One that would make a gift of myself.

Her waiting gaze burned the edges of my skin.

Unable to delay further, I rolled up my cuffs.

Inhaled.

Made my choice.

The opening melody revealed itself in a cascade of slow, single notes downward. Followed by an equally languid but hopeful climb upward.

The piece was indeed Vaughn's. The second movement from his Piano Sonata no. 3, the andante espressivo. When Cristofer had first performed the sonata, some audiences had responded unfavorably. Not to the music, which was widely praised, but the work's unusual form. Unlike the traditional sonata comprising four movements, his contained five.

The extra movement, placed second, was mine.

I swept deeper into the piece, aware that its simple beginnings belied a gathering tempest.

The music had arisen, as usual, from loss.

She was a woman of noble birth. Who had courted me. Whose honeyed hair and yielding skin and translucent eyes had left me breathless. She was a comrade in the arts. A writer. All manner of poems, novellas, and plays flowed from her pen to wide acclaim. Driven from the other side, she wrote night and day. Keeping a warm kettle and a full inkwell always at her elbow.

Soon after we met, I became her favorite subject. Fodder for comedy and tragedy alike.

She held me in the great palm of her imagination. Elevated me, body and soul.

She was married. To a mapmaker. And sometimes bounty hunter.

My mistress, I liked to call her. And though she did not enjoy the term, she allowed me to use it. Just as she allowed me to do all things.

And do them I did.

Until the candles smoked and the sheets clung to our skin with scented dampness.

Until her husband's ship returned.

But the rigor of our love outlasted me.

Immersed in work for Cristofer while simultaneously immersed in my mistress, I soon found my music fatigued. My blood anemic.

Frustrated by the exhaustion, I began to grumble at the perpetual need for secrecy in our rendezvous. At the nuisance of dashing into hidden lairs at bizarre hours.

Near collapse, I whisked her away to the seaside. There we spent the night opening and closing our shells, letting the tides pull between us. The next morning, I fell to my knees.

"Leave him," I begged.

She cast watery eyes along the ocean's horizon. Drew her tongue across a salty lip.

Her silence sealed her refusal.

She was, after all, an artist. She could not write if she were poor and untethered. If she were living in a housekeeper's cottage.

I understood her reasons, but still I pleaded.

To no avail.

The rejection caused spoil to set in at the edges of my ardor. Shortly after our return, the words "time" and "freedom" began to flow from my lips. (Even as I wished for no such things.)

Then one day she called for me and I did not appear. A declaration of autonomy.

When we met next, fear blossomed across her cheeks.

She demanded to know if I loved her.

I swore that I did. (And knew it was true.)

But my feet were restless.

She begged me not to leave.

But how could I stay?

The details of our end are too painful to recall. The turmoil too profound. Suffice it to say that for weeks I feared my head might become her husband's next bounty.

It did not. And this pained me further.

Together we had climbed to soaring heights of joy, and still I leapt, an act that dashed me to ruin upon the ground.

I might not have lived had it not been for the solace I found conceiving the movement that found its way into Cristofer's sonata.

I had not intended it for him, or for anyone, of course, but when he heard me playing it, he insisted that it be released into the world through his hands.

Heartsick and out of my head, I agreed.

For three nights I played the piece over and over for him until he had transcribed every note. The composition thus becoming his.

Upon retrospect, I wish I had not let the piece slip from my grasp to be poured into other ears. I would sooner stand naked before a crowd. Though even then I would not feel as utterly stripped as I do when the andante espressivo plays aloud.

Such were the thoughts roiling through my mind as the music unfolded beneath me. The piano's somber voice saturating the room.

After a few moments, I paused. Then, with some hesitation, I introduced the second theme. Its delicate melody swept forward on bright sails. At every turn there seemed the promise of eruption, of release. But on every occasion the piece quieted and drew back into itself.

The effect was tortuous.

In the midst of this tension, I felt someone step close. Sensed their heat along my side.

I struggled against the distraction of her perfume. The resonance of her skin.

Her proximity pulled me back into the present.

I bent again to my efforts.

The melody's tidal swoon continued. The waves receded, reappeared.

Each note a tentative step forward. A handkerchief tossed in farewell, in hope of safe return.

I churned on.

In the distance, I could see the moment of pause waiting. This was a singular silence I had inserted just before the final passage.

During the piece's conception, the pause had, in actuality, lingered for weeks. It was at that time that Cristofer, alarmed by my fading health, had hired a nursemaid to care for me. Each day the elder woman burned herbs and spooned bitter soup into my mouth. When I roused, she brushed rough sponges along my extremities. Forcing weak blood to flow.

One night, after several weeks of ministrations, I was awakened by an owl calling beneath a full moon. Unable to sleep, I laid still with open eyes and found the strength to push beyond the pause. But in order that I never forget the trial of that silence, I memorialized it within the music. A phenomenon that Cristofer had faithfully recorded, and magnificently reproduced in each performance.

My hands lifted from the keyboard, arching upward.

Ava drew in her breath.

I raised my foot from the pedal, deepening the hush, the moment's finality.

Would she think the piece over?

To be truthful, it was a rather long silence.

Unmoving, I stared down at the bars of black and white. Suspended between the intense pain of past and present, between shattering loss and the unattainable.

Terror threw her arms around me.

I faltered. Doubted if I could go on.

It seemed only disaster lay ahead.

My hands trembled.

The silence lingered.

I fought the urge to run.

Then I was struck with sudden insight, as though my life was passing before me. And I beheld in all clarity the folly of my pursuit: I had come in search of something that did not exist. Lured by a Beauty that, as before, would engulf me and regurgitate empty bones.

And worse, in performing the second movement, I had laid my soul bare before a virtual stranger. Before someone who, should she discover my identity, could bring catastrophe not only to myself but to those I loved.

Had I gone completely mad?

Richard's curdling laughter echoed inside my head.

Terrified, I made to stand.

I would excuse myself. Claim sudden illness. And never return.

Then.

She touched me.

Or rather, a token of her dropped upon my skin.

A tear. Fallen from her lashes to slip inside my collar.

I held still as the droplet crept down, curling its way over my collarbone. Descending toward my heart.

In its wake I felt a surge such as I have never known. As if her empathy had watered a dormant seed.

Then and there I decided that the silence had measured long enough.

I inhaled. Pressed fingers into ivory. And began to carve my way out.

A string of repeating bass notes stepped softly into the room. Atop these, the melody presented itself, a gentle, rising bridge of doublets.

Then, without warning, a violent propulsion. My hands leaping together and apart. Underneath, the torrent of our entire affair rang out, clapping against the walls, the windowsills. Soon, the melodic edges grew sharp enough to cut, to draw blood.

Then, as if dropped from a cliff, the music fell away.

I drew back, heaving. Took a moment to gather my strength, before ushering the piece to its tender end. I held the last note in suspension, its tone glowing deep inside the piano's belly. Until it followed its companions into silence.

I withdrew my hands. My cheeks shiny with tears.

Without a word, she lowered herself beside me.

I kept still. Unable to retreat.

She leaned closer. Closed her eyes as if against a painful thought.

"I am not a free woman," she whispered.

I choked back a sob.

She did not speak again. The only sound, our breath.

Having made her admission, Ava lifted a hand and drew her fingertips beneath my chin.

In the silence, she came to me.

Fusing the softest of joints between us.

CHAPTER 12

*C*ristofer sat at breakfast, crestfallen. A letter from Clara in his hands.

He had written to her while she was on tour, updating her on the children's conditions and activities (all were healthy and well occupied).

Further into his missive, however, he had felt compelled to reveal something of his heart. How it ached in her absence. How he longed for her physical presence, especially alongside him at the piano. How life seemed joyless without her.

Though Cristofer had written with sentimentality before, there existed a new and desperate edge in his language. An urgency. Especially when viewed in the light of recent events.

Prior to his sending of the letter, I had cautioned him against any effusiveness that might recast his relationship with Clara. Given the circumstances, I feared that such premature admissions would result in misunderstandings and conflict.

He had ignored my warning.

I set toast and coffee on the table. Sat alongside him.

"What did she write?" I asked.

He grunted. "It's all dashes and question marks," he complained. "Nothing but questions, questions, questions: How are the children? Have I seen Richard? Have the doctors made a report? How is the concerto coming? Other than that, not a word. Not a single remark addressed toward me nor my affections."

He tossed the letter aside.

I kept still. Unsure how to best assist. How to navigate the oncoming heartbreak.

But Cristofer surprised me, as he continually does.

Instead of sinking into depression, he scoffed and lifted the coffee to his lips.

"I suppose, now, there's no avoiding it."

I looked up, curious as to what he meant.

"With the first and third movements reasonably sketched, I must tackle the adagio."

He had fortified himself against the truth of things. This effort, I knew, would cost him.

"I am here to help," I said, a part of me wishing I had not. I had matters of my own that needed tending. Still, loyalty toward my liege owned the greater part of me.

Breakfast lingered between us.

"And how are things faring with the madame?" he asked.

I started as from a daydream. I had in fact been thinking of her.

Of how sweet her tears.

How tender her approach.

How lush her lips.

"Rather well," I told him. "She is not as poor a student as Jacque would have one believe."

Cristofer nodded. "I might have suspected that."

I refreshed his coffee. "What do you mean?"

He shrugged. "On the night of their soiree, one of his servants pulled me aside. He insisted that the madame was possessed of considerable talent. He said, though, that Jacque had forbidden her from musical pursuit. Going even so far as to lock away the instrument she'd had since childhood."

A weight sank inside me.

Cristofer tossed a hand, laughed. "The servant was young and profoundly intoxicated, so at the time I didn't take his tale too seriously. Still, I wonder if some part of it might be true." He looked over. "Has she said anything of the sort to you?"

I shook my head. "Not a word."

I thought back to when Ava had first approached the piano. Remembered feeling in her a certain sense of deprivation.

"Would you say, then, that she is?"

"Is what?"

"Possessed of some talent."

I made to answer, to gush over Ava's remarkable ability, a gift whose splendor could not even be overshadowed by her physical beauty.

Yet I hesitated.

Should I reveal what I knew?

Would doing so break a confidence? Or cause Ava difficulty?

"She is a competent amateur," I replied.

Cristofer mumbled something unintelligible. Looked uneasily at the pages of Clara's letter.

I marveled at how easily I had misled him.

And what of my great loyalty? The one to which I just sung praises?

The truth is, nothing tumbles allegiance more quickly than a lover's first kiss.

"Hmph," he grunted, wiping a napkin along his lips. "And what of your charade," he asked. "Is it holding up?"

"I believe so, yes."

"Good," he said with a shrug. "But still, do be careful, Henri. Jacque is no one to be trifled with. His ambitions are monstrous and his influence runs deep in those he employs."

He then flashed lionish eyes in my direction. "That said, I certainly hope you find more success in your escapade than I am finding in mine," he offered. Threw me a grin.

I returned his smile. Impressed again by his resilience. By his willingness to make light of that which I knew held his every fiber hostage.

"Patience, dear Cristofer. Everyone has been under enormous strain. And Clara's will have only multiplied being out of the country. Things will settle again and right themselves."

He looked toward the broken piano. Grew suddenly serious.

"Jacque has arranged for an orchestra to rehearse the concerto when it is complete," he said. "I am hoping to avail of this opportunity in a month or so, depending on how the adagio comes along. Hopefully the pressure of this deadline will leave my heart too winded for other pursuits."

I laid my hand on his forearm. Understood well his predicament. "Reach out to her through the music, Cristofer," I suggested quietly. "Leave the flowery verse to the poets."

He set his hand atop mine.

I winced at his tenderness. At his naiveté in dealing with matters of love. And at the fact that I had sullied our remarkable relationship with its first lie.

Is it possible that one's experience of time can contract and expand simultaneously?

If not, then how is it that the time spent with Ava rushed like the wind, whereas the days between our lessons lumbered like snails?

With Cristofer still spending most of his time at the Thornes', I was able to work on my composition freely at whatever hour I wished. Despite the luxury, however, I found it difficult to sit still. My focus elusive.

Often, after sketching but a phrase or two, my attention would drift and I would catch myself half an hour later staring at nothing. My ears deafened. My vision stained.

All I could see was aspects of Her. All I could contemplate—that she had heard the sentiments spoken beneath my music—and could trace my feelings, my thoughts, as easily as her own. Such a marvel contained within a lover was absolutely unknown to me.

For the first time I felt matched. Met by an equal.

The phenomenon held me spellbound.

I looked down again at the parchment. Hummed out the phrases I had scribbled. Grimaced.

What dross!

Drawing fresh ink to the quill, I slashed out the offensive efforts.

Where was my head?

I needn't ask. I knew exactly where.

Realizing I could not produce anything worthwhile in my current condition, I gathered my manuscript and re-stashed it inside its secret drawer.

That done, I turned for the door. I needed exertion to exhaust that part of myself, the whirring assemblage of lustful gears that would not cease.

So intent was I on dispersing my energies that I nearly collided with the postal boy tromping up our path.

Out of his pouch he produced a single letter. From Clara.

This one—strangely—addressed to me.

I took the envelope, dropped a coin in the boy's palm, and disappeared into the forest.

I had walked some five miles before I lifted Clara's letter from my coat pocket.

~~~~~~~~~~~~~~~~~~~~~~~~~~~~~~~

My dearest Henri,

I pray this letter finds you well.

For my part, I am withstanding the trials of touring as well as can be expected, though the distance is proving more difficult this time, as you no doubt understand.

I am certain, too, that you are surprised to have this letter from me. Please know I wish its contents to be of no burden. It is just that I can trust so few with the current situation. Because of this, I must make a request.

Would you go to see my Richard and inform me of his condition?

My worry is dreadful and, if left unabated, I fear it will soon interfere with my performance. You know better than most how deplorable that consequence!

In short, the doctors have made no report, yet continue to recommend against visits from myself or Cristofer.

Other than his, yours are the eyes and heart I trust most.

Oh, Henri, I despair at making this request yet thank you for granting me this one indulgence, this horrid imposition upon you and your time. I will not do so again.

Lastly, though I cannot instruct your decision, I would ask that you destroy this note and, most importantly, withhold its contents from Cristofer—I would not wish to create a misunderstanding during this time of supreme labor on his concerto.

With all gratitude and warmest affection,
Clara

P.S. Last night I performed Cristofer's Piano Sonata no. 3, a piece dear to my heart. Particularly the second movement—the andante espressivo—which, I must say, nearly overwhelmed me! It is true I am under some strain, but there is such a noble and authentic ache in that movement. It is enough to unseat one's soul.

P.P.S. Lastly (I promise!) remember to include some news of yourself in your reply, as it would help steady me against the public chatter ever at my ears.

I hardly knew what to make of the missive—the first ever from Clara.

My intuition told me that she was saying a great deal more beneath her words. Though of what in particular I could not be certain.

While I was happy to help—and given my esteem for her would gladly have done more—I was troubled by her request that I keep the matter from Cristofer.

Especially on the tail of my having so recently misled him!

I understood her reasons, of course. Still, I wondered at her dividing my employer and me in this way.

I read the letter several times. (Marveled at the uncanny coincidence of her mentioning the andante espressivo.) Then tore the pages into pieces, which I scattered beneath the shrubs.

CHAPTER 13

At last, the day of our lesson arrived.

Humming with anticipation, I dressed quickly and strolled to Cristofer's cottage. I'd heard him return home in the small hours and knew he would not rise until afternoon.

I poured coffee into a carafe to keep it warm and set out a tray of sandwiches.

That done, I turned to my journey.

Before I realized it I was crossing the plaza. Accompanied by a frothy mix of birdsong.

The serenity was cut short when a horse's hooves clattered behind me.

I reeled, expecting to see the stable boy upon Jacque's stallion. Instead, I found the estimable monsieur himself!

A fearless horseman, he urged the stallion in a galloping pace, the beast's path angling dangerously close to mine.

I leapt aside, stones kicking past my ears.

Jacque let out a whooping cry and skidded the stallion to a halt before the hitching post. No sooner had he done this than the stable boy appeared.

Jacque dismounted and tossed him the reins. To my horror, the back of his hand followed quickly behind, striking the boy square in the face.

"You've been letting him have his head again!" Jacque complained.

The boy shrunk before his master.

"The horse is to be fit for *my* tastes, not yours!"

"Yes, sir."

Jacque yanked off his spurs. Hurled them to the ground. "I will not be so kind as to remind you again," he growled.

The boy hinged at the waist, bowing with deference. Rising quickly, he ushered the horse toward the stable. As he trod off, the boy flashed an angry glare in my direction.

In that moment I felt certain he recognized me.

No sooner had I tasted this fearful thought than Jacque came up and clapped me on the back.

"Monsieur Worth!" he cried. "That stallion is a bully when left to his own devices. I do apologize for his misdeeds." He looked over the dirtied knees of my breeches. "I trust you have not sustained significant injury?"

"Not at all," I said, swallowing my heart.

"There's a good man!" he said. "In any case, I'm glad to have run into you. I'd like for us to have a little chat."

"But I ... the madame—"

"Not to worry!" he assured with a toss of his hand. "Ava is running late as usual. With any luck, you'll be able to conduct your lesson shortly."

He pressed his palm against my back. An unyielding plank.

By the time we arrived at his study, Audric had set down a tray of brandy and thrown open the curtains.

I glanced about, on guard.

The plastered walls were tall and laden with plaques, mirrors and filigreed commendations. Overshadowing these more peaceable items was a display of firearms that rose behind Jacque's desk, many of the weapons within reach.

"Sit, please," he said.

I resisted, feeling suddenly trapped.

Had the stable boy already informed him of my disguise?

"Please, I insist you make yourself comfortable," he urged. His look glanced off the tent at my crotch.

I sat. Remained alert.

Without looking up he said, "You've grown a mustache." He chuckled. "You artists, forever changing fashion!"

I smiled weakly. My eyes darting between my host and the bank of ready pistols.

"Brandy?"

I shook my head.

He looked disappointed. "Cigar?"

"No, thank you."

He squinted. "A purist, eh?" He wagged his head. "No indulgences before a lesson, is that it?" He yanked the crystal lid from the decanter. "I'm always leery of purists myself. Too much like altar boys. Clean on the outside, but oh what they will do in the dark!"

I froze at his comment. Realized he was already intoxicated.

He poured himself a generous glass. Circled the rim with the shiny stub of his lost finger.

I set my hands on my knees to cease their trembling.

"You are a brave man to be taking on my wife," he said. "As you've probably observed, she is strong-willed to a fault. Most unbecoming in a woman, I think."

I said nothing. Unsure what position I occupied.

He ambled toward his desk, his stocky build and thrusting chest reminiscent of a taller Napoleon.

"Of course, you have my permission to be as firm-handed as

you wish," he continued, "though I suspect that's not your way." He flashed a knowing look. Grinned.

My stomach grew queasy.

"Let us be frank, Henri," he said, turning his back to me. "The madame, despite her faults, is particularly alluring." He drew his fingertips along the handle of a crescent-shaped pistol hung on the wall. "For your part, you are young. And though poor, not unattractive."

I sat impossibly still, grasping at the thread of his logic.

He deflated as if shouldering a burden. "As I'm sure you understand, a man in my position has interests to protect. Fortunately, I sense in you a certain—and I mean no disrespect—but a certain *femininity*."

He turned to face me.

"Am I therefore safe in assuming that you will not find my wife to your liking?"

Comprehending the critical nature of the moment, I grabbed hold.

"If I am following you, sir, then I can only say that you are correct to assume I am not like other men. Not by half. And am therefore quite different in my attitudes and sensibilities." I returned his stare with one of equal weight. Were I to bend now, to falter, all would be lost.

He laughed, evidently pleased with my admission and the accuracy of his assessment.

"Good. Good!" he said. Made a show of lifting the weapon from the wall.

Turning back to his desk, he lifted a small bag of gunpowder from a drawer.

"And what of your friend, Monsieur Vaughn? Does he share your proclivities?"

I froze. Terrified that my answer might put Cristofer in jeopardy.

He smirked at my hesitation. "I assure you, monsieur, I will hold your answer with the strictest discretion." He loaded powder and shot into the pistol's iron muzzle. Rammed them down with a rod.

"Of such things I have no knowledge," I said, certain now that Jacque could not be trusted.

If the stallion were a bully, the master himself was even more so.

Jacque chuckled. "A loyal friend!" he cheered. "A fine quality in a man."

My eyes cut to the door.

Jacque dropped into a chair. Swung a leg over its pillowed arm. "There is one more matter," he said. "I must ask that you not discuss your undertaking here with anyone. In these turbulent times, the press is forever after men of rank. Seeking gossip of any kind with which to smear their reputation."

He eyed the flintlock.

"I therefore intend to keep my wife, and her private pursuits, safe from prying eyes." He cocked the hammer. Looked over. His weapon at the ready between us. "I assume I've made myself clear?"

I nodded slowly. Though I could not imagine how his wife's enviable talent on the piano might be used to smear his reputation.

"There's a good man," he said.

In that instant, a figure appeared in the doorway. Anticipating the butler, I stood on wobbly knees. But it was not the butler. It was Sarkov. His eyes darted about the room as if assessing its security.

"Come in, Sarkov," Jacque called. "Monsieur Worth and I have just now settled our business and, I believe, have a solid understanding between us."

As per our usual routine, Audric led me down to Ava's room. Thankfully, he did not notice the tremor afflicting my limbs.

After seeing me inside, he made a great show of disappearing but, I now realized, would not go far. Given Jacque's apparent insecurities, which I felt certain my ruse had only partially alleviated, he had no doubt instructed Audric to secretly observe our lessons from the hallway.

Thinking back, I realized Ava had known this all along.

When my eyes adjusted to the light, I found my student already at the piano.

She turned. Her beauty coiling about her.

I bowed. Tried to steady myself. "Madame. I apologize for my delay—"

"No need to explain," she said.

I was glad to hear this, as I did not wish to break her rule by speaking of him. Part of me, however, wanted to reveal what had occurred in the study.

She indicated the music propped on the piano rack. Swept fingers lightly down her throat. "I've been working on the materials you left for me."

I set down my satchel. "And how does it go? Are you making progress?"

Her eyes bore into mine. "I believe so, yes," she said, "though I hope I am not deceiving myself in this."

In the heat of her look, I felt her meaning.

So this was to be it, I thought.

Knowing that we were under scrutiny, we would communicate through innuendo. Through shielded whispers. And the vivid tongue of music.

"I doubt you are deceiving yourself, madame."

To this, she smiled.

Then, imagining Jacque's pistol at my back, I said, "But perhaps I should be the judge of your progress." I motioned toward the sheets of music. "Let us begin with arpeggios. Scale of F minor. That has proven a good key for you."

F minor was, in fact, the key of the piece I had last played for her.

I saw her eyes light and knew she had caught the reference. That she could read my interior with such ease set my heart aflame.

She whirled to the keyboard.

Her fingers spread and her wrists leapt. Without hesitation, she climbed her way up and down the chords.

"E minor!" I called out.

She shifted mid-flight.

I listened. Noted the edge in her playing, the urgent explosiveness. As if she were on fire and attempting to stamp out the flames beneath a furious tempo.

The pace continued to speed. The volume soared. It was a passionate performance, but she was not in control.

I flinched at the growing tension, my nerves raw after my encounter with her husband.

"Madame, enough!" I cried.

She looked up and I saw hurt in her eyes. I instantly regretted the harshness of my tone.

"Was it inadequate?" she asked.

I shook my head. "No, no, to the contrary," I said.

I looked over to see her face searching mine.

I sighed. "The level of emotion you bring to bear on the instrument is extraordinary ... I stand amazed at the intensity you can lend even a simple exercise."

She blushed. Traced the outline of my lips with her eyes.

Despite my anxiety, I leaned forward. My attention dropping to her hands. How I wanted to lift them. To press kisses between each finger.

From the hallway came the rasp of a throat being cleared.

I started. Drew back. My mouth gone dry.

I ran a hand through my hair and dragged a stool before the keyboard.

"The ability to convey such passion is truly a gift," I continued, raising my voice so that it would be audible on the other side of the door.

Her eyes stirred into mine. Undeterred.

I looked away. Realizing how dangerous the game had become.

"But music arises as much from discipline as it does catharsis," I cautioned. "As musicians, our emotions cannot be permitted to run unchecked. In playing, even in composing, we must always keep our heads, must always remain in command—however tentatively. Otherwise, the result of our efforts can spin into a pandemonium beyond our control."

I tilted my head toward the door. "Do you understand?"

"Of course," she purred.

She blinked slowly. Luxuriously.

She pressed forward. Her lips parting.

An invitation.

Held in the spell of her, I found myself lured, despite the hazard.

A click sounded behind us and I flinched, imagining it a flintlock.

Seeing my withdrawal, she fell back. Exasperated.

"I thought risks were part of the endeavor," she huffed, lifting a sheet of music to fan the heat from her breast. "To my knowledge I have not heard a great musician commended for a 'safe' performance."

"Of course, of course," I said, loosening the cravat at my neck. "But even risks taken in performance are nevertheless *calculated* ones."

What did she expect me to do? Hurl myself before the firing squad?

Her eyes sparked with dissatisfaction.

She stood and crossed to the window. Her chest heaving. When she turned back, I could see color rising to her cheeks.

"Tell me, monsieur, were you in *absolute control* when you composed the andante espressivo?"

My eyes went wide. "Madame, I ... I did not write that piece—"

"No, no, of course not," she said. Gave a wry smile. "It was Vaughn, of course. My mistake."

I stared in horror. Dizzied by the height of our innuendo. By the wrenching battle between fear and desire.

"Ava ..." I whispered.

She did not respond.

My middle iced with fear. Not at the terror of death.

But at the possibility of losing her.

I stared into the slender curve of her back.

What could I say?

Words and emotions tangled inside me. Not knowing what else to do, I rose from the stool.

Then sunk to the bench.

Rolled my cuffs.

And began.

The first notes fell from my fingers like raindrops. Earnest. Plaintive.

Heartbreaking.

Forgive me.

What I find beautiful about Chopin's berceuse, and the reason I chose the piece, is that it arises from the realm of purity. The left hand repeating a simple refrain of five notes. A dancing phrase, a slowly tumbled waltz.

Meanwhile, the unadorned melody begun in the right hand grows increasingly complicated with each pass. Its march toward complexity meek at first, then unrelenting.

Yet the simple refrain repeats as if unaffected by the turmoil around it. That lone kernel of innocence. Borne in our hearts. Unaffected by the mistakes of our pasts. The unintended entanglements of our longings.

Forgive me.

But I cannot stop wanting you.

She heard me.

Within moments, I felt her approach.

She came and stood behind, watching the music unfold from above, lightly pressing herself along my spine.

The air around us shimmered.

I sensed that she wanted to say something but could not. Dared not.

Why complicate our situation with words?

The music spoke plainly enough.

Toward the end, the piece shifted, shedding some of its effervescence to become solemn, meditative.

She lowered herself beside me.

I drew the piece to its conclusion on a cadence of two chords.

I turned. Our eyes met. Ticked back and forth. Searching. Seeking consent.

While the last note faded inside the piano, she pressed herself into my embrace.

Her head tipped back as I kissed her throat. Her breasts softening along my chest.

"Please," she whispered. "Take me from here."

Take her?

"Somewhere. Anywhere …"

I nodded, breathless. Intoxicated by the scent of her.

"Yes … I will," I promised.

But how?

Something tumbled outside the door.

We flew apart. Faces burning.

I reset my cravat. She smoothed her hair.

"Madame," I said, hoping to cover our tracks. "I think you will find it instructive to practice the material at a slower pace. That is not to say that I wish you to lessen the intensity, but rather to increase control."

She nodded dumbly. Biting down on enflamed lips.

"Shall we try?"

She retook her position at the piano.

I noted the tremble in her hands. "Start with C major," I said, offering a simple key.

Despite this, she flubbed several notes. I urged her on.

She bent to the keys, frowning.

I looked toward the door.

Eventually we came to the end of our time.

She looked up. "What would you like me to work on for our next lesson?"

I smiled. Gave the matter some thought. "I am hopeful we will be able to address movement."

She lifted an eyebrow.

I felt as though I should say something more. Something to acknowledge the passion, the eternity passing between us.

Before I could think of anything, she rang the bell.

In an instant, Audric stumbled into the room. Seeing us, he waited obediently by the door.

Had he suspected?

Ava stepped toward me.

"I found today's lesson most instructive," she said in a steady voice, her composure fully restored.

Then she did something unexpected.

She offered me her hand.

I looked up quickly. Searched her eyes.

Dare we do this?

She tilted her head. Waited patiently.

Not wanting to appear awkward, I swept my palm beneath hers.

"It was my pleasure."

I pressed her fingers to my lips. Tasted her warmth.

"Good day, monsieur."

With that, she departed.

Exhilarated, I took the dark stairs two at a time.

The train pulled into Endenich a few minutes after the hour. I lifted the carafe of coffee and sandwiches I'd brought and began the two-mile walk to my destination.

The linden trees lining the facility's entrance were as I had remembered. Though their canopies were fuller, their emerald leaves having richened with the approach of summer.

I entered the building and headed down the main passageway. The air smelled of camphor and porridge. The narrow hall opened onto a vestibule broadly windowed. A young man with curly hair stood before the glass staring directly into the sun. An older man, his face half-shaven, plucked repeatedly at his fingernails. A younger one sat in a deep chair, whimpering as he scratched infected wounds at his shins.

Horrified, I passed quickly. The patients' terrible state only heightened my fears as to the condition in which I would find Richard.

Before allowing me entrance, the orderly at the front desk insisted I open each sandwich in front of him. He needed to insure they were free of forbidden items.

My God, how could our man of brilliance be reduced to this?

I found Richard in the outer courtyard. Seated on a bench near a small flower bed. A bird, perhaps a titmouse, chirped out quick melodies in the pergola above him.

"Hello, friend," I said, lowering myself onto the bench.

He flinched. Startled by my presence.

"Hello," he said.

I set down two cups. "I've brought coffee and sandwiches."

"How nice."

I poured two steaming cups and divided the sandwiches between us.

He took the coffee in his hand but did not drink.

I tilted my head at the bird. "Lovely song."

He smiled. "Yes."

Then, as I watched, his eyes lost focus.

"My daughter once kept a bird," he said, as if to no one in particular.

I noted his use of the past tense.

"Really?"

His expression crumbled.

"Richard?"

His coffee spilled to the ground as he folded over his legs. He pressed a palm to his face and shuddered.

I was caught off guard and uncertain what to say. But, wanting him to know he was not alone, laid my hand along his back.

After what seemed an eternity, he gathered himself. Sat upright.

We remained silent. Side by side.

I handed him my kerchief.

He removed his glasses. Wiped the tears from his face. Laughed a little to himself. "One day it escaped from its cage. And met an unfortunate end."

It took me a moment to realize he was still talking about the bird.

"It was my fault. I was... I was not paying attention," he said. "She was devastated."

"Your daughter?"

"Yes. It was her first taste of real loss. For some of us it comes so young. While for others, it waits."

I felt a twinge in my heart. Knowing something of what he spoke.

"She stayed in her room for days. Weeping. Refusing to eat. When she emerged, she was angry. And threw a book at my head!" he said. Then, quieter, added, "Even now it is difficult to think of the rawness, the utter loss, she felt in her young body."

Saying this, he reset his spectacles. The right lens fractured with a web of cracks.

The lone bird above us was joined by another. Together they sang out.

He then leaned toward me as if in a conspiracy. Dropping his voice to a whisper he said, "That night. In a fever. The song came.

I couldn't sleep for the urgency of it. It was so hungry to *be*. My mind, its doorway. My fingers, its stairs." He put a hand to his forehead. "It was then that I finally understood. The gift. The price. The diabolic compensation. Her loss for my crea—" he broke off, his voice thickened with emotion. "I tried to fight it," he moaned. "For their sakes. For mine. I *tried*!"

I held the untouched sandwich in my hand. Feeling lost. Confused.

Then, as if someone had thrown a switch, Richard's countenance cleared.

I stared in amazement at the rapidity of the change.

With a strange tip of his head, he acted as if another person had come to join our conversation. He lifted an open hand to our invisible guest. "She can fan to a spread of fifteen notes," he said with admiration. "Most enviable."

I assumed he was speaking of Clara.

Just then the orderly arrived. My time was up.

When I stood, Richard's hand shot out and grasped my elbow.

Looking down at him, I found his expression suddenly lucid.

"You will be careful, won't you, Henri?" he said, his features wide with fear.

"Yes, of course I will," I assured him.

Holding the door for me, the orderly said, "So, you're Henri?"

"Yes."

"He often engages you in conversation," he said. "Imaginary, of course."

I frowned. "Of what does he speak?"

The orderly shrugged. "Nonsense, mostly. But sometimes he talks of music. And the Creator. And something he calls, 'The Most Exacting Sacrifice.'"

Back at the front desk, I signed the guest book then let myself out.

On my return to the station I realized I had come seeking some sign of improvement. Some hopeful detail I could pass along to Clara.

That was not to be.

Boarding the train, I wondered at his final words to me.

Of what should I be careful?

Of Cristofer and Clara's passions?

Of my own?

"*Please*," she had whispered. "*Take me from here.*"

As the train swayed steadily forward, I reflected upon my visit with Richard and soon found myself overcome with the strangest sensation. A feeling that it was not his mind that he had lost, but his heart.

My Dear Clara,

I saw your Richard today. I found him looking well, if not a bit thinner. Certainly nothing to cause alarm.

We enjoyed coffee and sandwiches in the garden, and he seemed generally content. I'm not sure whether he recognized me at first, though he did address me by name as I departed—a hopeful sign.

His mood definitely carries the mark of melancholy. I say this not to concern you but to paint an accurate picture—the duty with which I believe you have entrusted me.

One item that brought him some tears was recalling your daughter's loss of her pet bird. Apparently he held some responsibility in this? On the face it struck me as a trivial matter, but the look in eye suggested otherwise.

The doctors told me that "the maestro" (as they like to call him) spends a great deal of time alone. He has not yet inquired of his wife or family (it pains me to be the one to tell you this). The doctors insist that until he does so, it is best that he not receive visits from intimates. Doing so, they fear, would shatter his tenuous sense of self before he is able to wrestle truth from delusion. This effort, they say, would ensure a more enduring recovery.

I realize it must be difficult to receive this report secondhand. And hope that my observations serve to bring you greater peace of mind rather than less. If I can do anything more to assist, you have only to ask. Rest assured, it is not an imposition of any kind.

As for your request of news—there is truly little to report.

I continue my daily walks to the market to evaluate its treasures. Asparagus is finally in season! I will plan to feature this delicacy in your welcome dinner, as I know it is a favorite.

Meanwhile, Cristofer continues to work at a feverish pitch, and so I minister daily to his needs, in the hope that I can prevent his efforts from depleting him. From what I have heard, the work is one of massive beauty. Something you may look forward to.

I have also, as you likely know, been providing Madame Bertrand with piano instruction. This we do once a week at her residence. She has proven a ready and enthusiastic student, though I do not yet know the outcome of our endeavor. Nor her intentions for future study. Still, it has been edifying on a number of levels.

I hear the post boy outside and so must end here.

Please do not hesitate to make future requests of any kind.

I remain yours respectfully, and affectionately,
Henri

CHAPTER 14

I arrived at the castle early. My mind awash with anxiety at the plan I intended to unfold.

And its risk.

From where my courage (*recklessness?*) to make such an attempt had arisen, I could not be certain.

I only knew that despite the magnitude of potential penalty, I could not mobilize the strength to resist.

I had just passed through the gates when I heard men's laughter. On the far side of the plaza, I spotted Jacque encircled by a group of soldiers in full ceremonial attire. Plumage spouting from helmets. Tassels cascading down shoulders.

Wanting to avoid notice, I slipped behind a pillar. Within moments, a carriage clattered through the back gate, its coach jet black and shining.

With all haste, Jacque and the men boarded while three conscripts, well armed, leapt to positions on the outside, clinging like eagles on a rock face. Thus arranged, the carriage departed at full speed.

Stepping to the piano, I set the sheets of the Chopin nocturne Ava had played for me along the rack.

"Good morning, monsieur."

When I turned to address her, my mouth fell open. And all thoughts of carriages and armed guards fled.

Ava had dressed in a manner entirely different from that to which I'd become accustomed.

In place of her stylish and formal dress, she wore a simple charmeuse shift. Sleeveless and sky blue. Fitted at the waist. A petite oriental collar about the neck.

Her hair was pinned back in a loose, youthful manner. And her cheeks bore little of the rouge and inks with which she normally highlighted her features. At her ears hung but single pearls.

I stared. Dumfounded.

She noted my expression and hesitated. "Does something displease you?"

I shook my head. Unable to speak.

I then worried that my silence would upset her. Would lead her to think I did not take pleasure in her appearance.

Yet nothing could be further from the truth. In fact, I found the absence of glamour breathtaking. Divested of pretense, her natural beauty radiated.

I held as still as if she had come to stand naked before me. Without ruse or masquerade. Allowing me to observe the all of her.

Standing there, I felt suddenly emboldened, knowing that when a woman chooses to come before another stripped of artifice, she is entrusting them with a rare gift. With a trust that renders her most vulnerable. And, in my mind, most alluring.

Others standing in my shoes might have reacted differently. After all, many prefer their women painted and powdered. Ruffled and jeweled. I, on the other hand, possess an inherent weakness for women au naturel.

While it is true that the artistry of a fine costume can seduce, it is equally true that superficial trappings have no effect whatsoever on the quality of Light a woman exudes. And that this Light only shines more brilliantly within a bare setting.

So it was with Ava.

I took a step back.

Had she known the effect such an unveiling would have upon me?

"Is that music intended for me?" she asked.

It took me a moment to find my voice. When I did, I recommitted to my purpose. "Will you play it for me again?" I asked.

"With pleasure."

She settled to the bench. Drew in a breath. Launched the bass rhythm in her left hand, then lighted on the delicate melody with her right.

"Stop," I said, nearly as soon as she had begun. I pointed to the first measure. "Let us consider the opening phrase. Play it once more. Just the six notes."

She did.

"Again," I insisted.

She squirmed a bit, then repeated the phrase.

"Again."

She pouted. Relented.

"Again."

She looked up. "I have played the phrase five times. Each time the same. Is there a point you wish to make?"

"You have made it for me."

Her forehead crinkled.

I took a step back. "In your playing I have observed that you rely on instinct. On a musical liberty dictated by your heart. But for reasons I can't yet discern, you often seem hurried. And so perform phrases identically each time. This should never happen." I took a step forward. "Why do you rush?"

She averted her eyes.

I slipped in front of the bench, making to sit alongside her.

She moved to accommodate me. Though she did not move far.

"Listen," I said.

I played the opening six notes, giving the first, a deep bass, an extra sounding. The effect served to root the piece in place. The rest unfolded atop a fluid rhythm. I played the phrase a second time, hitting the opening bass with a light, lacy touch. Doing so, the rest unfurled upon a more courageous rhythm.

"Can you hear the differences?" I asked. "A phrase such as this invites limitless interpretation. It is susceptible to a thousand nuances. To play it by rote shrinks its essence."

She moved toward the keys. Eager for another chance.

"Wait!" I said, and touched her lightly on the shoulders. "Hold your position. Stay in the moment of silence. It is the point of entry that will serve as your bridge to new possibility."

I felt her shiver beneath my hands.

"Take a deep breath," I instructed. "You have all the time in the world. No one is coming to take the piano from you."

She spun at my words. Searched my eyes.

"A breath," I reminded her, determined to press on.

She inhaled. Made to approach the keys.

Again I pressed my palms along her shoulders.

"Wait," I whispered. "*Listen*. Imagine what is to come."

I felt her straining beneath me. After another several moments I released her.

She fell into the keyboard as into the arms of a lover. Her phrasing wrought with tenderness. Its tone demanding yet affectionate.

Yes, I thought to myself. But to her I said, "Stop."

She flinched back.

"Let us try again," I said, indicating some disappointment.

She scowled.

"Breathe."

She did. Then attempted to move forward.

As before, I restrained her.

"Find your balance. Set your feet on the bridge. But do not cross," I instructed.

Her chin thrust outward. A gathering storm.

When she released, the phrase launched in a new direction. This one less tender, more high-spirited.

It was brilliant.

I shook my head. "Enough, madame."

She pushed back from the keys. I felt the heat of her rising, settling in the crevice between our legs.

"Perhaps I am not making myself clear," I said.

Her cheeks reddened. "I would have to agree."

I ignored her irritation and laid a hand on my heart. "Every time you approach a piece, you must come from the most authentic place possible. No two approaches, therefore, will ever be identical. It is this spontaneity that results in rubato, the altering of time and tempo to enhance the beauty and meaning of a phrase."

She sniffed. "I am familiar with the concept."

"Of course," I said. "All the more shocking, then, that you seem unable to command it."

Her eyes flew open.

I did not relish her anger but adhered to my plan.

"Place your hands upon the keys, but do not draw a single note."

Her demeanor sparked with resistance. For a moment I thought she might slap me.

She then complied.

I looked down at her fingers. Slender and sensitive as violin bows. Arching with receptivity. To think of their responsiveness, of their feathery touch, made me...

I shook my head.

"Now. Lift your fingers. Hold them above the keys. Wait until you feel the sound rising of its own accord. Then, drop into place."

She did and banged several notes.

"Silently!" I urged. "You are only to make an approach. Not storm the castle!"

She writhed alongside me. Her aggravation intense.

"Again," I said.

She lifted her hands. Held still. Turned inward. Then, after a moment, allowed her hands to settle to the keys.

The effect was magical.

I could not tell her this. Instead, I exhaled and wagged my head in disappointment. "No, no. Again, that is entirely incorrect," I said. Crossed my arms. "Madame, I must be perfectly frank. If you cannot make the effort to master this simple but critical technique, I would have very little interest in continuing our studies."

She leapt to her feet, unleashing her outrage. "This is intolerable! Either you are speaking nonsense or I am a pitiful musician!"

She wrung her hands and paced along the bookshelves.

Remaining calm, I asked, "Do you enjoy walking in the garden?"

"That would seem a ridiculous question," she hissed.

I struggled to restrain laughter. Yet did not relent.

"Have you ever seen butterflies light upon blossoms?" I asked, indicating the flowers outside. "They never, ever land the same way twice."

"Is that so?" she spat. Boiling with rage.

I nodded. "It is in that spirit that you must approach the music before you. There are, in fact, several examples within nature that illustrate the technique clearly."

She whirled to face me. In that moment, I saw realization strike. Her eyes flit to the door then back to mine.

"I see," she said, her entire physique softening. "Perhaps, then, I have not paid nature's creatures sufficient attention?"

"Perhaps."

She broke into a coy smile. "Well then, monsieur, might I make one request before you forfeit our lessons entirely?"

I waited.

She cleared her throat. Lifted her voice. "Might you take me out of doors to show me directly these examples of the technique you wish me to learn?"

Keeping my tone serious, I said, "I could be persuaded to make one final attempt, madame. Though I would forewarn you, I expect you to work as diligently in the out of doors as you do before the instrument."

"The terms are understood," she said.

She drifted to the coat rack. Removed a long, silken scarf. Draped it along her shoulders.

"Let us go out this way," she said, standing near the door where Audric loitered, thus forewarning him.

My pulse raced.

I allowed the butler a moment to take cover, then threw open the door.

Ava swept across the threshold. Her body brushing against mine as she passed.

She paused in the hallway. Glanced up and down.

Audric was nowhere to be seen.

"This way," she said, turning toward the direction opposite from which I normally arrived. "There is a shortcut."

Without looking back, she led us down a dark, winding passage. Not far behind we could hear Audric's uncertain plodding.

We rushed headlong into a stone staircase. It appeared to rise to an exit. Without a moment's hesitation, Ava ascended, unlatched the lock, and threw the door wide. Emerging, we found ourselves awash in light, folded in the arms of the back garden.

I blinked in astonishment.

Ava re-draped the scarf about her shoulders. "Had you a place in mind for my instruction?"

I stared blankly.

She noted my hesitation. "Through here," she said, and wove her way between stands of cypress trees.

I followed.

The landscape grew dense, delivering us into a thicket of ivy.

"Is he still there?"

I glanced over my shoulder. "Yes."

The foliage gave way to a path. To the right, it swept up a

heavily wooded incline. I immediately recognized the trail from my morning walks.

Behind us, we could hear the butler crashing through the underbrush.

"This way," I said, pointing up the hill.

We fled, giddy with anticipation.

When we had gone a fair distance, I led us toward a deer path that branched from the main trail. "Here," I said.

Skirting along the narrow path, we descended and ascended several times, passing through copses of beech trees.

Ava glanced over her shoulder. "I think we've lost him."

I agreed. But wanted nothing left to chance. We turned again from the trail. Onto yet a smaller path. Heading for the spot where I often ended my walks.

Stepping ahead, I pushed aside vines and branches. Just when the foliage had grown too thick and it seemed we could advance no further, we burst into a clearing.

The air cooled instantly. The birdsong amplified. Airy ferns reclined around a bubbling spring.

Ava's eyes opened with delight. "How lovely!"

We looked about for several minutes, absorbing our surroundings.

Neither of us moved.

What now?

We had broken free of scrutiny. We were alone.

For a married woman it was an unseemly predicament.

Wishing to dispel the tension, I removed my coat and laid it atop a swell of moss.

She cast her eyes downward. "Thank you."

I took a perch on a nearby knoll. Pretending to scout a bird, I assessed the situation.

Normally, if a woman were to run off with me, I assumed a certain authority.

Such was not the case with Ava.

Desperate as I was to take her in my arms, I could not.

What was it I feared?

I had already considered what damages might befall my friends should the reality of my disguise be uncovered. And, with Cristofer's assurances, had come to peace with it.

That was not the eventuality holding me back.

What, then, was it?

Sensing Ava's proximity along my skin, the answer became unavoidable.

It was my love herself—not her person, per se, but the possibility of her rebuff, her rejection.

What if things went the way of my first dalliance with Tess?

What if she fled in disgust?

The mere thought of this prospect had me shaking.

And what about Ava?

Having come this far and at such risk, why had <u>she</u> not made an approach?

Until this point she had been forthright. Clear with her desire.

Had she changed her mind?

My confidence wavered.

"Madame," I began. "If you would prefer to return home, I can lead us there promptly."

Her face fell. "Is that what you want?"

Seeing her disappointment, I regretted my words. "No, no, of course not."

A meadowlark lighted in a nearby tree. Its song unfurled above us.

I studied my boots.

An awkward moment passed.

Then.

"You mentioned butterflies?"

I looked up. Saw her parted lips. Her knowing smile.

With that my hesitation fled.

How it is possible for a single look to change the course of one's resolve, I shall never know. And yet, it has always been this way for me. Despite the risk. Despite the possibility of self-annihilation. I cannot resist Beauty.

I rose and went to her.

Neither of us said a word.

Like lovers kept apart, our lips hunted. I drew hers between mine.

She spooled my hair about her fingers. Pulled me to her.

Together we fell back. I pressed along the length of her. Felt her hips widen beneath me.

I dizzied at her hunger. At the growl in her throat.

Closer now, I let my hands drift to her breasts.

She gasped. Shifted beneath me. Shifted again. I soon realized her body's objective. It was seeking the core of me. Confirmation of my lust.

Uncertain as to how the stuffing in my pants might perform under such strain, I cupped her breasts firmly and lowered my mouth to her belly. Traced my lips downward. Attuning to her cadence. Unleashing jasmine.

Arriving at the hem of her dress I clasped it between my teeth. Having done so, I listened for her moan. For the tone of acquiescence. Hearing it, I slipped beneath.

Hidden from view I gazed into the world above. Sunlight blazed through fabric as through stained glass. Igniting a sky blue empire.

I marveled at the heaven of her.

How could such a compact world as this contain the cosmos?

I ascended the taut arc of her thigh.

She rose and fell above me.

I set sail on her tides. Skimming shorelines. Nibbling stars.

Her final cry ruptured the forest. An opera of pleasure.

Breathless, we rolled onto our backs. Laid there. Seen by the clouds and unashamed.

A swallowtail flit overhead. Tossed on the wind.

Ava laughed. "I see what you mean about butterflies."

I looked over and she laughed aloud. Her cheeks full of roses.

I have never seen a woman more beautiful than she in that moment.

Gazing up, I thought how if one could choose their time of death, I would choose it then.

She turned to look at me. Her eyes gauzy. "When I first heard you play, I felt as though a wave had crashed and swallowed the ground beneath me. I remember actually thinking I might fall back and drown." She shook her head. "No one has ever done that to me."

I recalled my own undoing at the first sight of her.

She dropped her voice to a whisper. "I knew then that I had to draw you near." She waited. Then said, "I suppose you think that presumptuous."

I wagged my head. "No more than me having wished you would seek my instruction."

She smiled. "And did you wish that?"

"More than anything."

She drew my hand to her breast.

"Though I did not expect the enormity of your gift," I confessed.

"Does it displease you?"

"Displease me?" I said in shock. "I find it intoxicating."

She sighed. Nestled herself into the curve of me.

"When I was a child, I had a schoolmate whose father gave lessons," she said. "I remember distinctly the day I visited and heard him at the piano. He was playing a Scarlatti sonata. I found myself seduced by the instrument's tone, its flagrant sensuality. When he played, the music spoke to me clear as words. And yet, that which it shed its light upon seemed beyond all words." Her look grew distant. "I was so envious and wished more than anything to be his daughter."

"So he would teach you?"

She nodded. "My own family was quite … poor. When I told my mother of my desire to own a piano, she thought I was ill and sent me to bed."

I cringed. Remembering my own mother's bitter resistance.

"What then?"

"After some time, I approached my friend's father. Offered to be his housekeeper on the condition that he save my wages until I had enough."

"To purchase an instrument?"

"Yes."

A realization struck. "The piano you keep in your study?"

"Yes."

I nodded. "How long did it take?"

"Seven years," she said. "But during that time, I eavesdropped on a thousand lessons. Soaked up every word, every technique. At night, I read sheet music, memorizing notes, keys, time signatures. I etched a keyboard into the top of my bureau and practiced scales and arpeggios there. By the time I actually sat before a real keyboard, I felt as though the instrument were already a part of me."

"Do you mean, then, that you're essentially self-taught?"

She nodded.

I held still. Absorbing this remarkable fact.

Hers was a gift that needed—no—*demanded* nurturing.

At birth she had been marked a genius.

But her talent also rendered her an aberration. A perpetual outsider.

Like me.

I then recalled the servant's words to Cristofer.

"He does not like that you play," I said. She would know I was speaking of her husband.

Ava grazed her fingertips along my cheek. "I understand your curiosity," she said. "But let's not spoil this time on unpleasant things."

I reached up, wove my fingers between hers. Enraged that a man as cowardly as Jacque had the privilege of approaching her.

She propped herself on an elbow. "Now I must confess something," she said. A knit wrinkled her brow. "I have not been entirely honest with you."

I strained against my ball of socks.

She had not been honest?

"This has made it difficult for me to feel at ease," she continued, "so I am compelled to speak."

I swallowed.

"The truth is, I suspected your secret when we first met."

My blood iced.

"Secret?"

She glanced down. "Yes."

So.

She knew.

What had given me away?

A crooked sideburn? A curve of breast?

"Madame—" I began, trying to pull my hand from hers.

She held my fingers tight and continued as if I had not spoken. "I first suspected on the day you came to assist Monsieur Vaughn, when I overheard you playing on Beethoven's piano. It was the most otherworldly, heart-wrenching music I'd ever heard. And yet, somehow ... *familiar.*"

My eyes widened.

"Then, when we were alone, and you played the andante espressivo from Vaughn's Piano Sonata no. 3, I was certain of it."

So it was not my costume but my performance that had given me away.

How could I have been so careless!

She pressed closer. "Tell me, Henri. Why do you do it?"

Tess's words echoed inside my head.

"Why, Henri? Why do you go about as a man?"

I struggled to think what to say, what explanation might cause the least harm.

"Ava—"

"It wasn't just the stylistic similarities between the two pieces. But the visceral way with which you played them. As if they were bleeding from you."

I held still. Bewildered.

She sighed. "Your andante, in particular, surges with such heartbreak. Such yearning."

My andante?

She plucked a stalk of grass. Twirled it thoughtfully. "You know, they say yearning is expressed by those who let life's gifts slip through their fingers."

The meadow began to spin.

She took note of my distress. "I see you are not used to being found out!" she said with a quick laugh. When I said nothing she wagged her head. "Though no one has dared confront you, I should think anyone with a modicum of musical instinct would realize the truth." She looked off for a moment, then added, "Or perhaps the discovery requires a woman's intuition."

A tremor ran the length of me.

Had I heard her correctly? Was she inferring <u>not</u> that I walked in disguise but that (far worse!) I had conjured music for Cristofer? That I was the true author of certain pieces?

I prepared to dissuade her, but a sudden look of pain in her eyes made me hesitate.

"So is that what you do?" she persisted.

"Do?"

"Yes." she said. Traced the grass between my lips. "Do you let life's gifts slip through your fingers?"

A knot cinched my gut.

How awkward our pleasant interlude had suddenly become!

We had only just tasted one another and already she was making allegations.

She saw me blanch. "Forgive me," she said. "That was unfair."

She rolled toward me. Lifted her mouth to my ear. "You may keep your secrets," she whispered. "I already know what I need to know."

Saying this, she bit gently at my throat. Sought my lips with her own.

"Ava ..."

Saying nothing more, she rose above me.

The ground hollowed beneath us.

I reached for her just as the staccato of horse hooves shot between the trees.

Terrified, we flattened to the ground. Held our breath.

I covered her body and listened, expecting to hear the carriage returning to the castle. But as the galloping sped past, I could discern only a single horse, the rider following the main road.

Might he have seen us?

I listened deeper, struck by the rhythm of the animal's gait. Certain I'd heard it before.

In a flash I remembered.

Jacque's stallion!

CHAPTER 15

*T*he sun rose on a bed of strings. On a holy timbre that flew up and strained against the rafters. Elevating me until I woke and found myself suspended. Midair. My heart knocking at my ribs.

Then silence.

Into which entered a piano.

Its pitch heightened yet supple. Its pace serene yet increasingly insistent.

Soon a chorus of strings wedged itself gently beneath the melody. A lover slipping beneath the sheets. Together they wandered, one tone caressing the other, until the piano's melodic arc peeled upward. Its pitch rising until it seemed as if it might drift into ether. Just then a band of horns sounded. Their low drone swelling to provide solid ground. A safe place to land.

It was the honeyeater piece, to be sure.

And yet.

The bird had abandoned his branch. His song replaced.

By Hers.

Everywhere I turned, she emerged.

I felt soaked with her. Lathered.

The new theme's demands would not relent. The music rushing toward expansion.

Trembling at the lack of control, I became swept up in a rush far more powerful than I.

The tonality resonated equal parts worship and torment. Giving shape and sound to my passions.

Soon images rose alongside the tones.

Her face, now smiling, now lusty.

Her hands gripping my back.

Her moan at my ear.

Like a waterfall, the music spilled itself before me. Relentless in its reveal.

I could not judge its quality. I only knew it had to come.

Cast in a spell, I lay still.

Committing every note, every instrument, to memory.

How I longed to hear it played aloud!

Unfortunately our piano had yet to be repaired.

As I was thinking this, the bass strings dashed upward in a single devastating rush toward the sky. I noted within their departure a sudden change of key. And a rhythmic variation that demanded attention.

Hear me!

I listened.

"Hello? Anyone about?" a voice called.

I jumped as if beckoned from another world. Not expecting visitors, I roused quickly, tossed on my britches. Stumbled to the door.

To my surprise I found the piano tuner.

"I've come to finish the job," he said.

I turned the crank on the coffee grinder while the tuner angled over the piano with his tools. Every so often a hideous *ping!* shot from beneath the hood.

When he re-emerged, his face damp and purpled, he said, "Can you play something for me?"

I looked over. "You don't play?"

He laughed. "Not a note."

Sitting to the bench I executed a run of scales, putting the instrument through its paces.

"Hold it there, right there," he said. Lifted a wrench of some kind. Disappeared into the frame.

When he was finished, the piano sounded sublime.

I nodded in admiration. But wondered at one thing. "How is it possible you can perfect the instrument's pitch without knowing how to play?"

"Nothing mysterious about it," he said. Dropped his tools into a box. "My business is sound. Pure sound. Not the chemistry of it. Not the mixing of one tone with another."

I shrugged. "I suppose I haven't ground to stand on when I know so little of how the instrument works."

He wiped his beefy hands on a rag. "Would you like to?"

"Like to what?"

"Know more about how it works?"

I glanced down at the piano's fan of linear strings. Straight as corn rows. Bound in tension.

"Tell me about escapement," I said.

He grinned. "You're in luck." Returning to his box, he removed a jointed piece of metal and wood. "Behold, the miraculous mechanism!"

I stared blankly. It didn't look very impressive.

He lifted the coupling. "This is what differentiates the pianoforte from the harpsichord," he said. "This is what gives the piano its lush, rounded sound compared to the other's *plink-plunk*. It's also what allows you to modulate the volume as you choose. To shatter the glass, or lightly dust the sills," he said.

"Seems a lot of responsibility for those little bits of wood."

He laughed. Held the contraption lengthwise. "Imagine that this end is connected to one of your keys. And this other end attached to the hammer that will strike the string."

I examined the piece carefully.

"When you depress one of the keys, this lever tilts the arm of the hammer sending its head toward the string with as much force as you give it. The hammer then hits the string and, if nothing else happened, would remain pressed against it, dampening the sound and creating a plunky note. What the inventor Cristofori created was a way for the hammer to be separated, to 'escape' from the key at the last moment before it strikes the string. In this way, being in free-flight, the hammer promptly falls back from the string after contact. So that the resulting tone rings out and resonates entirely."

"If I'm hearing you correctly, then the hammer is essentially *thrown* at the string?"

"That's it exactly!" he said. He rubbed thoughtfully at the stubble on his cheek. "It's a lonely business unfolding inside these pianos. The hammer lives a life of being continually cast off from her earthly ties. To be hurled into the void. Alone. But, when the aim is true, she lands. And the sound—that only she can make—sublime!"

He dropped his hand and smiled. "Ah! Well. That's enough fancy rumination for today," he said and gathered his tools.

For my part, I stood still, my head hung in disbelief. I'd had no idea that the artistic endeavor that had arisen to dominate my life—the inspired yet disciplined creation of song—was enabled by a fundamentally reckless act.

A radical and solitary leap of faith.

Our reunion could not have been sweeter.

For days I remained with her. The sheen of her beneath my fingers. The breadth of her voice cupping my hands. My entire frame cradled within her borders.

Sitting at our restored piano, the music poured from me as from a swollen and dusty cask.

I felt every bit the vintner. Who waits. While maturity transforms ordinary juice into elixir.

I marveled at its ruby color. Its gushing intoxicating flush.

As in my bed, the instruments rushed to their places, swung the sky, dove the valleys. Pulled my heart apart in pieces.

The piece was not heated in its movement. Its pace not fleet of foot.

Yet its notes pierced the skin. With yearning. And noble blades.

Within the beats I heard the rhythm of her breath.

Felt the heat of her Light.

Tasted jasmine on my lips.

Sightless, I dared further inward.

Cristofer found me days later.

He started when he spotted me on the floor. Crumpled beneath the piano's shadow. Sheets of manuscript papering the rack, the fireplace, the loveseat. Vegetables rotting by the sink. Signore wailing in hungry circles.

"Henri!" he called, slapping my cheeks.

I opened my eyes. Smiled.

He fell silent at my queer expression. At my features infused with exhilaration.

"Ah, Henri," he said. "You've been there, haven't you?"

He needn't explain what he meant. We both knew.

He took me to his bed and there I slept.

Hours later, I woke to the smell of herbs and browning onions. Wrapping myself in his robe, I went to the kitchen.

Cristofer had set the table for dinner.

What had brought him home?

And made him take over his housekeeper's duties?

"Sit," he said when he saw me. He set down chunks of seeded bread and a ramekin of butter. Uncorked a bottle of wine.

I looked him over as he worked. Observed his crisp movements. His vibrant humming.

He had come home to celebrate. Of that I felt certain.

He set two bowls of minestrone soup at our places. "Mangiare! Mangiare!" he said.

I ate like a starving wolf, grateful for the sustenance.

When we finished, Cristofer raised his glass.

"To completion," he said.

I looked at him strangely.

He laughed. "The concerto, Henri. I've finished."

I turned to look at the pages of his manuscript sitting atop the piano. Stacked nearly seven inches high.

"Bravo," I said.

He dropped a mock bow. He was beaming.

I felt lightened by the accomplishment. As if it were my own. Knowing how critical this success to his self-esteem and career.

"And the adagio? It came?"

He sagged. "It came, yes. I believe it even has merit. And speaks to the heart of things."

I slapped the table. "My God, Cristofer! I should be indulging *you* tonight!"

He laughed.

His mood was jovial. His edges smoothed by the attainment of his milestone.

"Have you shared the news with Clara?" I asked.

He shook his head. "I will wait until her return. However, I have informed Jacque. And he is already working to secure a rehearsal with the orchestra in a week's time."

The mere mention of Jacque brought Ava crashing back into my thoughts.

Then I remembered.

My piece!

Where was it?

Cristofer caught my look of distress. Laid a hand on mine.

"Don't worry. I collected every page. It's waiting for you in your cottage."

I exhaled. Fell back against the chair. Appalled that I had left the manuscript out in the open.

Cristofer wiped a crust of bread inside the belly of his bowl. Squinted as if in thought.

Without looking at me, he said, "You're composing."

I flinched. Feeling as though he had caught me in some treachery.

He grunted. "A work of your *own?*" he clarified.

"Yes."

I watched a frown darken his features. Then, just as quickly as it had arrived, he covered it with a smile. "Good for you, Henri," he said. And left it at that.

I lifted another chunk of bread. Studied my liege a bit more closely. Noticed the sharpened angles beneath his cheekbones. He, too, had been held in that place, in that rapture where awareness of self diminishes almost to nullification.

"Is there more to tell?" I asked.

"Yes," he admitted without delay. Lifted his napkin. "The orchestral society has offered me a position."

I sat up. "The same position they refused you?"

He chuckled. "Yes. The very same."

I tensed. "And did you accept?"

He stared out the window. The dark turned back his gaze.

"No."

I sagged with relief. "Cheers! Good for you!" I raised my glass. "The time has come for you to concentrate on composing. Not on the musical chores of others."

He looked uncertain. "I hope that proves to be the case."

"Of course it will! You have completed a *concerto*, Cristofer. When it plays, all the world will beat a path to your door."

He shook his head. "Mine might be music born too early. It may take time, years perhaps, for the masses to understand. To appreciate the places I'm wishing to take them—"

"Then let the clock begin ticking toward understanding *now*, Cristof. There is no sense in waiting. Besides, you might be underestimating your audience."

He puckered his lips. "Perhaps."

He drew silent. In the quiet, our mutual exhaustion settled around us.

Cristofer looked down at his hands. "I would not be here without you, Henri," he said softly.

I shrugged. "Nor I without you."

He grew quiet. "Nor either of us without Richard."

"Yes," I said. Waited. Then, "Has there been word from the doctors?"

His head sagged. "They've seen no change."

I stared into my wineglass. My sadness having no words.

Later, Cristofer carried over a roast chicken. Reluctant, but hungry, we filled our bellies.

"Henri," he said over a plump drumstick, "I will need you to be at the first rehearsal."

"Of course!" I spouted. "Where else would I be?"

"It's a bit more complicated than that," he said. "Jacque will be there."

"Oh."

"So you'll need to don your costume."

"I see."

"And play my attendant."

I sniffed. "That should not be too difficult."

He stared hard at me over a scavenged bone. "Henri, the concerto cannot manifest without your ears. I must have your word."

I smiled at his compliment. Wondered if he had glanced at the pages of my manuscript. Decided he had not. He was too saturated with his own vision to take on another's.

Besides, he had no knowledge of the dreams I'd once harbored. And, therefore, no reason to show interest.

Yet why did I suddenly wish he would?

I looked over at my benefactor. As usual, the gravity of his genius tipped me out of orbit. Knocking me off the planet of my own concerns to align me, again, with his.

"I will be there, Cristofer. I promise."

CHAPTER 16

Rain pelted the ground in slashes. Cyclonic winds twisted the flags. I pulled my cape tight about my neck and sped across the plaza.

Audric opened the door and ushered me inside. He draped my sodden outer garments over his arm and offered a soft cloth with which to dry my hair.

Making myself ready in the vestibule I noticed a hush about the castle. There seemed a certain lack of activity. A vacancy.

When I made some comment in this regard, Audric said, "The monsieur is abroad."

I tried not to react to the news.

As we went down the dark stairs, I could hear Ava already at the piano. To my surprise, she was playing the rhapsody Cristofer had performed the night of the soiree. She had just begun to play the second theme.

My theme.

When her door came into view, however, my heart seized.

A fist-sized lock had been installed on the latch. Though unlocked, its mere presence served as an unmistakable warning.

Audric bowed in the threshold. "Monsieur Worth to see you," he announced.

Ava acknowledged him but kept her hands on the keys, continuing to play.

I stepped inside. Bowed.

Ava's attention remained on the piano.

The butler turned and closed the door.

Keeping still to listen, I flushed at the sound of my music spilling through her fingers. She was playing from memory.

Soon the music's allure swept all thoughts of husbands and locks from my head. Like a sorcerer's spell, it returned me to the night of the party. To the moment I first entered her presence.

Anew, I saw her radiance.

Her courtly gestures.

Her secret tears.

How I wanted to confess the effect she'd had upon me that night.

To recount the Beauty I had in her beheld.

But, of course, I could not do so. For that night I had come as nature dressed me.

I glanced outside and cursed the inclement weather. Given Jacque's absence, it seemed especially inopportune.

My eyes drifted back to the piano. Her body soared above the keys. The piece, a colossal deluge of emotion, churned and frothed around us, its level ever threatening to rise. Yet whenever it surged upward, she grasped handfuls of liquid and wrestled it down.

In this way she kept us afloat.

I marveled at her extraordinary ability. Her dynamics. Her vigor.

And wondered if I truly had anything to teach her. Anything at all to impart.

What can one contribute to inborn brilliance?

As she steered the piece through a turbulent channel, I found myself wondering at her choice.

Why had she decided to play the rhapsody?

To harp on the accusation that I had lent my vision to some of Cristofer's creations?

But I had denied that charge.

I listened again.

Her rendition vacillated wildly. Throbbing with remorse then storming in rebellion. The tempo bolted then lumbered.

Like a poet she seemed to possess an intimate knowledge of

every note. As if she had lifted each before the light, seeking to know facets, flaws, florescence.

Before her rendition I felt uncovered. She had spirited into the sealed chambers of my heart, holding a candle aloft.

Then, as I listened, her decision to play the music began to feel less like a threat.

And more like recognition.

When the final cadence sounded, she sat back. Her skin shiny with effort. Her eyes round with exhilaration.

She turned. "I assume you know the piece."

I said nothing.

With an open palm she fanned the heat from her chest. "Such vast emotional expression," she said. "It's hard to imagine it having been written by a man such as Vaughn."

I swallowed.

"Cristofer is a sensitive creature," I said. "That this tendency arises in his music should not be surprising," I said, feeling a strange sense of déjà vu I could not place.

She lifted an eyebrow. Her expression playful. "I wish you could have heard how it sounded on the night of our soiree. He performed it on the Broadwood, you know," she said, referring to Beethoven's piano.

"I imagine the effect was magical."

She looked off. Her visage grown distant, dewy. "Quite," she said.

She then looked to the door. Gave a little cough and settled back to the keyboard. "I suppose you want to begin today's lesson with the Mozart sonata?"

I looked up in surprise. I had never mentioned Mozart.

She began to play immediately. A quick, busy piece. Not a measure of silence to be found.

She tipped her head, indicating that I should sit beside her.

I did.

No sooner had I swept the wrinkles from my pant legs than she leaned her body toward mine. Her eyes silty, volcanic.

We had been kept too long apart.

She turned her head, her body performing of its own accord.

Our lips joined. Moans rumbling our throats.

It was then I realized the need for Mozart.

As the heat gathered between us, and my hands found her, she began to falter at the keys. When the sonata's precision crumbled, I reluctantly lowered my fingers to the ivory and took up the piece.

Music swelled the room.

Free to roam, she spun to envelop me. Her hands sifting into my hair, drawing me against her.

Cleaved in two, half of me attended to the music, the other half to my love.

The challenge proved a thrilling division.

My lips at her ears.

A run of minor flatted thirds.

Nibbling her throat.

A syncopated arpeggio in the tonic chord.

Then.

A knock at the door.

Ava jumped up quickly. Backing from the piano, she smoothed her hair. Her clothes. Motioned for me to do the same.

I patted down my mustache.

Still, our reddened cheeks and shining eyes spoke of impropriety.

"Come in," she said.

Audric stepped inside. His eyes whisked the room. The both of us. If he noticed anything untoward, he did not reveal it.

"Madame, I wish to inform you that the stable boy has come down with a fever and will not be at work today."

"I see." She drew in a quick breath, seeming unusually agitated by the report. "Anything else?"

"Yes. The stone masons have arrived to address a cracking wall in the west portal. If it is agreeable with you, I would be happy to oversee their work."

"That would be most convenient," she said.

He bowed and turned.

"Audric," she said, holding him back. "I appreciate being kept informed while the monsieur is away, but would request that you hold all further notices until the conclusion of my lesson."

"Of course," he said, and dutifully disappeared.

Weak-kneed, I sagged along the bench.

Ava waited a moment. Drew in a labored breath.

"Shall we begin again?"

I shook my head. Petrified.

"Please," she whispered.

I stared in disbelief. "Ava, I don't think—"

"*Please*," she insisted.

Did she wish to pretend nothing had happened?

I swallowed. My pulse racing with fear and unspent passion.

Uncertain what to do, I struck up Mozart's sonata. It wobbled at the start.

When I had moved some way into the piece, she came and settled beside me. Laid her head along my shoulder.

At her touch, an unexpected bitterness skittered across my tongue.

I needed to speak. To find release from this trap.

"Ava," I whispered.

She said nothing. Wound an arm about my waist.

"Ava!" I rasped with some force.

She curled a hand in my lap.

I drilled into the sonata. "There is a lock on the door," I said.

My tone harsh, impatient.

She pressed closer. "Yes."

The sonata unspooled between us. Smothering our voices.

I shook my head. "Why, Ava? What is his objection to your music making?"

"Please," she begged. "We have such little time to ourselves. Why ruin—?"

"Because this is killing me!" I cried before I could stop myself.

I hadn't meant to erupt. But hours of worry and aggravation, of caution and disguises, had overwhelmed me.

Ava leapt to her feet. Strode to the other side of the piano and faced me over the instrument.

"Killing *you*?" she hissed.

My head sunk before her anger.

The music droned on.

"I'm sorry," I said.

I had no right to pretend I bore the entire cost of our affair. It was true our situation had inflicted certain risks on my person. As well as on my friendship with Cristofer. But it was also true that Ava likely bore the lion's share of liability. In fact, hers was a risk I had yet to accurately assess.

The sonata slowed beneath my hands. The music's levity jangling my nerves.

I felt the sting of tears.

Ceased playing.

"Forgive me," I said into the silence. "It's just ..."

My words fell away.

She nodded. "I know."

She tipped her head toward the keys. Urging me to mask the silence.

Her request fanned my rage.

Determined to have my say, I yanked back my cuffs. Drew upward and pounced into Cristofer's nascent piano concerto. Carving into the first movement. The allegro. Its heroic theme.

I crashed headlong into the chords. Octaves leaping overhead. Then reversing to drill down into the piano's belly.

Sweating, I found my voice.

"He is a brute," I growled, "and has no comprehension of your beauty. He is possessed of no faculties to see or hear the essence of you as I do," I said, my heart aflame.

Standing above me, she blushed. Her poise tumbled by my bold declaration.

I writhed along the bench, the rigorous bass line demanding attention.

"Why do you tolerate his barbarity?" I asked between clenched teeth. Incensed, I wielded an ax over the melody, hacking at it in fury that such a man should have rights to her treasure when I could not.

Was it not enough that the very sight of her, the very sound, the very feeling of our spiritual allegiance catapulted my heart and imagination to greater heights than I'd ever known?

Unable to look up, I burst into a series of rapidly descending arpeggios. Finding bottom, they turned with a sudden pivot and fought their way back up in chains of percussive thirds, fourths, and fifths. The last hurled with force at the orchestra, daring retaliation.

Sweat beaded along my sideburns. Beneath my lip.

With little warning, the music slowed, hushed. Ushering the theme I had written. A hesitant upward climb of fragile tones. Minnows against the tide.

In my mind, I could hear the orchestration Cristofer had built beneath to sustain the delicate melody. Thus encompassed, I heard his voice all about me, declaring his agony. His impossible circumstance.

I shut my eyes.

How was it possible that we had both tripped upon the same snare? To have found the Light that sustains us only to be forbidden its glow.

What would become of us, twisted on this cruel nail of fate?

The piece developed, veering in a new direction, yet the echoes of our themes reared up, pushing again and again through the larger song. We would not drop the matter. Not surrender the point.

Lifted from the bench in a vigorous surge, I regained my footing and launched into the final dénouement. Runs pounded like horse hooves. Strings howled. Flutes pierced. A tireless, galloping anguish.

I rode on but found it difficult to breathe.

Eventually the end came into view. The final upward flourish.

I threw my fingers into the fray, spraying them across the keyboard, then collapsed.

It was several moments before I could rise.

To my surprise, I did not find Ava hovering over the piano but sitting in a chair at her desk. Facing me. Her expression shattered. I could not tell whether this had resulted from the piece itself or an external circumstance.

Without a word, she nodded toward the door.

I glanced at my watch. Our time was over.

My heart snagged in my throat.

In a rush of unreason, I hurried to her, fell to my knees.

"Ava, *please*," I implored. "I must see you. Away from here. Perhaps we could travel? Disappear to the coast …"

I heard the requests fall from my lips.

Wondered if I were mad.

Did I truly believe we could be together?

But how when I remained in disguise?

And she belonged to another?

She pressed her fingers to my lips. Gazed into my eyes. Tenderness muddied with regret.

She cupped my face in the petals of her hands.

"Henri," she whispered. "If such a thing were possible, I would be with you for all my days."

The dagger nested in my heart.

A knock fell upon the door.

I bolted upright. Breathless.

Ava motioned for me to collect my things.

I rushed back to the piano.

"Come in, Audric," she said. Turned to her desk. Took out pencil and paper.

"Pardon me, madame. Have you extended your lesson?" he asked, peering over to where I quaked above my satchel.

"Not at all, we were just finishing," she said, writing in order to keep her face hidden.

Only I saw the furtive hand that swept her tears.

After but a moment, she folded the sheet of paper and turned around.

Audric took this as permission to speak. "It's the stone masons, madame. They are requesting your assessment of the repair."

"I see," she said. "Very well."

She rose, the dignity of her carriage revealing nothing of our thorny interlude.

I watched the gem at her throat spark as she crossed toward us.

I bowed as she approached. "Well played today, madame," I mumbled.

"Thank you, monsieur."

She lifted the sheet of paper. Held it out to me. "I apologize for the delay in returning this assignment to you. But I am still struggling with the berceuse. All those horrid flats!" she said with a high-pitched laugh.

I grit my teeth in a tight smile, playing along as best I could.

I had, of course, given no such assignment.

It was then I noticed the page trembling ever so slightly in her hand.

Fearing that Audric might notice, I slipped the sheet into my satchel. Buckled it fast.

"I trust you will be gentle with your corrections," she added.

My mouth dry with fright, I found myself bewildered at how quickly she had collected herself.

Who was this clever chameleon?

And how many persons could she wield?

Out of my head and uncertain where to go, I dashed headlong for the woods.

Bit by bit the storm unraveled me. The wind tearing my coattails. Branches snatching my cravat. Showers dissolving the adhesive behind my false bristles. Like small drowned creatures, they slipped one by one from my face.

Panting with exhaustion, I burst into an open field. The ground rippled with rows of sodden green stems. The mud sucked at my boots, reached for my thighs, making the way forward difficult.

I heaved and struggled. Then tumbled into the muck.

The first cry to escape me sounded like choking. I strapped a hand over my mouth. Hoping to contain myself.

But there was no hope.

My jaw widened and unleashed a torrent. Harsh unpleasant cries that rasped my throat.

Outraged at my reduction, at the sheer impossibility of my love, I pounded fist after fist into the mud.

I had loved intensely before.

That was true.

Yet no other liaison had felt as dismantling as this.

But what had I expected?

Were my fantasies getting the better of me?

Could I no longer distinguish truth from illusion?

I wept as raindrops pelted my face. Feeling every bit the fox who finds his hindquarter cinched in iron teeth.

Like him, I had nowhere to run.

When the storm had drained the worst of my sorrow, I sighed.

Closing my eyes, I rolled onto my side. Felt the mud discover and accept the shape of my cheek.

Then, for the second time in my life, I gave thought to leaving.

A sudden cry shattered that notion.

"What in the hell are you doing mucking up my beet field?" she wailed.

I started. Looked up through the smear of rain and dirt.

A pair of rubber boots tromped alongside my head.

Tess.

What was she doing out in the storm?

"For the love of God, Henri." She took a step closer, wagged her head. "Looks like that little mustache of yours did the trick, eh?" she said.

I reached for her open arms.

Tess's tub was an old tin trough once used to water horses.

She stripped me down and helped me inside. Set tall pots of water on the stove. These she poured over my shivering body until I was submerged to my chin.

As before, I felt strangely at home.

Until I noticed an absence.

"Where are the hounds?" I asked, missing their floppy ears and boisterous slobber.

"At the neighbor's," she said. "He was watching them while I was away."

"You were away?"

She nodded briskly. "Aye. Just coming back when I found you up to your neck in beet greens."

I marveled at the chance of our paths having crossed.

"Just my luck."

"No luck about it," she said. Tossed a peat log onto the fire.

I settled into the warm suds, comforted by her portly shape and mystical outlook.

The crackle of flames clapped with the rain's syncopation on the roof, making me feel as though I were inside a drum.

A better place to be than inside my head.

The fire amply stoked, Tess carried over two glasses and a bottle. Pulled the cork with her teeth. Poured each glass full of whisky.

"I dare say today's not a day for tea."

The liquor scalded my throat. Opened a hot flame in my belly.

Tess drank a second glassful. Looked at me intently. Concentrating on a spot just above my head.

She frowned. "You shouldn't be here," she said.

I looked over the rim. Certain I was where I wanted to be.

On the way to Tess's house I had made up my mind. I would end my instruction with the madame. Have Cristofer make an excuse. And never see her again.

Tess leaned forward. "You're meant to be somewhere else."

I shrugged. "The bottom of a lake, I suppose."

"No." She closed her eyes. "Someone is looking for you."

I lowered further beneath the water. "Undoubtedly Cristofer," I mumbled.

She banged the bottle against the tub. "Pay attention, Henri!" she snapped. "Your little charade has stirred a hornet's nest."

She calmed. Poured us each another glass. Stared again over my head.

"I see lust about you. And love." She put a hand to her forehead. "I see one who seeks to possess you, another who yearns for this, and yet another who aims to harm."

I stared into the bubbles. Half listening.

"I'm already aware of that, Tess."

"Are you?"

"Yes."

"Then who is looking for you, Henri?"

"I told you. It's Cristofer."

She shook her head. "No. It's a woman."

After a minute Tess visibly calmed. Sailed her fingers across the water. Gave my arm a frisky pinch. "Why don't you tell me about her," she urged.

I shook my head, groggy with drink. "It's over. We are no more."

"Ahh." She gave an encouraging shrug. "But you can still tell me what it was like, can't you?"

"What's the point?"

"Well, if it was worth winding up face down in a field, it's probably worth recounting!"

I glared.

Was she poking fun?

She kept a straight face.

I sighed. Sunk beneath the bubbly warmth. Told Tess the story of how we'd met. Of Ava's private room. Her husband's lies. His veiled threats. Then onto our first lesson. Our passions and music. The butler's ear at the door. Carried away, I recounted our first kiss. Of how we spoke secretly, seamlessly. Sharing an understanding of one another without need of words. And how her beauty and gifts and spirit uplifted me. Enlivened my imagination and spurred my long-silent quill—to the point of beginning a composition. One entirely for myself. I then described the piece drawn from the honeyeater's song. And how I'd come to realize that Ava's presence in my life was its true inspiration. I even went so far as to sing a line for Tess. Then another.

It was at this point that I stopped. I couldn't continue for the look on the barmaid's face.

"What is it?" I asked.

Her smile broke its normal bounds. "Do you know that this is the first time since we've met that I've actually seen this?"

I sunk a bit, feeling guarded. "Seen what?"

Tess wagged her head. "You," she said. "Happy."

I gaped. Thrown by her remark.

Then, from somewhere within me rose an unexpected awareness.

"What is it, Henri?" she asked, leaning in. "You look like you've seen a ghost!"

"The *berceuse*!" I said, shaking.

"What?"

"The piece she mentioned at my departure," I explained, talking more to myself than Tess. "It means 'lullaby.' She must have been trying to tell me something. About sleep. Or, perhaps, the night."

I groaned at my imbecility and searched about me for a blanket. Finding none, I leapt from the water naked. My bottom pink with heat.

Tess cheered at my immodest display.

Ignoring her, I ran to where she had set my clothes. Lifted my satchel. Unsnapped the buckles and drew the sheet of paper from inside.

I skimmed the music assignment Ava had sketched. Saw immediately that it was nonsense. But there, embedded between the notes, she had written the words: *Garden window.*

My head spun.

"What is it?" Tess said, her curiosity aroused.

"She wants me to come to her," I said quietly. "Tonight."

Tess settled back in her chair. Her eyes ran the length of my steaming body. She grinned.

"Are you surprised?"

I began to shiver as the full import of Ava's message took root. We would spend a night. An entire one. Together.

I shook my head. "I can't do it."

"What? Why on earth not?"

"Because she will discover the truth."

Tess stared. Narrowed her eyes. "I'm guessing she already has."

"No," I said, recalling the details of our interludes. "On one occasion I feared she had, but now am certain she has not."

Agitated, Tess threw up a hand. "So what if she does? What is the worst that will happen? Is it any worse than the torment you already endure?"

Her question multiplied my exposure. I searched again for a blanket.

Noting my desperation, she threw me one. "Hate to cover all that up," she grumbled. "Now. Tell me the truth. What is so dreadful about her finding out?"

Resistance knit my brow. But I knew well enough Tess would not relent.

"Because ... when she learns the truth, she'll ..." I stopped, unable to bear the thought.

"Will what?"

I bit down. Squeezed my eyes. "Hate me," I said.

My imagination played out the shock of her horror.

Love's rejection was agony to be sure. Though, of course, survivable.

But to be dismissed by the Beauty and Light I revered? By that which enriched my veins? And tucked purpose inside my heart?

No. That risked not grief alone.

But extinguishment.

I sank to the floor. Drew the scratchy blanket about me.

Tess drank and drank again.

The fire crackled.

The house creaked, sodden with rain.

"Go to her, Henri," she slurred.

I stared at my knees. "I can't."

Tess reddened. "You can and you *must*!" she railed. "For God's sake, has having your face pressed in the muck taught you nothing?"

I cowered before her outrage.

"Look at you, Henri! You've been hollowed out. Drained of life. Guilt-ridden into paralysis," she boomed in a voice not quite her own. "You've tethered yourself to melancholy, made a sacrifice of yourself, but what has it earned you? Let go, Henri! Acknowledge your desires. Let them arouse you. Inspire you. Before it's too late!"

She paused. Deflated. Returned to herself.

I held still in the silence.

Trembling.

"Tell her, Henri," she urged.

"But what if she—?

"But what if she *doesn't*?" Her gaze bore into mine. Her forehead lifted, prompting me. "She's the one who urges your Light, Henri. Must you really know more than that?"

When she fell silent, I looked again at the sheet of manuscript. And its risky invitation.

I glanced outside. Saw dusk's arrival hidden in the rain.

I cannot say whether it was the whisky, Tess's fiery conviction, or the urgings of my own intuition that emboldened me. But in that moment I sprang up to find my boots.

Slipping first into my suit, I worked furiously to smooth the wrinkles. Found Tess's broken comb and slicked my hair.

Instinctively, my hands rose to my mustache.

Only to find it missing.

My stomach dropped when I recalled how the critical pieces of my disguise had slipped from my face in the rain.

Tess chuckled. "Looking for your furry bits?"

I nodded.

"You'll find them by the fire."

I strode toward the flames. Found my bristles carefully laid out and drying on a stone.

"Had a hunch you might be needing them," she chirped.

I ran to my satchel. Removed the jar of adhesive. Applied the elements as best I could. Then turned to face my friend. "How do I look?"

Tess's eyes widened at my transformation. "Well, I'll be," she gasped.

I went and knelt before her. Took her hands into mine.

"Thank you, Tess. Again. For salvaging me."

She scoffed. "You could thank me better with a kiss."

I grinned. Took her face between my hands. Pressed my lips to hers. Drew back. "Will that do?"

She smiled, kept her eyes closed. "Hmmm. A bit scratchier than I'd expected. But very nice indeed."

I gave her knees a squeeze. Then made my way for the door.

"Henri!"

I stopped. Turned in the threshold. The rain at my back.

She had opened her eyes. A dark expression weighting her face.

"I've had a premonition."

"Yes? Of what?"

She met my gaze. "That I shall never see you again."

I held still.

"Do your premonitions always come true?"

She nodded. Gravely.

"Not this time!" I cheered, convinced she was wrong.

Tess lifted a hand in farewell.

"See to yourself, Henri," she warned.

I gave a tight-lipped nod. Turned up my collar.

And dashed into the night.

CHAPTER 17

*T*he darkened castle loomed above, hunching like a vulture. Not a single light winking from within its massive walls.

I swallowed and wound my way to the back. Alert for any sound or movement.

Arriving at the garden, I decided against entering through the gate. That might attract attention. Instead, I slipped behind a band of trees that lined the perimeter wall.

Wedging my fingers into the stones overhead, I nudged my boot into a crack. With a grunt, I boosted myself up. Found another crack. Tugged. The rock was slick with rain and lichen, making the climb difficult. I tried not to think of the damage I might inflict upon myself should I fall.

When balanced along the peak, I threw my legs over as though dismounting a horse. Hit the ground with a thud. Waited to see if anyone had detected me. Hearing nothing, I scurried behind an ornamental shrub outside the madame's room. Peered through her windows.

Beyond the glass, I perceived nothing but darkness.

Had I misinterpreted her invitation?

Imposed meaning where none existed?

"*Go to her, Henri,*" I heard Tess say from within the greenery.

I approached the window. Looked once more over my shoulder. Tapped gently. Listened.

Heard only silence.

I squinted against the rain. Tapped again.

This time, the window opened. At first I could only make out a pair of dark shoulders.

Audric?

A hand grasped mine.

I panicked.

"Ava?"

"Shh. Come inside."

She closed the window behind me. Bolted the latch. Threw the curtains.

Keeping hold of my hand, she drew me forward. "This way."

I stepped ahead, uncertain, my balance lost.

Something soft brushed my cheek. She had drawn us through

the silk drapes. Into her private partition.

A bed of coals glowed in the fireplace.

"You're wet," she whispered. Slipped the cape from my shoulders. Lowered me to the chaise longue. Untied my boot laces. Set my socks near the fire to dry.

I shivered at her touch. At the burnished angles of her that appeared, flickering, in the firelight. Though it obscured her somewhat, I was thankful for the darkness, as I doubted the condition of my disguise. Anxious, my hands rose to my mustache.

Tell her, Henri.

I wanted to. Badly.

Her palms flattened along my collarbones. Pushed me gently to the mattress. She nestled in beside me. Lifted two eiderdown quilts and spread them over us. The scent of her skin rendering me breathless.

I glanced toward the curtains.

"Are you certain we're safe?" I whispered.

She drew a finger to my lips. "Yes."

Despite her assurances, I felt uneasy. Not wanting to delay, I lowered my hand to search out the seams in her dress.

Before I could proceed, her hand curled around mine. Held it still.

"We have time," she said. Drew slow liquid fingers along my cheek. My lips. Time.

Both gift and curse.

Tell her.

The firelight gilded her eyes with amber.

She brought her lips near mine. But did not touch. She waited, suspended before me.

My head was swimming. My britches on fire.

I drew her to me until our lips met. Gingerly. As though moving through honey.

We retreated then lunged. Seeking in each new approach a separate angle of softness. A refined sense of the other.

Our breath came in measures.

And so began our silent conversation. A slow unwrapping of our vulnerabilities, our shapes, our desires.

Minutes undressed into hours.

We kept our clothes on.

With each pause, I waited for her to speed ahead, to reach inside my shirt or down below.

Much to my relief she did not.

What was she waiting for?

What was I waiting for?

She reclined beneath me, arching with delight. A smile of contentment bowing her lips.

Unable to bear the tension, the impending possibility of my discovery, I looked away.

Long as this night, I knew it would not last long enough.

She draped a hand over my heart. "Henri? Are you alright?"

"Ava?" I gasped.

"Yes?"

"There is something I must tell you. Something you need to know." I shuddered. "I'm not—"

"Stop," she said.

"But Ava, you don't understand—"

"Shh," she said, silencing my confession with her fingertips. Without warning, she rolled over to pin me beneath her. Her face hovering above mine. Her curls brushing my forehead.

I flinched, unsure of her motivations.

"Hold still."

I froze when her fingers sought the edge of my mustache. Dipped beneath its bristles.

And then. Ever so gently. Peeled back.

Her eyes roamed over the truth.

Her expression ablaze. Unreadable.

As if in a trance, she lowered her lips. Feathered the length of my newly exposed skin with kisses.

She whispered, "Do you know how long I've wanted to do that?"

Hours later, the rain stopped. The sky lightened. The first hints of peach pooled between the stars.

Ava laid beside me. Fading in and out of sleep. Our naked bodies warm. Ripened.

I gazed down the length of us. My eyes dipping into our mutual valley.

During the night, she had revealed her preparations for our rendezvous. How she'd had one of the stable hands cajole Audric into drinking. Until he passed out and left the key to the lock on her door unguarded. And how that same stable hand had then misplaced the key in case Audric woke prematurely.

It all seemed carefully plotted. Assuming that her accomplice would not betray her. Which, she assured me, he would not.

Still, I felt somewhat unsettled by the impending dawn.

I looked over to the piano. Then down at my lover.

Saw her eyelids flutter.

How I wanted to wake her with music. To play for her the song, her song, that swelled inside my head as I lay there.

"Are you awake?"

She moaned softly. Kneaded her body into mine.

I brushed my fingers down her side. Drumming a tender arpeggio along her skin.

She opened her eyes. Broke into a guilty smile. "Well played, maestro."

I returned the grin. Felt the soft of her about me.

And marveled.

Still, a question had come to pester my heart.

I lifted onto an elbow. "Now you must tell me something," I said.

"Right now?" she asked, sleepily.

"Yes."

She frowned. "Alright, then. What is it?"

"I want to know how you learned of my disguise."

"Ah," she said. Drew in her lips, wetting them along one another. She seemed hesitant.

Had something in the question made her uncomfortable?

"The truth is," she began. "I fell in love with you on the night of our soiree."

I drew back. My mind reeling through recollections of that evening.

"But how is that possible? I was dressed as a woman. And we were never even introduced!"

"No, we weren't. Nevertheless—"

"I don't understand."

"I know."

"But—"

"Shh," she said.

Her expression wearied. As though caught in the recall of a distant sorrow.

I was baffled.

She sighed. Took my hand.

"I suppose the time has come for me to reveal a secret of my own."

CHAPTER 18

Bleary-eyed and having just arrived home, I set the kettle atop the flame. Turned the crank on the grinder. The coffee's pungent aroma stung my nose.

Signore brushed about my shins. Yelping for breakfast.

Sipping coffee, I assessed the contents of our larder. Found only a limp spray of green onions and some potatoes. A trip to the market would be the first order of business.

At the table, my rain-wrinkled suit hung over the back of a chair. Ironing it would be the second order of business.

Cristofer bounded through the front door.

"Henri, by God, look at you. Almost midday and not yet dressed!"

He noted my disheveled hair. Drooping eyelids.

"Late night?"

I shook my head. "Early morning."

He chuckled. Lifted the watch from his pocket. Clicked open its face. "Luckily you've plenty of time."

My eyes narrowed. "Until what?"

It was then I noticed his soaring spirits. The restless energies animating his limbs.

I was too tired to speculate as to the cause.

He pulled out a chair. Made to sit, then didn't.

I took advantage and dropped into the seat.

He paced along the bookshelves. Wrung his hands.

"Clara's just arrived back from her tour."

That explained his sudden vigor.

"I see."

He strode toward the carafe. Poured himself a cup.

I waited. Certain he had more to tell.

"As it happens, Monsieur Bertrand was also in Bonn and was able to attend her final performance. Afterward, he offered to escort her home in his carriage. She was most touched, and readily accepted."

My throat tightened.

"You don't say?" I said.

For the life of me I couldn't see why this news should make me uncomfortable.

But it did.

Still bubbling, he went on.

"Both were enthused from their travels and spoke vigorously during the ride."

I winced to think of our esteemed pianist in such a ruthless presence.

If I had disliked Jacque before, my disdain had only multiplied following Ava's recent revelations.

"Clara, of course, regaled him with her belief that my concerto would serve and, in fact, *must* serve as a salvo against the Wagnerians—a point that Jacque seemed to intuitively grasp and which led him to hatch the most spectacular plan."

I waited. Holding my breath.

"As a welcome home for Clara, he's arranged for she and I to perform a preview of the concerto this evening. At the castle. The guest list will include his most respected and influential colleagues."

I stared in disbelief. "But Clara has only just now returned. Surely she wishes to be with the children."

He shrugged. "She did not hesitate to accept his offer."

I looked away. "Of course she didn't," I muttered. My thoughts turned to Richard. His trembling fingers. His threadbare heart.

"Do you have a fresh suit?" Cristofer asked.

"What?"

He noted my wrinkled coat on the chair. "For tonight," he explained. "We need you to oversee the pages during our performance."

I stood half-dressed before the mirror. Frayed by inner tensions, I wanted only seclusion. Instead I'd been summoned to the lion's den.

In my hands rested the false mustache. Its storm-tossed bristles would require considerable attention were they to perform successfully that evening. I drizzled several drops of oil along its length. Teased a comb through the pelt.

Doing so, I avoided the reflection of my face.

My heart and mind were bursting at the seams with secrets and scandals. The whole of my circle, it seemed, had become ensnared in a web.

There was Cristofer. Hopelessly yearning for Clara, the wife of his dearest friend and most ardent supporter.

Then the tormented Richard, still willing to sacrifice his genius in order to gain the love of his wife.

And Clara, unavailable to husband and admirer alike (and, I believed, even her own children). Desirous only of achievement. Oblivious, it seemed, to the needs of the heart.

While I, myself, pined for Ava. A woman married to the man who held my benefactor's musical hopes in his clutches.

Meanwhile Jacque, according to Ava, sought the arms of any female who was not his wife.

Then there was Ava herself. The vine that tangled us all. The one who yearned for me—a housekeeper of little means. An impossibility trapped in disguise.

I shuddered at the dangerous liaisons binding us.

And what of the evening to come?

I wondered if Ava would be in attendance.

If so, I prayed we could keep the truth of us hidden.

I prayed that all of us could.

The carriage arrived in a timely fashion.

Cristofer maintained a thoughtful silence as we boarded.

Though dressed in his finest suit, his flowing hair oiled back, his fingernails trimmed and buffed, something in his posture lacked its usual vitality. His earlier enthusiasm seeming to have waned.

Chin on hand, he glanced out the window. I observed the gravity of his stare and knew immediately his state of mind.

To him it must have felt like ages since he'd seen Clara. During this time, he had battled the waves of ache and impoverishment induced by her absence.

Now, again, he would stand before her. The object of his desire. And cause of his suffering.

I had no doubt as to the conflicting emotions beguiling his heart. The first being nearly unbearable joy at her return. The second an awful-tasting bitterness that she had abandoned him in the first place. And lastly, muted rage at her steadfast dismissal of his affections.

Having simmered this same vile stew in my own heart, I feared for its impact on his behavior.

Cristofer was already given to impolite slips of the tongue. Especially in defense of his heart. And I could easily recall a half dozen such missteps. For example, when a musically inclined countess, for whose perfume-laden performances he had developed a fancy, rejected his advances on the grounds that she found him prejudiced against the fairer sex, he had explained it was not *all* of the fairer sex whom he found wily and offensive, only her.

Those who are not closely associated with my Cristofer assume such comments to indicate a cruel and misogynistic heart. But I who have benefited from his unyielding regard and sympathy know better.

Cristofer is a complicated creature. Equal parts enchanting and juvenile. Gentle and coarse. A tortured boy dressed in a brave man's clothing. His wayward comments and occasionally brusque nature were, I learned, not the result of base insensitivity but of infamies suffered in the folds of his youth. And so, feeling indebted to his tender heart, while admiring his ripening genius, I kept my vow to protect him.

Given the emotional turmoil likely to unfold that evening, I felt particularly vigilant. Despite being myself in a position of unenviable jeopardy.

The facade of the Thornes' residence came into view, igniting a spark in Cristofer's eyes.

As the horses' hooves clattered to a stop, he said, "Will you come in?"

"No, no. Go ahead. I'll wait," I said, not wanting to impose on their moment of reunion.

No sooner had he descended from the carriage than a commotion arose at the Thornes' front door. We looked up to see Clara stepping outside. Her face drawn. A gaggle of children encircling her. Grabbing at her skirts, her sleeves. Dragging themselves in her wake. Begging her to stay.

Clearly unsettled, Cristofer climbed the stairs and did all he could to appease them, dispensing a pat on the head to one, a sweet to another.

The eldest girl, Marie, joined Cristofer in his efforts. Cradling a toddler in the crook of one arm, she hopped from child to child, attempting to cleave each from her mother, imploring them to hush.

None, it seemed, could be placated.

Overwhelmed by the protest, Clara spun on her heels. "Enough!" she cried.

The children fell silent. Their damp eyes shining.

Taking a deep breath, the great pianist settled to her knees. I watched as she opened her arms and drew them toward her, one at a time. To each child she bestowed an intimate tenderness, straightening one's collar, smoothing another's hair. It was the first time I had ever seen the amazing sensitivity of her hands used for anything other than creating music along the keyboard.

I was left breathless by the authenticity of her affection.

A quick glance in Cristofer's direction told me that he, too, had been taken by her gentleness.

When she had conveyed her love to all, Clara drifted back to her feet.

"Mama's audience is waiting," she told them. "Now be good and go inside. It's nearly time for bed."

The children dutifully obeyed, herding themselves through the door.

Clara watched them go. The strangest expression on her face. *Relief?*

Fracture?

I had always thought Clara somewhat indifferent to her children, viewing them as impediments to her aspirations. Now I wondered if perhaps she, too, yearned for what she could not have.

The carriage creaked as we made our way. Clara sat on the bench opposite us and, for the first several minutes, entertained us with stories of her tour. The dukes she met, the princes, the tiresome critics. Whose piano had been out of tune, whose sublime. It was clear to me she was using the chatter to distance herself from the children. From the life she continually left behind.

I'm not certain that Cristofer recognized it as such. For his part, he leaned forward, relishing her every word.

I could not help but pity him.

The sheer magnetism of her person drew one to her as a chilled animal to the sun. Her effect, I had to admit, was inescapable.

And so he was again doomed to tumble into her snare.

Unable to stop himself, he commented upon her radiance.

Clara blushed.

Falling into silence, they formed a bridge with their eyes.

Even without looking, I could feel the heat.

Perhaps recalling my presence, Clara quickly turned their talk to logistics for that evening's performance.

As the two of them discussed key and measure and how to divvy up the concerto's movements, I looked out the window.

The rhythm of the carriage wheels drew me back to the previous night. To Ava's arms wrapped about me. Her voice in the dark.

She was telling me the story of her husband.

"He was born into nothing and always envious of those who had more," she said. "At an early age he was sent to work as a stable hand for a duke and his family. It was during this time that his ambitions grated heavily against his station. Fortunately, his employer noticed his initiative and rewarded him fairly. A few years later, the duke's only son died at the hands of a mysterious illness. Sick with grief, the two parents fled their home country, taking Jacque with them. At some point they decided to adopt him and raise him as their own."

When Ava recounted Jacque's secret past, my mind flashed back to the conversation we'd had in his study. To the casual way he'd thrown his leg over the arm of his chair. And loaded his pistol.

Recalling the strain of that encounter, I could not help but wonder at the nature of the "mysterious illness" that had taken the duke's son.

She went on.

"With the blessing of his new parents, Jacque went to work

forging every social and professional connection he could make. It soon becoming apparent that his talents lay in the political sphere. When he was offered his first diplomatic post, his supporters quietly suggested that he make it a priority to wed.

"As with all his undertakings, Jacque threw himself into the effort. Still, even as he forged ahead, he was haunted by the fear that his vulgar lineage would be detected. Very little evidence exists, of course, but if one were to investigate thoroughly, the truth could be learned. For this reason, he refused to pursue a woman of noble blood, certain that her father would have him investigated. He therefore set his sights on a peasant girl of, in his words, 'radiant and exceptional beauty.'"

I spun my fingertips in circles along her belly. "He certainly found one," I said.

She offered a brief smile.

"When I met him, I thought him charming. A man of the world. But when he asked for my hand, I refused. I told him that my family relied on the money I earned. And that this small sum made the difference between life and death for my little sister who suffers from a sickly constitution."

I scoffed. "I can only guess what he proposed."

She paused before continuing. "He immediately had an agreement drawn up. As long as our marriage remained in good standing, he would accept the obligation of sending my father a monthly stipend." She sighed. "I can fault him for many things, but in this he has kept his word."

My head fell. "So that is what keeps you under his thumb."

She blanched. Lifted the sheet to cover her breasts. "Does that reduce me in your eyes?"

"Because you made a sacrifice of your life?"

She avoided my gaze. The truth hard for her to bear.

I pulled her close. "It is no reason to be ashamed. My brother did the same. For me."

Her expression lightened. "You have a brother?"

A lump filled my throat.

"I did."

She rested her head along my shoulder. Together we stared into the flames.

Not wanting to sink beneath my sorrows, I said, "Tell me the rest."

She gathered me underneath the covers. Took my hand into hers. "We married in a celebration worthy of royalty and soon became the talk of the town. Invited to every gathering. Every event. It was glamorous and terribly exciting. I met all manner of people. And Jacque treated me like a queen. At first."

Her eyes narrowed. "Then one night we attended a soiree hosted by a well-known rival of his. A man with ambitions ruthless enough to match his own. Our attendance was meant to be a show of strength. The evening featured a pianist performing works of Mendelssohn. The host's wife noticed my interest and asked if I played. Without thinking, I said yes. Believing that if I were invited to perform, my abilities might further elevate Jacque's reputation."

"Did they request that you play?"

"They did."

I smiled gently. Imagining the glorious impact she would have had upon the unsuspecting guests. How every man and woman would have swooned at the beauty laid before them.

"I played Scarlatti's Sonata in D Minor. Then a Chopin nocturne. For which I received an ovation."

"Was Jacque not happy with the result?"

"He seemed so. Then his rival challenged him. 'Surely you can best your wife!' he said, insisting that Jacque play something as well."

"And did he?"

"No. He resisted, saying it would be unseemly to outshine his lovely wife. His declaration charmed the women, of course, and because of this the matter was dropped."

I mulled over her story. The truth coming at last to light.

I looked her straight in the eye. "He cannot play."

She shook her head. "No."

"And because of this," I continued, "he feared that his rival's request would raise suspicions, ones that might ultimately reveal his low birth."

"Yes."

Aghast, I waited for the rest.

"He seemed perfectly at ease the rest of the evening. But when we boarded our carriage for home and the door closed upon us, he became enraged."

"Of course," I said. "He felt betrayed."

"Yes. Instead of a strength, he viewed my talent as a risk. As a hazard to his ambitions. Unfortunately, after that night, I received several requests to perform."

"But after so narrow an escape, he could not accept further risk."

She nodded solemnly. "It was the reason we left Paris."

I sifted my fingers between hers.

"And once you arrived here, he forbade you from playing, in public *or* private. Lest suspicions about him be raised anew."

"Yes." Her expression narrowed. "I fought him, of course. And our arguments became increasingly vicious. His fears and paranoia escalating until—"

"It wasn't a riding accident, was it?" I said, leaping to the most obvious conclusion. "He himself cut off his own finger!"

"*Shot* it off," she corrected.

I recoiled.

"Problem solved," she said, breaking into a twitter, more out of horror than humor. She quieted, then said, "After that, he came to detest me. And though he would never admit this, he resents the creative domain to which I have access. The height to which I can ascend and where he cannot follow. My abilities plus his injury serve as constant reminders of his inferiority. And so, like any man of weakness, he sought to restore his sense of superiority in the arms of lesser women. *Many* of them."

"A habit he flaunted to hurt you."

She nodded. "It has been a difficult time."

I closed my eyes. "Yet you rely on one another."

She said nothing.

Sensing her discomfort, I took up where she'd left off. "And so, to further shore up his image in this new city, he cast himself as music's great benefactor. A collector of grand pianos. A connoisseur of composers. A confidant of famed performers."

"Yes."

I grit my teeth. "A safe disguise indeed. For who would dare question the hand that feeds them?"

"True," she said.

I immediately regretted my statement. Saw how it pricked her conscience. I drew the covers tighter about us. Sat still in the hush.

Until my mind lighted on something incongruous.

"But there is still one thing I don't understand."

"Yes?"

"If he imagines your abilities on the piano to represent such a grave threat, why did he suddenly allow you to take lessons?"

She slipped her hands slowly down my back.

"That," she said, "is a bit more complicated."

The carriage wheels clattered atop the plaza's cobblestones.

Unlike the previous night, the castle was lit to full effect. Candles burning along every rampart. Glowing tall inside windows.

Limber stable hands dashed between troves of richly decorated carriages, their guests emerging in the relaxed pace of the wealthy.

The sight of the castle adorned in such finery spun me in a whirl of déjà vu.

Clara noticed my distress and set her hand atop my knee. I glanced up. She took in my disguise. Tipped her head with a smile. "Ready?" she asked.

Just then the carriage door flew open and a long-coated footman stepped inside to usher the celebrated guests. As Clara and Cristofer emerged, all eyes turned to them. A round of applause spontaneously arose. The two, clasped arm in arm, graciously accepted the cheers, offering humble waves.

I fell behind, careful to keep my distance. Fortunately, my friends' celebrity kept everyone's attention off their lowly page-turner. Quite different from the first time I had approached the castle with Cristofer. But much preferred given the circumstance.

Inside, the atrium smelled of wax and French champagne. Lively conversation lit the corners.

The crowd drew apart as we made our way toward the drawing room.

"Clara! Cristofer!" Jacque boomed before we had crossed the threshold. He greeted Cristofer with a manly embrace. Dropped an elegant bow before Clara. Ignored me entirely.

"But where is Monsieur Thorne?" he asked.

"He was unavoidably detained this evening and sends his deepest regrets," Clara said. Her tone did not invite discussion.

"Ah, but this is my fault," Jacque said, genuinely upset. "There was so little notice given."

A butler approached Jacque from behind. Said something in his ear. Jacque's eyes lit up. He leaned toward his esteemed guests. "Everything is prepared," he told them. "Come this way."

As we crossed the drawing room, I scanned the crowd's fraying edge, hoping to lay eyes upon my love. But she was nowhere to be seen.

I froze when Clara and Cristofer drew back with a gasp. Startled, I peered between them to find whatever had caused their sudden reaction.

There, bathing in a pool of light, sat the great Broadwood, but this time it was accompanied by a second piano. An Érard, much like the Thornes' own, though this one of a far nobler birth. Her flanks glinted with dark chestnut, her fallboard inlaid with swirls of mahogany ivy. Rooted on finely sculpted legs, like fluted cannons, she contained a quiet elegance that one sensed masked a fiery interior. Much like the pianists who would soon approach her.

"Where on earth did you acquire this instrument?" Clara asked in a breathy voice.

Jacque allowed himself a smile. "She came into my hands after a long and laborious negotiation. But I believe the effort was worth the prize. See for yourself," he said, inviting her to sit.

Clara did, her body assuming its customary posture as a bird curves to its nest.

Without further ado, she charged into the introduction of a bagatelle composed by Richard. After only a few measures she drew back.

"Extraordinary!" she exclaimed.

Jacque pat his chest. "I am most pleased to hear this," he said. "I thought her a very fine specimen."

I scowled from the perimeter. Only I knew how tenuous his musical knowledge. How thin his facade of expertise.

My hands quivered, wanting only to wrap themselves around his neck.

Lured by the sound of the piano, the crowd began to advance toward the drawing room.

"Audric!" Jacque called.

The servant appeared instantly. I turned toward him. Dropped a polite nod. He, like his master, ignored me.

His uncustomary rudeness sent a chill through my bones.

Had he learned of our midnight encounter?

Had he informed his master?

"See that the audience is kept at bay until the artists are prepared," Jacque commanded.

Audric enlisted two footmen to redirect the crowd.

Jacque then turned to Cristofer. "You will be left in peace while you prepare. Should you require assistance of any kind, do not hesitate to inform me."

A cheer rose up as the host returned to his guests. Lifting his voice along with a glass, he cried, "My friends, we are in for a spectacular evening!"

When the roar died down, Cristofer turned to Clara. "Which instrument would you prefer?"

I set my case of music on one of the benches, awaiting their decision.

"I assume either will be a pleasure. What is your preference?" she replied.

The two pianos sat side by side so that their keyboards were aligned. As if to create the illusion of a piano with fourteen octaves rather than seven a piece. In this way, I would be able to move between the two instruments and turn pages for both performers.

Cristofer shrugged. "These people have come to hear *you*. Therefore, I think you should play on the Broadwood so that you will be more visible."

"But it is your concerto they have come to hear, not my performance," she countered.

Ah, artists. Forever shoring one another up!

"Please, I insist you play the Broadwood," Cristofer said. "And not another word."

The decision made, I spread the music along each rack. My commission being to turn the music whenever a performer was in action. Each preferring to turn their own pages when not playing.

In the first movement, Clara would take on the part of the piano while Cristofer would re-create the voice of the orchestra behind her. In the second movement, they would reverse the arrangement. Then share the lead in the third.

The undertaking before them, sounding an entire concerto through the channels of four hands, was an enormous one. And would undoubtedly prove even more of a challenge for Clara, as she was less familiar with the work.

Still, both musicians were masters of sight-reading. On several occasions, and for their own amusement, they had spontaneously transcribed one of Richard's concertos while seated at a single piano. Even then, light-hearted as its intent, the resulting performance had been thrilling.

The pianists sat at their respective instruments and strolled through the pages, passing whispers as they undertook small passages.

I could not help but notice the seamlessness with which they worked. The furtive intuition. They studied and considered and moved as though of one body, one mind. Seeming to communicate using the framework of the music itself.

Being able to share such a particular intimacy with Clara was the very thing that kept my liege ensnared.

After surprisingly little time, Cristofer turned to me. "You may tell Monsieur Bertrand that his musicians are ready."

I blanched. The last thing I wanted to do was approach him.

But what choice was left me?

I bowed and disappeared. Assuaging myself with the thought that I might perhaps spot Ava while delivering my missive.

Unfortunately, I arrived at his side without finding her.

"I beg your pardon, Monsieur Bertrand," I mumbled, stepping into the circle that surrounded him.

Every face turned in my direction. I noted several young women, each lovelier than the next.

"Yes? What is it?"

"The pianists wish to inform you that they are ready."

Several of the girls let their eyes run the length of me. Their fans lifting to hide lascivious smiles.

Their reaction was not lost on Jacque.

Turning his back to me, he shouted, "Everyone! Please! See yourselves to the drawing room!"

The crowd rumbled with approval. Jacque ushered his ladies and they slipped away on a sparkling wave.

All but one.

"Good evening, Monsieur Worth."

I turned. Immediately recognized the greasy face. The fat stare. Sarkov.

He had been standing amidst the gaggle of women.

He leaned closer, squinting.

I turned quickly on my heels. "Excuse me," I muttered.

As I followed the crowd, I felt his stare drilling into my back.

CHAPTER 19

*C*ristofer and Clara sat tall at their respective pianos. Waiting for the audience to settle.

From my position between the keyboards, I let my eyes wander across the assembly. Seeking her out.

Unable to find Ava, I began to fear her absent.

What condition could possibly cause her to miss such an event?

Was she suffering punishment for our rendezvous?

In the wake of her previous night's confession, and my being privy now to her most dreadful secret, I found it impossible to staunch the flow of anxiety.

I had nearly stopped breathing when Jacque's voice rang out.

"Darling!"

Heads turned. Necks craned.

She appeared in the hallway. Framed within an arched portal.

She was adorned exactly as she had been the night of the soiree. A velvet gown, stained like blood, low at the neck. The generous ruby seeping from her heart.

Her choice spoke clearly. A secret message meant only for me.

A hush fell over the crowd as she strode gracefully toward her husband.

Waiting in the front row, he offered his hand. She smiled. Laid her palm atop his.

Stones churned inside my belly.

Jacque lowered his wife into her chair. She turned to face Clara and Cristofer. Nodded warmly to each.

Avoided me entirely.

In her presence, the air about me turned fuzzy. Indefinite. I became vaguely aware of someone speaking. Jacque, no doubt. Introducing his guests.

Someone cleared a throat. Did so again.

The piano stormed to life. Rumbling in a low octave.

Someone pressed a heel into mine. It was Clara.

Jolted to attention, I turned and scanned the sheets of music laid across Cristofer's rack.

Below, his left hand trembled within a fearsome trill as he mimicked a cello's rolling growl—the ominous undercurrent beneath the concerto's opening theme. His right hand fired rounds of forceful chords. Then mimicked sharp runs carried by the strings. The notes recoiled from one another in strict angles.

From the corner of my eye, I noticed the audience members shift in their seats. I returned to the score. Deftly removed the first two sheets. Revealing to Cristof his new direction.

After a moment, the opening slowed. The strings smoothed. Their language turning introspective.

The melody's sudden tenderness came as a relief.

The pace continued to slow, luring everyone's heartbeat with it. A gentle sedative. Eventually winding down on three descending notes. An impossibly slow triplet that dropped into silence.

Cristofer stilled. Drew a breath.

I slipped two sheets from the rack.

Then he pounced.

A storm of abrupt chords swiped at the onlookers' heads.

The opening trill returned. Paired as before with its strident theme.

The crowd teetered again on the edge.

I could not help but smile. This was my Cristofer at his best.

Underneath all his finest works, no matter how alluring and melodious, lay an inner tension. An unspoken anguish. And never would he let its presence be forgotten.

The piano's plea chimed on, filling the air with ache.

As if seeking refuge, those in attendance turned their eyes to Clara. Watched her turn the pages of her score.

The question prodding everyone's mind: When would the famed pianist make her entry?

I needn't have looked at my watch to know that Cristofer and the orchestra had been holding sway for nearly two full minutes.

Yet Clara remained still. Her piano silent.

I could feel the collective angst rising.

Such a prominent delay of the featured instrument was unheard of. Even Beethoven, in each of his five concertos, had introduced the piano almost immediately.

Yet now nearly a full *four* minutes had passed.

Beside me, Cristof had begun to glisten from effort.

The audience passed looks of concern. Undoubtedly many of them were thinking that Cristofer had choked under the pressure. That Richard Thorne's public declaration—naming him as the second coming of Ludwig van Beethoven—had left him stricken and reluctant to lift the piano's voice lest its timbre be compared to past genius.

While their supposition might have carried a modicum of legitimacy, it did not encompass the entire truth.

I, on the other hand, had been privy to the forces that had led Cristofer to delay entry of the featured instrument.

The truth was, Cristofer viewed the concerto's commission as an opportunity for him to express his profound love for Clara. In his mind the concerto represented his grandest love letter. His most earnest confession. A testament of all he held sacred.

But just as his love for Clara was wrought with complication and tumult, so was his composition. From its earliest measures, Cristofer had attempted to master the love over which he, in reality, wielded only the weakest influence. His was a predicament that would not bend to his will. And so, through the delay of Clara's entry, he had endeavored, if only briefly, to exert control. To hold her passions at bay as she did his.

If words had been chosen to attend the music by way of narrative, they might have said something like, "You have now entered *my* world, Clara. I will tell you when you may approach, when you may lift your voice. In the meantime, you must listen to *me*. Must give ears to the urgencies of my heart. And wait to speak until I am done with my exclamations!"

I cannot say that his technique was altogether ineffective. During the opening, I noted an uncharacteristic tenseness inhabiting Clara's person. A wringing of her hands. A tightening along her brow. Held captive in the swell of his music, she had heard his message. Of this I had no doubt.

But what of the audience?

Cristofer's pace again began to slow. Approaching an idle.

At this cue, Clara sat up and shifted toward the keys.

The audience drew its breath. Held still as Cristofer floated back. His hands dropping upon his knees. His final note sustained by the pedal, which he seemed reluctant to release.

To my left, I sensed the pressure building inside Clara as she restrained herself.

Then.

Cristofer lifted his foot. Revealing silence.

Clara set upon the keys at once. A hawk to its prey. Her talons driving into the flesh of my theme.

My knees weakened to hear my work beneath her hands.

She distilled it into the purest tincture of pain and joy I have ever heard.

The melody surged on.

Moments later I found myself aroused by the rawness of Clara's interpretation. As if she had stepped into my interior chambers and read me from within. Thus affected, I dared not look upon her.

And in that moment I tasted the torture that Cristofer endured. The despair of his being kept from the soul who could most clearly see him.

Seeking distraction, I peeked at the audience. Found every eye fixed upon Clara.

Except hers.

Ava sat motionless. Breathless. Her gaze upon me.

I returned to my duties. Swept two sheets for Clara. When I did, the pianist's eyes flashed to mine. Sharply. I avoided her look.

The music leapt forward. My theme dissolving seamlessly back into that written by Cristofer.

When the composer leaned again to the keys, he did so gently. Slipping into his chords quietly. Lending harmonic support.

Having set aside his anguish and abandoned his need for control, he strove to create a space in which Clara could shine. Could be cherished and adored by her listeners, as by him.

Immersed, Clara's body swayed. Music dripping from her fingertips. The good and noble part of Cristofer now speaking. Temperately. Of forgiveness. Of hope.

The moment was sublime. The musicians held in the sway of a tide that pulled on them equally.

To watch them, each suspended in the thrall of the other, was to witness their common poetry. Their hypnotic affinity.

No one, I felt sure, could fail to notice.

For the first time since his departure, I found myself glad that Richard was not present.

But, as with all love that is not free to roam, and lovers who are not free to speak, the performers' sweetness soon turned acidic.

With a rapid escalation of volume, Clara grabbed hold of Cristofer's initial theme. Pounding its intent with a fury meant to match, if not overwhelm, his own.

But Cristofer had not left himself without ammunition. Armed with handfuls of weighty chords, he faced her assault head on.

In an emotional maelstrom, each pianist launched brazen phrases at the other like cannon shot. The main theme claimed by one then the other in a nerve-wracking exchange.

I leapt between the racks as the two faced off. Pulling sheets as though lighting fuses.

In the audience, no one stirred. The only movement, the frantic waving of ladies' fans.

Then came the crushing blow: my theme's return.

The unrelenting minor chords scaled toward the sky. Their desperate intensity heightened by the variation Cristofer had composed.

The sound traveled to grip every throat. Penetrating each listener with the most intimate of hungers.

I marveled at its impact. And the tears that came to their eyes.

But I was most startled when I bent before Clara and found even her eyes glistening. I had never seen her lose control during a performance.

Yet there was no time to ponder my observation. Needing to attend to Cristofer's score.

The performance rumbled on.

At last, Clara attacked her final notes. Striking them with feverish intent. When she had concluded, her entire body sagged. Sank limply from the keyboard. As though she might expire.

Alone, Cristofer struggled to bring the piece to a close. Tackling the final runs with reckless abandon.

Finally he stilled. Then, with considerable restraint, planted the final four notes.

When he removed his foot from the pedal, the silence rang as loud as the music.

No one moved.

I rushed to set the music for the second movement.

Unexpectedly, the spectators leapt to their feet. Roaring.

Normally, applause were held until the end. But not so tonight. The opening allegro had moved the audience beyond propriety.

In the uproar, I sought her eyes. Found her trembling. Her visage misty and lush. The directness of her stare conducting a bolt of heat into my person.

I turned away. Only to find Clara's eyes upon me with an equal intensity. Saying nothing she stood and went to Cristofer. Ringed an arm through his. Accepted the accolades.

After an appropriate delay, Cristofer escorted Clara back to her bench.

The audience settled itself amidst murmurs and the brushing of fabric.

Cristofer dropped to his seat. Lifted his cuffs. His expression darkening.

I knew well his intentions for the adagio. That he wished it to be a consecration. An exultation of his love.

And though I had never heard the movement, nor laid eyes upon the score, I expected its performance, given Clara's presence, to be difficult.

Wanting him to feel my support, I moved closer to his side.

He then pushed gingerly off the shore. Floating forward on a dramatic swell. An ever-expanding ring of dual chromatic scales. Blossoming with excess.

After hearing only a few measures, I knew the horrible truth.

He had missed his mark.

He'd allowed sentimentality to overcome musical awareness. The result being, much like his first attempt at the concerto's introduction, garish and overwrought. Milky with emotions that lacked authentic underpinnings.

I could sense Clara's displeasure.

Determined to see Cristofer through, I kept my presence alongside him steady. Knowing that, as before, a slight reworking and polishing of the piece would uncover its cache of hidden gems.

But that would come later.

Preoccupied with such thoughts, I was startled by the entry of Clara's piano. This time she took up the role of the orchestra. Unlike the ensemble that Cristofer commanded in the first movement, this one had a decidedly diluted tone. Its harmonies thin and uncommitted. Providing only a meager background for the main theme.

Meanwhile, Cristofer bent to his labors. His expression pained. His brow dripping.

I leaned closer. Drawn by the need for repair.

Peering over his shoulder, I scanned the music. Upon noting the phrases, I was overcome with the urge to stop him. Make suggestions. Lead him in a different direction.

Clara emitted a sharp hiss. I started and pulled back. Realizing I had been looming inappropriately close to the performer.

My participation would have to wait.

The rest of the movement unfolded without undue ceremony. Its conclusion arriving in a gale of exuberant arpeggios.

When it settled, the audience did not erupt with cheers but remained silent.

I looked over at Cristofer. His expression was elated. For him the piece had come off brilliantly. Adrift in his own passions, he had not noticed the audience's lackluster response. Or, if he did, held little regard for their opinion.

Seeming eager to put distance between themselves and the

adagio's overt sentimentality, Clara raised up and seized upon the presto. It burst open with effervescence.

Cristofer bent back to the keys. With a powerful lunge he took up the orchestra. Luring her onward.

I snuck at look at the crowd. Found them held again in rapt attention.

Then came the moment of exchange. When Clara and Cristofer would switch roles. She taking the orchestra, he the piano.

I bounced on my knees in anticipation. Knowing I would need to leap quickly to execute rapid pulls for each.

But when the moment arrived, nothing happened. Or, rather, something entirely unexpected happened.

Disregarding the agreed-upon cue, Clara did not switch to the role of orchestra, but marched forward with the piano's score.

Cristofer glanced up quickly.

Clara did not return his look.

Staring agape at his love, he recognized immediately the obstinate lines digging into her brow. And knew she would not relent. That she was determined to see the piece to its conclusion. With herself at the helm.

From my vantage, I sensed Clara wanted to unleash a performance so fiery and explosive that it would vaporize the mediocre second movement from memory.

And Cristofer's third movement was undoubtedly powerful enough to succeed. Setting aside sentimentality, it embraced a grand heroism.

Having quickly assessed the situation, and knowing his score by heart, Cristofer returned to the keyboard and dove back inside the piece.

Above, the chandeliers hummed.

Below, the ladies' fans flickered.

The performance swelled as the two rushed onward.

When Clara relented, the orchestra momentarily taking the lead, she fell back. But there was no time to rest.

Gathering herself, she leaned forward to pull two sheets.

When she did, I saw her cheeks drain to white.

I panicked at her response.

Had I misordered the pages?

I rushed to her side. Hoping I could right the matter in time for her imminent entry.

Following her stare, my eyes quickly lighted on the thing that had shaken her. Displayed on the rack was a sheet from an entirely different work.

Mine.

I lunged to tear it down.

Before I could get hold, Clara's hand shot out and seized my wrist.

I gasped at the crushing power of her grip.

Holding me firm, she examined the score.

Having seen our tussle from the corner of his eye, Cristofer turned a questioning look upon me. I returned a helpless shrug.

Seeing my distress, the audience let out a laugh, thinking our antics a pre-arranged part of the performance.

Ridden with anxiety, I turned to Clara. "Your entry approaches," I warned.

When she missed her cue, Cristofer hurled a more frantic look our way. Storming ahead, he then reversed direction to repeat the last several measures. Hoping, I assumed, that Clara would this time make her cue.

Ignoring the performance, Clara kept her eyes on my music. After what felt like an eternity, she loosened her grip. When she did, I reached up and tore down the page.

I rifled through the remaining score. Relieved to find it all in order, I set the proper sheets and returned to position.

Cristofer stormed ahead, approaching Clara's cue a second time. When it arrived, she leapt into a passage of brilliant proportions. Unleashed, she charged up and down the keyboard, the keys relenting beneath her strikes.

The audience erupted with shouts of enthusiasm.

Overcome, Cristofer laughed aloud.

Together they raced toward the finale. Each performer hammering out their final cadences. The conclusion leaving the audience breathless.

Barely had the piece ended when Cristofer leapt to his feet. His body abuzz. His spirits soaring. He rushed to Clara's side. Helped her to her feet. Embraced her with fervor.

The crowd burst into wild, jubilant cheering.

Not to be outdone, Jacque rushed onto the stage. Made a show of bestowing generous embraces.

The crowd soon broke its bounds. A gaggle of young females rushing forward to encircle the shining Cristofer. A band of men dropping bows before Clara.

I wilted with relief.

The percussive pop of champagne corks ricocheted high off the stone walls.

Jacque called out, "Everyone! Please! Join us in the banquet hall for refreshments and delicacies!"

I winced at his showmanship. His false gallantry. And wished immediately to return home.

But I could not.

Would not.

Abandon her.

The evening unfolded along a spine of sparkle. Those who had gathered having been electrified by the concerto and the privilege of witnessing its preview.

Witty conversation, laughter, and the clinking of glasses prevailed.

Intent on finding my love, I stirred into the crowd, ignoring the sometimes odd, sometimes lusty looks tossed by those I brushed past.

Eavesdropping as I went, I noted that most were singing the praises of the first and third movements. The exultation. Athleticism. Originality. Everyone proclaiming that the concerto would earn Jacque, Cristofer, and Clara the highest praises when it premiered abroad.

For all their effusiveness, however, not one person mentioned the adagio.

"May I refill your champagne, Monsieur Worth?" someone asked.

I spun. Startled to hear my name.

There before me stood the stable boy. A bottle of Veuve Clicquot tipping from his gloved hand.

"Thank you," I muttered.

"Brilliant performance," he said.

I sipped my champagne. Wished for him to leave. When he did not, I said, "Don't you normally see to the horses?"

"Yes," he replied. "But we were short a hand this evening. Too many officers to attend to."

"Officers?" I asked. Then noticed a large group of military types lingering nearby.

The boy nodded. "Here to show their support."

"Support for what?"

He made a strange face. "Haven't you heard?"

I shook my head. "Apparently not."

The boy leaned in. Slurred. "The chancellor has appointed Monsieur Bertrand to be his minister of foreign affairs."

"Ah," I said.

So, Jacque's acts of showmanship, however false, were paying off.

The boy ran the back of a hand across his lips. Glanced about quickly. In a low voice said, "I, myself, believe he tenders a wish to one day be emperor."

My eyebrows rose at his words.

"*His ambitions are monstrous*," Ava had said of her husband's desires.

Behind us, someone bellowed with laughter. We turned to see Sarkov heading in our direction.

The stable boy cringed. "Pardon me," he said, and darted into the crowd.

Seeking a place of safety, I sequestered myself behind a tapestry hung in a far corner. From this vantage I scanned the hall. In the center of the great room, I spotted Cristofer lifting sifters of brandy and cigars with Jacque and a handful of generals.

Cristofer said something and the men erupted with laughter. He was alive with charm. Gilt by victory.

Good for you, Cristof, I thought.

Searching a wider swathe, I then found Clara along the periphery. She, too, had absconded to a distant corner. Notoriously reticent and loathing of chatter, flattery, and spirits of every kind, she'd kept herself hidden. It was only after observing her for a moment that I noticed how the light of her attention remained fixed on a distant object. Curious, I turned my gaze to follow the trajectory of hers.

What had piqued her interest?

I shivered when I saw what it was.

Or, rather, *who.*

I watched as Clara lifted her skirts and advanced across the room. Some keen purpose animating her step.

Ava had just separated from a group of doting gentlemen when Clara approached. Stood before her. Said something I could not hear.

In response, Ava smiled and held out her hand. The two exchanging a tender greeting. But when Ava released her hand, Clara held it fast. Without a word, the elder woman spread our hostess's palm across hers. Observed it intently.

Ever poised, Ava submitted calmly to her guest's unusual scrutiny.

Without lifting her eyes from Ava's hand, Clara asked a question.

Ava answered. Gave another smile, though with less enthusiasm.

How I strained to hear what was passing between them!

But before more could be said, two men approached. Eager to pay their respects to the renowned pianist.

With an affable nod, Ava excused herself and disappeared into the crowd.

From behind me, a voice declared, "You seem to have quite a fancy for her."

I whirled to face the speaker.

"I beg your pardon?"

Sarkov laughed. Spread a palm along his plump jowl. "For the monsieur's *wife*," he said.

"Certainly not," I protested. Fear taking root in my bowels.

"No? Then perhaps it is the great pianist for whom your ardor burns?"

I said nothing. My limbs trembling.

"But no, I would not think Madame Thorne to the liking of someone so dashing as yourself," he said. "Far too plain. Too prudish." He pinned me with a stare. "Unless, of course, your main obsession is for *married* women."

Uncertain how to respond to his accusations, and not wishing to lift my voice any more than necessary, I attempted to push past.

He snagged me with a beefy paw. Drew me close.

"You've tasted how jealous a character our Monsieur Bertrand. And how well armed," he hissed into my ear. "Just imagine what unpleasant consequences might arise were someone to plant a seed of doubt in his mind."

"You're mad," I said. Tore from his grasp. "I have no interest in the monsieur, nor his holdings."

Saying this, I fled into the crowd.

All of us were silent on the carriage ride home. Each lost in their own thoughts. Cristofer and I intoxicated. Clara exhausted.

We had been seen off by Jacque and Ava. While the four of them shared flattery and embraces, I had stood at a distance.

When we turned to depart, I'd sought again to catch Ava's eye. Desperately wanting to know the nature of what had passed between her and Clara. But instead of making a connection, I watched as Jacque pressed a hand against the small of her back and steered her back to their guests.

Emboldened by drink, I determined to follow. And had taken a step in their direction when Clara hooked her elbow through mine.

With a firm yank, she spun me round, ushering me toward the plaza.

The horses' hooves churned the gravel as our carriage made its way home.

We were nearly to the Thornes' when Clara broke the silence.

"Have you scheduled a rehearsal with the orchestra?" she asked.

Cristofer nodded. "In a week's time."

"Good. Very good," she said.

The carriage jerked to a stop in front of her home. A single light glowed in the kitchen window. The children long asleep.

The driver opened the door.

Cristofer hopped out. Held up a chivalrous hand.

Before exiting, Clara turned to me. "Henri, I have a small favor to ask. If you would be so kind as to drop by at your leisure, we can discuss it in more detail."

I knew immediately her desire for a meeting had nothing to do with a favor of any kind.

"Of course," I said.

I watched as the pair strode to the front door. Stood outside speaking in hushed tones.

I tensed. Dreading the nature of the remarks that alcohol might be loosening from my liege.

After some time, Cristofer took a nearly imperceptible step forward. When he did, Clara glanced over his shoulder. Seeing the driver in full view, she pulled back. Noting this retreat, Cristofer lifted his palms. Waved his arms about. Pleading. Then, without warning, dropped to his knees before her.

Clara stiffened at this grossly inappropriate gesture. Then whirled around and disappeared inside.

When the door slammed, Cristofer's head dropped as though by guillotine.

I kept silent as the carriage shuttled us homeward. My patron stewing in the shadows. The night's success diluting with heartache.

"Let's be off to the Hedgehog!" he burst out, referring to the local tavern where he often planted his sorrows and harvested young ladies.

His sudden request caught me off guard.

"Now?"

"Of course!"

I could hear the slur in his voice. Knew I should accompany him. Lend a sympathetic ear. Yet I felt tapped. My heart craving isolation. And silence.

"I would, Cristofer. It's just that ... it's that *time*," I explained, implying I was in the throes of a woman's monthly inconvenience.

"Oh," he said, unsettled. "In that case we shall take you straight home."

When I stepped down, Cristofer leaned out the window. Laid

a hand on my arm. "Thank you for tonight, Henri. You performed wonderfully."

"It was *you* who performed," I said. "A massively brilliant preview."

He allowed himself a wan smile. "See you in the morning?"

"Of course."

I gave a small wave, knowing he would likely not return for days.

"Driver!" he shouted. "To the Hog!"

Standing in the wake of his departure, I prayed, as I always did, for his safety.

The downy bed softened about me, cradling my bones. Weary, I breathed into the dark. Happy to finally have rest.

Outside the night simmered with churring crickets. Screeching fox.

No sooner had I closed my eyes than I felt my consciousness thinning. Its curling and intoxicated tendrils conspiring to transport me back to the previous night.

To the glowing fire.

Her delicate touch.

And sad confession.

In my recall, I had just inquired as to why, given his prior refusal, Jacque would suddenly allow her to take lessons.

She rolled away from me.

"Ava?" I pleaded.

She drew inward. Seeming at battle with some internal fear. After a moment, in a voice husky with emotion, she said, "On the morning of the soiree I woke and realized I could not go on."

I stared into the dark.

Had she really meant what I thought?

She rolled back to face me. Her expression earnest. Weighted.

My heart iced over.

"What are you saying?" I asked, terrified she would confirm my worst fear.

"When he forbade my making music, life left me," she said. "And so, that morning, I decided to leave."

I pitched over a wave of nausea.

She let out a little laugh. "It was all carefully plotted," she said. "I'd purloined one of his firearms. The necessary accouterments. And hidden them in a tree."

She swept a curl from her cheek.

"My plan was to attend the soiree, then, after the guests had departed, disappear into the forest and never return."

I kept silent.

"Darling, you're shaking," she said.

My mind reeled as she drew me closer. "But what about your

sister? And the stipend to your family?" I asked, shocked that she would consider abandoning them.

"Under the terms of our agreement, he would be required to continue his support," she confirmed. "His obligation would cease only if I were to leave him."

Somewhere beneath me, the earth slipped.

"Please," she urged. "Know that my wish to depart was not because I did not want life. But because I wanted it *too much*. With all possible relish. And intensity. Having learned to drink from a goblet, I could not be condemned to sip from a thimble."

She lifted my face close to hers. "Do you understand?"

I did, indeed, understand.

A dog howled in the distance.

"What stopped you?" I finally managed.

She smiled.

"You did."

"What? Because you saw me?"

"No, because I *heard* you."

I balked. Prepared, yet again, to deny her accusation that my music lived inside Cristofer's.

"Ava, I think you were misunderstanding—"

She interrupted with a strange laugh. "Actually, I understood perfectly."

Her gaze lost focus as she returned her mind to that evening.

"The approach of death is a queer phenomenon," she mused. "One usually thinks of it as an increasing darkness. The slow cessation of sight and sound. And yet, having accepted my end, having tasted it along my tongue, a new reality unveiled itself before me." Her eyebrows furrowed. "It was as if a mask had been peeled away. Revealing the purity of things—the light beneath." She held perfectly still. "Though that night I was staring death in the face, never in all my life had I felt so vividly *alive*."

I shivered. Recalling how luminous her Beauty. How brilliant her Light.

"But that still doesn't explain how, or why, as you claim, you fell in love with me."

She grinned.

"When the footman announced Monsieur Vaughn's arrival, we all turned in anticipation. And whereas everyone's eyes fell upon the composer, mine fell upon you."

"But I was dressed as a lady … "

"True. But it was not your costume that drew me." She took my face between her fingers. "It was your shine."

A coal popped in the fire.

I flinched. My heart on edge.

She continued. "I feel it almost futile to describe the entirety of what I beheld that evening. But you were … *alight*. Like the sun. Ablaze with color. To be honest, it hurt to look upon you. And so I turned away."

"But you must have looked again?"

"No. I gathered myself. Recommitted to my plan. And withdrew."

"Then what happened?" Having asked this, I looked between the velvet curtains. Saw dawn's inky approach. Tried not to let the length of our visit concern me.

Ava sighed. "Then Monsieur Vaughn came to the Broadwood." Her breath caught. "His music. The lush tone of that piano. It spread over my heart. Like a healing balm. But then the music suddenly shifted. It transformed. And instead of soothing, it pierced my soul."

I knew the exact moment she was describing—the passage when my theme settled over his.

"I cannot tell you how that music dismantled me. Shucked me from myself. Inflating me with a longing that swelled beyond the bounds of my body. And then I spotted you for a second time. Hidden in the shadows. And I knew. Deep in my marrow. I just *knew*." She squeezed her eyes against the intensity of her recollection, then said, "In that moment, thoughts of death left me. And all I wanted was to live. If only in the faintest hope that—someday—I might know you."

She laughed, swiping at tears. "You must think me a fool."

"No," I breathed.

Soothed by my assurances, she lowered her face. Pressed her cheek to my chest. Told me the rest of her story.

"Shortly afterward, I told him of my plan. And swore to him that I would carry it out if he did not allow me certain freedoms." I considered this.

"He would be terrified of losing you," I said, "because of the damage it would inflict upon his reputation—even more so were you to perish by your own hand. So he permitted you to seek instruction, but only on the condition of utter secrecy. And a veil of amateurism."

She nodded.

"And that is why you initially agreed to a female instructor. Because you were hoping Clara would recommend *me*."

"Yes," she said. Blushed.

"But when I returned for the second time, with Cristofer, you saw me in disguise."

She laughed. "Of course I wasn't entirely certain at first. But then, when I heard you play…" her voice trailed off, her eyes lowered, "I knew it was you. And your daring masquerade only enticed me further."

This time it was my turn to blush. I laid back, giddy from the revelations.

Outside a rooster crowed. His cackling a sharp reminder that soon the world would wake.

I did not want to leave. But knew I could not remain.

"My love," I said, "I should go."

Her head dropped into the pillows. Her lashes sparkling. Webbed with tears. "I know."

Despite my conviction, we remained still. Neither wanting to be the first to rise.

But as the minutes passed, my giddiness drained, leaving only fatigue. And a sadness.

For Jacque would soon return.

Who knew how long it would be until we could spend another night?

Or ...

If ever?

CHAPTER 20

When Cristofer did not return the following morning, my mind began to expand into what I anticipated would be several days alone.

I could not remember the last time I'd enjoyed such a generous span of solitude.

Cradling my coffee, I went to the piano. Lingering before her, I wondered briefly how it felt to always have one's innards on display.

"It was not your costume that drew me. It was your <u>shine</u>."

With a heat inside that bordered on fever, I set down my demitasse and strode to the drawer that contained my manuscript.

Sitting at the piano, my mind turned to the accident that had occurred at the Bertrands'—the sheet of my score having become tangled in Cristofer's. Determined not to have such a calamity repeat, I set about reassembling the entire manuscript.

When every page had been accounted for, I set the emerging score along the rack and launched into it.

As the music unfolded, I found myself suddenly unsettled by its ambiguity.

To begin with, the piece had no particular form. Up to that point, I'd merely followed the honeyeater's inspiration, allowing it to inform the voice of a piano. That lone voice, however, had eventually called forward an instrumental accompaniment. But the wandering meditation did not conform to any distinct classification—neither chamber music nor symphony.

What, then, was its purpose?

And without a traditional form, who would ever hear it?

I sat back. Irritated.

The ambiguity had never bothered me before. I'd merely allowed the spirits to convey me wherever they wished.

Why, then, did it bother me now?

I got up. Roamed the room.

"If such a thing were possible, I would be with you for all my days."

Hearing these words again, I felt my gut thicken. And soon realized the source of my irritation. I'd become bloated with ambiguity. Stuffed with the unknown.

I leaned against the steady horizon of a windowsill.

Would nothing I wished for find its skin? Would all I love drift into formlessness?

Was this the sad fate the soothsayer had foretold?

As I wondered these things, something swept before me.

A sound.

I tilted my head. Heard an irregular pulse. A hollow rapping along the roof of my skull.

Then a tone, burnished, of woodwind, sheathed itself about the rhythm. Enriching its voice. Meshing flesh to body.

Thus defined, the rhythm flowered.

I pressed my palms against my head. Notes, harmonies, counterpoints coming fast. Of their own accord. Splashing about me in gorgeous downpour.

Then came a flash.

Hot and bright.

When it relented, I saw a bridge. Yet to be built. One stanchion lay anchored in the piece beneath me, its future span arching toward Ava.

Seeing this, I understood.

Each ambiguity possessed an aim for the other.

The piece I was composing was meant for Ava. Was *of* her.

In her, the work would find its form.

And she, upon hearing it, would find hers.

Ours.

Lured by this notion, I dropped once more to the bench. Lifted my quill. And without hesitation began inking silent notes onto parchment.

Composition is a strange act in this regard. Such enormity of song arising from muted symbols. From the soundless mind. For I have yet to hear anyone putting their ear to a composer's skull and detecting a melody within. Which sometimes makes me wonder if heaven itself may not be a silent world. Our music, then, but a gross impersonation of its rich and pure peace.

Despite this contemplation, a timpani belted percussive beats against my ears. Its copper belly resounding.

I shut my eyes against the world. And returned to work.

Raising stones into the arch, one note at a time.

I cannot say for certain how long I lay curled within the chaise. My breath steady. My heart content.

Day had shifted into night and back again while I'd slept.

The manuscript lay stacked on the piano.

Complete.

Roaming in the dream world, I imagined greeting Ava for her

lesson. Sitting at her piano. Waiting for her to settle. Then launching into the piece whose every note and counterpoint I had polished with devotion. With a passion I could not restrain.

My heart rose with joy to imagine her unbridled response. Her utter acceptance of my invitation.

Be with me, the music urged.

I saw her stand. Begin to approach.

Then something clattered.

I sat up quickly. Scanned the cottage. Saw that the breeze had knocked over the broom.

Everything else was as I'd left it.

Cristofer, it seemed, had not returned.

I felt a twinge of worry.

Held in the thrall of composing, I had given little thought to my benefactor's whereabouts.

Should I go look for him?

I recalled the depth of his despair and decided to give him one more day. He undoubtedly needed the company he was keeping. For I knew that, despite its depravity, it wielded for him a restorative power.

And besides, I had another errand to which I should attend.

Having wended my way through the forest, I soon found myself upon the street. I paused to let a carriage go by. Felt the grind of wheels against cobblestone drawing me down into that dark place.

Fortunately, the music of a piano halted my descent. Drifting slowly through a window.

Its effect stronger for the fact that the window was open.

And stronger still in that the window belonged to Clara Thorne.

I mounted her doorstep and listened. It was a lovely piece. Forthright and audacious. The introductory movement from one of Richard's early sonatas.

Listening, I glanced down the road. Toward town. Toward the bridge. And the swift waters he had begged to drown his life.

I wondered what he had seen on that final stroll.

Had he noticed the row of willow trees to the left? The children's bicycles balanced along the fence? The splash of scarlet tulips beneath the neighbor's stairs?

Or had his eyes been fixed in darkness?

I shuddered, recalling Ava's confession. *"My wish to depart was not because I did not want life. But because I wanted it too much."*

Inside, the music ceased.

I knocked.

Heard footsteps. The creak of door.

"Henri!" Clara exclaimed when she saw me.

I bowed. Apologized for arriving unannounced.

"No, no!" she said. Drew her hands down the front of her dress. Righted a loose pin in her hair. "Now is an excellent time. Please. Come in."

After hanging up my cape, she led us into the kitchen. Set the kettle on the stove. Drew down cups and saucers. A tin of tea.

Watching her work, I noticed the taut arc of her belly. Her condition slowly becoming visible.

Not wanting to stare, I inquired, "Where are the children?"

She brought a tray of cream and sugar. "With their tutors," she said. "Hopefully learning their letters."

"And if not?"

"Then perhaps chasing frogs," she said. Leveled a weary smile. "I do hope they amount to something."

I laughed. "They come from good stock. How could they not?"

"Yes," she said. Drifted back to the stove.

I regretted my comment. Sought a way to move beyond it.

"You mentioned a task I might help with?"

She placed a tray of biscuits between us. Poured our tea.

I had the distinct impression she intended to broach a difficult subject.

She blew across her cup. Her keen gray eyes softening behind the steam.

I reached for a biscuit.

"I met Richard when I was quite young," she said.

The biscuit froze at my lips.

It was not just the fact that she had mentioned Richard, but that she was sharing such an intimate memory with me, the housekeeper.

"My father did not want us to marry," she said. Tossed a hand. "In fact, he went to great lengths to prevent it."

I had heard the stories from Cristofer. Clara's father had so gravely objected to his young daughter's intentions, and those of her elder suitor, that he'd launched a lawsuit in order to prevent matrimony.

"It was not out of cruelty, mind you," she said. "But arose from his singularly focused desire for my success."

It was widely known that Clara's father, a gifted pedagogue, had devoted his life to honing and shaping her extraordinary musical gift.

"But it would have been impossible to halt our joining," she continued. "I had already recognized Richard's genius. And unfortunately, to the young, to the innocent and uninitiated, such a glow is irresistible. Such recognition taking on a holiness that cannot be denied."

I shifted in my seat. My thoughts having lighted upon Ava. And the heated recognition that had passed between us.

A glint came into Clara's eyes. She leaned forward.

"There are those, Henri, who are born possessing a lantern inside their soul. Whose capacity for light is receptive to Creation itself. And it is Creation that compels such souls to give body to what they feel and see and hear—to manifest artistic forms through which their majestic glimpses can be shared. And it is these same who nourish humanity, who draw us forward toward what is ever possible."

I kept silent. My hands on the table. I had not expected to hear such philosophies. And could not imagine the purpose in her conveying such thoughts.

"Such was the capacity I recognized within Richard." She narrowed her eyes. "And, as time has passed, it is the same capacity I have come to recognize within you."

I sat back with a jolt. Instinctively fending off her effusion.

"It is *you* who possesses such capacity, Clara, not I."

"No. I have not been gifted that particular channel, the intense receptivity that you and Richard possess," she insisted. "For my part, I am an interpreter. No more. As such I am called upon to reproduce the works of others. To let them sing forth. *Not* to create them. In this way, we interpreters forge the structure of the shrine—but are not its animating spirit. Do you see?"

I didn't know if I did.

Her voice fell to a whisper. "But you, Henri, have inherited the power to liberate eternity. To instill human life and endeavor with meaning."

I shrank back. Her intent now fully transparent.

"Those are large assertions to make based upon one page of scribbles," I said, foolishly thinking I could undermine her conviction.

Clara huffed. "Those were no mere scribbles, Henri," she asserted. "And I hope you don't plan on wasting more of my time with foolish disclaimers."

I froze. The air about me roaring.

For the life of me I could not conceive how Clara had divined the dream that laid dormant inside my heart. How she could have unearthed my longing from one glimpse of a single sheet.

I knew only that I had to make some protest, any protest, that would throw her off the scent.

"Clara, I have no interest in a composer's life," I began. "In any case, following such an avenue would not even be possible for me. Firstly, as you know, I lean entirely toward solitude and could not endure the required publicity. Secondly, I have no credentials to speak of. And thirdly, I am a woman and would, therefore, not be received."

The latter was a hard argument to make when I sat before her dressed as a man. But I made it nevertheless.

Clara sat up. Broke into a victorious smile and said, "For your objections, I have obtained solutions."

"You've done *what?*" I sputtered.

She returned to the stove. Set about refilling our tea. Calmly. As if she had not just made an incendiary remark. As if she had not just slipped the floorboards from beneath my feet.

"While on tour I made an acquaintance," she said. "A very wealthy and influential individual. A count. Who, though possessing little musical ability himself, is keenly attuned to the talent in others. He is also a lover of novelty and does not flinch from the eccentric. After coming to know him, I explained your situation and outlined what I felt you would require to develop your particular gifts—"

"You *mentioned* me?"

How dare she invade my privacy. Open my secrets to the world!

"Calm yourself, Henri!" she roared back with a ferocity that cowered my own. "I did not give away your name nor your location. Merely your circumstance."

I kept to my seat. Fuming along with the tea.

No stranger to opposition, Clara pressed on. "After some period of discussion, he became duly intrigued and requested that I make you the following offer: That you become a resident of his estate. That you make composing your primary occupation. And that you relinquish half your profits, including all royalties, to him."

My eyes widened.

The windows began to smear.

"In exchange, he will keep your identity a secret. Further, he will serve as your ambassador to the world at large, delivering your music into the hands of the finest talents—thereby absolving you of all public duties—while at the same time guaranteeing your work a grand and enthusiastic reception."

I stared at her, blind.

It was not just the presentation of the offer that had me riled.

But the question of *why* Clara, with all the predicaments and difficulties she faced, had gone to such lengths to secure it.

Despite my obvious distress, she excused herself from the room.

Her abrupt departure only increasing my exasperation.

I sprang to my feet and careened along the cabinetry. My mind spinning with competing and contradictory thoughts.

What if I were to try and make a life composing?

Not just writing under the shadow of another, but for myself, in my own name?

Just contemplating the possibilities unsettled me. Made me want to laugh out loud and scream at the same time.

But what of Cristofer?

He relied on me. Utterly. For comfort. For vision.

And I owed the man my very life.

To abandon him now would deliver a crushing blow.

I couldn't possibly forsake him.

Certainly not for my own gain.

I halted, having become trapped in a corner of drawers. Thus stilled, my mind collided with yet another impediment.

And what of Ava?

If I were to take a commission, I would have to resign as her instructor. Relinquishing the only avenue through which I might ever see her.

Before I could even contemplate an answer to either obstruction, a strange thought arose. This novel thought felt prickly. Unfamiliar. A new coat untried.

If I were to remain in service to my benefactor and in thrall to my love—what, ultimately, would become of me?

The question yawned wide.

I reeled from it.

"Well? What have you decided?" Clara demanded, storming back into the kitchen.

I jumped.

"Good God, Henri. Are you alright?"

I opened my lips to speak but could not issue a sound.

"Please, sit," she urged.

She pulled her chair alongside me. Pressed a hand to mine.

"Forgive me. I should have anticipated the impact my news would have. Such an extraordinary opportunity, arising out of the blue, must certainly come as a shock. I should really have done more to prepare you."

I felt my heart dividing.

Clara shone her eyes into mine. "Henri, you cannot keep your sheen hidden forever. Creation wishes to speak through you. And I am imploring, *begging*, you to listen!"

I broke my gaze from hers. Rushed back to safety. "No. I cannot," I said. My head shaking wildly. "Thank you for your efforts, Clara. But I cannot do this."

"Henri—"

"Please! Say no more! And I beg of you. Do not mention this again."

She sat back. Her eyes burning through me.

"It's because of her, isn't it?"

"What?"

"Because of Ava. You've fallen in love with her."

I laughed. "Madame Bertrand? Don't be absurd! She is a student. And a mediocre one at that."

Clara's mouth tightened. Her demeanor hardening.

"I held her hands and felt for myself the truth of things," she said. "She is an artist. Possessed of a certain talent. This has drawn you. But Henri, believe me, I know of what I speak when I say that her luster will fade. Will pale in compare to that held before you. And, having given your best to her, you will one day find yourself with little to show for your efforts. With little of your life's purpose fulfilled. *Please*, Henri. Listen to me. You will wake to a tragedy that will have deprived not only you, but the entire world."

I laughed again. This time with less conviction.

"Clara ... please ... this is all too much. And your assumptions far too romantic for reality. It is not an affair of the heart that would make me defer," I said. "It is rather out of loyalty to Cristofer that I must refuse. His star is poised on the verge of ascension. How could I desert him now? Leaving him at this critical time with no one to cook and clean and look after his moods? And, further, I cannot entertain such an offer because, I regret to say, I am not the consummate composer you think I am."

Clara slammed a palm atop the table. Rattling the porcelain.

"You're lying!" she cried.

I felt tangled. The last thing I'd wanted to do was upset her. Especially given her condition. Still, she had a point.

I was.

Lying.

Clara leapt to her feet. Stalked about. "Do you understand the magnitude of what you're risking, Henri? What lies at *stake*?"

I balked. Overshadowed by her rage.

"Those who are fated to attune themselves to Creation cannot simultaneously pledge their soul to another, to the bartering of human emotions," she continued. Her fists clenched at her sides.

"The mind, the *heart*, cannot sustain such an intense duality. It is impossible. And should one attempt it, he would simply crumble and ... *fall to pieces!*" Saying this, she slumped into her chair, weeping.

For a moment I could not move. Stunned by her raw emotion.

As in a dream, I bent forward. Pressed a hand to her shoulder. "Clara," I whispered.

A long moment passed before she looked up. Drew fingers across her tears.

"I made a grave mistake in marrying him," she said. "I was young, naive. I wanted only to support him, to be near his light, feeling so strongly that it was my duty, my privilege, to usher his genius."

I shook my head. "But Clara, you have done this. You more than anyone have illuminated Richard. And brought his music to the people. How, then, could your joining have been a mistake?"

She released a low moan. "Because he loved me. Adored me. Cherished me with a passion beyond reason," she said. "And because of this, because of his marvelous devotion, he found himself driven to please two masters. One calling from earth, the other from heaven. And this tremendous effort, this lifetime of attending to us both, has destroyed him." Saying this, she issued a choking sound.

I kept still. Moving only to sweep the hair from her eyes.

When she could speak again, she said, "Listen to me, Henri. The human muse burns more brightly at a distance. She is not to be coddled nor domesticated. Hers is a liaison best savored in the imagination. To draw her close only invites disaster."

I drew back. Shocked and offended by the nature of her words. By the subtle suggestion that I should cast my love aside. As if she were nothing.

Exasperated, I lashed out. "Is that why you keep Cristofer at bay? Why you lead him on but do not surrender? To ensure that his own muse is kept at a safe distance?"

I expected her to fly into a rage.

Instead, she burst into laughter.

"Yes, yes, my dear. You're onto me there," she said. "Our dear Cristofer." She sighed. "He, too, is possessed of a brilliance, one no doubt grander than us all, though I believe it will take him longer to realize his gift entirely."

I frowned. "You didn't answer the question."

"Yes, I will admit it," she sniffed. "I use the little power I have over him to prevent him from committing to another. To initiating something as foolish as marriage. He most certainly shares your tendency in that regard. Yet I am hopeful he will outgrow it."

Hearing this, I reviewed the times I had witnessed them together. Heating themselves by the fire, conspiring alongside the piano, hushed and reverent during the other's performances.

I drew in a quick breath. Struggling to contain my suspicions.

My belief that her love for him burned just as brightly.

The silence between us grew awkward.

Clara blinked slowly. A queer expression dappling her face. With the tip of one finger she pressed at crumbs on the tabletop. "You are young, Henri. There is much you do not understand. Perhaps someday you will realize that sacrificing one's own beauty for that of another is itself a certain kind of death." She stopped. Sat back. Lowered her eyes.

Afraid of what I might say, I peered into the stain at the bottom of my cup.

"I understand your aggravation," she said. "And that you are not accustomed to others interfering in your life. But Henri," her voice closed off. She cleared her throat. Tried again. "I sought to obtain this offer because I cannot watch what happened to Richard, happen to you. I could not bear it."

After several minutes of silence, I looked up. Found Clara restored, her eyes clear, her cheeks dry.

She lifted our cups. Carried them to the sink.

"The children will be home soon," she said.

I understood this as my cue to depart.

Standing inside the door as I tossed on my cape, she said, "Promise me you will think it over."

I drew a hand through my hair.

"Clara ..."

I wanted to tell her it was impossible. But could not risk upsetting her further.

Standing before me, she broke into a smile. Drew my hands into hers. Placed kisses on my fingertips.

"Thank you for coming," she said.

When she had closed the door, I bounded down the steps without looking back.

As I crossed the street, I heard her again at the piano. This time sweeping into a new piece. I froze when its melody became clear. It was a passage from my work. From the page she'd accidentally glimpsed during her performance.

My mouth fell open.

A bicyclist yelled out, angry that I had blocked his path.

But I could not move.

Amazed that in such a brief amount of time Clara had memorized the entire passage. And astonished further by the sheer pathos she was loosening from its fiber.

CHAPTER 21

Signore Minore wove about my shins as I drew back the curtain to peer outside.

Could he sense my anxiousness as I stared down the empty walkway?

The concerto's rehearsal, with full orchestra, lay only hours away.

And Cristofer had yet to return.

I shivered at the unfortunate scenarios that might have befallen him while haunting the Hedgehog.

Had he encountered the villainous mermaids?

Had they played their ruse upon him as they had me?

Did he now lie broken and bloody in some dark, rat-infested alley?

I jumped at the sound of bacon fat snapping in the pan.

Going to the front door I looked again down the walkway. Seeing only butterflies at play, I rushed back to the stove and extinguished its flame. Placed a swatch of linen over the skillet.

With so little time left, I had no choice but to scour the city.

Stepping into the bedroom, I double-checked my preparations for Cristofer. His boots sat on the floor, laced and buffed. His suit and cravat pressed. His manuscript sorted and wrapped in its case.

Turning to the mirror, I took stock of my costume. Knowing Cristofer might re-appear in a less-than-tidy state and would likely need assistance in arranging himself, I had already attended to my own appearance. Noticing a slip at the edge of my mustache, I set about righting it with a small patch of glue. I had no sooner mended it when the pound of galloping horse hooves flattened Signore to the floorboards.

A rushing horseman might signal an urgent, perhaps even tragic, message.

An icy fist gripped my heart.

Cristofer!

I dashed for the door and threw it open.

Prancing and shuddering before me was Jacque's stallion. His brazen tail lashing the air. The rider dismounted.

It was the stable boy.

He stepped forward. Stared me in the face. He nodded officiously, his brown curls sweaty from his efforts at the reins.

I wanted to run, to hide. But was trapped. And the boy would no doubt have a message from his master. One in regard to the rehearsal. Its contents therefore vital to my dear Cristofer. My dear *absent* Cristofer.

Given the circumstance, I had no choice but to stand my ground.

My mind whirled. Trying to recall how the boy had encountered me.

As a man? A woman?

Certainly he'd met me as a woman. Here at the cottage. When he'd brought the missive from the madame.

But had we not also met on the evening of Clara and Cristofer's performance? Had he not served me champagne? Man to man?

My hands went numb.

What had I done?

"Good day, Monsieur Worth," he said. If he thought anything amiss, or suspected my dual identity, he was not betraying it.

"You have a message for Monsieur Vaughn?" I inquired. "I will take it here," I added quickly, hoping he would not insist on presenting it directly.

The boy shook his head, wiped the back of a wrist across his upper lip. "My missive is not for Monsieur Vaughn, but for you, sir."

"Me?"

To which "me" was he referring?

I struggled to maintain composure, feeling caught in the web of some torrid Shakespearian plot.

I then realized that Cristofer must have told Jacque that I rented a cottage on his property, or something similar. For why else would the stable hand come looking for me here?

"The madame wishes you to know that she and the monsieur have been unexpectedly called abroad," he announced. "Therefore, all lessons of the piano must be forfeited until their return, the time of which is presently unknown. She promises prompt communication when such information becomes available to her."

I stared.

Forfeited?

Unknown?

"Sir?" the boy asked. "Have you understood? I cannot leave without you saying so."

"Yes—yes, I have," I stuttered.

"Good day to you," he said, scrambling atop his muscular beast.

Despairing, I asked, "Has she—I mean, have the Bertrands yet departed?"

The boy nodded, "Early this morning, sir." Saying this, he turned the horse and walked him some distance, undoubtedly to spare me a shower of stones, then gave the animal its head and bolted down the path.

I could not move for the implications of his message.

There would be no more lessons.

No more Ava.

I glanced out at the world to see its every slant and curvature drain of color.

The clock in the sitting room chimed the hour. Alerting me to the urgencies at hand.

If we were to make the rehearsal, I would have to find Cristofer.

Quickly.

In warm weather, the Hog had a stench all its own. A sinewy mix of barley, sweat, and desperation. Highly pungent. Decidedly male.

Squinting through the dim light, I made out a barmaid wielding a mop. She drew slop along the floor, working around the outlines of fallen patrons sleeping off late night revelries.

"He was 'ere a couple of nights before. But not last night," she said without so much as a look in my direction. She had served Cristofer and I many a draft.

"Any idea where he might have gone? Or with whom?" I asked.

She shook her head, the tentacles of her filthy mop sucking at a patron's cheek.

"Seemed in a queer state, he did," she said. "Not much for talking."

I tipped my hat and left her to her labors. Eager for air.

Outside I scanned the crenellations of the city's rooftops.

My thoughts drifted back to the last night I had seen him. To his heated confrontation with Clara. His falling on bended knee. Her gasp of reproach.

How cruel the blade that must have entered my sweet Cristofer in that moment.

I wondered at his capacity to withstand such injury.

And strained to deduce the particular refuge he would crawl to with such a dire wound.

As the hour advanced and Cristofer's whereabouts continued to elude me, my anxiety rose to near panic.

Had someone, perhaps from the Liszt and Wagner school, found him in a weakened state and brought him harm? Had they heard of his forthcoming concerto and sought to extinguish the threat?

But no. I had turned every corner. Rifled every establishment. Inquired of a dozen colleagues without uncovering so much as a trace. If something untoward had happened, someone would certainly have caught wind of it.

I entered another alley. Found nothing but vegetable bins and a pile of old clothes.

Frustrated, and feeling the mounting pressure of my own untended emotions, my worry began to veer dangerously toward resentment.

Was this to be it, then? All his hopes, all his labors—our labors!—amounting to nothing but humiliation and defeat?

I bit on metal.

And what of Richard? And Clara? And all their efforts to elevate him? To extend their brilliance for the assurance of his?

Was this to be his final regard of them?

I spat onto the street.

With precious little time remaining, I decided to walk back home. Praying that Cristofer had come to his senses and returned there.

Turning on my heels, I determined that the shortest route home involved taking the bridge from which Richard had leapt.

Soon I approached its arch of heavy wood and stone. It was vacant. No fisherboy to animate its gravity.

As the clomp of my boots reverberated against the water below, Richard's voice rose to my ears.

"The demand of genius is that it be allowed to flourish in one's life without bonds. The surrender to its needs must be utter and complete. I was never able to do this."

I startled as if I had run into the man himself.

Quickly on its heels, the conversation with Clara drifted back to me.

"He found himself driven to please two masters. One calling from heaven, the other from earth. And this tremendous effort, this lifetime of attending to us both, has destroyed him."

My countenance clouded in confusion. Clara seemed to believe it was her love that had ruined Richard. My assumption had always been it was because she did *not* love him that he had been broken. And yet both husband and wife seemed to insist the opposite was true.

Another voice entered my head. This time it was Cristofer.

What would he have to say? I wondered with some irritation.

Not much, it turned out. No more than a few pathetic moans.

Moans?

I spun to lean over the handrail.

"Cristofer!" I cried in relief, spotting him under the arch.

I dashed back to the end of the bridge, scrambled down its steep embankment to where he slumped, his back pressed against slimy stones, his boots submerged in muck.

I should have known, I thought, lifting his face into my hands.

When he responded with a certain dullness, I became more forceful.

"Cristofer!" I urged, slapping a cheek. His breath stank of dampness and whisky. Next to him sat a pile of rags and gnawed-over chicken bones. Refuse left by the foreign vagrants who camped there.

"The rehearsal begins within the hour!" I cried.

I saw his eyes burst open. Mired in mud and anguish, he'd lost all sense of time.

"Not to worry. Just come with me," I said, with as much confidence as I could muster.

I didn't have the heart to mention that Jacque would not be present. Given Cristofer's tender place, I feared he would take the news as signifying a loss of his patron's conviction. Or worse. His interest. Neither of which I believed to be true, yet felt uncertain I could convince him otherwise.

With a bit of struggle, we managed to be on our way.

As we lumbered homeward, my mind busied itself with the progression of preparations. I would insist he disrobe outside and hang his clothes on the bushes, then set water to heat on the stove for coffee and washing, revive his breakfast as best I could, provide hot towels (no time for a bath), attend to his matted hair, and so on.

Being deeply occupied by the process, I failed to notice the man shadowing our steps with his own.

"Hello," the stranger said. "Is that not you? From the forest?"

I recognized him immediately.

It was the scientist. Hefting his sound machine.

Fearing any type of delay, I said, "Yes, yes, but we're in a terrible hurry."

"I see that!" he said, his face reddening as he strove to keep apace.

Peering over his glasses he asked, "Are you Cristofer Vaughn? *The* Cristofer Vaughn?"

Not relishing anyone to see my friend in such disrepair, I prepared to deny the man's query.

However, Cristofer saw fit to answer for himself, our swift movement (and no doubt his terror at the upcoming rehearsal) seeming to have revivified him considerably.

"Yes, sir, I am."

The scientist smiled. "It's an honor to meet you," he said. "Perhaps your friend here has told you of my experiments? In regard to the collection of sounds?"

I grimaced. I had never in fact mentioned them.

"I don't believe so. Not entirely," Cristofer answered.

The scientist brightened. "Well, then, perhaps I could provide a demonstration. In fact, it has been my wish for some time to capture your performance for posterity. It would be a most fine specimen!"

Cristofer blinked. "Capture?"

The man struggled to keep apace.

"I know how strange that must sound," he huffed. "Just think of it as a photograph. Not of light. But of tone. If you would imagine—"

"Regrettably, sir, this is where we must part ways," I interrupted. "We take this path to the left, and have not one minute to spare. Perhaps another time."

The scientist seemed relieved, his person having come under considerable strain bearing the weight of his mechanical load.

He bid farewell as we continued on. "I will reach out again, Monsieur Vaughn! A fair adieu to you both!"

We were nearly through to the edge of the trees when Cristofer, now seemingly himself again, asked, "What did he mean by a photograph of sound?"

I shook my head in annoyance. "There's no time for that now, Cristof. We must prepare for the concert hall with all haste."

Yet somewhere deep in my heart, I yearned to know if the man could indeed make Cristofer's music sing in perpetuity.

If, in fact, he could make *any* of us sing forever.

CHAPTER 22

*W*hen we arrived at the concert hall, the burnished bellow of a French horn reverberated in its domed ceiling. I took this as a positive sign, as it is one of Cristofer's most favored instruments.

"How do I appear?" he asked, adjusting the case of music under his arm.

"Dashing as ever," I said.

He drew in a staggered breath.

"Henri," he said, casting his eyes down. "I feel every bit the fool. Had it not been for you—"

"Stop," I said, cutting off his words with my finger. "I believe you've pulled me out of a waste bin or two."

He smiled.

"It's what we do," I added. "What is required. No more."

He blushed.

I wiped a bit of egg from his cheek. "There is one more thing," I said, wanting to gird him against the bad news.

"Eh?"

"It's Jacque. He's been called away. He will not be present. But I've no—"

The boom of a man's voice cut my assurances short.

"Monsieur Vaughn! You're here!"

Sarkov approached us at a rampant clip.

Cristofer searched me with his eyes, still digesting the terrible news of his patron's absence.

When he arrived, Sarkov greeted Cristofer and led him toward the hall.

"Everything has been prepared according to your specifications. I believe you will find the conditions superlative," he said, nodding with a certainty that did not invite contradiction.

Passing through the great doorway, we beheld the stage, brightly lit. Its floorboards shiny with polish. Atop these sat the musicians, arranged in a gentle horseshoe, each busily attending to the peculiar demands of their instrument. The sheets of the concerto's score already set neatly on their stands.

In front of the players rested the protagonist. A spectacular piano. Not the Broadwood, of course, but an instrument of sublime craftsmanship.

Sarkov led the composer to his musicians. Cristofer mounted the stage with vigor, making a great show of handshakes and other pleasantries. I smiled at his efforts, knowing the awful toll our stressful approach, not to mention his dark escapades, had taken on him.

Having delivered the composer to his rightful place, Sarkov turned to me next.

"And for you, Monsieur Worth, we have set up a table for the taking of your notations." He drew me toward a desk. Its surface decorated with a stack of fine parchment, a tray of quills, and three bottles of ink.

When we arrived to stand before it, I noticed a key lying directly in the center of the blotter. I was preparing to inquire about its presence when a flash of recollection shook me. In that instant I recognized the gently curved legs of the desk. Its matching chair upholstered with rich green silk.

It was hers.

Ava's.

From her private room.

I struggled to conceal my horror.

"Ahh, there's where I left it," Sarkov said from behind. He made a show of leaning forward to collect the key off the blotter—the one, no doubt, that fit the lock on Ava's door.

Just then the strings released a maddening screech as they tuned.

"I trust you find everything to your liking?" Sarkov asked, his eyes searing into mine, his face split along a terrible grin.

I fumed. Wanting to ram my fist down his fat throat.

The strings screeched again.

Sarkov said nothing more and departed.

Alone before Ava's desk, I faced the awful realization. He had invaded her private space. Ransacked it.

I strained to think of any evidence he might have discovered.

Were there any assignments or notes we had passed that spoke of our affections? Any artifact of mine unwittingly left behind?

And then a far more sickening thought …

Had she recorded anything of our affairs? In a diary, perhaps? Or a letter to her family?

"Henri?" a voice hissed. Then again, "Henri!!"

Cristofer was kneeling at the edge of the stage.

"Where is she?" he asked, his eyes bulging.

I stared. Mute.

How in God's name should I know where Ave was? His bully of a benefactor had taken her without leaving so much as a date of return!

"Where is *Clara*?" he urged, provoked by my failure to respond.

I started.

Clara!

Lost in the shock of seeing Ava's desk, I'd forgotten about our brave pianist.

I turned to scan the hall. Nowhere did I catch sight of her proud silhouette.

Cristofer ran his fingertips nervously along his baton.

Behind him the musicians waited, their preparations nearly completed.

"Concoct a delay," I advised, then dashed for a side door.

Outside, I ran to the street and searched for any sign of a carriage. But the only thing I saw was an old street sweeper. Hunched over what appeared to be human regurgitation on the concert hall steps.

"Looking for someone?" he asked.

I ignored him.

"Maybe the lady with the sour stomach?"

I turned. "Lady?"

He nodded. Whisked his bristled broom. "Aye. Here no more than a minute ago. Think she went down that alley," he said, nodding to the left.

Within a minute I found Clara bent over a broken wheelbarrow.

"The mornings are the worst," she said, lifting the kerchief I offered.

She kept her back to me, taking a moment to gather herself. Having removed all evidence of the episode from her dress, she stood. Pressed a hand to her swollen belly.

Though deathly pale, her coal-colored eyes still shone with an intensity I have seen in no other.

She steadied herself against my shoulder. "I'm ready," she said.

"Are you certain?" I asked. "I could offer an explanation, apologies—"

She shook her head. "That will not be necessary."

I knew enough not to question her a second time.

I felt significant envy at the quality of relief that washed over Cristofer's face when he spotted Clara. How I wished to have my own agony so utterly abated.

With a regality borne of decades onstage, our pianist ascended. Took the hand Cristofer extended and bid him a firm greeting. She then turned her attention to the musicians and, with a courtly nod, sealed the bond between them.

This done, she turned to her instrument. Slipping in front, she sunk gently to the seat. Rearranged her skirts while glancing at the sheets of music before her. It was apparent from the efficiency underscoring her movements that she was done with pleasantries and wished to get to work. Nothing about this behavior would have seemed unusual, of course, but I could see by the expression on Cristofer's face, by the slightest kink in his brow, that he felt slighted.

The rehearsal progressed brilliantly, Clara easily integrating Cristofer's revisions, nodding throughout with approval, which visibly cheered him.

Though the music no doubt proved a challenge, its themes being dense and complicated in timing, the musicians seemed to relish it, the brass in particular, their cheeks ruddy with energetic exhalation.

Throughout the performance, Cristofer shouted out notations and ideas, which I duly transcribed in the proper places on the score. While so doing, I occasionally looked across the hall. To where Sarkov stood. Obscured in shadow.

His looming presence sent sheets of ice burrowing under my skin.

If he and Jacque were willing to ransack Ava's private domain, what other precincts were they willing to invade?

In fact, could _any_ limit be assumed for a man who would shoot off his own appendage?

I recalled the stable boy's words.

"I, myself, believe he tenders a wish to one day be emperor."

I shuddered.

Felt a maddening desperation to find Ava. To warn her.

Onstage, the orchestra pounded through the concerto's first movement.

As never failed, the allegro's insidious building of tension grabbed me by the throat.

Marching toward dénouement, the orchestra growled like a feral animal, unleashing deafening chords and smashing timpani. Yet from within, the piano fought back. Clara's arms hinging like powerful jaws, consuming the keyboard with massive runs spanning one end to the other.

When silence fell at last, I looked up at Clara. Expecting to see her collapsed. Instead, fully upright, she took the kerchief offered to her by the page turner and briskly dabbed the perspiration from her cheeks.

I then checked on my employer's condition.

Now, I have seen my Cristofer through his share of triumphs and sorrows. Of love and loss. And so I can say with full authority that he never shown with more luminosity than in that moment. His love for Clara, his admiration for her gift and for the sheer beauty of the sound they had made together, had stoked the fire within him to a radiance more befitting a star than a human.

Had the occasion of this performance occurred before an audience, those in attendance would have leapt to their feet to welcome Beethoven's rightful heir. In fact, the desire was palpable among the musicians, and even myself, to do just that.

However, with Clara's mood setting the tone, all kept their seats. Simmering.

Then, from within the hood of silence, I saw Clara lift her gaze to the conductor. As she did so, I felt certain she would scoff once she observed the degree of Cristofer's pleasure. His blatant ecstasy.

But in this I was wrong.

Rather than looking away, the two artists locked eyes. A nearly imperceptible smile coming to each of their lips. Though no one else noticed the exchange, I felt the magnitude of its significance. In that brief moment, each acknowledged to the other what they had created. Not just beauty. But Beauty itself. The force that ushers Eternity and sweeps aside human limitation.

Held in mutual astonishment, I could see that what had transpired between them had far surpassed either of their expectations.

Burgeoning with newfound confidence, Cristofer nodded to his pianist then returned his attention to the orchestra. Standing to his full height, he lifted his baton. With shuffles and clicks of wood and metal, the players refreshed themselves, braced.

Then, with the deftest arc of wrist, Cristofer let slip the concerto's second movement, the adagio.

The Italian word *adagio* literally means "at ease." This description, when applied to the infamous musical movement itself, is a misleading euphemism. The term was likely adopted owing to the slower pace of a concerto's second movement, often a much-needed respite following the majestic fanfare of the opening *allegro*.

Still, there is nothing easeful about the adagio. It is a movement, and a moment, that requires the listener to be still. Utterly. To listen. Pliably. And to fully inhabit the world of another. So inwardly focused are its tones. So attuned to the sorrows and contradictions and aches of a particular life that the adagio possesses the power to lead one into the root cellar of another's soul.

And herein lies the danger.

From the vantage point of a composer, no movement is more revealing, more eviscerating to the point of spiritual undress.

For Cristofer, the vulnerability inherent in his own concerto's adagio was further aggravated by the fact that in his heart he had dedicated it to the very woman, the very artist, who would perform it.

And so I held my breath at its launch. Recalling its flat reception at the soiree. And Clara's lack of comment.

Perhaps no one was more surprised than I when the music lifted off to lovely effect. The strings laid a bed of feathery chords upon which Clara's quiet, dreamy melody could repose. I turned to see Cristofer raise an eyebrow. He, too, had noticed a new depth in Clara's commitment.

The first theme then settled, extending a farewell as the second arose.

The normally seamless moment proved jarring, however, as Clara was late in her entry. As untidy as it sounded, it was also unprecedented. I watched as her lips pressed into a terse line, her eyes darting about the score as if seeking different notes to play.

The error in her timing struck like a contagion. The solo flute fell behind by a half-beat. The cellos' solid tone thinned.

It was then I realized that the promising open had resulted not from the quality of the music but from the afterglow of the heroic allegro. And as its trail of fairy dust began to fade, so did the performers' glimmer.

It was not that Cristofer's second movement lacked emotion. Rather, it *seethed* with it. Garishly. A woman donning heavy face paint. Impossible to ignore. Yet entirely unconvincing.

Cristofer waved his arms with exaggeration.

The orchestra responded.

But the slide into mediocrity gained momentum.

Then the piano fell silent.

Cristofer steered the orchestra onward, no doubt thinking Clara had mis-stepped and would soon rejoin.

When she did not, his head whipped up.

He found her sitting still. Hands in her lap.

Stunned at the sight, his body lost animation, sagged.

This had a calamitous effect on the orchestra. The rhythm of its various sections veered out of control, then toppled.

An uncomfortable silence followed.

"Clara?" Cristofer asked.

She stared him dead in the face.

Cristofer swallowed. Loud enough for all to hear. "Shall we take it from measure twenty-five?"

Clara's expression darkened. "I cannot," she said.

Cristofer shrugged. "Alright, then. Let us try again from the beginning," he offered.

The players lifted their instruments. Prepared.

"No," she said.

Everyone stiffened.

The conductor cleared his throat. "Are you needing a rest?" he asked, a tender tone coming to his voice.

Clara shook her head. "No. I need to move onto the third movement."

My heart sank.

Cristofer stared in disbelief. "But we have not yet finished with the second …"

"But *I* have," she stated.

The conductor's cheeks drained of color.

Apparently her opinion of the music had not changed.

Please, no, I thought. *Please do not eviscerate him in front of all these witnesses. Do not expose his deepest confession as a farce.*

I wanted to mount the stage, fall to her feet, beg her to cease.

I coughed lightly, hoping to catch her attention. But she made no effort to notice me. In fact, she had not looked once in my direction since arriving.

Cristofer tried again. "Perhaps you could offer some explanation as to—?"

Clara lifted a hand. I could see the morning's illness cracking its way through her patience. Her decorum.

"The music lacks merit," she said.

I cringed at the venomous words. Expected to see their target falter. But despite the cruel barb, or perhaps because of it, Cristofer stood his ground. The hinges of his jaw swelling.

"Perhaps it is not the music, but its *subject* that lacks merit," he retaliated.

My eyes widened at the treachery of his insult.

Would neither side relent until it had wrought permanent damage?

Caught between the adversaries, the players squirmed in their chairs. Fortunately, they were not privy to the subtext of the words passing over their heads. Still, such a flagrant dispute between composer and performer was unseemly. And while Cristofer might easily succumb to his lower tendencies, it was unfathomable to see the noble Clara Thorne making a similar descent.

With neither side showing any sign of capitulation, I wondered who held the superior position. Who had more authority in the matter of artistic decisions—the composer, or the star performer whose husband had commissioned the piece?

Another minute passed in silence. Deafening in its tension.

"Well, then," Clara said calmly, breaking the spell. "It appears our rehearsal has come to an end."

Stepping from behind the piano, she turned to the orchestra. "You played with exceptional tone and enthusiasm today," she told them. "I look forward to repeating the occasion when the score is properly revised."

I dared not look at Cristofer. But prayed he would keep his lips sealed as I doubted their collaboration, much less their friendship, could survive another bitter turn.

Fortunately, he refrained.

Clara descended from the stage.

With all haste, Sarkov escorted her to a waiting carriage.

Having come home by separate means, I approached the cottage with dread. Expecting to find my employer inside, dejected. I also anticipated that I would be required to tend the damage. Yet given the unsettledness in my own heart, even the mere contemplation of such a duty left me drained.

Strangely, I did not find Cristofer at home. Nor any sign that he'd been there. That surprised me. And I worried that he might have gone to confront Clara.

But what could I do if he had?

Had I not done all I could to protect him?

I set my notes down on the piano. Looked toward the kitchen. The afternoon's rush had left it badly disordered. Even Signore seemed bent out of shape.

Intending to set things right, I went to the fireplace and stacked its belly with wood. The flames leapt quickly. I held still, letting the heat soak into my cheeks, my hands, my thighs. The sudden warmth turned my mind to my lover. And her whereabouts. Presently unknown.

Craving her, I turned all the capacities of my mind toward seeking.

Surely we were connected on some level beyond the physical?

I strained to intuit her. To tease her essence from the air.

I waited. But, like Clara, my patience had thinned.

Frustrated at the lack of communication, I kicked the fire.

Where had she gone? Had she been taken? Or left voluntarily?

And for how long?

I wheeled around. The piano sat quietly. Her feet rooted in the hardwood.

On top sat the pages of Cristofer's concerto.

Longing for distraction, I thought I could perhaps dive into his adagio. Find some way to repair it.

I fanned out the pages. Hummed through the bars.

But for all my desire to help, I found little energy in reserve. My limbs became tense, then twitchy.

Where? my mind kept crying. *Where was she?*

I paced back and forth, hating to be held captive. Wanting only to work. To turn sideways and slip into the truth of things.

"Dammit!" I roared, slamming the fallboard.

Startled, Signore scurried under a table.

Overcome, and in need of answers, I put on my hat and breached the approaching twilight. Able to think of only one person who might help me.

CHAPTER 23

*A*s I approached her land, I noticed that Tess had harvested her beets. The mighty field lay upturned and fallow. Clods of dirt hulking where bouquets of scarlet-tinged greens had once flourished.

Plodding ahead, I waited to hear the bellow of her loyal beasts. Braced for the pack's clumsy advance. Yet as I drew closer, I heard nothing save for a gentle, cyclic clanking of metal on metal. No barks or shouts or hellos.

By the time I arrived at the door, I could sense the vacancy.

Not a soul was at home. Not beast nor barmaid.

I fought back a sense of agitation at her absence.

A breeze lifted and the clanking came again. This time, I found its source. It was a collection of flattened spoons and forks Tess had hung on strings. Her version of wind chimes.

I hesitated at the door. I did not want to invade her privacy yet needed to determine when she would return.

Finding the door unlocked, I proceeded inside.

The dwelling was as I remembered. Its beams pinned with sprays of drying herbs. The kitchen table heaving with jars. A great kettle nestled in the now cold fireplace. And waiting atop the cupboards, her crystal ball.

How I desperately wished the clairvoyant herself was there to peer within its watery prism. To divine from its crystal the answers I sought.

Thinking she had taken her harvest to market and would soon come home, I lifted a scrap of paper from the butcher block. Set about looking for something to write with.

It was during this brief search that I spotted the gift she had left for me.

For there, carved into the butcher block, was my name. Above it rested the regal flight feather of an owl. Its shaft carved into an expert quill. Lifting it, I felt how its arc rested perfectly in my grasp. The feather, I noted, had come from the animal's right wing. Its curvature, therefore, a perfect fit for those disposed to write with the left hand.

Still, I was confused.

If she'd known I might be coming, why hadn't she stayed to meet me?

To <u>help</u> me?

Given all that lay at stake what I needed was guidance, not a writing implement!

Irritated, I wrapped the quill in its leather sheath and pushed out the door. The tangled wind chimes clanking behind me.

I journeyed home through the dark forest, festering.

As I came into the clearing before our cottage, I heard the piano. Spotted lamplight pouring through the windows.

Cristofer had come home. And was working.

I suffered a pang of guilt, remembering the disrepair in which I had left the cottage. For a moment I thought to go inside. To tidy the kitchen. Prepare him a meal.

But even as I thought these things, I hesitated. I hadn't the strength for dealing with his anguish. And while his playing did not reveal an underlying tumult, I knew he would need to process the rehearsal's horrifying events. And this I could not bear.

Tonight I had my own sorrows.

"Henri?"

The voice was soft. Angelic.

"I didn't realize you'd come home."

Yes, I heard myself saying. *I've come home. To you, Ava. The only one who—*

I turned my face toward her light.

"Oh! I'm sorry. I didn't realize you were sleeping."

It was not Ava.

But Cristofer.

His image came slowly into focus.

"I saw you in the chair. With the candle lit," he said. "And I thought—"

I sat up.

"My apologies, Henri."

I nodded dumbly.

Waited for him to go. Eager to slip into my bed.

But Cristofer remained where he was.

"Are you very tired?" he asked. "I thought we might share a nightcap."

"Perhaps another time," I mumbled.

I ignored the pained expression my words brought to his face.

"Of course, of course," he said. "I just wanted to thank you for today. I went through the notes you made. They're splendid."

"You're welcome."

Still he did not leave.

"I'm sorry the rehearsal did not go as you wished," I offered. But even saying this felt draining.

"Yes, the rehearsal," he muttered. "It certainly did not bode well, did it?" He gave a heavy sigh. "Henri?" he said, his tone suddenly tinged with a distress I could not ignore.

"Mmm?"

His eyebrows stitched together in a painful seam. "Richard has made a horrific request."

Richard, I thought, ashamed that I had recently given him and his suffering so little attention.

"He wishes not to see Clara nor the children—ever again."

"What?" I sputtered.

He nodded. "His letter arrived this morning. Just before rehearsal."

Shaken, I looked past Cristofer, into the web of stars framed by the open door. The ramifications of his words rattled about my head. Connections and meanings forming and breaking.

"That would explain Clara's behavior at the rehearsal," he said quietly.

I looked over.

Did it?

Entirely?

And in the way he thought?

"Yes," I said. Unable to conjure anything beyond agreement.

Cristofer turned as if he would leave. "I'll let you get some rest."

I was glad to hear this.

But still he did not go.

He paused again on my doormat. "There's one more thing," he said. "A favor—" His eyes met my darkened glare. "No. Never mind," he said, retreating. "It can wait."

The morning arrived despite my reluctance to face it. A robin's jaunty song drifted in alongside hints of timothy and honeysuckle. I looked up. Noticed the mice scurrying about. Noticed too the light. How it gripped the walls at a lower angle, a wild animal exposing its underbelly.

The day was full of herself.

I groaned and shut my eyes. Wanting nothing to do with it.

But even the inky darkness beneath the covers could not smother the call. Enticed by the morning's pulse, my mind chugged to life. Began to whirr softly.

The first unwanted thought arose.

Of Ava.

Of how the light knew her face.

Then came the inescapable ache. It had lessened by a degree in the night but now rose anew.

I studied the ceiling.

Could I will it to collapse?

Sensing the edge of despair, I tried to console myself with the knowledge that she had not gone forever. And would return.

But even as this thought served to steady me, the previous night's doubts came back to roost.

Why had she gone with Jacque? my mind wailed.

With someone who had pillaged her world and forbidden her passions?

The thought that she had left with him—willingly—worked its poison.

Would that always be her choice, then?

Was her commitment to me that sheer?

I felt rage sprouting alongside the ache. Unfurling expansive leaves. Choking the hurt beneath its shadow.

Rage. That cruel drug of diversion.

From previous involvements I knew how tempting it was to employ it against heartache. To engage its hostility in order to supplant the truth. To render the beloved less desirable.

But to employ that false defense against Ava?

It struck me as wretched.

Yet for how long could I keep these ruinous tendencies at bay?

CHAPTER 24

*T*he coffee streamed into my demitasse thick and black as licorice. I took a sip. Grimaced at the flavor's sharp edge. "A good day's work in a cup," Cristofer fondly called his morning beverage. And indeed, under its influence, I had restored life and order to his living space. The cottage's doors and windows had been flung open, the carpets beaten, the kitchen scrubbed, the market visited and a lunch prepared, Cristofer's room tidied, the piano polished, inkwells refilled, and a sheaf of new parchment set out.

Though I had little left in me, my duty to Cristofer would not allow me to wallow. He, too, had great obstacles and struggles before him.

Upon my arrival, I'd been disappointed not to find my employer at the piano working on his concerto. As I knew he must. If Clara would not accept his adagio, he needed, with all haste, to repair it. Or devise another.

Aware of this urgency, and mindful of my role in supporting him, I'd spent the morning manifesting the perfect conditions for his creativity. And girded my character to receive him.

While cleaning, I'd been running through Cristofer's first movement in my mind until, from that place unknown, a theme suddenly occurred to me. Being itself distilled from the concerto's opening, I felt that its notes and tone might provide the seed for a brilliant new adagio. When I had collected most of the theme into my memory, I dashed to the parchment and jotted it down. Attempting the theme on the keyboard, I found it of surprising worth. And could only imagine the heights to which my liege would soar.

Relieved at having this gift to offer him, I sagged along the bench.

Staring at my scribbles on the manuscript, my mind turned to Clara.

I thought back to her pallid appearance on the morning of the rehearsal and considered the effect Richard's request must have had.

Her husband. Lover. Confidant. And father of her children, including the one yet to be born, had banished her—entirely—from his life.

No wonder she could not stomach Cristofer's overtly effusive adagio.

With Richard having abdicated his station, Clara's ability to ward off the dashing composer's ardor had been significantly reduced. She likely worried, too, that her altered circumstance would lead Cristofer to take all manner of liberties. These might even possess a greater potency than his errant music.

If Clara did not plug the leak now, the dam would break and drown them all.

Of course this assumed that she did not secretly harbor a love for Cristofer. Which, despite her denials, I still thought true.

I felt disheartened by the difficulties besieging the great artists. As immobilized by them as by my own.

A breeze swept through the cottage. I breathed in deeply.

I cannot say how the scent of that late afternoon affected me. Only that it did. Lured by a sudden compulsion, I set again upon the keyboard.

But it was not the new theme for Cristofer that sprung to life before me.

But a piece most foreign. One I had not played in years. Nor given any thought to.

It was the nocturne. Written for my brother.

The very work that had drawn Cristofer into my life. And me into his.

The piece began with the firing of a single theatrical note, a sudden boom in the lower octave.

It quickly retreated from this opening shot and commenced to wind its way daintily along an easy footpath. A decorative perambulation. Frilly to be sure, but not delicate. Despite the apparent ease of its melody, the drama boiling beneath could not be ignored.

After several interlacing detours and variations of stride, the mood darkened. And my hands wandered, almost unaware of each other.

So immersed had I become that I had little time to marvel at the fact that I'd remembered the piece entirely.

I took the final run, a rapidly descending arpeggio of three octaves that shored up the final four chords. When the resonance of the last had died, my head fell.

The bench creaked as I sat back.

When I felt the familiar deluge of guilt rise, I stood quickly. Unwilling to surrender, I strode to the kitchen, intent on setting some beans to soak.

No more than a minute had passed when I heard the piano play behind me. Its voice scratchy. Its tone thin.

I spun. "Signore?" I called, thinking our feline had traipsed across the keyboard. But when I looked, I found no one near the instrument.

I listened again.

The run of chords was unmistakable.

It was a section of the nocturne I had just played.

The phrase repeated. Hollow and jangly.

Baffled, I tapped the side of my head.

The sound came again. Repeating itself. An eerie echo.

This time I noticed a detail that elevated my confusion to horror: The echo had faithfully captured an error I'd made, a missed C sharp.

The phrase came yet again. The past somehow trapped inside my head.

Terrified, I pressed palms against ears. Applied pressure.

In addition to all my recent torment, was I now to suffer that notorious ailment? That infamous corruption of hearing that afflicted so many of our kind?

"Nooo," I hissed.

Shaking, I glanced at the dark liquid in my cup.

Hadn't Cristofer once said that too much of it made his ears ring?

I cursed myself for having steeped such a potent brew. Knocked the cup into the sink. Then paced the room, praying the phrase would not repeat.

But it did.

And again registered my flubbed C sharp.

In a panic, my mind flashed on Richard. On the bloody jab marks he'd made about his ears.

Was this the hellish demon he'd been fighting?

Again, the ghostly chords repeated. My error intact.

Then came a shriek. And banging on the door.

I fell back. Scrambled across the floor.

Had the furies come to take me?

What in God's name was happening?

"Hello? Monsieur Vaughn? May I speak with you?" the voice cried out.

I scurried to hide underneath the piano.

Was it Cristofer they wanted?

"Monsieur Vaughn? It is I. Professor de Martineville."

Who?

Through the glass of a side window I saw a familiar face. The scientist from the forest. The sound collector.

I scurried from under the piano. Struggled to my feet. Opened the door.

"Greetings, mademoiselle. I wonder if I might have a word with Monsieur Vaughn who I've just now had the pleasure of hearing at the piano," he said, looking over my shoulder.

I hesitated. Knowing the man had never met me as a woman. Much less in my apron. He glanced up earnestly, his eyes reaching over the wiry tops of his spectacles.

"He is not at home," I managed.

"But I just heard him," he insisted. He then scrambled to an open window where he'd propped his sound machine. The wide mouth of its horn gaping at the room.

With some effort he lowered the device and brought it to the front door.

"I've captured a bit to show him the nature of my invention," he said, pointing to the black cylinder at the machine's center.

I stared in disbelief at the jagged white lines etched around its middle.

His forehead wrinkled. "I hope I've not offended. I came to pay a visit. Heard the piano. It elevated me in such a way that I … I could not help myself. And could think of no more efficient way to explain this device than by demonstration. And a fine specimen it is," he said.

I swallowed a lump as the man's meaning came clear.

"You have my music on there?" I asked, pointing to the cylinder.

He smiled. "You heard it, then?"

I shook my head. Took a step back.

Without another word, he knelt over his contraption and turned the crank.

Though I knew it impossible, I heard the notes I had played not more than moments ago. Resurrected exactly. Every nuance identical.

But how?

Was it magic or science or witchcraft?

I did not know.

I dropped to my knees, shuffled to the device.

"Do it again," I said, incredulous. Then watched as the cylinder spun and a silvered needle lowered into the narrow groove along its surface. Moments later, shimmers that had died in the past emerged faithfully from the horn.

"Again," I insisted. Still unable to believe my ears.

And yet it came again and again—wending through hiss and crackle—the song for my brother—my flubbed C sharp repeated with perfect fidelity, just as it had occurred.

I sunk further, supported only by my ankles. "How is this possible?" I croaked.

The man removed his glasses. Set to cleaning them with a cloth.

"After collecting many specimens of bird songs, I ruminated for months on how I might resuscitate them. Toward that end, I conducted hundreds of experiments and devised all manner of machines. But nothing worked. Until one night I had a dream. And in it I saw the entire solution laid out whole!"

My mind returned to that day. In the forest. When I thought I'd heard the honeyeater. The *particular* honeyeater. Singing again.

Then, as now, I was certain I had misheard.

But had I not just before me heard my own playing returned—a sliver of my past brought back into the present?

The man had mentioned photographs, the news sent from Paris. Of how a person's appearance could be captured. Burned onto a plate.

But how could the same detainment occur with sound?

Bodies at least had solidity to them. Something to be detained.

A bird might be trapped in a cage.

A pianist thrown in jail.

But their *voices*? These had no physicality. No qualities that could be held in the hand. That could sit still while chemicals mixed and dried.

No.

They were but phantoms. Ephemerals. How could they be sieved from the air, scraped into wax and imprisoned on a cylinder?

And worse, be made to sound again whenever the warden wished!

Was this not a corruption of time itself? An unnatural over-turning?

I looked down at the contraption in fear.

What perversion had the scientist unleashed?

Would rivers soon run in reverse? The moon rise in the west?

And might the dead—God help me—live again?

One exceptional thought chased another. Flapping about my head like birds blown from branches.

Then.

Tess.

"You claim sorrow at impermanence. Yet the ability to touch Eternity has been granted you."

Unaware of my extreme vexation, the man broke into the silence, saying, "You are quite gifted on the piano. How is it that I've never heard of you?"

I was unable to answer.

He shrugged. "But look here, I've really come to speak with your instructor. It is *his* particular sound I wish to capture. For I believe Monsieur Thorne is quite correct when he says that someday we will hear great things from him."

Even after convincing the scientist that Cristofer was not at home and the time of his return unknown, he refused to depart. And in fact remained on our front stoop for hours.

I found his presence irritating, mainly because I wanted to forget what he had shown me. If I did not, if I stared into the jaws of his aberrant world, I would be unable to function.

Finally the man agreed to leave, but only after obtaining promises that I would not relay to Cristofer anything of what I had seen. The scientist wished to witness for himself the impact his invention might have on the composer.

I felt glad when, at last, he and his contraption disappeared into the forest. Certain that Cristofer would be in a precarious mood when he returned, I did not think it a good hour to spring such unsettling news upon him.

"Hey ho! Henri? Are you about?"

The voice rang out with such alacrity that at first I did not identify it as that of my employer.

"In here!" I called.

He bounded through the door as though propelled by wings.

Signore rushed toward his master.

Cristofer looked about. "My heavens, you've set this place more right than it's ever been."

I smiled. Glad to have him notice the efforts.

He rushed forward to give me a hug. "Oh, dear Henri! Have I been always neglectful in telling you how grateful I am for your presence in my life?" His gray eyes sparkled. Literally.

In a bit of shock, I said, "You're certainly in a better mood than expected."

"Ha!" he bellowed. Slapped me on the back as though I were a drinking cohort. Then allowed his noble head to droop. "Yes, of course," he mused. "You must have thought I'd be overcome by the need to write an entirely new adagio, eh?"

I frowned. Further annoyed by the understatement. I was elated to see him happy, of course. But irked at having to endure the vicissitudes of his mood. Especially having so recently suffered my own.

"Apparently, you have found some remedy," I said.

He smiled in a way that hid a secret.

My hackles rose. Distrustful of whatever could so abruptly erase the previous day's damage.

He slapped the top of the piano.

"*You* are my remedy, dear Henri."

I squinted, unsure of his meaning.

Had he somehow seen the recent sketches I'd made?

But he could not have. He'd only just now returned.

My thoughts ceased when he opened his case, removed a manuscript, and set it upon the rack.

With unexpected care, he sank to the stool. Drew in a long breath. Slid up his cuffs. Then leaned into ivory.

When he began to play, the breath left me.

The silver-sided chords descended. A somewhat strained procession. Drawn with ache. With hunger.

The notes were falling from his hands.

But spoke of another spirit.

My own.

It was my piece.

For Ava.

The melody in his right hand attempted a rise. Relented. Turned slowly to follow the left downward.

I held completely still.

Cristofer kept on. Settling with care into each chord. Lingering at the melody beyond reason. Even beyond decorum.

Unable to support myself, I sunk into a chair.

Before I could even consider the reasons he might be performing the piece for me, she appeared.

Or rather, emerged.

It was not her face that came before me. But something less corporal. More pervasive. An effusion, I suppose. An imperceptible lattice of scent, touch and affection.

Suspended upon its frame, my heart pounded as though I were running.

And yet, I could not have been more still.

Without fair warning, tears leapt to my eyes. Drained down my cheeks.

Her sudden nearness seemed only to amplify the actual distance between us. Not just in miles, but in probability.

I suddenly wanted Cristofer to stop. To stay his hands.

But he was gone to me. I could tell by the stubborn jut of lower lip.

He, too, was lost in a love denied.

It was the second time that day I had heard my own music

returned to me. Yet despite their grossly different avenues, something about the two experiences felt similar. For when Cristofer began to weave in the second more fluid melody, I realized it wasn't really him playing.

It was me.

He was playing for me. *Of* me.

This was not Cristofer sitting to my pages. Interpreting them. No.

There was no ownership. No assumption.

He was playing exactly as I would play. A needle to my cylinder.

Goosebumps lit my flesh.

This act of his, this selfless dissolution, was meant to convey a message. Of this I felt certain.

Such was the nature of our intimacy. One being unable to conceal anything from the other.

When he placed the final chords, his head dropped.

We sat. Motionless. All manner of silent communication passing between us.

Finally.

"Forgive me. But I found the manuscript in the drawer while looking for some notes."

Another moment of silence passed before he spoke again.

"Henri ..." he tried. Hesitated. Tried again. "If this is what comes

… if this is what she elicits from you, then you must—"

He turned suddenly. His eyes glistening.

"Henri. I've been a fool. Paying attention solely to my needs without any regard for your predicament."

His sudden candor, his earnestness, elicited an automatic response. A reflex. Before I could stop myself, I endeavored to soothe him.

"No, Cristofer. Your dilemmas far outweigh mine. There is the concerto. The difficult rehearsal. Clara's obstinacy. Richard's agonizing request. So much. So very much. And all under the pressure of limited time. Why should you spend but even a moment on—?"

"Henri, *please!*" he shouted. "This is a most serious matter I am raising."

It was the first time he had ever raised his voice with me.

He turned and laid a palm upon the face of my score. "This, Henri. *This* ..." he shook his head. Closed his eyes. "It is—magnificent."

Before I could protest, he went on.

"This work of yours reflects a height to which we all yearn to climb. Can you not see that? It is all anyone, musician or artist or *priest*, for God's sake, could dare hope might result one day from his steady labor and devotion."

He opened his eyes. His expression wistful.

"Henri, there are so many things I do not understand. But one thing I know to be true is that many seek to touch the toes of the

Creator, to feel the brush of that grace and magic, yet only the rarest few are ever granted such access.

"But for you, Ava has bestowed this entry. What you find in her, what you *feel* for her, has brought you to the holiest of holies." He paused. Set firm hands upon his knees. "Such a gift must be cultivated. And nothing allowed to deter it. *Nothing*." He looked hard into my eyes. "Not even your loyalty to me."

"But—"

He cut me off with a loud grunt. "Do you think me unaware of what has been passing between you and Clara?"

The room tilted.

What?! my mind screamed.

What confidences of ours had she divulged? My accusations of her feelings for Cristofer?

I looked down. Praying he could not read my thoughts.

"It's alright, Henri. I understand it's because of me that you would refuse her."

Refuse her?

What had I ever refused Clara?

Other than her request that I turn my hand to—?

"She told me about the count's offer," he confessed.

I gulped. The direction of the conversation was unexpected. "Cristofer. Please—"

"No!" he said firmly. Getting to his feet he began pacing the way he did when chasing down a theme. "What she's offering you is rare and precious. It's the only way for you. And you must accept. I *insist* you accept, and will support the handling of this matter in whatever ways I can."

Feeling cornered, I longed to run outside for air.

But Cristofer was not finished. He came and stood before me. "Henri, I am ashamed of my greed for you. Yes, we have had an agreement. And one of mutual benefit, to be sure. But since that first moment I heard you play, I've known somewhere deep inside that you possessed a grander destiny." He rubbed his palms together. "Over the years, you've made it easy for me to forget this. Nevertheless, I can no longer deny the truth. My conscience will not allow it."

"Cristofer …" I began weakly.

"Of course it's not ideal for me," he interrupted. Slipped a fingertip along the polish of our piano. "And I will miss you terribly." He wagged his head. "But this is a matter beyond personal requirement. And you have already done me much service."

That Cristofer would make such a sacrifice uplifted me entirely. Altered the course of my blood. Gave hope a northward swing.

Still.

There was so much I had not told him. So much he did not know.

How could I explain everything?

466

Of Jacque's ambitions and insane jealousy? Of the necessity to hide his ordinary birth? Of his stealing Ava's piano? Of Sarkov and the lock? Of their ransacking Ava's private domain?

"It is unknown whether she would come with me," I muttered, not wanting my hopes to falsely rise with his.

He looked up with a start. "Why on earth wouldn't she leave Jacque?" he asked. "Because he's so handsome?"

I searched his eyes. He searched mine. Sensing the absurdity, we burst into laughter.

Shaking his head he asked, "What could possibly tether her to that man?"

When I did not answer, he again grew somber. "Clara is opposed to your being together, of course," he said. "And perhaps she's right—perhaps I'm young and don't understand these things. But for the life of me I can't see the benefit in barring such passion." He paused. "But I *can* speak to the pain of its denial."

I waited a moment before saying, "I appreciate all you have said, Cristofer. Truly. Still, there are reasons—"

"Of course, of course," he said briskly. "There always are, aren't there?" he added with a bitter huff. "But all things can be worked out. All impediments reduced."

I wanted to insist otherwise. But could feel his rigidity. He had made up his mind: If *he* could not have his love, I would have mine.

Nothing would dissuade him. It was the quality of his stubbornness that made him a brilliant musician. A loyal confidant. And, sometimes, an impossibility.

He then began to speak of the count. Relating the details he'd heard about him. His creative tastes, quirks, proclivities, and so on.

But I did not hear a word. My imagination had escaped to ponder the vast possibility that had opened before me.

I imagined Ava and me at liberty in a fruited garden. Sharing tea and the day's news. I imagined her hand in mine. Our coupling under no one's scrutiny. I then imagined us turning to our separate endeavors. She to a glistening, round-mouthed piano. Me to a table littered with sheets of manuscript and quills.

A warmth rose to surround me.

"Henri? Did you hear what I said?"

I turned to my liege. My eyesight dappled. His grim expression brought me crashing back to the drawing room.

"I'm sorry. What?"

"I had tried to make the request of you earlier," he said, "before I transcribed the work. But last night you seemed so sorrowful. I did not wish to inflate your troubles."

The topic had apparently changed.

"Transcribed what?" I asked, lost.

A look of vexation wrinkled his forehead. "Your piece, Henri," he said succinctly.

I fell silent.

"*You are my remedy*," he had told me earlier.

And had been to visit Clara.

Oh God …

Please say he has not done it. Please say it is not what I fear.

For what Cristofer did not know—could not possibly know—was that Clara had already seen a section of the piece. And knew it to have arisen from my hands!

"I spent the entire night copying it out," Cristofer continued. "And just this morning performed it for Clara."

My mind rushed back to Jacque's castle. To Clara's hand shooting out and grasping my wrist. Her eyes pinned to the errant sheet of my composition.

Cristofer leaned back against the fireplace. "She was astonished, to say the least," he said. "You cannot possibly imagine the effect it had upon her."

I tried to imagine the thoughts passing through Clara's mind when Cristofer began to play, claiming the piece as his own.

"In fact," he continued, "not since Richard presented her with his "Variations" have I ever seen her so visibly shaken. It were almost as if—" he began, but stopped himself.

"She found it with merit?" I blurted. Worried that my silence would convict me.

"Yes," he said softly. "And expressed enormous relief that my concerto now possesses a worthy adagio."

I drew back at his words.

Momentarily forgetting the hazard, I marveled at Clara's observation.

I should have known.

My most tender creation.

For my love.

An *adagio*.

Yes.

Clara had seen the truth immediately. Naming what I could not.

"Of course I share in her relief," he whispered hoarsely. "Still, it's a devil of a blow."

I watched as the hurt of his work being replaced took root. Knew I should say something. Something to comfort his wounded ego. His broken heart.

But I couldn't trust my lips.

"I haven't upset you, have I, Henri?" he asked suddenly. "I was terribly reluctant to use this first piece from you. And I never would have, had the situation not been so *dire*." Thus saying, he reluctantly swiped a tear. "But, in truth, part of me also wondered that if you were to hear your music come through Clara's hands, it might …

Well, at any rate, it's the last favor I'll ask from you. The very last."

I looked away before he could see my face. His promise ringing more true than he could possibly know.

He then began to speak of contacting Sarkov and making arrangements for another rehearsal.

But I hadn't ears for his plans.

All I could think was … *she knows.*

Clara knows.

CHAPTER 25

I lay in the meadow beneath the castle. Staring up as clouds wandered by.

I had run to this spot because I knew of no other that could annihilate me. Disperse my person away from itself.

Bright flowers—pink, white, blue—danced about. Their tender green stems bending to the wind.

Above, the castle's flags snapped in the breeze.

I breathed deeply, trying to slow my racing pulse.

I had no disguises left. No confidants. No harbors.

All had been lost.

These thoughts were interrupted by the scent of singe.

I looked down at my hands. The creases of my palms and fingers were black with ash. The soot all that remained of my original score.

As soon as Cristofer had left the cottage, I'd burned everything. Now, even if Clara were to confront him about plagiarism, there no longer existed one shred of evidence—the only remaining manuscript of the adagio written entirely in Cristofer's meticulous script.

When a piece of ash drifted down from my cuff, I saw within its burned edges a single note.

The sight drove hurt into my heart.

What had become of me?

What would become of me?

Without warning, Tess spoke into my thoughts.

"Your desire did not cause anyone's death, Henri. Though denied much longer, it may bring about yours."

For the first time, I acknowledged the gravity of her prophecy. My own death feeling close at hand.

Floundering, I recalled Cristofer's assurances, *"All things can be worked out. All impediments reduced."*

But could they?

I thought again of the count's offer.

What if I were to accept?

I conjured a scene in which my love returned from her journey to find her world pilfered. And my safety threatened.

Unwilling to tolerate the confines of her existence any longer and the dangers it cast upon her lover, she would pack what few things she could, evade her keepers, and abscond with me.

It was a delicious thought. My savoring making it seem all the more real.

I laid back along soft earth. Imagined its gentle scoop to be hers.

Even just contemplating the possibility of our escape left me feeling wild and dizzy and alive.

Turning, I found the flowers about me glowing with renewed incandescence.

Emboldened, I jumped up.

This was not a time for despair.

But for action.

Thinking quickly, I concocted an imaginary request I could make of Audric to trick him into revealing what he knew of Ava's return.

With my newly hatched plan, I strode up the hillside. Believing for the first time that our love would prevail.

I had but taken only a few bounding steps when—

BOOM!

The deafening blast flattened me along the ground.

BOOM!

BOOM!!

BOOOOOM!!

One report resounded after the next. Tearing through leaves and birdsong.

Petrified, I covered my head.

The gunfire sounded angry. Predatory.

I kept still. Hoping I was not the target.

From the castle ramparts came shouting. Raucous laughter.

Had Jacque returned?

Did my love now inhabit her world?

On this hope, I surged forward.

BOOM!!

BOOM!!

My entire person shook from the shattering reports.

As invincible as my will, I knew my flesh too soft for bullets.

My advance—and my intentions—would have to wait.

When there came a pause in the explosions, I spun and fled down the hill. Praying I would not feel the pierce of lead.

CHAPTER 26

*D*espite the unseen rot festering in its foundations, life at our cottage resumed a somewhat normal rhythm.

Yet my entire being felt taut. Held in unbearable distress. A constant state of hope, dread, and anxiousness.

At any moment, I expected Clara to bang on the door. Deliver earth-shattering accusations.

At the same time, we'd had no news from the castle.

Had Ava, in fact, returned?

If so, when, and under what conditions, might I see her?

Cristofer seemed unaware of my nervous condition. He was too preoccupied with preparations for the next rehearsal.

One morning, as I was clearing our breakfast dishes, he addressed me from the piano. A quill poised in one hand.

"Henri, would you be able to fetch us some ink?"

"Of course," I said, eager for any errand that might occupy me. "I'll stop in town on my way back from the market."

To this he did not respond, having become reabsorbed in his work.

I returned from the market later that afternoon. The yellowed head of a chicken poking from the mouth of my sack alongside the feathery fringe of fennel. Several jars of ink clinked together with my step.

The walk had helped to clear my head and ease some of the stress from my bones. On the way back I had taken a short detour past the castle. This time, thankfully, my advance was not shattered with gunfire. Which left me free to imagine my love breathing somewhere close by.

If only I could get word to her.

Telling her to meet me in our secret glen.

If only ...

The pleasure of this thought dissolved the instant I stepped from the forest trail. For there, in front of our cottage, stood Jacque's stallion.

My eyes flew to the stable boy lingering on our front step. Seeing him, I hurried back into the cover of branches. The ink jars clinked as they settled to the ground.

I could hear the boy delivering his missive to Cristofer but could not make out the words.

I watched as Cristof gave a slight bow, then returned inside.

The boy leapt onto his animal. Bending forward to adjust a stirrup, his eyes drifted to where I knelt.

To my horror, I saw a discrete smile curl his lips. It was not a friendly smile. But a knowing one. As on the face of someone who has detected more about you than you wished.

Without hesitation, the boy stood up in the stirrups then dropped his full weight upon the saddle. The animal reared at the sudden jolt and exploded in a wake of pounding hooves and dust.

I waited several minutes after the boy had departed before stepping toward the cottage. My knees suddenly weak.

Inside, I could barely face Cristofer. Terrified of what the boy's message might portend.

Thankfully, I found him unscathed. In fact, he seemed invigorated.

"Ah, Henri, you're back!" he said as I placed the new jars atop the piano. "Some wonderful news to share."

"Oh?" I said, heading for the kitchen.

"Yes. Jacque has returned and already spoken with Clara," he began.

I felt my heart skip.

She is near!

Cristofer went on. "She has apparently worked him into quite a state of arousal about the concerto. Particularly its new movement," he said.

"Ah, very good," I said, hoping to mask a twinge of agony.

"Yes! And he's arranged for a rehearsal the day after tomorrow. With full orchestra. And this time Jacque himself will be in attendance."

"Marvelous," I said.

I set my sack atop the counter. The chicken's transparent comb jostled.

"There was also a message for you," he added, lifting a jar.

I stiffened. "For me?"

"Yes. The madame has requested that you resume your lessons. As soon as practicable."

I tried to say "I see," but very little came out.

Cristofer smiled. "I thought you would be pleased to hear that."

"Yes. Quite," I said, keeping my back to him.

I flinched at the sudden pop of a cork. Cristofer already stirring the ink.

"You know, that's rather funny," he said, squinting into the distance. "Why would that boy deliver a message for Ava's instructor to *my* cottage? I've never told Jacque or anyone else that this was where you resided."

My hand froze around the neck of the chicken.

Cristofer shrugged, gave a short laugh. Then sunk to his quill and sheets of paper.

My mouth went completely dry.

From the outset I'd assumed that the stable boy delivered my messages here because Cristofer had told Jacque I lived on his property.

But he had not said anything of the kind.

Had someone, then, discovered the truth?

Sarkov? Jacque?

Or, perhaps, the stable boy?

As I stood before the mirror, I could hear Cristofer out in the carriage calling my name. We were late for the rehearsal.

I had finished dressing, yet could not get my shaking limbs to cooperate, to carry me toward the door.

All I wanted, all I craved, was the chance to see Ava again. To be held in her presence.

But set against this desire was prodigious fear.

On the one hand, Ava had sent word that we should resume

our lessons. Presumably, she would not have done so were it to put me in jeopardy.

On the other hand, what if Sarkov or the stable boy had informed their master of my disguise? And what if, during their travels, Jacque had turned his wife against me? Convincing her that my depravity would be her ruin?

Was Ava leading me into a trap?

I shook my head.

No.

I could not believe that of her.

Would *not.*

"Henri!" Cristofer shouted again, this time with some urgency.

I looked back into the mirror. Struggled to slow my pulse.

The risk, I realized, was one I must run. For my desire to be near Ava would not abate, nor would it allow me to choose otherwise. Even if it meant my end.

I clutched Cristofer's manuscript under my arm.

"Coming presently!" I called.

By the time we arrived at the hall, the orchestra's musicians were already on stage attending to their instruments.

Sarkov approached from a side aisle. "Greetings, Monsieur Vaughn!" he called. Then led the conductor to his podium.

Free to look about, I scanned every seat, every balcony, every shadow, seeking her contours.

Neither she nor Jacque were present.

Onstage, Cristofer nodded to his musicians. Then went to speak with the first violinist.

As he did, I mounted the stairs and set out Clara's score. Having done that, I stepped down and headed for my desk. And there received a shock.

The desk set out for me was different.

Not Ava's at all.

A clatter came suddenly at the main doors. All heads turned, no doubt expecting Jacque.

But it was Clara.

As she approached the stage, Cristofer offered his hand. They ascended arm in arm, Clara's condition now well apparent. He drew her immediately to the piano bench where they sat to study the new score. The way between pianist and composer seemed easy. Mutual. Once again, they were in tune.

I could see relief drizzle down the players' faces. No doubt the previous rehearsal's poor ending had left them anxious.

Everything was in order, and the musicians eager to begin.

However, even after an hour's delay, the benefactor had still not appeared.

Lifting his watch, Cristofer stepped off the stage to confer with Sarkov. After a brief conversation, he returned to the podium. There, he promptly tapped his baton, bringing a halt to idle chatter and page turning.

I again scanned the hall. And still did not find her. My heart sank.

I would have continued searching had I not become distracted by the feeling of someone's eyes upon me.

Clara's.

From her perch at the piano, she held me in an intensely piercing gaze.

Not wanting to confront her or her accusations, I pretended not to notice.

The walls then shook with a deep bellow. Cristofer had let slip the orchestra.

The allegro rolled forward. Its themes taking root, as if preparing the ground for the piano. Given the unusual delay before her entry, Clara returned to a position of repose, her hands in her lap.

Yet when her moment finally arose, she snapped to life. Pounced on her opening chords, while still allowing them their ache. Their haunting rise.

I noted that the balance in volume between soloist and orchestra had improved greatly since the previous rehearsal. It was a note I had made for Cristofer.

As if reading my mind, he spun around to face me, arms pumping.

I smiled broadly in acknowledgement.

Indeed, the rehearsal had gotten off to a brilliant start.

CHAPTER 27

lara's face shone. The folds of her dress clung to her swollen belly. She and the orchestra dove at one another. Exchanging volleys.

How I wished their benefactor were there to receive their efforts. To see Cristofer occupied in glory.

I no sooner had this thought than Sarkov sprung to his feet and rushed up the aisle.

I hoped his sudden motion would not upset the rehearsal.

As it turned out, it was not the rehearsal that was upset.

But me.

For when my eyes fell upon her, my world and all its contents upended.

She swept in like a fragrant mist, her arm upon Jacque's. Her attentions fixed on his movements. When he paused to share a word with his henchman, she waited delicately alongside him.

She looked paler than I remembered. Thinner. But no less radiant. Her auburn waves tumbling about her shoulders. Her throat sparking with fresh jewels.

Fortunately, Cristofer had his back to the new arrivals and his efforts flowed uninterrupted.

I knew I should not stare. But for all my fears could not tear my eyes away.

Ava, for her part, ignored my presence.

Jacque led his wife, with unusual care, toward their seats.

Once settled, they cast their eyes solely upon the performers.

Having seen to his master, Sarkov returned to his post in the shadows. On his way, he threw a sharp look in my direction.

I responded quickly. Returning my attentions to the conductor. Praying my interest had not been noted.

The allegro's finale reached its final crescendo. Its themes and breadth widening to unleash a wall of impetuous chords.

Clara leapt at the final bars like a cat striking its target.

When the final note faded, the hall fell into a strange ringing as though it had become an enormous tuning fork, its stone and wood resonating.

It was at this point that Cristofer turned around. I saw he and Jacque find one another. The benefactor pumped his fist triumphantly in the air. From his perch, Cristofer gave a quick, jaunty bow. Clearly pleased with Jacque's reaction.

As the two men shared their exchange, her eyes shifted to mine.

I flinched at the sudden acknowledgement. But no sooner had I recovered than I found her attention returned to her husband.

"Henri?" a woman's voice rang in my ear.

I turned, dazed. Found Sarkov's eyes fixed upon me. Watching.

"Henri!" she called again.

I blinked and glanced toward the stage. Found Clara. It was she who was beckoning.

I rose as if in a dream. Approached the stage.

From her bench she leaned as far forward as her condition would allow. "I need you," she said. "To turn the pages."

I hesitated. "But my notes …" I sought out Cristofer. He'd seen our interaction and indicated that I should assist.

I swallowed.

As I mounted the stairs alone, I suddenly wished I'd attended better to my disguise. Endeavored more ironing. Applied more adhesive.

I sought an empty chair and swept it alongside Clara's bench. As I dropped into my seat, she gathered the pages of the first movement and set them on the floor.

She then sat back with a huff.

On the rack before us waited the notes of my adagio.

Written in Cristofer's hand.

I felt a burn at my cheeks. And prayed that Clara would not mention the ruse.

Thankfully, before any words could be spoken, Cristofer lifted his baton and, with impossible tenderness, let slip the strings.

The hall, and all its occupants, settled as a delicate sigh rose from the violins. It glided, ephemeral, into the air. A water bird taking flight across a morning lake.

To say that the tones cut into my soul would sound inappropriately ornate. But I know of no other way to describe it.

I had imagined this song, this gentle step toward love, a thousand times. Never once, as I walked through forests, or endured the darkest hours of longing, did I ever expect to hear it come to life.

Not in the hands of a full orchestra.

With my Cristofer at the helm.

Clara Thorne at the keyboard.

And my beloved in the audience.

As the wooded bassoons and cellos entered, their tone hefty as an ark, I swooned.

Clara noted my reaction but kept her attention on the music.

Still, I could feel her disapproval.

The bench creaked as she adjusted her position.

Get ahold of yourself, Henri, I commanded.

As I settled, the oboe's mournful cry arose, signaling the piano's impending entry.

I watched Clara's spine lengthen.

Knowing what was to come, it took every bit of strength to resist peering into the audience. To seek Ava.

Then.

Clara unveiled the chain of silver-sided thirds.

They came descending, reluctant, bottomless.

I braced myself against the music's effect. But the effort proved useless.

At Clara's signal I pulled one sheet of music to reveal the next. Then cast an eye to Cristofer.

Though maintaining his position at the podium, he appeared to be melting. The edges of him softening. The horns entered, but his attention did not waver.

He had chained himself to Clara.

The piano swept forward, flirting now with discord. Each hand wandering into separate thoughts.

Clara growled softly. The passage challenged with its irregular rhythm and incandescence.

I listened fully, hoping Ava would hear what I wished her to hear.

That she might know of my love.

Might step upon the bridge.

Clara's arms blurred. Tremolos cascading into swift and lengthy arpeggios, one after the other.

The strings then took hold, soaring toward upper octaves. Their cry splitting me open lengthwise.

Before I could stop it, my vision soaked with blue.

Her sky blue empire.

Traced with butterflies.

And pressing moss.

Submerged in memory, and no longer able to contain myself despite the hazard, I peered into the audience.

In that instant, her eyes rushed into mine. As if they'd been waiting.

Her cheeks shone with tears.

Yes, I thought. *She has heard.*

My mind raced. Conjuring how I might commandeer a carriage to have waiting at our next lesson, so that we might abscond—

Clara growled again. Louder.

My eyes snapped back to the piano.

The pianist struggled to tame the unsettling theme beneath her. Sliding suddenly along the bench. Pouncing upon the lower octaves.

Flayed open, I heard Clara's playing as though for the first time, and was transported.

With each measure, she revealed far more than I could ever have rendered. Or even been aware existed.

Perhaps she knew me better than myself?

"Henri!" Clara hissed.

Her remonstration hit like a fist.

Adrift in her realm, I had missed my cue.

I leapt forward and turned the page.

Having returned full attention to my duties, I was nearly unaware of the piece drifting toward its end. Its rifling passion turning slow and ponderous.

The woodwinds chimed their last note in a plaintive and hopeful upper register, then released.

The hall fell into silence.

No one moved.

Transitions between movements are always awkward. Audiences sit, either quelled or ecstatic (or worst of all, disinterested). Depending on their reaction, the conductor either holds a space for appreciation or quickly cues up the next movement.

But Cristofer was not giving instructions.

He just stood with his arms at his sides. His eyes pinned to Clara. The oddest expression on his face.

Even I, who know Cristofer better than most, could not read the emotions angling his features.

Perhaps it was a mixture of sentiments.

Whatever the case, I could tell by the tensing of Clara's carriage that she did not appreciate the attention.

"Well, then," she said, breaking the spell.

She got to her feet. Bowed to the musicians. Turned to Cristofer. "Resume at a quarter past?" she inquired. Her tone formal. Devoid of sentiment.

I looked on, stunned at how quickly she had resurfaced from the depths.

Cristofer appeared equally astonished. For it took him a moment to conjure an answer.

"Yes. Of course," he finally said, waving a hand to free the musicians.

Eager for a rest, or perhaps to be free of the renewed strain between conductor and performer, the players scrambled noisily to their feet.

Fearful of where my eyes might light should they remain unoccupied, I set to gathering the sheets of manuscript off the rack. Seeking to right my appearance without detection, I intermittently wiped a cuff across my cheeks and pressed fingertips into false bristles.

A hand landed on my shoulder.

I started, thinking it was Jacque.

"Henri," Clara said. She stood uncomfortably close. "The balance of this bench is not to my liking," she said. "If you go to the storeroom below the stage, you will find the one I prefer. The mark of its maker is burned underneath the cushion and resembles a sideways B. Will you bring it to me, please?"

It took a moment for her request to focus in my mind. A bench? A storeroom?

"Yes, yes, of course," I said, relieved to have a reason to leave the stage.

As I descended toward the audience, I kept my eyes averted. Still, the sheen of her caught in my periphery.

I willed myself not to look but indulged in the traces allowed by a sideways glance.

Through this same lens of indirection, I saw Jacque produce a cigar. Amputate its head with a clip. Billow smoke about himself and Ava.

Enraged, I stormed to the bottom of the stairs. It was then that I spotted Sarkov. His right hand stuffed disarmingly inside his waistcoat.

I swallowed my anger and struggled to appear at ease. Praying my disguise remained intact.

I then scurried down a second set of stairs located near the base of the podium. At the bottom, I slipped inside the sunken storeroom. Closing the door behind me, I fell back against it.

My heart was pounding.

What a brute! I screamed inside. *What an utter bully!*

Seething, and emboldened by Ava's response to the adagio, a plan for our escape began to formulate more concretely in my mind. I would accept the count's offer. And bring Ava with me. His mansion would provide all the safety and shelter we required.

After all, according to Cristofer, the count had a penchant for androgynous sorts. As well as inciting gossip among his set. It would bring him no small amount of pleasure to sequester a talented but mysterious composer within his domain.

And if the count was the kind of man to guard one secret, why not two?

I smiled at the plan's perfection.

The ceiling above me wailed as someone dragged a chair across the stage.

Were the musicians retaking their seats already?

Prodded into action, I searched through the dank, poorly lit room. All manner of furniture and props had been stored there. Some items covered with cloth, others stacked in corners.

Along a far wall I found a row of waiting benches. At first I wondered how Clara had known of them, then realized the hundreds of performances she and Richard had given within the hall. They no doubt knew the building as intimately as their own children.

This last thought gave me pause.

I shook my head to ward off the oncoming murk. I could not tend to that sorrow now. To the Thornes' unborn child. Rather, I needed to locate the bench with the sideways B burned in its belly.

Determined, I knelt to my task, upending each seat in turn.

I had made little progress when I heard the creak of door hinges. They swung open quickly then closed. I squinted through the dim light. I hadn't known there was a second entrance.

"Hello?" I called out.

No answer.

Only the sound of breathing. And footsteps.

I held still. Uncertain of what I faced.

"Henri," she said, her face emerging from the dark. "It's me."

Clara.

She rushed into the room. Noting my distress, she said, "Sit down."

I did as she asked.

Her eyes burned through the room's dimness. Alight with purpose.

I felt certain she had come to accost me about the adagio's subterfuge. And my secret alliance with Cristofer.

My mind reeled. Yet it then occurred to me that I needn't defend myself. I need only tell her of my intention to accept the count's offer. This news, I felt confident, would placate her entirely. After all, she certainly couldn't wish to harm Cristofer's reputation.

But what she said next took me by surprise.

"Do you have money with you?"

I stared. Baffled.

"What?"

She shook her head in frustration. Reached inside the waist of her dress. Removed a considerable stack of notes. Pressed them into my palm.

"But—?"

"Listen to me," she urged. "You're in grave danger."

I kept still.

Where had I heard that warning before?

Time folded in on itself. The cylinder faithfully reproducing the past.

"There are rumors going about," Clara said. "Of Monsieur Bertrand's wife. Of an infidelity."

My heart skipped then raced.

"His opponent has pounced upon these rumors. Using them to cast doubt on Jacque's virility. They're stirring up gossip. Saying he is more dilettante than soldier. Asking how he could possibly rule a government when he can't even rule his own bed."

At this I heard Sarkov's voice in my head.

Just imagine what unpleasant consequences might arise were someone to plant a seed of doubt in his mind."

Clara's lips tightened.

"You need to leave, Henri. You must disappear."

"Yes. I have been intending ..." I trailed off. Dizzying.

Ava.

She went on. "I've arranged for my carriage to deliver you to the train station immediately after the rehearsal. Cristofer can ship your personal effects later."

I swallowed. "And the madame?"

Clara scowled. Her expression alternating between pity and disgust.

"I won't go without her."

Her eyes rolled. "This is not a game, Henri."

"I'm not playing it as one."

She lowered her voice. "I don't think you understand the gravity of what's at stake."

"I'm afraid that's *all* I understand."

She pressed toward me. "He's desperate to make an example of someone. And after today's ... performance ... I think there can be little doubt as to his target."

I glowered.

She leveled a stare. "No one in that hall could have missed what was passing between the two of you," she said.

Just as I had perceived Cristofer's heat for Clara, so had she detected mine for Ava.

My hands then rose to the bristles on my lip. Fearful that perhaps even more had been detected.

"Has anyone questioned that I am a man?" I asked.

"Of course not!" she said. "But don't you see? That's what makes you so dangerous. And why Jacque—"

"I'm sorry, Clara," I interrupted. "You know how thankful I am for your efforts on my behalf. And how deeply I admire you and Richard. But I will not leave her. I cannot."

Clara's hands began to tremble at her sides.

Her reaction surprised me.

Why had she suddenly become so personally invested in my life?

I knew she was under an inordinate strain.

But did that explain her persistence? Her sudden fury?

What did she want from me?

The silence between us grew unbearable.

Then.

"Would you rather stay and humiliate Cristofer?" she asked.

My head snapped up. Our eyes locked. Her expression cold as ice.

There could be no mistaking her threat.

Like the consummate performer, she was drawing upon her every resource.

I felt a surge of anger. I had no wish to upset her, nor overstep my bounds.

Still.

My affairs were none of her business.

"With all due respect, Clara—"

"No!" she roared. Lips shining. Cheeks aflame. "You have no respect. None. Not for me, nor yourself, nor Cristofer, nor the rare and precious gift that has been given you." She drew in a ragged breath. Swept damp hairs from her forehead. "If you possessed even a modicum of respect, you would not be so ready to sacrifice everything that is true and good and *enduring* to pursue some ... confection," she spat.

I stepped back. Stunned by the furor of her outburst.

She turned away. Drew out a kerchief.

Standing there, watching her back heave with emotion, I finally understood.

Clara's life was not playing out as she wished. She could not have the love for which she yearned. And the love she *could* have would no longer have her.

This woman of consummate control and self-determination could not get her life to lay down before her. Could not tame its events as she could sheets of music.

I did not wish Clara harm. But I could not allow her to stand in my way. Nor could I allow her to tarnish Cristofer's reputation.

I searched for the ground beneath my feet. Steadied myself upon it. And drew upon my own arsenal.

"I'm not the only one with secrets," I said. "I know what passes between you and Cristofer," I told her, unleashing my long-held suspicions. "Do you think no one sees? Do you think I believe your claims that the passion between you is unilateral?"

I drew a great breath and loaded my most lethal ammunition. "And do you truly believe that Richard did not notice your ardor?"

Her face blanched. To my horror, her dress billowed as her knees buckled.

"Clara!"

I leapt to her side. Wrapped my arms about her. Guided her to one of the benches I had inspected.

She sat, slumped. Staring across the floor as though across an ocean. Her focus unfixed.

I held her close. Ashamed.

I waited for her to punish me for my impudence.

But she didn't.

She just shook her head, over and over.

"Oh, Henri," she whispered. Her hands, strong as vices, enfolded mine. "No …"

When she saw my confusion, she smiled. A curious smile. Unbalanced.

She chortled. Lifted a hand to contain herself. Then started to laugh. The sound escaping despite her obvious efforts. As the volume of her laughter grew, her mirth veered into delirium.

I held still, terrified.

She slapped her leg with an open palm. Her screeches setting my spine on edge.

Just when it seemed she might never recover, she let out a long sigh.

"Oh my heavens," she said. Then pealed into another round of merriment. Thankfully, this one faded far more quickly than the first.

"Oh my heavens," she said again, daubing tears from her cheeks.

She allowed herself a brief respite before whisking hands through hair and clothing. Restoring her composure with instinctual efficiency.

She then returned her attention to me. Her gray eyes softening from the color of iron to dove. "Henri," she said. "If you truly believe that's my secret, then I'll allow you its amusement. But no. How could I be in love with Cristofer when, truly, my heart belongs to another?"

Richard's face, drawn and sorrowful, flashed before my eyes.

I filled with remorse.

"Clara, I— "

"Please," she said. "Don't."

Upstairs, a trumpet burst out with a coppery cry. A French horn erupted into a trill. The clattering of music stands and footsteps rattled the ceiling.

Clara pressed her palms to her belly. Spoke quietly, despite the commotion above us.

"You and I share an affinity," she said. "We lean toward both soul and bone. But Henri," she went on, her voice dropping further, "one cannot serve both masters. Attempting this draws only loss."

Running her hands once more over her dress, she rose slowly to her feet.

"You are young, Henri. And your way not yet clear. Perhaps I'm foolish to think I can influence the tendencies within you. But when I—" She broke off, her voice catching in her throat. Tossing back her shoulders, she began again. "When I see, when I *hear* what wishes to speak through you ... "

Middle C sounded on the piano upstairs. The first violinist calling the orchestra into tune.

At this cue, Clara fell silent. Holding the moment between us.

Then, without saying anything further, she fled.

Cristofer peered down from the podium with a puzzled look when I re-emerged from the storeroom.

"Did you not find the bench?"

I shook my head. "It's unavailable," I said, knowing the request had been a ruse.

At the piano, Clara busied herself removing the rest of the score from the rack. She would not need it. She would play the third movement from memory.

I returned to my desk and began setting my notes in order.

As I did so, I intentionally dropped my quill to the floor. Bending to recover it, I looked into the audience from below.

But her seat was empty.

Despondent, I sat up.

Only to find Sarkov looming over my desk.

He grimaced and slapped a leather glove on top of my notes. "You have dishonored the monsieur's wife, and therefore the monsieur himself," he said. "I hereby notify you of his challenge: A duel of pistols. At three o'clock. To the death."

My body went cold.

A duel?!

With me?

In that instant, Clara leapt upon the keyboard, firing a round of chords that brought any possibility of further exchange to a halt.

Cristofer told me later that she had discharged the finale as though besieged by furies.

At the rehearsal's conclusion, Clara ushered me quickly into her waiting carriage. She had learned of Sarkov's treacherous missive and was overcome with terror. The driver latched the door and stepped to his horses.

Clara waited beneath the carriage. Its window framing her face. "The count will be expecting you," she said. "And will keep you safe," she added, looking quickly over her shoulder.

Our eyes soon found one another's. And lingered. Searching for what, I cannot say.

"Will I see you again?" I managed.

She gave a queer smile. Seemed as though she might say something but held it back.

The horseman snapped the whip. The carriage lurched forward. As we pulled away, Clara called out, "Send me your music, Henri!"

I waved, and then the great Clara Thorne faded from view.

CHAPTER 28

*H*alfway to the train station, I signaled the driver. Instructed him not to take me to the agreed upon destination but to the Hedgehog instead. When we arrived, I hopped out. Paid. Rushed inside.

Seeing me, Cristofer sagged with relief.

"My God, Henri! What took you so long? I was worried sick!"

"I'm sorry," I said, checking about me. "I had an errand to run."

He nodded absently and steered me deeper into the establishment. To a bank of semi-covered booths reserved for influential guests who wished not to have their tawdry activities detected.

We dropped into seats across the table from one another. He took my hands into his.

"Did you accept? Did you agree to the duel?"

"Yes," I said.

Not more than an hour ago I had sent word to the castle. Accepting the summons. Agreeing to meet fire with fire.

"Henri," Cristofer said hurriedly. "I've given it all some further thought and I must beg of you not to do—this thing you intend."

I shook my head. I had anticipated his wavering. Which is why I'd insisted that he not tell Clara of my detour—nor our plans.

"Why can't you just reveal yourself as you are, as a woman?" Cristofer tried. "Jacque cannot fire upon a member of your sex!" he insisted.

"I cannot do that. I cannot bring that humiliation to you and the Thornes. I cannot be the cause of your losing a commission so dear to your hearts."

"But Henri! What is the loss of one commission if it means the loss of *you*?"

Though I did not show it, his words, his steadfast loyalty, brought courage to my heart. And salve to the cuts our recent conflicts had inflicted.

I smiled.

With his one declaration, all had been righted in our world.

Still. I could not grant his request.

I lifted his eyes into mine. "There is no other way for me, Cristofer. You of all people should understand that."

He sunk. Kept my hands in his.

"I do," he whispered. "I do understand. I just—"

He looked up, his eyes misting. "I just could not bear the loss if ..."

I held tight to his hands, feeling within our grasp the bond that had endured long enough to save us both.

Outside, the church bell chimed. Twelve o'clock.

I felt an immense emotion welling up from within me and strongly suspected Cristofer was under the same influence. I knew the longer we delayed, the greater the chance his resolve would fail.

"Do you remember what to say?" I asked.

Without looking up, he nodded.

I peered outside. Hoping the second carriage had arrived.

Turning back to my liege, I thought of the many things I wished to express. My gratitude for his ten thousand kindnesses. For having restored me to life. For having helped elevate me to the highest of creative heights.

But before I could say anything, Cristofer spoke.

"Henri, I want you to know something," he said, his voice wavering. "I hope someday to be worthy of the gifts you have bestowed so generously upon me. And I pray that, should we survive this day, your name will eclipse mine from history."

A lump lodged swiftly in my throat.

Was I truly going to release the hand that had held me aloft for so long?

Was I ready to push from our settled shore?

Unable to speak, I lifted his hands to my lips, kissed each finger. Then turned and let him go.

By the time I arrived at my hiding place, my clothes were damp with sweat. My false bristles slipping dangerously out of place.

I searched between the nearby trees and outcroppings of rock, ensuring I had traveled there unseen.

Satisfied I was alone, I peered down. Below, I could see the castle's dense outline. Its billowing flags. Its proud stanchions.

I could see, too, men from the newspapers milling about. Some with notepads, others setting unwieldy cameras upon braces. Their mouths no doubt watering at the prospect of a slaughter.

To the right of the plaza, a cadre of military men loitered along the buttresses. Some smoking. Others cleaning rifles.

Into this scene stepped my Cristofer.

Upon seeing him, a wave of panic crashed along my shoulders.

How could I have sent my tender-hearted employer into the arms of such danger?

What sort of unrecognizable horror had I become?

My teeth chattered as he nodded to the conscripts and made his way toward the main door. I marveled at how confident his steps when I knew the fear occupying his heart.

To my relief, he was let in immediately.

I fell back, losing my sight to the sky. The clouds dark and heavy with rain.

As I laid there I prayed over and over for Cristofer's safety. For his success. For *our* success

Though I may never know what actually occurred inside the castle, I relied, as ever, on the faculty of my imagination.

This is what I saw:

Audric led Cristofer down the hallway, past the Broadwood, and into the study. Jacque welcomed the composer with his usual bravado while Sarkov sat, unmoved, in a far corner.

Jacque offered Cristofer a glass of brandy. He accepted, in the hope of steadying his nerves. Upon lifting his glass, Cristofer caught sight of the pistol set on Jacque's desk.

"Today's performance was sublime," Jacque said. "In fact, *beyond* sublime."

"Thank you," Cristofer said with all humility. Then, girding himself, he pressed on. "Monsieur, though I have only the deepest of gratitude for your compliments, I did not come here to discuss music. Not in particular."

Jacque raised an eyebrow. "No?"

Cristofer shook his head. "No … I came to apologize."

"But for what, my friend?" Jacques asked, surprised.

"For the appalling behavior of my assistant," he said.

Jacque's visage narrowed.

Even Sarkov lifted his head.

Cristofer pressed on. "I had no idea the lack of honor marring his character and will forever regret having exposed you and your household to a spirit of such duplicity."

Jacque rubbed the stump of his finger with a thumb. "Is that what you came here to say?"

"Yes," Cristofer said, as earnestly as he could. Squeezing the glass to still the tremble in his hands.

Then, for a moment, he lost courage.

Without warning, Jacque burst into a cackle. "You artists!" he exclaimed. "So intolerably *sensitive!*"

Cristofer froze, uncertain.

Jacque blew a cloud of smoke into the air.

"Do you think I hold you responsible for that young ruffian's perfidy? Not on your life!" he said. "We in the upper tier are all, at one time or another, subjected to the wiles of our subordinates and there is no accounting for a man's impulses. Especially in the young." Waving his cigar, he continued, "Do not give it another thought, Cristofer. Your energies are too valuable to waste on such matters."

He drew in a long drag and exhaled slowly. "If it will bring any relief to you at all, you may rest assured that your former charge has made his last mistake." His deathly tone made clear his meaning.

Wanting to cover any horror that might leak from his face, Cristofer dropped forward in a deep bow.

"Now be off with you!" Jacque said, returning to his desk to hover over his pistol. "This afternoon's events will not be suited to a man of your refinement."

"Of course, monsieur," Cristofer said. After shoring himself up with another swig of brandy, he added, "But before departing, I feel I must make an apology to yet another."

Jacque looked up. "To whom?"

"To the madame, sir." Then, before his patron could protest, he said, "Madame Thorne insisted I do so."

For the first time in their conversation, Jacque seemed caught off guard. Stalling, he took a step back, looked toward the shadow under which Sarkov hid.

(Earlier I had told Cristofer of Jacque's desperate reliance on Clara. Of how his ascension relied on strategies such as associating himself with her stardom. And while Clara had made no such request, Cristofer had agreed to pretend it so. Knowing my life depended on it.)

"Clara requested this?" Jacque said, expressing disbelief.

"Yes," Cristofer confirmed. "She was most vehement about it."

Jacque threw a hand into the air. "Oh, very well, then!" he declared, his irritation evident. He signaled to the footman who departed immediately.

After but a short delay, Ava stepped into the room.

"Madame," Cristofer said.

Ava approached and offered her hand.

Cristof took it gently. Planted the softest kiss.

"You wished to see me?"

"Indeed," Cristofer said.

Then, turning to face the cliff, he leapt.

"Madame, I am compelled to apologize for the behaviors of my assistant, which I understand have deeply offended you."

Ava stiffened. "I see," she said.

Cristofer cleared his throat. "I am not sure how I could have failed to notice the potential for such aberration. I suppose my only excuse is having *cocooned* myself so utterly in order to fashion a concerto worthy of your generous patronage."

At his words, Ava's cheeks went suddenly pale.

Cristofer met her eyes with his, holding her gaze for just a moment more than appropriate.

Jacque pretended to rattle about his desk, though his ears, like Sarkov's, were glued to the conversation.

After a moment, Ava said, "Thank you, Monsieur Vaughn. I am, of course, grateful for your apology. However, I am equally thankful for your having wrapped yourself away, as the concerto you have composed is as enchanting and breathtaking as any butterfly."

Cristofer blushed deeply.

"You are too generous with your compliments," he said. "And I can only have faith that the music itself will see us through."

Ava gave a gentle laugh, her eyes now sparking. "I assure you, I share in your sentiments entirely."

And so as not to further delay his departure, Ava again extended her hand.

"Thank you for taking the time to see me reassured," she told him.

He tipped his head in that gentile way of his and replied, "I considered it my most solemn duty."

I had been waiting what felt like hours, though the motionless shadows contradicted my perception. Finally, I spotted Cristofer.

Having been let from the castle, he strode back across the plaza. His steps purposeful. Undiluted.

I pressed my palms together in thanks. Grateful that he, from what I could perceive, had suffered no maladies on my behalf.

As his footfalls approached the main gate, I held my breath.

Would he give the signal?

When he reached the opening, he paused between the iron doors. Sifting a hand into his waistcoat, he lifted his pocket watch, clicked open its cover, and pretended to read the time.

I covered my mouth to suppress a yell.

She had heard!

And would come to me!

CHAPTER 29

M oments after Cristofer left the castle, I scurried down the hillside.

From there, I slipped onto my hidden path and followed it to the berms of moss and springs where Ava and I had spent our first time alone. Where butterflies had traced our silhouettes.

My heart rose upon seeing the place.

But now was not the time to contemplate sweet memories. Too much danger lay in wait.

I scoured the area to make certain I was not being watched. Then hiked up the hill toward the main road. From a safe distance I spied the carriage I had hired with the funds from Clara. It sat at the designated spot. Its driver having fallen asleep atop his perch.

Assured, I returned to the clearing.

Below, I heard the church bells strike two o'clock.

Soon the castle would be buzzing with activity as all prepared for my arrival. During the rush, Ava would be able, I hoped, to slip away.

Unsure what else to do, I paced around the spring. Watched its misshapen crown of water bubble and dissipate. With every passing moment, I listened for her arrival. For the sound of rushing steps on soft ground.

Without warning, a deafening *crack!* knocked me from my feet. I slapped hands to my ears, but too late, I could already hear the ringing inside them.

A bolt of lightning crisped the sky.

The storm had rolled in quickly. The sky having grown dense as a bruise.

I peered again down the path, praying she would arrive before the downpour.

About me I could feel the air thickening. Growling. Becoming more and more predatory as time passed.

Seconds later, a single drop of rain, big as a coin, struck the top of my head. Another hit the rock at my feet. Yet another struck my shoulder.

The sky tilted its chest and spilled the treasure, unleashing a torrent of silvery doubloons. I fled beneath the canopy. The pathway beyond filling with thick puddles.

Held inside the uproar, I could no longer hear the possibility of her approach.

"Ava!" I cried out. "Ava, where are you!"

The rain swallowed my voice.

A sudden gust stripped the cover from overhead. I dashed to an outcropping of rock, though it hardly mattered. I was already soaked to the bone. My clothes heavy as a drowned man's.

Still, I waited. Unable to imagine my love seeing rain as an obstacle. Unable to bear the consequences should she arrive and find me missing.

Yet she did not appear.

As the storm's fury escalated, so did my own.

Inside I raged, but could not move for the lashing of wind and rain.

Quick as it came, the storm abated. The sky lightened, its bruises fading.

I stepped from underneath the stone ledge. Seeing how the squall had ravaged the terrain, my rage turned to panic.

Had she tried to make it only to be caught in mud and fallen branches?

Had she fallen and become injured?

Stirred by these thoughts, I fled down the path. Scrambled up ridges and down embankments.

She was nowhere.

Below, I heard the church clock peal.

The dreaded hour had arrived.

I recalled the particulars of Cristofer's warning: When the time of the duel arrived, I was to flee, no matter what. For Jacque would launch a manhunt that would be extensive and swift.

"Ava!" I called as loudly as I dared, my voice hoarse from the dampness.

I waited.

Nothing.

Then came the clomping of horse hooves. And the shouts of men.

Could it be?

I listened again. Heard distant galloping. Barking dogs.

The hunt had been unleashed.

"Run, Henri! Run!" I heard Cristofer scream.

A strange cry slipped from my mouth.

Fighting mud and bramble I tore back to our meeting place. I arrived panting, a painful stab gutting my side.

But Ava was not there.

Below, the wails of dogs and men grew louder.

Shaking, I darted up the hill to the main road. And the waiting carriage.

Bursting from the trees, I shouted to alert the driver, "Wake up! We've got to go! *Now!!*"

From then on it felt as though time had slowed. As if every moment were glomming onto the next, refusing to release. In this gluey motion, my eyes swept up and down the road. But the carriage was gone. The tracks of its departure rutting the mud.

With leaden legs, I ran after it, crying out. But there was no end to the trail.

The driver had left. Without me.

Within seconds I heard the hooves of a single horse. Charging up the main road.

The pace of time resumed. Accelerated.

Looking down, I saw my footprints in the muddy road. Fearing they would give me away, I snatched up a branch and dragged it across to erase them.

Crashing back down the hill, I found myself returned to our meeting place. But the bubbling spring and gentle moss brought no comfort.

The yelping of dogs had grown louder.

My thoughts reeled, blurry with panic and lack of breath. I had to decide on a path. On a direction.

I could not descend in any way I normally did. Any of my usual routes would lead me too close to the castle. The only choice, then, was to risk the ravine at the backside of the mountain. I had never attempted to traverse it. Nor was I certain if it were humanly possible. However, if I *could* scale down the incline, I would be brought to the northern-most end of town. And from there, could surely find a means of escape.

The thunder of hooves rose and fell as the rider navigated the road's steep turns.

Feeling no choice left to me, I dashed back into the woods.

Within minutes the trail vanished and the forest thickened. Sharp branches attacked like hornets. Stinging my cheeks. Tearing holes in my coat.

I fought back like a wildcat and cried out when something sharp pierced my ear.

Soon, and much to my amazement, I reached the ravine.

I scurried to its edge. Looked down. Grew sick at how quickly the land plunged away.

I grabbed onto a sapling just below the ridgeline and lowered a foot into the ravine's mouth. In a flash, the rain-slickened ground slipped from beneath my feet. Crashing onto my back I began to slide downward. I yelped and clung to the sapling with all my might.

Thankfully, the tree held.

Digging into the mud, I scrambled back up to the top. From there I scoured every inch of precipice, searching for a drop-off that was less severe.

There had to be another way to get across!

The sound of pounding hooves beat the air.

He was close now. In a moment he would be upon me.

Certain that I would soon be shot in cold blood, I could feel the cessation of rational thought. And the rise of animal.

I will never understand why or how I did what I did.

Such things may never be known.

Suffice it to say, I stepped to the edge.

And leapt.

Of the hurtling crash, or where I landed, I remember nothing. All that remains is a memory. Felt from time to time within my body. Of falling. Of the weightless and unknown. The shapely arc projecting toward nothing, and everything. A queer elation it is. A liberty seldom felt on earth.

And what was going through my mind as I fell? The last thing I remember?

Only these words:

The hammer lives a life of being continually cast off from her earthly ties. To be hurled into the void.

Alone.

But, when the aim is true … she lands.

CHAPTER 30

I wasn't sure at first what woke me.

I tried to open my eyes but could not for the light. It shone around me like a holy blaze.

I suspected I was dead.

With some effort, I lifted a hand to shield my eyes.

Dismayed, I found that the light was not from heaven.

But the sun.

The clouds had parted. The storm having sauntered off to haunt other lands.

Turning my head slightly, I found the edge of the ravine looming far above.

It took some time for me to gather enough consciousness, but finally I was able to process that ... I had jumped.

And lived!

I laughed out loud at the realization.

But no sooner had the laughter shaken me with joy than a searing pain stabbed my side. I bit down hard on my lip. Tasted blood.

Terrified at what I might find, I raised my head to look down the length of me.

Uncertain as to what I beheld, I stared in silence.

The arm that had traveled with me all my life no longer looked my own. Appearing more like an expired trout. Or a curvy water snake.

In how many places my limb was broken, I could not say.

For a moment, I marveled at its strange new geometry.

Then the pain struck anew.

My head knocked back against the ground. I thought I might burst into tears. Indeed, my heart felt heavy enough for it. But, in truth, I hadn't the strength. And could already feel the sense leaving me.

For how long I lay there, I will never know. There was no time in that place.

Not time as we know it.

I only know that a honeyeater landed nearby. And sent its song winding down to meet me. When it did, it elicited a reverberation that rang out from my core.

A perfect, never-before-heard note.

The wave of it amplified inside every crevice and capillary of me. And above it, or rather from *within* it, arose the most enchanting music I had ever heard.

So ethereal was its refrain, so generous its cadence, that I could sense nothing beyond it. And so, surrendered.

You've been a fool, Henri. Lost to guilt and fear, you could not acknowledge the truth set right before you—that you, yourself, are a part of the Beauty you desire. To deny this is to deny what you ardently seek.

This recognition, and the music arising from within it, carried my heart to a new place. And there, despite the pain and anguish, I came to understand one thing:

I had been spared.

CHAPTER 31

❝ Henri?”

A voice called from deep inside the fog.

The celestial song was gone.

I forced my eyes to open through the pain. And peer through the murk.

The form before me sifted into shape.

Sweet angels! Come for me at last, have you?

But it was not an angel that had whispered my name.

It was the stable boy.

In one hand, he clasped the reins of his horse.

In the other.

A pistol.

Though I was not fully present at the time, this is what I imagine unfolded:

"Can you stand?" he asked, lashing my good arm about his shoulders.

Bracing me against his torso, he shuffled us to a high shelf of stone. Knelt me at its edge, then returned to his horse below. Once he'd gotten the animal in place he returned and maneuvered me carefully down. Finally setting me upright on the horse.

With great agility, he then sprung to a position in front of me.

My body collapsed against his back.

"Put your arm around me," he said. "And hold tight."

How long we rode, I could not say. Was it minutes that passed? Hours? Days?

Finally, "Henri. We're here."

He had ridden us to the river.

Just beyond it waited Clara's carriage.

On the arch of the bridge stood a figure.

Her body draped in hood and cape.

Clara?

I looked again.

Ava?

Is it?

You?

EPILOGUE

*F*ollowing the act of escapement, wherein the hammer strikes the string and rebounds, a supportive arm rises immediately, as if from nowhere, to catch the sailing hammer as it falls back. Thus caught and cradled in a cushion of felt, the noble hammer is lowered gently and returned to its original position of rest. There it remains until the master again calls upon it to produce its unique and ringing tone.

—*The Artistry of the Piano, 1877*

The count's citrus gardens are legendary. The exotic fragrance that lifts from slender blooms intoxicating. And a fine match for strong coffee.

It is under the shade of these trees that I like to read my mail. The volume of which has become significant in recent months.

It was here, amidst this sweet scent, that I read the only letter I have ever received from Richard Thorne. Though his script was frail, he had written to thank me for the songbirds I had sent him (my final errand before departing). He went on to say that the creatures' chirping recalled for him many cherished hours.

In the margin of his letter, almost as if written in another hand, he had added, "Our efforts are but dim echoes of Creation ... yet ... despite the cost ... they bring us ever closer ... in this I have absolute faith ... for, my dearest Henri, someone or something is leading us onward ... "

He wrote more, but these things, excavated from deep within his soul, are best held in private.

He closed his letter by sketching a musical staff and lining it with notes sung by his new birds. Beneath this, he included a brief accompaniment that he had no doubt improvised while humming along with them. This image, of the great Richard Thorne at work, composing with songbirds, was to be my last of him.

For not long after, I received a letter from Cristofer. The first of many. This one informing me of our dear Richard's passing. During the night. Alone. Having never met his youngest son. Or seen again his beloved.

Other than this difficult news, life here, in service to the count, has been sublime. He has granted me use of a small room overlooking the mountains. The space holds within it nothing more than an elegant Erard piano and a modest desk. The desk contains but a few precious items: manuscript pages, ink bottles, dried butterfly wings, my recently acquired reading spectacles, and Tess's owl-feather quill (which, miraculously, survived the fall).

It is here in this high room that I do the lion's share of my composing.

When finished for the day, I like to stroll off into the mountains. To think. And, mostly, to listen.

In the rhythm of these days, the music comes and is shared with ease. This at once provides me with comfort, strength and, dare I say, joy.

Of the rest, I will say only this:

If Clara Thorne was wrong in her assumption, and the truth be that one *can* honor both the earthly and divine simultaneously—wherein bone and soul vitalize one another—then you will find my name etched into the pantheon of great composers.

But.

If Clara was correct, and one's earthly being cannot withstand the unnatural strain of serving two masters—then you will have never heard of me.

However.

A third possibility exists.

Perhaps, one day you will find yourself listening to a piece of music when its mood suddenly and unexpectedly swerves to dive under your skin. Arousing your blood. Forcing your heart to veer toward forest, or ache, or the beauty of a woman remembered. And in that moment of tender incursion, perhaps you will come to wonder if it is not my music, my sounds, nesting inside you—disguised—beneath the name of another.

And so, in whichever of these ways it comes to pass, may the cylinder that spins within me spin also within you.

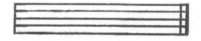

MUSIC THAT INSPIRED *ESCAPEMENT*

Johannes Brahms

Piano Concerto in D Minor, op. 15, no. 1
Sonata for Piano in F Minor, op. 5, no. 3
Rhapsody in B Minor, op. 79, no. 1
6 Piano Pieces, op. 118. No. 2: Intermezzo in A Major

Frederic Chopin

Berceuse in D Flat Minor, op. 57
Barcarolle in F Sharp Major, op. 60
Nocturne in E Minor, op. 72, no. 1
Nocturne in C-sharp Minor, op. Posthumous

Robert Schumann

Album for the Young, op. 68. No. 16: Erster Verlust (First loss) in E Minor

Henrietta Worth

Piano Concerto in A Minor, op. 1, no. 1

Dear Reader,

I am grateful for you.

In our world today no one writes, or even reads, a book alone. Page by page we're building a global community that connects our collective minds and imaginations. And your opinion truly matters!

Given this powerful new reality, would you please take five minutes and share a review of ESCAPEMENT somewhere?

If you bought the book online, the easiest option is to return to the site where you downloaded it, for example: Amazon, Barnes & Noble, Kobo or Apple.

If you bought the book from an independent bookstore or borrowed it, you can share your thoughts on:

- A community reading site such as Goodreads or LibraryThing

- Your social media sites such as Facebook, Twitter, Instagram and Pinterest

If you enjoyed ESCAPEMENT, you might also like my first novel, THE WAY. To learn more about the book, and receive the latest news on all my projects, please sign up for Updates at: www.kristenwolf. com/subscribe

If you'd like to receive a monthly email featuring curated morsels of Wonder, subscribe to my blog at: www.wonderchews.com/subscribe

And lastly, I always love to hear from readers. Burning questions? Comments? Insights? Send them all to me at: kristen@kristenwolf.com

Thank you again for all your help in supporting writers and readers everywhere!

~KW

Made in the USA
Coppell, TX
25 May 2020

26465964R00310